The Tides That Bind

HEARTSTRINGS AND HOPS

KATIE EAGAN SCHENCK

ISBN-13: 9781965807910

Cover design by: 100 Covers

To my siblings and their partners who demonstrate every day that love conquers all.

Chapter One

Though Emily Gallagher plastered a smile on her face as her third graders filed out of her classroom for lunch and recess, her stomach churned. The idea of spending her lunch period begging her siblings for help nauseated her, especially since she was conflicted about why their assistance was needed. But what choice did she have? They must return to their Maryland hometown as soon as possible.

Steeling herself for an unpleasant conversation, she closed the door after the last student and walked to her desk. She FaceTimed her younger brother and sister, figuring it would be easier to tell them both the news at once.

Cassie answered on the first ring, and Emily resisted the urge to roll her eyes at her sister's unnatural red hair. The Gallagher trademarks of dark hair and brown eyes were lost on Cassie. Beyond the hair color, Cassie's bright hazel irises appeared to change color with her mood. A bright green when she was happy; a dull, muddy brown when she wasn't; and varying mixtures of the two for everything else.

"Hey, sis," Cassie chirped.

Her joyful demeanor caught Emily by surprise. Cassie wasn't a huge fan of unexpected phone calls. Text messages were more her style.

"I'm not interrupting you, am I?" Emily tried to keep the worry out of her voice. Cassie had started what felt like her ninetieth job of the year, and the last thing Emily wanted to do was distract her. She had hoped Cassie would settle down at some point, but she bounced from one thing to another with little direction or purpose.

"Nah, I'm due for a break. I've been researching case law for hours," Cassie said, leaning back in her office chair. "What's up?"

"It's Mom."

Cassie's perfectly shaped eyebrows furrowed. "Is she okay?" Her tone lost its bubbly warmth.

"Physically, yes," Emily said, hurrying on. "But she's overwhelmed." She hesitated, noting her brother had yet to join the call. "Let's wait for Pete, so I can tell you both at the same time."

Cassie nodded. "That's a relief. How's your class? Are they excited about summer break?"

"It's still a few weeks away." Emily laughed. "But yes, they're getting restless. They're all trying to one-up each other with their summer vacation plans."

Before Cassie could respond, Peter joined them. His black hair was longer than usual and disheveled. His dark eyebrows pulled down over his brown eyes as he glared at the camera. "What is it, Emily? I'm busy."

"Well, hello to you too," Cassie said.

Peter pinched the bridge of his nose, and Emily suspected he was working to keep his tone in check. "Hello, Cassie. Hello, Emily. How can I help you?"

"Better," Cassie said. "Emily was calling to tell us some news about Mom."

Emily cleared her throat. "I was just thinking how, you know, it's Mom's first summer without Dad and she's having a hard time keeping the pub going." Her voice cracked with emotion, and she blinked back tears.

"I can imagine," Cassie murmured, her own eyes a bit misty. "What can we do?"

"Well..." Emily said. "The thing is, the pub isn't the only business struggling back home, and the mayor is working hard to build the economy back to what it was in its heyday. One thing he's trying to do is attract a boutique hotel chain that has opened hotels in remote locations to great success. He's hoping if they build in the area, it'll increase tourism. Put Blue Heron Bay on the map." She hadn't meant to say that last line with such a distasteful tone, and she forced a smile, hoping her siblings wouldn't notice. "Which would be really good for the pub in the long run."

"I hate to do this to you both, especially so soon after you started yet another new job, Cass." This earned Emily an eye roll. "But could you come home and help? It'd mostly just be filling in on some of the shifts, as Mom has been short-staffed and fixing up the place. I wouldn't ask if it wasn't important."

"Of course I'll come," Cassie said. "Anything for Mom."

"Shouldn't you check with your boss first?" Emily raised an eyebrow.

"It's a family emergency." The sound of rapid typing drifted through the speaker as Cassie shook her head. "I'm sure he'll understand."

"I wouldn't go that far—"

"Mom needs us," Cassie interrupted her. "And anyway, things slow down over the summer here. Besides, it's a temp-to-hire position, so the agency can always send someone else if need be."

"If you say so," Emily muttered, not convinced her sister wasn't about to move on to job number ninety-one. "What about you, Peter?"

"Can't you and Cassie handle it?" Peter asked. "You know I have a deadline."

"I'm aware, yes, but this is bigger than just us. The mayor has asked all the local businesses to do their best to make the town appear like a good investment." When he didn't immediately respond, Emily huffed. "Come on, Peter. When was the last time I asked you for anything?"

A silence fell, and Emily checked her screen to make sure her siblings hadn't dropped off the call. Cassie was still merrily typing away at what Emily assumed was an email that would get her fired, and her brother stared off into space as if he was considering mutiny. She ground her teeth and waited, preparing to launch into one hell of a guilt trip if necessary.

Cassie punched a final key and frowned at the camera. "Jeez, Peter, what deadline could you possibly have that is more important than

Mom? She's been all alone since Dad died. Besides, it's almost summer —aren't you finished with your classes?"

"I'm working on my dissertation." Peter lifted his chin. "I know you're not familiar with deadlines, Cassie, but they exist for the rest of us."

Cassie opened her mouth to respond, with a sarcastic retort, no doubt, but Emily jumped in first. "Can't you work on your dissertation here?" She stifled a sigh of relief when Cassie flipped her hair and went back to typing. Even with an entire country between them, her siblings could always find something to bicker about.

When Peter still hadn't given her an answer, she grabbed the stress ball on her desk and squeezed the life out of it. Of course he would be the difficult one. She should have known. Though it was more than a little ridiculous. Unlike Cassie and herself, Peter wasn't even working; as Cassie had pointed out, the spring semester was over. Emily loved her brother, but sometimes his choice to put academia above everything else drove her crazy. She took a deep breath, ready to drill into him about getting his priorities straight, when he turned back toward the camera.

"Fine," he said with a heavy sigh. "When do you need me there?"

Emily's shoulders dropped, and the knot in her chest eased. "The sooner the better. After all, Monday is Memorial Day and the unofficial start of the summer season."

"I'll look at flights and let you know. But please don't ask me to take part in any stupid town events. I'll help with the restaurant, but I need to spend every free moment I have writing."

"So, don't allow Pete to have any fun, check!" Cassie teased.

Emily ignored her sister's antics. "Thank you both. I appreciate this and can't wait to see you."

She ended the call and slumped back in her chair. That was one thing she could cross off her list, but she wasn't looking forward to their shared task ahead. Blue Heron Bay was a beautiful small town by the sea. In her opinion, the natural shoreline on one side of the peninsula and the dense forest along the sound made it Maryland's best-kept secret. And she would prefer to keep it that way. When her mother had called to ask for help with the pub, Emily hadn't hesitated to agree. But as her mother had explained the deal the mayor was trying to broker with a hotel chain, Emily's enthusiasm had wavered. While she would do anything to save her family's pub, the idea of changing the town's idyllic façade just didn't sit right with her. If she could find a way to save her father's legacy *and* Blue Heron Bay's natural charm, she would do it in a heartbeat.

She glanced at the clock and realized she had spent most of her planning period on her family and not her students. Piles of ungraded assignments sat before her, and the notebook where she had started outlining her substitute plans was mostly blank. Sometimes taking time off was more trouble than it was worth. Trying to develop a lesson plan for her absences was her least favorite part of her job. She always felt the need to include a lot of detail or else her students would accomplish nothing while she was gone. Though she supposed, with only a couple of weeks left of school, it wasn't the end of the world.

"Knock, knock." A voice came from the classroom door. She looked up to see Jennifer Reynolds leaning against the doorframe. Her best friend was dressed in a blue blouse and gray pants, and her blond hair hung loose around her face.

"Hey, Jen, what's up?" Emily cleared the paperwork from her desk.

"Is it true? Are you really going to be gone for the entire summer?" Jen came over to help, her blue eyes filled with concern.

"'Fraid so," Emily said. "My mom needs help with Fiddler's Green. The pub was my father's legacy..." Her mouth went dry, and she swallowed a few times before continuing. "I need to do what I can to save it." She filed one stack of ungraded work into a folder she would take home that evening. "But Cassie and Peter are coming, too, so it's not all on my shoulders."

Jen pouted. "But I was hoping to get your opinion on the latest Mr. Right."

Emily chuckled. Jen had as many "Mr. Rights" as Cassie had jobs. "Shouldn't there only be one man who gets that title?"

Jen shrugged and leaned back against a desk. "Okay, fine. How about 'Mr. Right Now'?"

"Better." Emily pursed her lips. The students were due back soon, but Jen clearly wanted to share. "Tell me about him."

"He's in the navy and is stationed down at PAX," Jen said, gushing.

"You know how I love a man in uniform. We're going on our third date this weekend."

"Sounds promising." Emily narrowed her eyes. "But I know you, and the third date is usually the pass or fail."

Jen's face broke into a broad grin. "Exactly. Which is why I need my bestest friend here to overanalyze every detail."

"There is this new invention called a cell phone."

Jen moaned. "It's not the same."

"It'll have to be enough for now." Emily sighed. "I leave Friday right after school."

"We could grab dinner before you go. How about tonight?"

"I can't tonight. It's Wednesday, which means Thai takeout and—"

"*The Masked Singer*," Jen said, finishing for her. "You're so predictable. It wouldn't hurt you to change your routine."

Emily gave what she hoped was a nonchalant shrug. It wasn't the first time they'd had this conversation. "You know what they say, if it ain't broke..."

Rolling her eyes, Jen shook her head. "With that attitude, how will you ever find your Mrs. Right?"

The sound of children's voices and laughter floated down the hall, growing louder. Emily ducked her head to hide the flush on her cheeks, though her eyes darted toward the door, hoping no one had heard. While she didn't hide her sexuality, it wasn't something she openly discussed at work. Most people wouldn't blink an eye, but she preferred to keep her private life separate from her professional one.

"Sounds like lunchtime is over. I'll call you later," Jen said, her blond hair bobbing as she maneuvered around the desks in Emily's classroom and exited through the side door. Emily loved that they shared a wall. It made it easier to pop in to have a quick consult, and she couldn't ask for a better teaching partner.

As her students entered the room, Emily's warm smile returned. She'd lucked out finding a position at this tiny school in the rural community of Hidden River. It was within driving distance of her hometown, but far enough away that visits required planning.

Her students' parents were farmers, military personnel, or employees at the town's various shops. She'd set up her classroom to reflect their differences. Posters of warships and planes adorned the walls for their history lessons, an alphabet with a farm-animal theme surrounded the bulletin board, and newspaper ads featuring the town's annual festivals were hung throughout the room. The community had welcomed her when she moved here, and she couldn't imagine her life anywhere else.

The rest of the day passed quickly, and before she knew it, the dismissal bell rang. As the last of the children headed home, Emily sank into her chair with a satisfied sigh, feeling a little relieved she wouldn't be here for the last few weeks of school. Her class was already struggling to concentrate as the end of the year approached, and their lack of attentiveness would only worsen.

She arrived home that evening to a dark and empty house, a tiny cottage a good distance from her school that she'd bought with the hopes of avoiding impromptu parent-teacher conferences while grocery shopping. So far, she'd had much success.

After setting her Thai food on the coffee table, she wrapped herself in a warm fleece blanket and turned on the television. As she emptied her school bag, she set up the piles of assignments waiting to be graded next to her on the couch. Since she spent most of the day talking, she appreciated a long, quiet evening. Still, sometimes she wished she had someone to come home to. Someone to talk to about her day, or who enjoyed the gross mini corn cobs in her Thai takeout.

Her mother was convinced the thing missing from Emily's life was romance and would undoubtedly try to set Emily up with someone while she was home. Julie Gallagher was a hopeless romantic and truly believed everyone had a soul mate. Emily's must have gotten hit by a truck early in life, because she certainly hadn't found her yet. Living in a small town didn't help matters. Most of the women she met were already married. Emily had tried dating apps, but they weren't her scene.

She shook her head and moved on to the next pile of worksheets, trying to push her love life, or lack thereof, out of her mind. For now, she hoped to successfully wade through her mother's hopelessly romantic ideals without any of them rubbing off on her while she was home.

A few days later, Emily had packed her car for a summer away and headed to her hometown. Once she passed by the bustling city of Annapolis and crossed the Chesapeake Bay Bridge, the road opened significantly. This part of the state was even more rural than where she'd left. Better known to locals as the "Eastern Shore," it was famous for its expert watermen, estuaries, and, most notably, chicken farms. The hot and humid summer months made it impossible to escape that ripe smell on the way to the beach.

It was almost seven in the evening by the time Emily reached the two-lane bridge which would take her onto the peninsula. The sun sank low on the horizon, and the lights of the town reflected on the waters of the Assawoman Bay. Just the sight of Blue Heron Bay after a long absence filled her with a sense of peace.

Her childhood home was in the middle of the peninsula and only about a block away from the family restaurant. Emily pulled into the driveway of the small Cape Cod and smiled wistfully. As she climbed out of her car, the screen door banged, and she turned in time to be engulfed in a hug.

"You're home," her mom sang out, squeezing Emily so hard she thought she would burst.

"Hi, Mom," Emily wheezed.

Her mom released her with a laugh. Her graying hair was pulled back on the sides with a clip, and visible shadows appeared beneath her blue eyes. "Sorry. I'm so glad to see you. Here, let me help you with your bags."

"It's okay, Mom. I've got it," Emily said and stepped around to the trunk of her car.

Her mom opened her mouth to protest then seemed to think better of it and headed toward the house, calling over her shoulder. "How was your drive?"

"Not bad." Emily pulled her suitcases out and followed.

She set her bags in the hallway and took in the room, searching for any changes since her last visit over Christmas. A painting of a rowboat on a sandy shore adorned one wall, and a Thomas Kinkade painting hung on another. A blue couch and matching love seat faced each other on opposite sides of the room. Two gray recliners separated by an end table were closest to the hallway, and a television sat under a window on the far wall. Everything looked the same, though she couldn't help noticing how different the atmosphere felt since her father's death. It was subtle, but she sensed the melancholy hanging in the air. The formerly vibrant home was subdued, and Emily swallowed past the lump in her throat.

"Your old room is as you left it." Her mom went into the living room and slid down into a recliner. In the dim evening light outside, Emily hadn't noticed the deep lines etched into her mother's face. But when she was sitting by the lamp, the changes in her appearance were obvious.

"I'll put my stuff away in a minute." Emily perched on the arm of the couch. "How are you, really?"

Her mother looked up sharply. Was she going to fake a brave face? But then she slumped in the chair. "Not good. Things with the restaurant haven't been going well. And now, with the mayor trying to drum up business to attract a new hotel, it's just more than I can handle."

"What can I do?" Emily took her mother's hand.

"Just having you home is more help than you know," her mom said with a tired smile. "And I wouldn't say no if you offered to serve tomorrow. I can't seem to keep staff. They don't make near as much here as they do in Ocean City."

"That's one reason I'm here," Emily said to reassure her. "I'm happy to help. But…" Emily didn't want to upset her mother, but she needed to know. "Is it going to be enough? What will happen at the end of the summer when Cassie, Peter, and I leave? Can you manage?"

Closing her eyes, her mother shook her head. "I wish I could tell you, honey, but I honestly don't know." She massaged her temples with her forefingers. "Since your dad died, it's been tough in so many ways. This restaurant was more his than it ever was mine. He was its heart and soul, and I'm not sure how to revive the pub to its glory days, especially since we're not the only business in town struggling for customers."

Emily nodded. This was what she feared. Blue Heron Bay used to be a hub of tourism, but unlike the neighboring town of Ocean City, it hadn't managed to keep up with the changing times. Many families weren't looking for a quiet beach vacation anymore. They wanted more nightlife than the town offered. But that was why she had rushed home. She wasn't ready to let go of her father's legacy—not without a fight.

"We'll see what can be done once Peter and Cassie get here," Emily said with as bright a smile as she could muster.

"Are you hungry?" her mother asked, sitting up. "I could fix you something to eat."

"I ate on the road." Emily stood and stretched. "I'm going to put my stuff away and then go to bed, if you don't mind. If I'm going to be slinging hash tomorrow, I'd better get some rest."

"Do you need any help?"

"No worries. I've got it, Mom." Emily quickly grabbed her bags and hauled them up the stairs before her mother could argue.

Emily's old room was at the top of the stairs to the right and was the second largest room in the house. Her white canopy bed was still on the far wall, and her old white furniture was in relatively good shape. She had two nightstands, a dresser with a mirror, and a simple desk where she'd completed her schoolwork. The walls were still a dark purple, though she had removed the old teen magazine posters.

She set her bags on the bed and immediately began unpacking, as she wouldn't be able to sleep until everything was put in its proper place. While she waited for her siblings to arrive, she would do whatever she could to help her mom out with the restaurant and around the house. It'd been years since she'd worked as a server, and she was surprised to find she was looking forward to the change of pace. She and Cassie had worked many shifts as teenagers at Fiddler's Green. Maybe having the Gallagher sisters serving again would drum up some much-needed business.

Chapter Two

CASSIE GALLAGHER'S EYES GLAZED OVER AS SHE STARED AT the computer screen. She'd been researching this one legal question for what felt like days, but was only a few hours, and she wasn't any closer to finding a comprehensive answer for her boss.

It had only been six months since she'd landed her latest paralegal position, and already she was looking to leave. After working in prestigious law firms in Washington, D.C., she'd expected to be a big fish in a small pond just outside the city limits. But the firm was a bit *too* small, and she was overworked and underpaid. Emily had teased her about being like Goldilocks when it came to her constantly changing employment, and Cassie supposed there was some truth to that. Though she would argue she just hadn't found the right place for herself yet.

Her phone vibrated beside her. She blinked and rubbed her eyes as she looked down at it. Her sister's name popped up, and she clicked to read the message. Emily had arrived safely in Blue Heron Bay, and Cassie couldn't help wishing she was already there with her.

While on the call with her siblings the other day, she'd drafted an email to her boss about her need to take time off, copying her temp agency. Right after she hit send, her boss's door opened, and Logan hurried over to her desk. The scene had gone exactly as she'd hoped.

"Is everything okay with your mom?" he had asked, his heavy black eyebrows pulling together to the point of almost forming a unibrow.

Cassie shook her head. "My mom is very sick, and she needs me to come home right away and help her. Our family business is at stake." It was mostly true. Grief counted as a sickness, right?

Logan ran a hand over his bald head. "How long do you think you'll be gone?"

"I'm honestly not sure, which is why I let the agency know." Her phone rang. "This is them. Do you want me to put it on speaker?"

At his nod, she pressed the button. "Good morning, Linda."

"Cassie, are you for real?" Linda's irritation was palpable through the phone.

"Linda, I'm on with Logan, and we were just discussing the terms of my departure," Cassie said quickly.

The silence on the other end of the line was deafening. Cassie vacillated between annoyance and worry. While there was no way she would waver in her choice to leave abruptly, doing so was going to put her in a precarious position when she came back to the city at the end of the summer. Her agency's policy with long-term assignments usually required more notice than she was willing to give. Would they even work with her again after this?

Finally Linda said, "My apologies, Logan," and the anger in her voice had been replaced by professional detachment. "I wasn't expecting Cassie's email." She cleared her throat. "Cassie, this is against company policy, and you'd be leaving a very important client hanging while we locate your replacement."

Cassie widened her eyes at Logan and jutted her lip out in a convincing pout. A tactic she'd learned when she was younger that usually got her anything she wanted: new clothes from her parents, a warning instead of a speeding ticket, and hopefully, a quick exit from this job with a good reference.

Logan heaved a sigh and rubbed his forehead. A stab of guilt hit Cassie right in the gut, but she worked to keep the pleading look on her face. The case she was researching would be a tremendous boon for the firm, but she couldn't cave now.

"What if I continue to work on this research project remotely?" she asked, hoping that the offer would drive the point home. "Then I can catch my replacement up to speed with where I am so that they don't have to start over from scratch?"

Logan's face brightened, and he straightened up. "Great idea! Does that work for you, Linda?"

"That sounds good to me," Linda said. "I'll get started on finding Cassie's replacement right away. And, Cassie, let me know when you're back in town so we can set you up with a new assignment."

"Will do!" Cassie chirped. "Thank you both so much for being understanding!" She hung up the phone and gave her boss a grateful smile.

Logan had nodded and gone back to his office. *Easy as pie.*

Cassie grinned at the memory as she sent a text to her sister, confirming she would head over the next day. In an act of good faith, she'd decided to stay late that night, hoping to make a dent in her research and reduce the need to work remotely.

Lifting her coffee mug, she went to take a sip only to find it empty. She stood and stretched, letting her gaze travel over her tiny office. Her boss hadn't found the greatest building when he'd started out, but it sufficed for what he needed. There was a small receptionist area right inside the front door, and then her and Logan's offices branched off from there. A potential third office had been turned into a conference room and doubled as the break area. Cassie carried her mug over to the Keurig and chose a dark roast blend. She debated adding a dash of cream, but she decided against it. The bitter taste was exactly what she needed to get through the rest of this day.

Fortified, Cassie headed back to her desk and steeled herself for an evening of research. None of the case law search results were related to the legal issue at hand. She glanced down at her list of keywords and crossed out "jaywalking." Perhaps there was a different connotation for what her firm's client had done. So far, she'd tried "no crosswalk," "pedestrian and intersection," and a few other combinations, but was coming up empty on answering her assigned question concerning whether their client could be found contributorily negligent after being hit by a car in an unmarked intersection. Maryland remained one of the few states which still held onto the archaic principle of throwing out personal injury cases if the court found the victim had contributed to their injury through their own negligence. Most states dealt with comparative negligence, which, while reducing the amount a plaintiff could win, would still allow them a percentage of damages.

She still had a robust list of keywords to go through. Hopefully, one of them would hold the key to supporting Logan's argument in this case and win their client the damages they deserved. She sipped her coffee and typed in the next set of terms. It was going to be a long night.

Emily woke up bright and early. She dressed in a pair of slacks and a dark-green T-shirt with the logo for Fiddler's Green on the front and the quote "May the Road Rise Up to Meet You" on the back. As she pulled her long brown hair into a ponytail, she was overwhelmed with nostalgia for the last time she had donned this uniform. The Christmas before her last semester of college, her dad had asked her to pitch in when one of his servers had called out with the flu. It wasn't how she had planned to spend her winter break, but looking back, she was glad she had done it. Working today was going to be bittersweet without her dad there.

When she came downstairs, her mother was in her robe and slippers, making breakfast. Emily shook her head. Her mother had asked her to come home because she needed help, but she couldn't seem to turn off her inner nurturer. Suppressing a sigh, Emily wrapped an arm around her mother and gently maneuvered her to the side as she took the spatula from her hand.

"What are you doing?" her mother asked, her hands on her hips. "I'm not an invalid. I can still cook eggs."

"I'm sure you can, but since I'm here, you don't have to," Emily said matter-of-factly. She could feel her mother's scowl at her back, but she chose to ignore it. "Anything I should know before I start my shift?"

Her mother sat down at the kitchen table with a grunt. "Don't expect to be busy. It's been slow the last few weekends."

Emily bit her lip as she turned the eggs over in the pan and tried pushing her fears aside. "Things might pick up as schools let out." She glanced over her shoulder with a forced smile. "Especially in June, with senior week."

"I hope so." Her mother's tone suggested she didn't buy into Emily's optimism.

While the eggs finished cooking, Emily threw a few pieces of toast into the toaster and poured herself a cup of hot chocolate. She'd never been one for coffee, but there was something soothing about a cup of cocoa on a cool spring morning. Wrapping her hands around the mug, she let the warmth spread through her fingers and hoped it would keep the chilling sense of dread at bay.

The toast popped up, startling her, and she grabbed two plates from the cabinet. She scooped the eggs onto the plates with the toast and set one dish before her mother. Grabbing her own breakfast, she sat in her usual seat across the table.

"When did you learn to cook?"

Emily rolled her eyes as she sprinkled salt on her eggs. "I didn't, but anyone can scramble eggs, Mom."

"You'd be surprised," her mom muttered as she took a bite of toast.

They ate their breakfast in companionable silence. Emily had missed spending time with her mother. While she usually visited at least once every summer, she also enjoyed traveling to new destinations. Occasionally, she'd regretted not moving back and finding a job at a local school, and it had weighed more frequently on her mind in the last year following her father's death. Knowing her mother was here alone tugged at her heartstrings, and if she hadn't recently gotten tenure, she might have given up her job to find something closer to her hometown. But the idea of starting over after she'd worked so hard at her current school made her anxious. Besides, if her mom really needed her here full time, she'd ask. At least, that was what Emily told herself.

Emily cleaned up the breakfast dishes then joined her mother for the short walk to the restaurant. A cool breeze coming from the ocean broke up the humid morning air. It surprised Emily how quiet the streets were. While it was still technically the off-season, the promise of summer usually brought a more robust crowd.

When they reached Fiddler's Green, her mother unlocked the heavy green door, and they dropped off their purses in the office. Tony, the cook, would arrive shortly to fire up the kitchen, so Emily busied herself with taking the chairs off the tables and wiping them down to prepare for opening.

Wood paneling covered the bottom half of the walls, while the top half was painted a shamrock green. Various booths of dark mahogany were set up along the perimeter, with several tables spaced throughout the center of the restaurant. The bar ran along the back wall, with stools stacked on top. Wall sconces and a few hanging lights gave the place a more intimate feel. The once-vibrant Irish pub had dulled in the last year, and Emily closed her eyes as memories of her father sprang to mind.

Sean Gallagher had been a kind and funny man. He'd loved his Irish heritage and dreamed of opening a pub to celebrate it. Before Fiddler's Green, he'd worked as an accountant for the town and was therefore well versed in how new businesses struggled to keep their books in the black. Emily's mom had been hesitant to sink their life savings into such a risky venture, especially with three young children to feed. Emily wasn't sure how her father had eventually won her mother over, but whatever he had done worked, and Fiddler's Green was born. She recalled spending countless hours here as a child with various age-appropriate jobs. Between rolling silverware in napkins, washing dishes, working the hostess stand, and then eventually serving, she'd almost had the run of the house. The only job she hadn't done was cook, and, well, considering her aversion to the task and her lack of skill, that was probably a wise move on her father's part.

His death had been a hard loss, not only to her family, but to the town itself. So many people had turned out for his funeral. For the first few months, the people of Blue Heron Bay had bonded together to lift the Gallagher family, and the business had done well. But the cracks had started to show over the winter. Even with the Christmas tourists, the pub wasn't doing as well as it should have been. With the continued decline of customers, Emily worried they wouldn't last the summer.

"Well, well, well, if it isn't Emily Gallagher." A deep, familiar voice sounded behind her.

"Hello, Tony." Emily turned to greet him with a smile. His once jet-black hair was a softened salt and pepper. The wrinkles around his gray eyes crinkled as he grinned down at her. Despite all her growth spurts, he still towered over her at six foot five.

"It's so good to see you." He pulled her in for a hug. "And you have no idea how much we need you here." His voice was barely a whisper, and Emily's heart sank. Tony was never one to beat around the bush, but his blunt comment only confirmed what she already knew.

She sighed, and he pulled back to look at her. His broad grin had given way to a grimace.

"How bad is it?" she asked.

"Bad." Tony swiped a hand over his face. "And as I'm sure your mom has told you, it's not just us. The mayor's hotel venture is the town's last Hail Mary. If we can't pull it off, I'm not sure we'll be able to keep our doors open until the end of the year, let alone what will become of the town."

Emily bit her lip and nodded. "That's what I was afraid of." She sank down into the chair she had set out. "If it's any consolation, my siblings are coming too." She raised her eyes to his. "Hopefully, with the three of us, we can not only help spruce the place up for the hotel but also find a way to keep it in business."

"It'll be good to have all the Gallaghers here again." He jerked his thumb over his shoulder. "But so long as we're open, let me get the kitchen ready for today. Maybe now you're here, our luck will change!"

Emily gave a weak smile but didn't reply as Tony left her. She'd never been one for superstitions, but she could use the luck of the Irish right about now.

The morning passed by with few customers coming to the pub, and most of them were seeking a cup of coffee and conversation. Many were familiar faces, which wasn't surprising. Blue Heron Bay was a small town, and she was sure news of her arrival had traveled fast. She hoped the trend would continue once her siblings were home.

While Emily was pouring a cup of coffee, a young woman in a navy dress suit walked in. Emily stared so hard she almost overfilled the customer's cup. The stranger was about Emily's height, with raven-black hair and dark-brown eyes.

There was something about her. She was attractive, to be sure, but Emily had seen many attractive women in her lifetime. Her outfit, complete with a string of pearls around her neck, was much too fancy for this town, particularly on a Saturday when offices were closed.

Emily finished with her current customer and stepped over to the hostess stand to greet the new guest.

"Hi, can I help you?" She pasted on her best customer-service smile.

"I'd like a booth, if possible, please." The woman held up a laptop bag.

"Of course, right this way," Emily said as she led the way to the back of the restaurant. She gestured to a booth, and the woman sat down. "Can I start you off with something to drink?"

"Water is fine, thanks," the woman said.

Emily nodded and took a step toward the kitchen.

"Wait."

Emily turned back with a raised eyebrow. She couldn't possibly be ready to order, could she? "Can I get you something else?"

"Actually, I was wondering if I could pick your brain." The woman glanced around the restaurant. "If you have a minute."

Emily followed her gaze to the mostly empty dining area before she registered what the stranger had asked. What could this attractive woman possibly want to ask her about?

When she glanced back at the customer, she found the woman staring at her expectantly. She cleared her throat. "I have one table waiting for food. Let me take care of them, and then I'll come back with your water."

The woman nodded, and Emily rushed away, not wanting to risk making a bigger fool of herself. When she returned after serving the other customers, the woman had pulled out her laptop and was typing away. Emily set her drink down and went to leave, not wanting to disturb her.

"Would you mind sitting with me?" the woman asked, not looking up from the screen.

Emily sat and waited, hoping whatever the woman planned to ask her was within her wheelhouse. After a minute, the woman finished whatever she was doing and glanced up.

"So, first, my name is Anna Mae Wakefield." She held out her hand, and Emily took it automatically. Her eyes fell to the logo on Anna Mae's bag, and something clicked in Emily's head. She met Anna Mae's gaze and stared, dumbfounded.

"W-Wakefield? As in Wakefield Hotel Group?" Emily stammered. That was the name of the group the mayor had pitched.

Anna Mae's face broke out in an amused grin. "I see you've heard of my family. Yes, that Wakefield." When Emily said nothing else, Anna Mae raised her eyebrows. "And you are?"

A warm flush crept up Emily's neck and spread across her cheeks as she realized she hadn't introduced herself. She swallowed. "I'm Emily Gallagher."

Anna Mae's face brightened. "Oh, your family owns this pub!" Emily's mouth fell open, and Anna Mae winked. "We do our research whenever we're looking at opening one of our hotels in a new town."

"I'd heard the mayor had pitched you, but I wasn't aware it was a done deal." Emily shifted in her seat. She'd hoped to find out more about the planned hotel before anything was finalized.

"It's not," Anna Mae said. "We're trying to branch out into smaller communities with either a large tourist appeal or locations with untapped markets. After Ryan reached out to us, I visited Blue Heron Bay around Easter and thought it did well, but I was hoping for a more year-round venture." She took another cursory glance around the pub. "I'm surprised by what a ghost town this place is with summer so close."

Ouch. Emily ducked her head to hide her wince. "Our town used to draw a larger crowd. But in recent years, the people willing to make the trek out here prefer our neighbor, Ocean City. We're at least two hours from Annapolis, depending on bridge traffic."

"Hmmm." Anna Mae gnawed on her bottom lip as she pulled open her laptop. "Any particular reason?"

Emily thought fast. The real reasons weren't going to paint the town in a good light, but she couldn't bring herself to lie. "I'm not sure." She sighed. "The town has tried multiple approaches to entice people. Cheaper prices, hotel and restaurant packages, various events."

"And none of that has worked, I take it?"

"Not to my knowledge," Emily said. "But honestly, I'm not usually here this early in the season."

Anna Mae cocked her head. "Oh, I'm sorry. I thought you were a local."

"Used to be. I grew up here." Anna Mae looked a tad disappointed at the news, and Emily's heart fluttered in her chest. "I teach in the southern part of the state, but I came home early to help my mom."

"So, you'll be here the whole summer?" Anna Mae asked, her eyebrows raised. Was it Emily's imagination, or did she sound hopeful?

"Yes," Emily said, and a small knot formed in her belly. She wasn't sure where this conversation was going.

"Good. Maybe we can help each other," Anna Mae said brightly as she turned her computer around. "You see, I've fallen in love with this little town, and I think it's exactly what we've been looking for. We want to break into coastal settings but not ones that are overly developed. Basically, we want to be a big fish in a small pond, which is why Ocean City didn't make the short list." She pointed to a graph on her screen. "As you can see, we've checked out several locations, but they're either already bursting with hotels and resorts, or the local government has placed too many restrictions on building. Blue Heron Bay is ripe for development with a mayor and city council who are open to negotiations." She grinned. "Plus, it's an absolutely beautiful place. Unfortunately, my father still needs some convincing as he's worried about the lack of tourism. I might have a proposition that'll help both of us get what we want."

Emily leaned toward her, her emotions warring within her. On the one hand, she didn't want some high-rise to ruin the town's quaint charm. On the other, it was hard to resist the optimistic future Anna Mae was describing—and the captivating way she talked about it. Despite her qualms about the potential changes, she promised herself to keep an open mind, especially if it would save her family's pub.

Chapter Three

THE NEXT MORNING, CASSIE WOKE LATER THAN SHE intended and began rushing around. She should have packed earlier, but she'd been exhausted after working so late the night before. Besides, she worked better under pressure, even if it was self-imposed because of her procrastination. She hoped she wouldn't forget anything, as she hated buying toiletries while on a trip. Everything was always more expensive while traveling than when buying them at the local store. But maybe that was her tiny paycheck talking.

When she'd finally stuffed all her things into her bulging suitcase, she dragged it out of her basement apartment and to her bright-green car. She'd gotten a great deal on her hatchback, thanks to her father. He'd helped her pick it out and had cosigned the loan, a necessity since her credit was less than stellar. It'd been difficult keeping up with the payments with her rotating employment, but Cassie had managed, and now the car was about paid off. As proud as she was of herself, she wished her father could see her progress.

As she pulled into the drive-through at the local coffee shop, she glanced at the clock on the dashboard. She was leaving way later than she'd promised Emily, but she didn't think it would be a big deal. Peter hadn't given a straight answer about when he'd be there. As long as she made it before him, she wouldn't be the bad sibling. She fired off a quick text to Emily, letting her know she was on her way as she waited for her turn.

Coffee in hand, Cassie drove toward the dreaded beltway. Traffic was snarled, as usual, but she made up for lost time when she hopped on Route 50 east toward the Bay Bridge. Most people hated the almost four-mile-long bridge because it rose high above the choppy Chesapeake, but Cassie loved it. Being near water, if only briefly, brought her a sense of peace, and the views from the top of the bridge were spectacular. During the summer months, when traffic was bumper to bumper, she enjoyed watching the various boats on the water. Memorial Day weekend was the unofficial beginning of summer, and several boats were already out celebrating and likely catching their dinners. Crab season was in full swing, and she looked forward to cracking open a few with her family while she was home.

A couple of hours later, she crossed the two-lane bridge to her hometown. It filled her with warm anticipation after several months away. The last time she'd been home was Christmas, but her father's absence had put a damper on her family's holiday joy. Her homecoming now was bittersweet. How would it feel to work in Fiddler's Green again without its heart and soul? She could almost picture her father behind the bar, leaning down and telling jokes with a local fisherman. His wide smile and boisterous laughter could light up any room.

Pushing those memories from her head, Cassie bypassed her childhood home and headed straight for the pub. She expected her sister and mother would be there prepping for the dinner rush. After being cooped up in her car for roughly four hours, she was more than ready to stretch her legs.

The parking lot was empty, but it was still early. Maybe things would pick up later in the evening. She climbed out of her car and headed into the restaurant. Her optimism dimmed as her gaze traveled over her family's business. The atmosphere seemed subdued, and the few customers within did little to liven up the place. She didn't immediately see Emily or her mother, and she wandered into the backroom area.

"Emily? Mom? I'm here," she sang out as she entered the kitchen.

"Well, aren't you a sight for sore eyes?" a familiar voice called from the other side of the counter.

"Tony?" Cassie asked incredulously. "You're still here? I can't believe some big-city establishment hasn't scooped you up by now."

Tony grinned and pulled her into a rib-crushing hug. "You always were my favorite Gallagher. How've you been?"

"Not bad. I just got in. Any idea where the rest of the clan is?" Cassie asked breathlessly as he released her.

"I think your mom's in the office, and Emily should be out on the floor somewhere."

Cassie nodded and gave him her best thousand-watt smile. "Let me go say hello to them. Then we'll catch up, okay?"

"Deal." Tony returned to prepping for dinner.

Cassie left the kitchen and headed back to the office. Her mother was sitting at her father's old desk, poring over a complicated spreadsheet with a furrowed brow.

"Hi, Mom," Cassie murmured.

Her mother jumped. "My goodness! I didn't hear you come in." She stood and embraced Cassie. "When did you get here?"

"A moment ago. I figured I'd come straight here to help with the dinner rush."

Mom's smile faltered the slightest bit, but enough for Cassie to take note. "I doubt there will be much of a rush. Don't you want to go put your stuff away?"

Cassie gave a one-shoulder shrug. "There's time for that later. Where do you want me tonight? I'm always up for serving, but I've been moonlighting as a bartender recently."

"A bartender?" Emily's voice came from behind her. "Exactly how many jobs do you have at this point?"

"I lost count," Cassie quipped, taking the dig at her employment history in stride. She took in Emily's disheveled hair and wrinkled apron. "Looks like you could use all the help you can get."

"Even though it's slow, I've been handling both the bar and the floor, which has run me a bit ragged," Emily grumbled as she tucked a stray lock of golden-brown hair behind her ear. "If you can take over the bar, I'd appreciate it. It's the main attraction these days."

"Sounds great." Cassie gestured to the door of the office. "Lead the way."

The next few hours flew by. Emily wasn't kidding about the bar being the most popular spot in the restaurant. Few of the patrons were ordering food, but she was making a killing in tips serving drinks. Several college guys from the nearby university had come in, and Cassie relished the opportunity to flirt. After all, she'd only finished college a year ago herself, despite being almost twenty-five.

Around eight in the evening, things were slowing down. Cassie took advantage of the lull in customers to wipe down the bar. It would make closing easier if she started cleaning early. The door to the pub opened, and a light breeze followed a new customer. She looked up as he approached the bar. A baseball cap covered his head and obscured his face, though strands of blond hair peeked out from the sides.

"What can I get you?" she asked as he sat down.

"You're new," he said, raising his head and giving her a quick once-over.

"Actually, I'm not," Cassie said. "I'm filling in. My family owns the place."

He did a double take. "You're a Gallagher? Emily or Cassie?"

Wow, personal much? Cassie took a giant step back as she folded her arms across her chest. "Who are you?"

He gave her a sheepish grin. "My apologies. I'm Ryan Caulfield, the mayor of Blue Heron Bay, thanks in large part to your father." He held out his hand, and she hesitated before she took it. "Your dad meant a lot to me, and I like to stop by and check on the place whenever I can."

She worked to swallow past the emotion that welled in her throat whenever someone spoke of her father. He'd mentioned working on a local campaign, but as she'd never much cared for politics, she hadn't paid attention to who the candidate was.

"I'm Cassie," she said. "The youngest of the Gallagher brood."

"It's wonderful to meet you. Did you move back?"

Cassie shook her head. "My siblings and I came home to help our mother, but I'll be leaving at the end of the summer."

"That's too bad, though I'm glad your mother found help." He folded his hands on the bar. "I was afraid I'd asked too much of her when I told her about the hotel group I've pitched to build here."

Cassie nodded absently. She vaguely recalled Emily talking about a hotel during their FaceTime the other day, but truthfully, she'd been more focused on the time off from work than the reason it was needed.

"Now that you're here, I hope to make the most of your time," Ryan said with a wink.

She blinked, unsure what to make of it. Was he flirting with her? She, of all people, should be able to tell, especially after spending much of the evening flirting herself. But he was different, more sincere, more... purposeful. Like he knew what he wanted from life and had a plan for getting exactly that.

"So, can I get you anything?" Cassie asked again.

"Sorry, yes, I'll have a Sam Adams."

She nodded and grabbed a glass before heading over to the taps. The weight of his gaze followed her every move, and she shifted uncomfortably from foot to foot. While there wasn't anything wrong with him necessarily, he wasn't her type. For one thing, he appeared much older than her—maybe mid-thirties?

"Thank you," he said as she set the glass in front of him. "Are you planning to go to the town's Memorial Day parade?"

Cassie gave her one-shoulder shrug. "I'm not sure. I only arrived today."

"And you're already working?" he asked with raised eyebrows.

"I wanted to. Besides, it was a long drive. Feels good to move around."

"How far away are you?" Ryan asked.

She stared at him. *Again, with the personal questions.*

As if he read her mind, he hurried on. "I mean, if you don't mind my asking."

"I'm right outside of D.C.," she said, not wanting to give out too much information. A girl could never be too careful, regardless of his connection to her late father.

"Wow, that's quite a change of pace from here. Do you prefer the city?"

"Usually," Cassie said, the tension in her shoulders easing. "I love being able to walk most places, and there's so much life there. Every day, I meet new people. But I do miss the ocean."

"What do you do?"

Cassie rolled her eyes. Of course, the inevitable professional question. Sometimes it seemed like that was all that mattered to some people: a job, a profession, a neat and tidy box into which they could categorize someone.

"I'm sorry. Did I say something wrong?" Ryan's brows furrowed.

"Not exactly," Cassie said with a sigh. There wasn't much point in explaining it to him. He struck her as a stuffed shirt, and he was clearly established in a career path if he was mayor. There was no way he'd understand. "I'm a paralegal."

His face cleared, as Cassie expected it would, now that she fit into a box in his mind. Typical. And before he spoke again, she knew exactly what he was going to ask.

"Have you ever considered going to law school?"

There it was. She'd known his type from the second he walked in, and he hadn't disappointed. That was the question she was most often asked by business professionals. The question that had been the bane of her existence since she'd finally finished her legal studies degree. Everyone wanted to know what her next move was, her career goals, her ambitions. The truth was, she didn't have any. Why did everyone else adhere to a strict timeline of events for their lives? College, career, marriage, then family. Cassie swallowed another sigh.

"Probably not," she finally said. "I barely finished my bachelor's, so the idea of more school doesn't appeal to me."

Instead of pressuring her, as people often did, he laughed. "I don't blame you. I've thought about going for a J.D. with a focus on tax law, but I don't need to take on more student loan debt."

She couldn't help wrinkling her nose. "That sounds incredibly boring."

Ryan grinned. "It is, but it's also very lucrative." He took a swig of his beer before setting it back on the counter. "I like to keep fallback options in mind, especially since politics is hardly a stable career."

Stability wasn't really a word with which Cassie was well acquainted. She flew by the seat of her pants, and that method hadn't failed her thus far. The idea of having a fallback option more boring than her current job was about as appealing as getting a root canal.

"It was nice to meet you," she said as she moved away. "But I better check on my other customers."

He nodded. "I'm sure I'll see you around while you're in town."

Cassie wasn't sure if that was a threat or a promise.

Emily hid a smile when Anna Mae walked into the pub on Sunday evening. She had provided Anna Mae with a robust history of Blue Heron Bay the day before, and they planned to discuss potential options for how to bring the town back to its heyday.

Anna Mae slid into the same booth and pulled out her laptop. Emily finished up with the only other customers in the dining area before she walked over.

"Water again?" Emily asked.

"I actually thought I might try a cocktail." Anna Mae eyed the bar. "Anything you suggest?"

"Depends on what you like." Emily glanced back at Cassie, who was shaking some concoction before straining it into a martini glass. "My sister can probably make anything you want."

"She's your *sister*?" Anna Mae craned her neck, and Emily shifted her weight, trying to hide her discomfort. Was this beautiful woman really checking out her little sister right now?

"My youngest sibling, Cassie."

Anna Mae looked back up at Emily. "You two look nothing alike."

Emily laughed, pulling up a picture on her phone of her and Cassie when they were younger and Cassie's hair was brown. She handed the phone to Anna Mae. "We do when Cassie's hair isn't dyed."

"Oh, her color isn't natural?" Anna Mae pursed her lips, studying the photo before returning her gaze to the bar. "She wears it well."

Emily worked to quash the burning sensation in her chest. *You barely know this woman. Why are you acting jealous?*

Anna Mae leaned closer. "But I prefer brunettes."

Warmth spread up Emily's neck and into her cheeks. She cleared her throat and tried not to read anything into that statement. "I'll, uh, keep that in mind. So, what can I get you to drink?"

Anna Mae pressed her lips together, as if she were trying to hide a smile. "How about something local? What do people drink around here?"

"The Orange Crush is pretty popular. It's got vodka, Sprite, and orange juice, along with orange liqueur."

"Sounds fun. I'll try it."

Emily nodded and headed to the bar just as Cassie finished serving a group of college guys. She looked up at Emily as she approached.

"One Orange Crush, please," Emily said.

Cassie peered around her. "For the fancy suit?" She arched an eyebrow. "She doesn't strike me as the type."

"She wanted to try something local." Emily shrugged.

"Can't fault her for that." Without another word, Cassie gathered the ingredients and poured them into a glass. After giving it a quick stir with a straw, she stuck an orange slice on the rim as a garnish. She handed the drink to her sister as the pub door opened. "Oh no."

Emily glanced over her shoulder. The mayor was back. Mom said he checked on her regularly since their father had died, but tonight he made a beeline straight for the bar. Biting her cheek to keep from laughing, she had an inkling as to the purpose of his visit this evening.

"What's wrong?" she asked. "He's a nice guy."

Cassie grimaced. "He's so *boring*. He told me all about his career aspirations last night, even though I didn't ask." Her eyes swept over the pub, as if searching for an escape, but it was too late. Ryan had already slid onto a bar stool.

"Good evening, Emily, Cassie."

Emily smiled as she greeted him. "Welcome back. I'd love to stay and chat with you, but I've got to get this drink out." She could feel Cassie's glare on her back as she walked away.

"Here you go." Emily set the cocktail in front of Anna Mae. "Are you ready to order?"

After ordering a Waldorf salad, Anna Mae tilted her head. "Any chance you can join me?"

"If things continue to slow down, I should be able to. Let me put this in, and I'll come right back." Emily headed to the kitchen to give Tony the order then stopped briefly in the bathroom to check her reflection. Her brown hair was pulled back into a ponytail, but some loose tendrils had fallen out. Ignoring the butterflies in her stomach, she combed her fingers through her hair before resecuring it into her hair tie. With a deep breath, she squared her shoulders and headed back out to join Anna Mae.

"Thank you for your overview on the town yesterday," Anna Mae said after Emily sat down. "I did some research and noticed that Blue Heron Bay has almost no social media presence."

"I'm not surprised. Most businesses still advertise open positions around here with Help Wanted signs and newspaper ads."

Anna Mae shook her head. "That's a problem, but it's one I think we can fix." She turned her computer around. "I've created a few advertising campaigns for the town events we discussed."

Emily read the ads on the screen. There were options for the Memorial Day parade, one for the beach bonfire, and another for the Fourth of July fireworks. They included simple designs with photos and GIFs.

"I'm thinking we can post these on different platforms. Some of them will allow us to create event pages. We can also advertise on the college's website and work with the few businesses who do have social media to get the word out."

"Makes sense." Emily tried to sound like she knew what she was talking about, but Anna Mae might as well have been speaking a different language. Social media campaigns? Would that really work?

"We can start with the Memorial Day parade," Anna Mae said. "We don't have a lot of time, since it's tomorrow, but it'll be a nice test run." She clicked off the ads and closed her computer. "What do you think?"

"I'll admit, I'm not well versed in social media, at least not for advertising. But it looks good to me and is much better than the little effort the town has made so far." Emily spread her hands on the table. She was still struggling to wrap her head around all of this. Bringing in tourism, securing a new hotel, and trying to save her father's legacy. "I'm not sure where I come in."

"We can discuss it more over dinner," Anna Mae said, her lips curving into a smile.

Emily's heart skipped a beat. Her growing attraction to the woman in front of her wasn't helping. Emily's legs were wobbly as she stood and went to check on Anna Mae's food. While in the kitchen, she put in an order of her own. A few minutes later, as she carried their food back out into the dining area, she couldn't help wondering why this felt less like a business meeting and more like a date.

Chapter Four

Peter ordered his favorite coffee, a caramel frappe with extra caramel sauce and extra whipped cream, layered. The airport bustled around outside the coffee shop, and he dreaded how full his flight might be. He hated red-eyes, but he didn't have much choice after hanging up with his sisters. The holiday weekend likely meant a lot of travelers, but he held out hope of having a row to himself.

The last thing he needed was an impromptu trip home when he was making such progress on the edits to his dissertation. Sometimes he truly wondered if his family understood how important his doctorate was to him. His dream was to work in public policy, specifically in urban development, providing housing to the less fortunate. But sometimes, his family saw him as a professional student, not interested in getting a so-called "real" job. For him to be the best in his field and to have the ability to teach others, he needed a doctorate, and he was so close, he could almost taste it. If only he could get some support on the home front.

He'd just turned twenty-six earlier that month, and his goal was to complete his program by the end of the year. All he had to do was finish this last round of edits from his advisor, and then he could defend his dissertation to the committee and be cleared for graduation. He was going to lose precious time flying home and dealing with his family's flailing restaurant, but he would do his duty as the only son, with lots of grumbling along the way. Though he expected to assist with the day-to-day running of the pub, he doubted his presence would make much difference in saving it. Still, family was family, and he would be there for them.

Drink in hand, he chose a table near a wall and plugged in his laptop to keep it charged for the flight. Despite the many distractions in the airport, he was more focused than he'd been in days. Was it because he was finally embarking on the trip he'd been dreading, or had he simply accepted his fate? Whatever the reason, he spent the next hour revising various sections of his dissertation.

"Caramel frappe with extra sauce, extra whip, layered," called the barista. Peter looked up with a frown. Had he ordered a second cup? He didn't remember doing so. As he stood to go collect his order, he bumped into a shorter man with wavy black hair.

"Sorry," he said. The man turned, and Peter gazed into the darkest pair of brown eyes he'd ever seen. There was something familiar about the man, though he couldn't quite place him.

"You're fine," the man said. He picked up the caramel frappe.

Peter stared at the drink. He'd never met anyone who ordered his drink the way he did. Sure, people asked for extra whip and extra caramel sauce, but most people swirled the mixture together. Nobody asked for it layered.

"Can I help you with something?" the man asked, and a flush traveled up Peter's neck. He must look like a total idiot, standing in the stranger's way, staring at his drink.

"No, I..." Peter cleared his throat. "Sorry, I've just never heard anyone order the same coffee as me."

The man gave him a brief once-over, and his lips quirked up in a slow smile. "You have good taste."

Before Peter could respond, they announced his flight over the intercom for boarding, and he stumbled back to his table and packed his things. He hurried over to the gate. The eerie sense of familiarity followed him, and he wracked his brain, trying to determine if he knew the man from somewhere.

"Heading to Baltimore?" a voice said behind him as he joined the line of passengers waiting to board.

Peter turned to find the same man from the coffee shop. He nodded. "Going home for the summer."

The man raised an eyebrow. "It's a bit early, isn't it? Are you in college?"

"Grad school," Peter said, feeling sheepish. "For my doctorate."

"Wow, that's ambitious!" He held out his hand. "I'm Ricardo Capeluto."

Peter accepted his hand; the warm brown of Ricardo's skin was a stark contrast against Peter's pale fingers. Despite spending the last several years in L.A., Peter never managed to get a tan. He blamed his Irish genes.

As he opened his mouth to respond, his own name caught in his throat. He'd finally connected the dots on where he knew Ricardo from. Yanking his hand away, he shoved it in his pocket.

"Something wrong?" Ricardo asked with a quizzical frown.

Peter forced his expression to remain neutral. "I'm surprised you don't recognize me."

Ricardo's eyes narrowed. "I'm sorry. Do we know each other?"

"We went to the same high school. I'm Peter." His fist clenched involuntarily when Ricardo didn't immediately recognize his name. "Peter Gallagher? Valedictorian?"

"Oh! I can't believe I didn't realize it sooner. Which is sad because you look exactly the same." Ricardo flashed a broad smile, which caused flutters in Peter's traitorous stomach. "How've you been?"

"Fine," Peter said through his teeth. *Is he serious?* High school might have been over a decade ago, but Peter couldn't imagine how Ricardo could have forgotten how much he and his jock friends had tormented Peter over the years. Unless... Was Ricardo only pretending to remember him?

"Man, what are the odds we'd both end up in California?" Ricardo shook his head, oblivious to Peter's tense demeanor. "I'm heading home as well, though, for business first and then to visit family."

Curiosity got the better of Peter. "What do you do?"

"I work for a resort as an acquisition lead. I find locations for new properties. I'm actually heading home because I just pitched the idea of building right in our hometown to my boss."

"Good luck with that," Peter said with a smirk. "I can't imagine why any big resort would want to build in tiny Blue Heron Bay."

Ricardo frowned. "For starters, it's by the beach, which is a big selling point. But my sources tell me there's another hotel group already sniffing around there."

Peter shrugged noncommittally as he stepped up to hand the gate attendant his ticket and ID, though Ricardo's words triggered a memory of something Emily had said. He'd been so focused on the terrible timing of her request that he'd forgotten she'd mentioned the mayor was hoping to convince a hotel to build in town. He couldn't help rolling his eyes. Who would have thought humble little Blue Heron Bay might be the subject of a hotel bidding war?

As Peter had hoped, he was the only person in his row, and he set up his things just as he liked them. He'd splurged a bit for this trip to give himself more legroom, as he struggled to fold his six-foot-four frame into the tiny space provided. To his surprise, Ricardo had stopped at the row across the aisle.

Ricardo caught his stare and laughed. "I may not be as tall as you, but I like to stretch out."

Peter's face warmed, and he focused on putting his carry-on into the overhead compartment. The last thing he needed was a distraction. He hoped to discourage any walks down memory lane, especially since they'd likely prove to be more painful than wistful for him. Despite how well he had done academically, high school was not a time he wanted to revisit.

"You look wired." Ricardo sat across from Peter and buckled himself in. "I take it you don't plan to use this time to nap."

"Unfortunately, no." Nor did he plan to use it to chat, particularly with his old high school nemesis. "I'm hoping to defend my dissertation in the fall, and I have several revisions to make before it'll be ready."

"Ah, so you're almost done then." Ricardo's voice was tinged with awe, and Peter swelled with unexpected pride. At least *someone* understood what a tremendous accomplishment this was, though he wished it wasn't the bane of his teenage existence. "What's your focus?"

Peter glanced at Ricardo from the corner of his eye, unsure if he was truly interested or just placating him. "Public policy, specifically in housing. I want to increase access to safe and affordable housing for the disadvantaged and homeless."

"My mom and I could have used something like that when I was growing up," Ricardo said. He gave a small smile that didn't quite reach his eyes.

"What do you mean?" Peter asked and then immediately regretted it. What did he care about Ricardo's childhood?

"Just that things were pretty tight when I was in high school. My mom still struggles to find a job in the off-season."

"I, uh, didn't know that," Peter murmured, and he wished he could unknow it now. His growing empathy for Ricardo's plight almost made him want to forgive Ricardo for some of the things he and his friends had done to Peter in high school. Almost.

Peter turned away. He was eager to get airborne and hoped he could get back into the zone he had found in the coffee shop. The more work he finished before he arrived home, the better chance he had of meeting deadlines. Somehow, he suspected that though he had told Emily and Cassie he wouldn't take part in town events, they'd somehow convince him otherwise.

Before long, they were taxiing down the runway, and Peter allowed himself the momentary distraction of watching the world whiz by. He glanced over at Ricardo as the plane lifted into the air and ascended toward the sky. Ricardo gave him a lopsided grin that made Peter's treasonous heart pound.

So much for no distractions.

Memorial Day dawned, and Emily's head was still swimming with all the information Anna Mae had shared with her the night before. She jumped out of bed to prepare for her morning shift at Fiddler's Green. The house was quiet as she slipped down the stairs to the kitchen.

She hadn't told anyone yet about the plans she'd worked on with Anna Mae. They were still brainstorming ideas, and Emily wanted to wait until they had a clear path forward before broaching the subject with her family. What her mother needed most was her children there, rallying around her and helping with the business. Most of Anna Mae's grand ideas would take time to come to fruition, and Emily wanted to make sure she approached the proposals appropriately.

Peter was due to arrive that afternoon, though she didn't think he would be up for too much discussion. She suspected he'd spend his entire red-eye flight working on his dissertation. As proud as she was of her brother and his academic accomplishments, she didn't fully understand the rush to complete his doctorate. Their father had died almost a year ago, and Peter had barely taken enough time away from school to attend the funeral. Emily wasn't sure he'd allowed himself time to grieve.

Sean Gallagher was many things, but a lover of school was not one of them. He was famously quoted in his school yearbook as saying, "School's a drag." And she knew better than anyone how little he comprehended his only son's continued education. As far as their father was concerned, education was only necessary if it helped advance a career. Anything beyond a bachelor's degree was pointless to him.

The floor squeaked above her, and then a door opened. Soft mutterings confirmed Cassie was awake and none too pleased about it.

"Good morning, sunshine," Emily called as Cassie came into the room.

A grumbled, incoherent sound came from Cassie, which Emily assumed was her version of a greeting. She chuckled under her breath and set a mug of coffee on the table. Cassie's unnaturally red hair was tousled about her head, and her bright hazel eyes were dimmer than usual, but she gave Emily a tired smile as she slid into a chair at the table.

"You shouldn't be up yet," Emily said, scolding her lightly. "I told you I'd handle the morning shift since you worked so late last night."

Cassie shrugged. "Couldn't sleep."

"Eager to see our mayor again?" Emily teased, which won her a glare. Ryan had stopped by again the previous night. Since her sister continued to maintain a polite distance, Emily suspected the interest was one-sided. Ryan seemed nice enough, but he was not Cassie's type at all.

Pity. Emily so rarely liked the men her sister dated. His obvious concern for their mother and the success of the pub won him points in her book.

Emily opened the refrigerator and peered inside, trying to determine what she wanted for breakfast. Nobody had made it to the store since she had arrived, and they were running low on supplies. She wondered if she could find some time after her shift ended but then remembered the parade was that afternoon.

"Since you're up, would you mind going to the store this morning?" Emily asked.

Cassie gave her one-shoulder shrug. "Sure. I told Mom I'd be at the pub after the parade."

"Thanks," Emily said. "Peter should be here this afternoon, but he'll probably be too jet-lagged to join us."

"If he's not busy typing away," Cassie said, and Emily detected a note of bitterness in her tone. She snuck a glance at her sister, but Cassie's face betrayed nothing.

Emily stifled a sigh as she pulled out two pieces of bread and popped them into the toaster. Was it a good idea to have Cassie and Peter under the same roof again? They'd never gotten along, and she imagined spending a few weeks in close quarters would not help things.

But what other choice did she have? This was an all-hands-on deck situation to help their mother run the pub and find a way to save it from going under. They were both adults, and they'd figure it out, eventually.

Emily took her toast and a cup of hot cocoa to the table and sat across from Cassie. Her sister had perked up with the help of caffeine, but she still looked worse for wear.

"Maybe you should take tonight off," she said as she buttered her toast. "I can't imagine we'll be that busy."

Cassie shook her head. "There's a game tonight at the university, and I'm hoping some guys will stop by if they win."

"And you don't want to miss a chance to flirt?"

"I only flirt for tips." Cassie playfully swatted her. "Besides, I like bartending. It's mindless in a way. Not that it's easy, but it's a different skill set, which gives the analytical side of my brain a rest."

"You're not happy in your new job?"

"I'm not." Cassie's shoulders drooped forward. "It sounded like such a great opportunity at first, you know? Small law office, a chance to grow with the practice." She rested her hand on her chin. "But my boss sounded a lot more ambitious in the interview than he acts in real life. It's like he's waiting for some sort of Erin Brockovich case that'll put him on the map instead of building up his clientele more naturally through referrals and advertising." Her fingers fiddled with the handle of her mug. "At least it was only temporary. They'll probably offer the permanent position to my replacement."

"I'm surprised you went with law in the first place," Emily said before taking a bite of her toast. She gazed at Cassie thoughtfully. "Have you completely given up on writing?"

"It's not a very lucrative profession. And I'm not cut out for the starving-artist lifestyle." Cassie flipped her tangled hair over her shoulder. "I'd like to get back to it once I've established myself somewhere, but it's hard to be creative when I'm always worrying about money."

"Why don't you go back to D.C.? You did well at the bigger law firms."

"No, thank you," Cassie retorted, crossing her arms over her chest. "Between the commute and the pompous lawyers, it's not my scene."

"Okay..." Emily wasn't sure any type of work fit her sister's *scene*. "What about the government?"

With her head tilted toward the ceiling, Cassie tapped her chin. "It's a thought, but it's so hard to get into."

"Could be worth a shot." Emily sipped her cocoa and smiled, an idea forming in her head. "You could, uh, ask your friend the mayor for a job with the city."

Cassie scowled. "Not funny."

With a laugh, Emily patted her sister's arm. "You never know, it might not be such a bad idea." She walked to the sink to rinse out her mug. "Think about it. You could move back home for a while, get yourself situated. There's probably some promotional potential in the city government too. And then you could work part-time at the pub."

"But I have a life in Silver Spring," Cassie protested. "Besides, it's too quiet here. I need the hustle and bustle of the city. Great museums within walking distance or vibrant nightlife a short metro ride away."

"I don't get the appeal," Emily said as she pulled a notepad from a drawer and began jotting down items for Cassie to pick up. She handed it to her sister when she was done. "But to each their own, I suppose. I've got to get ready for my shift. Don't forget to ask Mom if she needs anything before you go."

"Will do."

Emily headed up the stairs to dress and prepare for her day, her heart pounding at the idea of seeing Anna Mae again.

Her phone rang as she was brushing her long brown hair. She glanced at it and grinned as Jen's face lit up the screen.

"So, how'd it go with Mr. Right Now?"

"Really well," Jen gushed. "We went to this wonderful seafood restaurant on Solomon's Island and then took a stroll along the water." She sighed. "It was so romantic."

"Does this mean we're dropping the 'now' and just calling him Mr. Right?" Emily asked, teasing.

"Maybe Mr. Perfect is more appropriate." Jen laughed. "How are things with the pub?"

Emily closed her eyes, wishing she had better news to share. "Not good. But they might look up." She told Jen about her meetings with Anna Mae.

"Do I detect a personal interest in this hotel heiress?" Jen asked.

"I-I'm not sure what you mean." Emily swallowed.

"Uh-huh. When are you seeing her again?"

"She's coming by today."

"Oh? For a lunch date?"

Emily bristled. Sometimes her friend's tendency to romanticize every little thing got on her nerves. "It's not a date. We're trying to brainstorm ways to increase tourism to the town, and hopefully, in doing so, we'll improve business at the pub."

"You keep telling yourself that."

"Even if I was interested in her, which I most certainly am not, what good would it do to get involved when I'll be heading back to Hidden River at the end of the summer?"

"You never know," Jen said. "Besides, it wouldn't kill you to have a little fun while you're there. When's the last time you had a date, anyway?"

Emily wracked her brain. "Probably the political pundit you set me up with last election season."

"Oh, goodness." Jen guffawed. "I'd forgotten that. What a train wreck that turned out to be."

"Yeah, thanks for that. She still messages me sometimes with campaign contribution requests."

"I'm sorry," Jen said, though her tone suggested she wasn't sorry at all. "But in all seriousness, I'd love to see you happy."

"Now you sound like my mother," Emily grumbled. She glanced at the time. "Look, I've gotta go. My shift is starting soon, but I'm glad things look promising with Mr. Perfectly Right."

"Have fun!"

Emily ended the call. Jen meant well, but she played fast and loose with her heart, which wasn't Emily's style.

"It's just business," she said to herself, but the expression staring back at her suggested she didn't buy her insistence any more than Jen had.

Chapter Five

CASSIE WANDERED DOWN THE AISLES OF THE GROCERY store, throwing into the cart many items that weren't on her list but sounded delicious. She'd forgotten the first rule of food shopping: don't do it on an empty stomach. Still, her mother had given her enough money to feed an army, and that was exactly what she was preparing to do. Her cart grew heavier with each new item, and she struggled to maneuver it around the tight turns in the store.

She hesitated at the end of an aisle near the cash registers, trying to see around the corner. She pushed the cart forward, only to hit something hard.

"Ouch!" cried someone in a deep voice.

She hurried around the cart. "I'm so sorry. I didn't see you." Her eyes met the now-familiar green eyes of Ryan Caulfield, and she stifled a sigh. So not what she needed right now. "Oh, hello, Ryan."

His face broke into a broad grin. "Cassie." He leaned against the edge of her cart. "You know, were it anyone else, I may have pressed charges. Since it's you, I'll let it slide."

"I appreciate that," Cassie said politely, wishing she could find a tactful way out of this conversation. Unfortunately, tact was a skill she'd yet to acquire.

He surveyed her items and whistled. "Are the Gallaghers having a party I wasn't invited to?"

"I'm restocking before my brother's imminent arrival," she said.

"Ah, the prodigal son returns." He gave her a wink. "I've heard a lot about him. He's quite famous in town."

Cassie choked back a groan. *Oh yes, perfect Peter.* Everyone's favorite golden boy. She'd hated following him through school. He'd set the bar so high, Cassie had no hope of ever reaching everyone's expectations. She was a mediocre student at best. Even now, as an adult, she still couldn't escape his shadow.

"That's him." She tried to keep the bitterness out of her voice. "If you'll excuse me, I need to finish shopping before my shift at the pub."

She tried moving past him, but he placed his hand on hers. "Here, this looks heavy. Let me help you."

"I-I can manage," she said, protesting, though it was clear from the fact that she'd almost run him over that she was struggling.

"I wouldn't want you to cause any further casualties," he joked as he stepped beside her and began steering the cart. "Where to next?"

Figuring the fastest way out of this situation was to humor him, she gave in and pointed to the next aisle. They walked through the rest of the store together, with Ryan doing most of the talking.

"The parade today looks to be well attended," he said as they turned the corner. "I'm hoping it's a sign that things are looking up for Blue Heron Bay."

Cassie nodded absently as she looked for the next thing on her list. It was easier to just let him drone on than actively engage in conversation. Especially since he had a habit of asking her a lot of personal questions. She wasn't usually a private person, but something about him put her on guard. Sometimes he could be a little *too* friendly, and she didn't want to encourage his apparent interest in her.

When they reached the checkout, Ryan helped empty the cart, and Cassie's eyes widened at how much she had gotten. She wondered if she'd overdone it, but with Peter coming home, she figured it couldn't hurt to have extra food around. Besides, if the total came to more than her mother had given her, she was pretty sure she had enough to cover the rest.

As the cashier rang up the last of her items, it shocked Cassie to hear she owed over three hundred dollars. What on earth had she bought to make the price so high? Her mother had given her just over half that amount, and she swallowed as she pulled out her credit card.

On the bright side, maybe she wouldn't need to come back to the store in the near future, which would mean one less chance to run into Ryan. And if she was lucky, he wouldn't bother to stop by the pub now he'd gotten his daily dose of Cassie-time. She discreetly crossed her fingers as she took her credit card out of the machine and signed.

"Well, thanks," she said as Ryan pushed the cart out to the parking lot. "But I can manage from here."

"I've come this far. Might as well help you unload," Ryan said.

She suppressed another sigh and led the way to her hatchback.

"I recognize this car," he said. "Did your dad help you pick it out?"

Cassie nodded, bewildered by how he knew so much about her when she didn't recall her father ever mentioning him. Or perhaps he had, and she'd forgotten. "He also cosigned the loan."

"You should know, your dad was so proud of you," Ryan said as he stopped beside the car and waited for her to unlock the trunk. "He was thrilled to help you buy it. It was the proof he needed to know you were going to be okay."

Cassie blinked back tears and tried hiding them with a frown. "By buying a car?"

"Mm, I think it was more what the car represented." Ryan began unloading the bags. "He took it as a sign you were settling into your life, finding some stability."

While she bristled at the word *settling*, Cassie couldn't deny his words touched her. When she had asked her father for help with the loan, it was with swallowed pride. Despite having worked through college, her credit was a mess, and she'd needed a cosigner on the loan in order to get a good deal. She'd feared disappointing her father by not standing on her own two feet as an adult. To hear that this decision made him proud was validating in ways she'd never imagined.

"It's almost paid off," she said. "A few more months and I will own it outright."

Ryan's answering smile brightened his entire face, and for a moment, he looked much younger than she'd assumed, closer to Emily's age of thirty. He still wasn't her type, but she had to admit, begrudgingly, that he was kind of cute.

"Thanks for your help," she said, surprised how much she meant it.

"Anytime. Will I see you this evening for my usual?"

"I'll be the one pouring the beer," Cassie said, for once not dreading the interaction. Who knew? Maybe they'd even become friends. But that was as far as it'd go. He not only wasn't her type, but he also didn't quite fit the fairy-tale romance she had in her head. Her parents had been high school sweethearts, and while it was far too late to hope for a similar outcome, Cassie held them up as her ideal. She refused to settle for anything less.

She climbed into her car and headed back to her childhood home, warmed by what Ryan had shared about her father. Cassie had always been the misfit, some might say the black sheep of the family. Her parents had worried over the years about whether she'd ever find her footing, so it meant the world to learn of her father's faith in her.

As she turned into the driveway, a car sat idling at the curb, and her brother stood on the sidewalk. He was shaking the hand of a handsome man with a deep tan and a thick head of black hair. Cassie's eyes traveled over the stranger with interest. But as the handshake lasted longer than was customary, it dawned on her she might not be this man's type.

"Peter," she called as she got out of her car and walked over. "We weren't expecting you until later."

"Traffic was light," he said, greeting her with a brief one-armed hug.

"Glad you made it in one piece." Cassie assessed his companion. "Who's your friend?"

"Wow, Cassie, I almost didn't recognize you with red hair. It looks good on you," the man said.

Cassie stepped back, confused. She tilted her head as she tried to match the face before her to a name. After a moment, it clicked. She turned to her brother. "How'd you score a ride with the best lacrosse player in the state?"

Peter glowered at her, but Ricardo laughed. "I don't know that I'd go that far, but definitely the best on the Eastern Shore."

Though she suspected her efforts would be in vain, Cassie couldn't resist an opportunity to flirt. She playfully placed her arm on his bicep. "Oh, don't be so modest. You were amazing back in the day."

"It was a long time ago." Ricardo shifted closer to Peter, unfazed by her charms.

Cassie nodded, her suspicions confirmed. *Definitely gay.*

Ricardo gazed up at their family home. "This place still looks the same." He turned to Peter. "I bet you miss it."

"Oh, Pete rarely graces us with his presence these days," Cassie said. She poked Peter in the ribs. "Everyone's been asking when the prodigal son will return."

Peter glared at her. "Don't you have somewhere to be?"

"Actually, dear brother, I could use your help." Cassie jerked her thumb over her shoulder. "I've got a trunk full of groceries. Would you mind carrying some of them inside?"

"I won't keep you," Ricardo said. "It was nice to see you both again. And Peter, I'd love to catch up while we're both in town. You have my number." He held Peter's gaze for a moment before getting back into his car and driving away.

"Oooh," Cassie cooed. "Looks like someone has a new boyfriend."

Peter scowled. "Oh, grow up." He pushed past her and stalked over to the car, grabbing two handfuls of bags before stomping to the house.

Cassie hid a smirk as she followed behind him. Between Emily's hotel heiress and Peter's blast from the past, Cassie wondered if all the Gallagher children were going to have summer flings.

Well, except for me. If her only hope of romance was with the mayor, she'd just as well stay single.

Emily paced from the bar to the host stand and back as she waited for Anna Mae to arrive. The morning had been disappointingly slow and provided little distraction. While she tried to tell herself she only wanted to see Anna Mae for the pub, she couldn't deny the way her heart stuttered whenever she looked into those lovely brown eyes.

A blast of warm air hit Emily from behind as she was clearing a table, and she turned to find Anna Mae bustling into the pub, her lips set in a determined line. She gave Emily a brief nod before heading to her usual table.

She seems... different today. Emily finished busing the table and took the dishes into the kitchen. When she returned, Anna Mae had already set out her laptop and was furiously typing away.

"Can I get you anything?"

"Please sit." Anna Mae lifted her left hand briefly from the keyboard to point at the bench opposite her in the booth before resuming her manic typing.

Emily's stomach churned, and she wiped her clammy hands on her pants. "Is something wrong?" She cringed as her voice came out all squeaky.

Anna Mae looked up at her. "I'm sorry. I'm all business this morning." Her eyes trailed back to the screen. "Give me one second to finish this email, and then I'll give you my full attention."

Emily nodded and took several deep breaths to calm herself. If something was bothering Anna Mae, it likely had nothing to do with her. Still, she clasped and unclasped her hands beneath the table, her leg bouncing so hard it vibrated.

A few moments later, Anna Mae clicked the mouse on her laptop and then set it aside. She clasped her hands in front of her and forced a smile. "There have been several developments lately. I'm afraid things aren't looking good for the hotel."

"Oh? Why?" Emily asked.

"My father expected more business in the off-season, especially since this is a holiday weekend." She leaned her elbows on the table and rubbed her temples with her index fingers as she closed her eyes. "He's coming to see the town for himself. If we don't put on one hell of a show, he's likely to look elsewhere, though our remaining options are limited." She opened her eyes and stared at Emily. "I've exhausted most of the towns that met the criteria of less development with open-minded government, and I really don't want to go back to the drawing board of finding new locations, especially since I'd hoped to get a new project off the ground before the end of the year. If I have to start from scratch, that won't happen." She grimaced. "And apparently, we're not the only group scoping out this town."

"What do you mean?" Emily cocked her head. She couldn't imagine two large hotel chains were interested in tiny Blue Heron Bay.

"Sunrise Oasis Resorts has sent a representative to scout out the place. They're looking for underdeveloped oceanfront towns as well, but they'll build a monstrosity that'll require clearing several city blocks." Anna Mae frowned. "And it won't help the town's small businesses because they'll bring in restaurants and stores of their own. If they get their hooks into this town, they will put a lot of places out of business."

"Even Fiddler's Green?" Emily's stomach dropped.

Anna Mae nodded gravely. "Even Fiddler's Green." She fell back against the bench and sighed. "It would certainly help with tourism, but it wouldn't be the same town anymore."

"What can we do?" Emily asked. Somehow, the ideas they had discussed the other day felt like child's play now that another developer was in the picture. And she doubted the resort representative would be open to hearing the ideas of the daughter of a local business owner.

"Convince my dad to stick to the plan." Anna Mae leaned forward as she peered at Emily. "I can't guarantee that would keep the resort away; however, it might be enough competition to keep Sunrise from taking over the whole town. While we incorporate restaurants into some of our hotels, our goal here is to limit our footprint while still bringing in business to the town through our loyal customers."

"But how do we convince him?" Emily frowned as her mind whirled through the possibilities. She didn't know the first thing about increasing tourism.

"We need to bring people into town before he gets here." Anna Mae pulled her laptop back in front of her. "I'm working on more publicity for the events we discussed before, but I don't think it's enough. Maybe if you held nightly events here, that might help. Other than the parade, the bonfire, and the fireworks, there isn't much in the way of nightlife. You're already bringing in the college crowd, but we're going to need more than a few frat boys if we're going to pull this off."

"We normally start doing trivia and karaoke nights every week in June." The events were a lot of work, which was why the Gallaghers discontinued them in the off-season. "Maybe we could start sooner and make it a family-friendly event. Or host kid trivia nights in addition to our normal trivia. Like Disney or other kids' shows."

Anna Mae's face brightened for the first time since she'd walked into the pub, which only made her more beautiful. Emily struggled to breathe. "And we could have some sort of trending karaoke, where the options are popular songs on social media or from kids' movies. That's genius!"

"We could have themed drinks as well, both nonalcoholic for the kids' nights and alcoholic ones for the adults," Emily said, her heartbeat quickening as the ideas tumbled out of her.

"Like a Shirley Temple but named after a Disney princess or YouTube star."

"Exactly!"

"We may be on to something," Anna Mae said as she opened a Word document. "How long would it take you to put this together?"

"Not long. We print and laminate the menus ourselves, so updating those isn't a problem. I could ask Cassie to help me with the trivia and karaoke."

"Perfect. And I can get started on the social media campaign." Anna Mae grinned over the table at her, causing Emily's heart to kick into overdrive. "We're going to give this town a summer it'll never forget!"

Chapter Six

After helping Cassie carry in the groceries, Peter took his things up to his room and immediately set up his laptop. He'd lost precious time on the plane, as he kept getting distracted by his attractive former rival sitting across from him. But now, he desperately needed to get some work done.

Though he knew he should go to the pub and greet his mother and Emily, he wanted some time to himself. Besides, he was going to be stuck here for the next few weeks. What difference would an hour or two make? The sounds of Cassie's movements around the kitchen drifted up the stairs as she put away the groceries. She said she was working the lunch shift at the pub but had promised not to tell Emily or their mom he'd arrived. He'd told her he wanted it to be a surprise, and she hadn't seemed to care either way.

Hours later, eyes bloodshot and glazed over, Peter pushed back from his computer. He'd more than made up for the lost time on the flight. If he could find a few hours each day to dive into it, he'd be able to send his revisions back in no time. He stood and stretched, trying to get the kinks out of his back. The jetlag was kicking in, but if he tried to sleep now, he'd never get on the right clock.

His phone buzzed. A text message from Ricardo. He tapped the notification.

Thank you for making a long drive enjoyable. Hope to see you soon.

Peter wasn't sure how to take the text. While Ricardo had talked for most of the ride, Peter had vacillated between stewing in uncomfortable silence and fighting his growing interest in what Ricardo had been up to since high school. He'd thought about confronting Ricardo, but he didn't want to make things awkward. Perhaps he should let the past stay in the past. After all, Ricardo wasn't an active participant in bullying Peter. He just hadn't stopped his friends and teammates from doing it.

Peter decided not to respond to the text. It would be difficult to avoid Ricardo in this tiny town, but he would do his best.

When he arrived at the pub, an uneasy feeling settled in the pit of his stomach. It was quiet, too quiet. Maybe Emily had been right to call them home. The pub was in real trouble if things were always this slow. Come to think of it, the town itself seemed to be lacking in tourists. That weekend was usually the kickoff to the summer, but Blue Heron wasn't boasting the usual beach crowd.

"Peter!" Emily called as he entered. "You're here." She rushed over and pulled him into a warm embrace. "Oh, I've missed you."

"Missed you too," he said as he wrapped his arms around her. Despite his reluctance to come, he was happy to see her again. It had been too long. He stepped back and surveyed the pub. "So, I'm here. Where do you want me to start?"

Emily bit her lip. "We were actually in the process of shutting down to head over to the Memorial Day parade."

Peter frowned. "Are you sure that's wise?" He glanced at the televisions over the bar, where the local university was playing baseball. "The game's on. Maybe some of the college kids will show up."

"I'd hoped for the same thing, but it's not looking likely." Cassie slid out from behind the bar and came over to them. "If they were winning, they might come out to celebrate, but they're losing."

"We see little action when it's a home game. And most people will go to the fireworks on the beach afterward," a blond man said as he stepped up behind Cassie. He held out his hand to Peter. "It's nice to meet the last of the Gallagher clan. I'm Ryan, the mayor of this town."

Peter shook his hand. "Nice to meet you." He looked around the pub for their mother, but the only other person there was a young woman with black hair standing behind Emily. "Where's Mom?"

"She's in the back," Emily said. "Peter, I want you to meet Anna Mae Wakefield, Director of PR at the Wakefield Hotel Group." The dark-haired woman stepped forward and smiled. "She's the reason we're all back home. I've been working with her on a publicity campaign for the town to make it more attractive to her father's hotel group."

"It's nice to meet you," Peter said, working to keep his expression neutral. *A publicity campaign? In this town?* He wished her luck. She was going to need it.

"So, are we going to the parade or what?" Cassie demanded, tapping her foot in impatience. Peter resisted the urge to roll his eyes. Getting out of work early was one of Cassie's favorite pastimes.

"I'm happy to stay and hold down the fort while you all go to the parade," Peter said. After all, he'd come all this way to help save the pub, not waste time attending silly town events.

"Let me check with Mom and see what she wants to do." Emily headed to the back, leaving everyone else awkwardly standing by the bar.

"Emily tells me you're working on your doctorate," Anna Mae said to Peter, breaking the silence.

"Trying to," Peter said, running a hand through his hair. "I'm hoping to graduate next spring."

"That's such a significant accomplishment," Ryan said. "Your mom must be so proud."

Peter shrugged. He wasn't sure what his mother thought. She was likely proud of him for anything he did, and she certainly put more stock into education than his father had. But that still didn't mean she, or anyone in his family for that matter, truly understood what he was trying to accomplish. He'd tried to explain it before, but as neither of his parents had gone to college, they didn't see the value in continuing an education beyond a bachelor's degree. His dissertation on the housing crisis alone demonstrated how much work there was still to be done to fight homelessness, and that was why he had continued through school. He hoped to take all of his research and apply it to reducing the homeless epidemic in the country.

Emily came back a moment later with Mom trailing behind. The dark circles under his mother's eyes concerned him, and the worry lines on her forehead seemed deeper. It struck Peter in that moment how much of a toll their father's death must have taken on her.

Her face brightened. "Peter! Welcome home." She rushed forward and threw her arms around him.

He returned the embrace, bending down slightly to kiss her head. "Hi, Mom."

She pulled away just far enough to look at him and touched her hand to his cheek. "I'm so glad to see you. How was your flight? Have you eaten?"

Peter couldn't help smiling. While she might have physically aged since he'd last seen her, she was still the same overprotective mom she'd always been. He nodded reassuringly and cupped her hand with his own.

"My flight was fine. I had a late lunch."

"Yes, yes, we're all happy the prodigal son has returned," Cassie grumbled behind them, flipping her unnaturally red hair over her shoulder. "Can we please go to the parade now?"

His mother shot Cassie a look before turning her gaze to the empty pub. "I don't see why not. Between the parade and the fireworks, I doubt we'll see another soul in here." She turned back to Peter with a tired smile. "And I want to hear about your progress in your program."

Peter stifled a sigh. It looked like there was no chance of him getting out of this outing. Even Tony had cleaned up the kitchen and seemed ready to head out the door. Without a cook, there wasn't much point in sticking around the pub.

Well, one town event won't kill me. He offered his mother his arm, and they all filed out of the restaurant.

As they walked to the parade route, everyone fell into pairs of twos. Anna Mae and Emily led the group, with Mom and Peter in the middle, which left Cassie and Ryan bringing up the rear, much to her chagrin.

"Have you been to the parade recently?" Ryan asked.

"It's been a while," Cassie said. "We used to go every year when I was younger, but when my dad got sick, things changed." She stared at the ground. "It was one of his favorite events of the summer." Blinking back the tears that threatened to fall, she turned to him, hoping to change the subject. "What made you decide to run for mayor?"

"Your dad actually encouraged me. I was at the pub one night, complaining about the state of Blue Heron Bay." He shook his head. "It used to be such a popular destination, but the last several mayors we've had... They just drove the city into the ground. After so many budget cuts, the town's upkeep efforts fell into disarray."

Cassie looked at the city around them. Sure, some of the streets could use some repaving and the sidewalks were a bit uneven, but otherwise, it didn't look much different to her.

"Your dad told me I should put my money where my mouth is and run for mayor." His face broke into a broad grin. "I thought he was crazy, but he even offered to be my campaign manager." He cleared his throat. "But then he was diagnosed, and I worried it would be too much for him. He still helped out. I ran on promises to clean up the town, and we did that." He gestured to the streets. "There used to be litter everywhere, but now it's better, which is good for both the people and the environment." His expression changed as he frowned. "But it's not enough."

"What do you mean?"

"Well, you grew up here. Do you remember it ever being so empty?"

With a frown, she thought back to how empty the pub was the night she arrived. Come to think of it, the town seemed to be lacking its usual beach traffic. "It has seemed a bit quieter than I'm used to."

"Exactly," Ryan said. "That's why I asked the local businesses to do what they could to attract customers. We need everyone to pitch in if we have hopes of saving our town." He glanced at her. "I'm glad you're here."

Before Cassie could respond, they'd arrived at the convention center. Ryan bid Cassie and her family a quick farewell before disappearing into the crowd. As the mayor, he would participate in the parade. She would never admit it to anyone, but a part of her was sad to see him go.

She followed her family behind the building to the small back road that was the start of the parade route, their feet crunching on the gravel. A small crowd had gathered, and Cassie couldn't help seeing it with new eyes. There were a few families, some college kids, and a smattering of older couples, but otherwise, the mass of people who used to attend were nowhere to be found. Guilt needled her stomach. The last few times she'd come to visit, she had relished the open space on the beaches, so much different from neighboring Ocean City, where if she didn't arrive early enough, it was hard to stake her claim on a large enough spot for her towel and beach chair. But the reality of what those empty stretches of sand meant hit her like a bucket of ice water being dumped over her head. No wonder the pub was in trouble.

"Let's sit over there," her mother said, waving her hand toward a bench on the sidewalk.

They'd barely made it in time. Soon after they sat down, a whistle blew, and then the sound of drums beat through the air. The marching band appeared a moment later, and they launched into a loud rendition of "The Star-Spangled Banner." Cassie and her family stood, hands over their hearts, as the band marched past them.

The few floats were nothing terribly elaborate. A fire truck came through, covered with American flags. Several groups marched, including the local Boy Scout troop, the police department, and a unit of the Maryland National Guard. Cassie particularly enjoyed that part. Was there anything better than a man in uniform?

A horse-drawn carriage sporting Ryan and some of his staff brought up the end of the procession. Cassie couldn't help noticing how distinguished he looked, waving to the crowd and smiling. His eyes met hers as he went by, and he winked before turning to the other side of the road. Her cheeks flushed, and she dropped her gaze, hoping no one had seen that. The last thing she needed was for rumors to start flying just as the summer season kicked off. Or worse, risk Emily upping her matchmaking game.

Once the carriage had rounded the bend, the small crowd that had gathered behind the convention center began dispersing. Cassie stood and stretched, turning to her family.

"Are we heading back to the house or the pub?" Emily asked.

Her mom sighed. "Honestly, I'm not sure it's worth it to reopen the pub. Tomorrow is a workday, so I doubt people will be going out after the parade, and we've never had much business on Memorial Day, even before tourism started to decline, because people prefer to be outside." She turned to Anna Mae. "I'm hoping you and Ryan will join us. We usually sit around the firepit after the parade. It's part of our tradition to welcome summer."

"I'd love to!" Anna Mae said.

"Cassie, why don't you stay a minute to invite Ryan," Emily said, a smug smile on her lips.

Cassie glowered at her. What game was Emily playing? Had she seen his wink or Cassie's reaction? Before Cassie could argue, Ryan himself appeared at her side.

"Oh good, you're back," her mother said. "I've invited you and Anna Mae back to our house, if you're free."

"Sounds great." Ryan immediately turned to Cassie. "If that's okay with you?"

"Of course," Cassie said with a forced smile. "Any friend of Dad's is always welcome."

He frowned, and she imagined that wasn't the reaction he was hoping for, but she didn't want to encourage him. After all, she was only here for the summer, and he seemed really devoted to the town. She didn't see the point in starting something that wouldn't last. But she wasn't about to be rude. That wasn't who her father had raised her to be.

"This was fun," he said as they followed her family back to the pub.

Cassie nodded. "The parade is such a great kickoff to summer. Brings back a lot of memories from my childhood."

"You definitely seemed in your element." He touched her arm, allowing the others to move ahead of them. Her skin prickled, and she braced herself for whatever he was about to say.

"I was wondering if you'd like to have dinner sometime," he said, and when she didn't immediately respond, he added: "With me."

Cassie swallowed. Knowing her father would have approved of the match gave her pause. On the one hand, one date wouldn't hurt anything, but on the other, it would likely mean much more to him than it would to her, and she didn't want to hurt his feelings. He was a nice enough guy, attractive and kind, but he seemed like he was looking for more than a summer fling, and she'd head back to the city in August. Besides, she liked her men less buttoned-up and a heck of a lot more fun.

"I-I'm not sure I'll have much time for dating while I'm home," she finally said, wishing she had a better excuse. Maybe she should have told him she had a boyfriend. He'd never have known the difference. "Between helping at the pub and spending time with my family, I don't expect to have much time to myself."

"Oh," Ryan said, and his disappointment was tangible. "Well, you're here for the whole summer, right? So, if you find yourself free one evening, let me know."

She didn't reply, and he didn't press. For that, she was grateful. The tension in her shoulders relaxed as the house came into view. She hurried inside after her family, hoping to put a little distance between her and Ryan.

Chapter Seven

EMILY WAS THRILLED WHEN MOM INVITED ANNA MAE OVER. She had given up on convincing herself that her interest in the beautiful woman was solely business-related. The truth was, she'd never met anyone like Anna Mae. She was both kind and fierce, going after what she wanted but not trampling on people in her quest to get it.

Her mom asked Peter and Ryan to help her set up the firepit while Emily, Cassie, and Anna Mae put together snacks and drinks in the kitchen. As Emily gazed over the full cabinets, she found herself both happy that her sister had gone shopping and worried that Cassie went a little overboard on the supplies.

"Anything I can help with?" Ryan asked as he entered the kitchen. He looked right at Cassie, who turned toward the cabinet to get glasses.

"Why don't you take these outside and start roasting some marshmallows?" Emily handed him a bag of marshmallows, bars of chocolate, and graham crackers. Ryan chanced one last look at Cassie before he reluctantly left the kitchen. Cassie sighed with obvious relief once he was gone.

"Everything okay?" Emily asked quietly, not wanting to draw their mother's attention.

"It's fine," Cassie said, though her tone suggested it was anything but. Still, Emily didn't want to press. Maybe she would be more willing to talk when their guests were gone.

Cassie and Anna Mae set about pouring chips into bowls while Emily and her mom took turns bringing beers and wine outside. Once everything was ready, they all took seats around the fire.

"It's such a lovely night," her mom said, a hint of awe in her voice. "Your father would have loved it."

Emily lowered her eyes to her glass of wine to keep the tears at bay. Being home these last few days had been hard. She half expected her father to come in at any moment, his salt-and-pepper hair parted to the side and his hazel eyes twinkling. Compartmentalizing her loss was easier when she was far away from those memories.

"To Dad," Cassie said, raising her glass to the fire.

"To Dad," Peter and Emily said in unison while her mom, Ryan, and Anna Mae said, "To Sean" at the same time.

They were quiet for a moment; the only sound was the crackling wood as the flames licked the logs. Then Cassie set her glass down and grabbed a stick, skewering two marshmallows. Emily followed suit, but Peter didn't move, his eyes never leaving the ground. Cocking his head, he bent forward and picked up a rock.

"Do you remember when we painted these?" he asked, holding up the rock to Emily.

"One of the many crafts Mom tried to occupy us with whenever we were bored in the summer." Emily laughed.

"How could you be bored, living so close to the beach?" Anna Mae asked, her tone teasing.

"Well, both of our parents worked before they bought the pub." Emily kicked at a rock near her foot, dislodging it from the ground. "So going to the beach was a treat." Nudging the multicolored stone toward Cassie, she grinned. "Check this out."

Cassie covered her eyes. "Ugh, I can't believe we kept that one. It's such a mess." She wasn't wrong; the rock in question looked like someone had tried and failed to create a rainbow. The colors were splashed all over the place, with no rhyme or reason to their placement.

"One of yours?" Ryan smirked as he picked it up and tossed it from hand to hand.

"I'm ashamed to say it was." She turned her pleading hazel eyes toward Emily. "Can't we just conveniently 'lose' that one?"

"Nope! I think we should prominently display it in the rose bed out front."

While Cassie groaned, everyone else laughed.

"Are there any embarrassing items you've made that I can see?" Anna Mae asked in a low voice as she scooted her chair closer to Emily.

"I'm sure there are," Emily said as heat crept up her neck, as much from the question as Anna Mae's close proximity. "But I'm hoping you won't find them."

"Aww, but it'd be an honor to see something you made as a child," Anna Mae said. Her warm smile made Emily's heart thump erratically.

"What are your family traditions?" Emily asked, hoping to change the subject.

"Well, the summer months usually involved visiting a lot of our hotels since we were out of school. It wasn't as glamorous as it sounds as my father spent most of the trip working." Anna Mae inclined her head thoughtfully. "We didn't go on many family vacations outside of that, but we did go to the beach a few times. Though it was always on the Gulf of Mexico."

"Had you ever been to the ocean before you started assessing new locations for your hotels?"

"I've been many times since becoming an adult." Anna Mae laughed, and warmth vibrated through Emily's entire being. "Though I'm looking forward to checking out the beach while I'm here. I build pretty impressive sandcastles." She nudged Emily with her shoulder. "You should see them."

"I'd love to, especially if it means a day on the beach with you." Emily bit her lip, worried she'd said too much too soon.

"Sounds like a date." Anna Mae gave Emily's hand a squeeze, and Emily's chest filled with warmth.

As the evening wore on, the sky changed from a bright-orange haze to a purple hue. Emily lost count of how many marshmallows she'd roasted, but she was filled with chocolate and graham-cracker goodness.

"It's getting late," Anna Mae said as she checked her watch. Emily swallowed her disappointment. She wasn't ready for the night to end.

"Yeah, I should go too," Ryan said, and he snuck a glance at Cassie. Whether or not her sister noticed, Emily couldn't tell, but Cassie's eyes never left the fire.

"Thank you both for coming," Julie said warmly, giving them each a hug. "I hope to see you tomorrow at the pub."

"I'll be there," Anna Mae promised.

Ryan nodded. Emily wondered if his daily visits would continue. Something must have happened between him and Cassie on the way home. She'd corner her sister later to get to the bottom of it.

Everyone said their goodbyes, and soon the Gallaghers were alone again. Peter disappeared to his room, presumably to get more work done on his dissertation. Their mother said her goodnights and went to bed.

As Emily doused the fire, Cassie cleaned up the area around the pit. Emily cleared her throat, hoping her sister might be more open to talking now that they were alone. "Did something happen with you and Ryan?"

Cassie didn't answer immediately as she focused on her task, but then she closed her eyes and exhaled heavily. "He asked me out."

"Wow, really? What did you say?"

"I gave some lame excuse about being too busy with the pub."

"If you actually want to go out with him, I'm sure we can spare you for a night."

"I don't," Cassie said quickly. "He's not really my type. And besides, I'm only home for a little while. What's the point of a summer romance?"

Emily frowned as she considered Cassie's words. She hated to admit her sister had a point. When the season was over, they would return to their lives, and Anna Mae lived quite far away. As much as Emily enjoyed spending time with her, what future could they have beyond her time here? Even if her father built the hotel, she had told Emily she wasn't involved with the construction. She would probably move on to seek out their next location soon after closing on the deal. And where would that leave her and Emily?

"Well, there's no harm in going on one date," Emily said, not sure if she was trying to convince Cassie or herself. "I wouldn't want you to work all through the summer and not have any fun."

"I'm sure I'll have fun," Cassie said. "Just not with Ryan." She wrinkled her nose. "He seems like the polar opposite of fun."

Emily laughed and covered her mouth with her hand. "Cassie! You shouldn't say that. He's such a nice man."

"I know." Cassie groaned. "But I don't want 'nice.'"

"Somehow that doesn't surprise me, though it'd be good for you." Emily gave her a pointed look. Cassie always picked the worst sort of guys. She'd yet to bring home anyone her family actually liked.

Cassie threw a marshmallow at her. Emily laughed as she ducked and then stood and stretched. It was late, and she was working the breakfast shift again at the pub the next day. She gave her sister a quick hug and then went upstairs to her room.

After changing into her pajamas and pulling back the covers, Emily climbed into bed. Tomorrow, she hoped to tell her family about the plans she and Anna Mae had come up with over breakfast. They hoped to host the first trivia night on Wednesday and the first karaoke night on Friday. Emily closed her eyes and smiled. Whether a summer romance was a good idea or not, she wanted to enjoy it while it lasted.

When Cassie woke the next morning, she decided to spend a few hours on the beach before her shift. She needed to shake off the lingering guilt over Ryan and clear her head. A cool ocean breeze provided some relief from the hazy humidity that hung heavy in the air. She threw on a cotton T-shirt over her bikini and wrapped a sarong around her hips. Packing her beach bag with a book, sunscreen, and her towel, she debated bringing her boogie board. Would she have time to catch a few waves before her shift? She supposed it couldn't hurt to bring it.

The sun had risen only an hour before, and the streets were quiet and still. She imagined most people had either already left for work or were just waking up. It was nice to have a leisurely morning all to herself.

She crossed the street and climbed up the steep stairs that would take her over the sand dunes. The sound of the waves hitting the shore grew louder the higher she climbed, and she breathed the scent of brine deep into her lungs. Her favorite place was by the water. It soothed her soul in a way nothing else could.

Once she reached the bottom step, she kicked off her shoes and dug her toes into the sand. The grains scraped her skin in a pleasant way, sloughing off her winter skin. She raised her head and scoped out a good spot.

The beach was empty, save for a few people walking their dogs or setting up fishing poles. Off in the distance, the pier jutted out from the water, and Cassie headed in that direction.

She kept her eyes on the horizon, enjoying the way the morning sun reflected on the rippling water. Several boats were already out there. Likely watermen trying to get the day's catch before the heat and humidity became unbearable.

As she neared the pier, a lifeguard ran across the beach to one of the many white chairs that spotted the shoreline. He was shirtless as he pushed the chair closer to the water, and Cassie admired his broad shoulders and tanned skin. There was something familiar about him, though she couldn't place it.

I could use some eye candy. She settled her towel on the sand near the lifeguard and began applying sunscreen. Her eyes strayed in his direction more often than she'd like to admit as she rubbed the cream into her skin. If he'd noticed her staring, he didn't give any indication.

Once she was fully protected, she lay down on her towel and pulled out a book. But within a few minutes, she was bored. She'd never been one to sit on the beach and tan. A water baby at heart, she wanted to jump the waves. Grateful for her forethought in bringing her bodyboard, she picked it up, wrapped the Velcro strap around her wrist, and bounded toward the sea.

The water was much colder than she anticipated, and she gasped. She stood for a moment, letting her body acclimate to the temperature before pressing on. Foamy tide caressed her skin, and she sighed. It felt like coming home.

She waded farther in, jumping up from her tiptoes as the waves rolled in, holding the board above her head. The undertow was strong, and she struggled to keep upright as she moved past the breakwater to greater depths. She slid her bodyboard under her and turned herself parallel to the shoreline as she watched for the perfect wave.

It was peaceful. Only a few surfers ventured as far out as she did. The majority of the beachgoers preferred to remain along the shoreline, the water barely brushing their ankles. The roar of the waves and the wind blocked out every other sound. For a while, she simply enjoyed the gentle rock of the sea, bobbing up and down like a bottle in the tide.

A sudden shout caught her attention. She jerked her head back toward the shore and saw that a small crowd had gathered on the beach. She scanned the horizon, trying to figure out what was happening. It took a minute, but eventually, she realized they were staring at her. The lifeguard she'd admired earlier was waving his orange flotation device and calling to her, while everyone around him covered their mouths in horror.

What the—but then she saw them. Fins, three of them, cutting through the water.

She'd seen *Jaws* enough times to understand the fear on the faces of the people on shore. But she'd also grown up here, and as the fins crested and disappeared beneath the waves, she couldn't help rolling her eyes. *Tourists.* Could they not see that those were not sharks circling prey, but curious dolphins?

Sure enough, a puff of air came from behind her. She turned and smiled as another dolphin surfaced to her right.

"Well, hello there." She held out her hand, and a gray bottle-shaped nose bumped against it. With a giggle, she stroked its rubbery skin. She'd always wanted to swim with dolphins, though this was hardly what she'd expected.

The dolphin clicked before it dove back under the water. Cassie turned back to the shore to reassure the people on the beach, but she was much farther away now, and she couldn't make out their faces anymore. What she could see was that the crowd of spectators had grown.

She started paddling toward shore, the dolphins swimming alongside her, unaware of the havoc they were creating. Despite her attempts to maneuver herself away from the circling fins, her new gray friends seemed as concerned for her safety as the people on the beach. The life-guard had grabbed a surfboard and was paddling out toward her.

As he approached, he called out. "Are you all right?"

"It's okay!" she yelled back. "They're not sharks."

He moved closer, keeping himself at a safe distance from the circling fins. Did he not hear her? She was about to yell again when his face broke into a smile, causing her stomach to swoop. It should be illegal for someone to look that good.

He shook his head and laughed. "I never saw them surface, so I assumed the worst." By this point, he was right next to her. "Still, they are wild animals. Best not to get too close."

"They're harmless," she said with a scoff. As she trailed her hand in the water, one of the dolphins skimmed the surface and bumped her fingers again before diving back under.

"At any rate, we need to head in." He inclined his head. "You've caused quite a stir on shore." With one hand on the board to steady himself, he held his other out to her. "Climb on, and I'll help you back. There's a strong undertow."

As tempting as the offer was to sit with him on his board, she wasn't ready for her fun morning to end. "But why do I have to go in? Can't you just tell them it's a false alarm?"

He raked his hand through his blond hair. "It's not just the dolphins. You're too far out for adequate supervision."

A quick glance confirmed she was continuing to drift out to sea. "Okay, then I can just swim back toward the shore." She lowered herself on her board and began kicking underwater, propelling herself forward. The dolphins continued to swim around them in lazy circles, which wasn't helping the situation. It appeared other lifeguards had joined the crowd on shore.

"Look, just come back to shore with me. I can't leave you out here by yourself, not with people thinking there are sharks about."

As much as she hated to admit it, he had a point. Better to swim in and explain than risk making the situation more ridiculous than it already was.

With a sigh, she let go of her board and took his hand. He pulled her in front of him and wrapped his strong arm around her bare waist. The feel of his warm skin on her own caused her breath to catch in her throat. Maybe this wouldn't be so bad after all. She was about to turn to thank him when he spoke again.

"What's your name?"

"Cassie, Cassie Gallagher."

"No way! I thought you looked a little familiar, but the red hair threw me off. Your family owns Fiddler's Green, right?"

She gave a brief nod, curious how he knew her. Though, really, her family's pub had been a staple in town for years, so it wasn't all that surprising. Still, there was *something* familiar about him. She wracked her brain as she pulled on the rope attached to her boogie board until she could reach it, then she settled it on the surfboard in front of her.

"We went to high school together, though we didn't run in the same crowds," he said as he paddled back to shore. "I'm Derrick Barnes."

Her heart stopped and then proceeded to thump erratically in her chest. *Derrick Barnes.* The *Derrick Barnes?* She'd only had the biggest crush on him throughout all four years of high school. And now, here she was, finally in his arms with no makeup and her wet hair plastered to her head.

She turned her head to look at him, careful not to upset the delicate balance required to keep the board upright. How had she not recognized him before? His hair was still the same sun-kissed blond she remembered, and his eyes were just as deep a blue as the ocean surrounding them. But he'd filled out over the years. His once rail-thin physique was well defined, if the hard muscles of his forearm pressing into her belly were any indication.

"I can probably make it on my own from here," she said as they approached the breakwater line, though she wasn't sure that was entirely true. Her whole body felt like jelly in his arms. Still, staggering onto shore on her own two feet was better than being carried by the man who'd unknowingly broken her heart.

"What's your hurry?" Derrick asked, pulling her tighter against him as he pushed her legs up onto the board with his own, almost upending the boogie board. He paddled with his other hand to catch a wave as it crested. They rode the wave smoothly onto the sand.

"Thanks." Cassie climbed unsteadily to her feet, the adrenaline pumping through her veins having nothing to do with her wildlife encounter and everything to do with the unexpected reunion.

Someone wrapped a towel around her, and she turned to find the crowd of people who had watched the whole ordeal close in. They broke into spontaneous applause, with many cheering for Derrick's heroic rescue. She waited for him to correct them, but he had stepped away to converse with his fellow lifeguards. Questions flew at her from all sides, while others expressed concern for her welfare. Her cheeks heated. Maybe she should have taken her chances with the not-sharks, especially if she was about to die of embarrassment.

"Give her some room," Derrick said, pushing people back and sliding an arm around her shoulders. He pulled her through the crowd, heading toward the stairs.

"But my things," she cried, turning back.

"I've got them," an unfamiliar male voice said.

"Thanks, Jimmy." Derrick tossed him a set of keys. "You can put them in the Jeep."

"Sure thing," Jimmy said as he headed toward the street.

She twisted around to look back at the crowd. "Shouldn't I give a statement or explain about the dolphins?"

He shrugged. "No need. I gave my supervisor a brief summary of what happened and promised a full report later." A sly smile brightened his face. "I told him it was more important to get you somewhere safe before you went into shock."

"Shock?" She frowned. "Why would I go into shock?"

Instead of responding, Derrick led her up the stairs over the sand dunes and down the sidewalk toward a building. A moment later, he unlocked a door which she assumed was to his apartment. The coolness from the air conditioner caused her to shiver, and she pulled the towel tighter around her shoulders.

"Sorry about the cold. Do you want to grab a shower while I find you something dry to wear?"

Cassie nodded, gritting her teeth to keep them from chattering. There would be time for questions later. He led her to a small bathroom with a shower stall.

"I'll see if my neighbor has some clothes you can borrow," he said before closing the door behind him.

Grateful for a moment alone to collect her thoughts, she considered her situation. Her high school crush, the boy she'd pined for all four years, had just pulled her out of the ocean and brought her back to his place. High school Cassie would be freaking out, but adult Cassie forced herself to get a grip. She hadn't seen him in almost a decade. In fact, she thought he'd gone to college in Florida and never come back. Not that she'd kept tabs on him since they graduated or anything. *Just a random social media search here and there.*

But he was here, in the flesh. And not only that, he *remembered* her, by name! The fact that he even knew she existed was enough of a shock. All those years, she'd attended every one of his lacrosse games, tried to catch his eye in the hallways, and even tried to get a job at the surf shop where he worked. That last one had been vetoed by her dad. The family needed her at the pub, but she found excuses to go by there whenever she could after school.

Once, she'd finally gotten up the nerve to ask him out, but she was too late. He and Jessica Gregor, the head cheerleader, started going out at the beginning of senior year. Cassie heard they broke up the summer after graduation, but by then, she was already in DC.

As excited as she was to have this second chance, several things weren't adding up. Why was he in such a hurry to get her off the beach and away from all those people? Why hadn't the other lifeguards wanted to talk to her? Wouldn't they have wanted to confirm the animals were dolphins before addressing the crowd?

A knock at the door interrupted her thoughts. Cassie peered out from behind the curtain.

A young woman with an armful of clothes and towels came in before setting the pile on the sink. "I've got some clothes, though they may be a little long on you."

The woman left the bathroom to give her some privacy. As Cassie stepped out of the shower, she covered herself in a towel and called through the door, "Thank you so much!"

"No problem. It sounds like you went through quite the harrowing ordeal. A school of sharks!" The woman paused before saying, "I'm Stephanie, by the way."

"Cassie." Her brow furrowed as she dried off with a towel. Was Stephanie on the beach? Had she seen the dolphins and assumed the worst? Why hadn't Derrick corrected her? Something wasn't right.

She pushed the thought from her mind as she pulled on the clothes Stephanie had brought. Between the steam from the shower and the fresh clothes, Cassie was feeling more like herself. As she opened the door to let the bathroom air out, she looked down and laughed at how much the clothes seemed to swim on her petite frame.

"Like I said, I knew they'd be long, but at least you don't have to put back on a wet bikini." Stephanie flipped her blond curls over her shoulder and handed Cassie a brush. "Thought you might like to look more presentable before we see the guys again."

Cassie gave her a grateful smile in return and began brushing the tangles out of her hair.

"Derrick sent Jimmy to grab you something to eat and drink. I'm afraid they don't have much here aside from stale chips."

The door opened, and Derrick peeked in. "How's it going in here?" His eyes met Cassie's in the mirror as she brushed through the last of the tangles.

"Much better," she said, lowering her lashes. He grinned as he moved closer to her.

"Glad to hear it. We've got food if you're hungry."

Stephanie took that as her cue and left the apartment, promising to check in on Cassie in the future. *Alone at last.* Cassie followed Derrick into the kitchen. His place wasn't much, just a one-bedroom apartment. She slid into the seat he indicated, where a cup of what she assumed was coffee had been placed. A bag of food sat in the middle of the table, and from the delicious aroma, Cassie surmised it was some sort of baked good. She lifted the cup to her lips and blinked in surprise as the velvety taste of chocolate caressed her tongue.

"I wasn't sure if you were a coffee drinker," Derrick said, gesturing to the cup. "But I figure most people like hot chocolate."

"Thank you, this is perfect."

Cassie took in the room. The kitchen was cluttered but clean. A few cabinets were missing doors. She reached over and pulled the bag of baked goods closer to her and found a chocolate croissant, a few donuts, and a muffin. Pulling out the chocolate croissant, she took a bite and relished the warm, gooey center.

"I took a chance and called the pub," Derrick said as he sat across from her and pulled out a donut. "Your sister is on her way."

Cassie finished the croissant and tried to hide her disappointment. Why had he called Emily? She didn't want to leave yet. There were questions she wanted answered.

She studied him out of the corner of her eye. After waiting four years for him to notice her, it figured that it would take a brush with not-so-dangerous sea creatures to catch his eye. What had he been doing since high school? Had he lived here the whole time, or did he move back after college? And of course, the most burning question of all, was he single?

"Are you going back to the beach to finish your shift?"

He swallowed a bite of his donut and nodded. "Just wanted to get you away from the crowd. It looked like they were bothering you."

"I was a bit overwhelmed by their concern." She eyed him over the top of her hot chocolate. "You'll tell everyone it was a false alarm, right? We don't want any parents afraid the beach isn't safe."

His face became guarded as he sent her a wary look. "About that." He shifted in his seat. "Listen, I was wondering if you would mind if we kept that our little secret."

A knot formed in her belly. She cocked her head. "What do you mean?"

"It's just—a lot of people are calling me a hero. I think I might get a promotion for it, which I could really use." He raised his head, his eyes pleading. "It won't hurt anything to just let people believe it was a school of sharks, right?"

Her teeth worried her lower lip. White lies to get out of a temporary job was one thing, but to outright lie to her family, to the town? That seemed extreme. Still, he had come to her rescue, even if she hadn't actually needed rescuing. The longer she stared into those deep-blue eyes, the more inclined she was to keep this a secret. Besides, as he'd said, what could it hurt? Even if people thought the dolphins were sharks, she hadn't been harmed. So a few newspapers might report a shark sighting, which happened all the time. People only paid attention to shark attacks. While a sighting might deter people from swimming in the ocean, it wouldn't stop them from visiting the beach.

She nodded, and his face broke into a broad grin. "Thanks, Cassie. You're the best." He slid his hand across the table, and she slipped hers into it, relishing the warmth of his skin against hers.

The doorbell rang, and Cassie slumped in her chair. Her sister had probably broken several traffic laws in her panic to get there, and now she would have to leave. She hoped to at least get his number so she could thank him properly.

Emily rushed into the room a moment later, her brown eyes wild with fear. "Cassie, what happened? Are you hurt?" She slid her hands over Cassie's arms and legs, checking for anything amiss.

Cassie squirmed away. "I'm fine. I promise." She looked up at Derrick under her eyelashes. "Thanks to my hero."

Derrick gave her the heart-stopping grin he was known for as he bowed his head. "It was my pleasure."

Emily looked like she was resisting the urge to roll her eyes, but she kept her comments to herself as she helped Cassie to her feet. "We need to get you home. Mom's worried sick."

"Wait," Cassie said as she stepped toward Derrick. She touched his arm and was momentarily distracted by the size of his bicep. If she was going to keep up the pretense of his heroics, she wanted something in return, but she had to play this just right. "How can I ever thank you for saving me?" Her lips twitched as she fought a smile.

"Well, maybe you'll let me take you out sometime," Derrick said, leaning back against the counter and giving her a quick once-over.

His response thrilled her. When he handed her his phone, she quickly typed in her number. "Thanks again."

"Anytime."

Emily grabbed Cassie's hand and pulled her to the door. As disappointed as she was to leave, her heart was lightened by this unexpected second chance.

Chapter Eight

Emily insisted on taking Cassie to the outpatient clinic, just to rule out any lasting effects. She had been terrified when she received the call from Derrick and was relieved it hadn't turned out worse. Surrounded by sharks but lived to tell the tale! How her sister managed to get into these situations was beyond her.

Of course, had Derrick not called her, Emily never would have known anything was amiss. Watching her sister flirt shamelessly with her rescuer had annoyed Emily more than it should have. Cassie had always been boy crazy, and Derrick was objectively handsome, but after witnessing the way Ryan had looked at Cassie last night, Emily's heart went out to him.

I guess she's learned the value of a summer romance. Emily smirked. She dropped Cassie off at the house, and their mother took over her care. Peter was manning the bar tonight. He wasn't as personable as Cassie, but he got the job done, and that was all that really mattered.

Anna Mae was coming by the house that evening so they could share their plans for the pub with the rest of the Gallaghers. Emily hoped her family would be amenable to the changes they were proposing, as she truly believed they would bring in the customers they were sorely lacking.

Tonight was turning out like every other night since Emily had returned home. There were a few college kids and a couple of regulars, but overall, things were pretty dead.

The door to the pub opened, and a blast of humid air followed Ryan inside. He hurried over to Emily, his green eyes filled with concern. He must've heard about Cassie's shark encounter, and she resigned herself to telling the story once more.

"Emily, is Cassie here? Is she okay?"

"She's fine. We decided it would be best for her to rest tonight, but I took her to the doctor, and there was no harm done." She started clearing a table, and he stepped over to help her.

"I can't believe this happened." He ran a hand through his blond hair. "We've never had a shark encounter before."

"Lucky for Cassie, a lifeguard was able to get to her and bring her in unharmed." Emily lifted the bin of dirty dishes she'd just cleared and headed for the kitchen.

"Any idea who he was?" Ryan asked as he followed her.

"Derrick something or other?" Emily shrugged as she unloaded the bin and started filling the sink. "He lives on Sand Dollar Lane."

"Derrick Barnes?" Ryan's eyebrows drew together in a way that suggested he wasn't pleased to hear the identity of Cassie's rescuer.

Emily studied him. *Does he know Derrick? Is it better or worse if Ryan is familiar with the guy who is apparently sweeping Cassie's feet out from under her?*

"That might have been it," she finally said. "Truthfully, I paid little attention to him once he told me what happened."

"Which is understandable, considering," Ryan murmured, lost in thought.

"You're welcome to come by the house tonight to check on her." Emily began washing the dishes. To her surprise, Ryan stepped up beside her with a towel, ready to dry. She handed him the first dish with a grateful smile. "Anna Mae and I have plans for the pub we want to discuss with the rest of my family."

"Oh? What sort of plans?"

Emily wiped her forehead with the back of her hand before washing the next plate. "Her dad is disappointed in the tourism for the start of the season, and he's reconsidering building in town. So we've been brainstorming ways to bring in people. We thought we might start with some events at the pub. Bring back karaoke and trivia nights and maybe make them more often."

"That would be a huge help, and I hope your idea works." He stared off into space as he dried the plate she'd handed him. "This town could use it."

They finished up the dishes while Peter cleaned the bar and the front of the pub. The dinner rush had long ended, and the dining area was empty. Once everything was prepped and ready to open for breakfast the next day, the three of them walked back to the Gallagher house.

Cassie was sitting in the living room, covered with a blanket, when they returned. Ryan immediately went to her side and began peppering her with questions. To Emily's surprise, Cassie didn't try to avoid Ryan and answered him warmly. Had her near-death experience softened her?

The doorbell rang, and Emily went to answer it. Her breath caught in her throat at the sight of Anna Mae in a checkered tunic and black leggings. Her dark-brown hair was pulled back in a French twist, and she looked so beautiful it almost hurt.

"Are you ready?" Anna Mae asked by way of greeting.

Emily nodded, not quite trusting herself to speak, and led the way back to the living room. Anna Mae greeted Emily's mom before she perched on the edge of the reclining chair and began removing several documents from the bag she had brought. She glanced up at Emily and inclined her head. Emily took a deep breath and began their pitch.

"While I have you all here, I'd like to discuss some ideas Anna Mae and I had to increase business at the pub."

Her family turned to her with curious gazes, and she willed herself not to lose her nerve. She explained how well the events they'd held previously had done and how they hoped increasing the number of events might drive traffic to the pub and, in turn, the town. As she detailed their plans for the themed events, her mom's blue eyes grew bright with hope.

"Those both sound great," Cassie said enthusiastically as she leaned forward on the couch. "How can I help?"

"We were hoping to use the Gallagher talents," Anna Mae said. "I understand you're creative, so if you could work on drafting the trivia questions and answers, that would be great." She glanced at Ryan. "And we should include some local color, so maybe Ryan can help you with any Blue Heron Bay traditions he's learned of since becoming mayor."

Cassie nodded. "Sounds good to me."

"Peter, since you're working on your dissertation, we won't ask much of you," Emily said as she turned to her brother. "However, if you'd act as the emcee on event nights, we'd appreciate it."

"I can handle that," Peter said.

"Great," Anna Mae said. "Emily and I are putting together a song list of karaoke favorites. We should be able to load those into the machine. Now it's just a question of when we want to host the events." She looked at each of them in turn. "Hosting two events each week is a lot of work, but I think it'll be worth it in the end."

Cassie raised her hand. "I think we should space them out and vary when we hold them, at least in the beginning. Some weeks we can have trivia on a weekday and karaoke on a weekend, and then we can switch. That way, we can cater to different groups of people throughout the summer. After we have a few events under our belt, we may find one night works best for karaoke and another works best for trivia. If that's the case, we can schedule the events for those nights for the rest of the summer."

Anna Mae pointed at her. "You're an event planner in the making." She reached over and grabbed Emily's hand, catching her off guard. "All right, team. We have a plan."

Since Anna Mae and Emily's plan didn't require much from him, Peter hadn't objected to the part they'd asked him to play. While he would have preferred the events only happen once each, he understood the logic in having them weekly throughout the summer. At least they hadn't asked him to download songs or come up with trivia.

Unfortunately, the addition of those events meant both the pub and the house were bustling with people, as Anna Mae seemed to have deployed her PR team to get the word out. After the first week, he discovered the best place for him to work on his edits in peace was the local coffee shop, Grounded. There was a perfect table, tucked away in a corner with an outlet, that had become his go-to spot when he wanted to escape the hubbub.

He arrived at the shop early one morning, laptop under his arm, and placed his usual order. As he took his cup of coffee and a bagel over to his table, he groaned. Someone else had gotten there first. Should he say something or look elsewhere? Maybe this intruder would leave soon. When the individual in question raised his head, Peter's stomach dropped.

"Peter! It's good to see you." Ricardo gestured to the seat across from him. "Please join me."

Not knowing what else to do, Peter sank down into the seat and set his laptop on the table. A plethora of conflicting emotions surged through him as he took in Ricardo's damp hair and lightly stubbled chin. He hadn't been able to stop thinking about Ricardo since the flight home, but that didn't mean he'd forgiven him.

"How's the dissertation coming?" Ricardo asked as he leaned forward, resting his elbow on the table and his cheek on his hand.

"Not bad," Peter said, trying to focus on the conversation and not on how much Ricardo reminded him of one of those perfectly chiseled sculptures often found in an art museum. It wasn't fair. Why did someone who had contributed, albeit indirectly, to some of Peter's least-favorite memories have to look so *good*? "How's your resort proposal going?"

"It's going well, I think," Ricardo said with an almost too-perfect smile. "I've been checking out potential locations in town that could work for our next resort." He glanced around the coffee shop, which was empty, despite it being the prime time for grabbing breakfast on the way to the office. "And the town could use what we offer to boost tourism, which would help my mom and people like her."

"That's great," Peter said. "It's funny you mention tourism. My sister and her friend are planning a bunch of events at my family's pub to entice people to visit."

Ricardo cocked his head. "Who is your sister's friend?"

"Anna Mae... somebody." Peter wracked his brain. Names were not his forte.

"Wakefield?"

"Yeah, that's it. Do you know her?"

"You could say that." Ricardo smiled enigmatically. "We run in similar circles, as it were. I didn't know she was in town. Is she often at your family's pub?"

Peter nodded, though he sensed there was something Ricardo wasn't telling him about his association with Anna Mae. Leaning back in his chair, he studied Ricardo.

"Are you going to the beach bonfire?" Ricardo asked, and Peter blinked at the subject change.

"I've been told I don't have a choice." Peter shrugged, hoping to appear nonchalant. Inside, he was still stewing about his sisters' insistence he join them. Apparently, his declaration that he wouldn't attend any town events had fallen on deaf ears.

"Aw, it won't be so bad." Ricardo winked. "I'll be there."

To his irritation, Peter's stomach flip-flopped. He was *not* interested in Ricardo. Even if he had time for dating, which he most certainly did not, there was no way he would ever consider the bane of his high school existence.

As if reading his mind, Ricardo began gathering his things. "Well, I know you've got a lot of work to do, so I won't keep you." He put his hand on Peter's shoulder as he passed on his way to the door. "See you tonight."

The sudden heat from his touch shot through Peter like a jet stream, cascading across his chest and pooling in his stomach. He looked into Ricardo's deep-brown eyes and swallowed. *Oh no.* This couldn't be happening.

But it was. *Fine, he's attractive. So what? I have many more important things to do.*

Yet even as he told himself that, he couldn't stop himself from turning to watch Ricardo stride to the door. When he caught Peter staring, Ricardo grinned and waved. Peter's cheeks burned as he whipped back around and hunched his shoulders, wishing he could disappear into the vinyl seating.

Focus. He opened his laptop and struggled to concentrate. His shoulder was still pulsing from where Ricardo had touched him. Closing his eyes didn't help because every time he did, an image of Ricardo's handsome face appeared.

It wasn't fair. As if it wasn't bad enough that Peter had to come home to help with the pub, now he was forced to endure impromptu meetings with his high school nemesis, who had only grown more attractive in the intervening years. And why did it seem like Ricardo was oblivious to his animosity? Did he not remember high school and the way his friends had treated Peter? The relentless bullying and the stupid pranks they pulled? While Peter would never consider himself a jock, he'd run track and cross-country. But he'd also been captain of the debate team and a member of the Future Business Leaders of America. And those clubs, unfortunately, gave Ricardo's stupid jock friends more ammunition for their harassment.

Was it possible Ricardo didn't know or—more likely—that he didn't remember? After all, they didn't bully *him*, just Peter. Taking a deep breath, Peter considered that. High school was well over a decade ago. Maybe Ricardo thought Peter would be over it by now. And he was. At least when he was on the other side of the country, as far away from this town as possible.

Pushing those thoughts away, he pulled a pair of headphones out of his bag and slid them over his ears. He had saved a few podcasts discussing the housing crisis in the country, which had helped refocus him in the past. As he pushed Play, he prayed they would perform their magic again.

The podcast was specific to California and the disparities plaguing the southern part of the state. To Peter's utter relief, a few minutes of listening to the discussion was exactly what he needed to push Ricardo out of his mind, and he resumed his edits, distraction-free.

Chapter Nine

Emily swelled with pride at how her family had jumped in to assist with the events for the pub. Her sister had already put together a series of questions for their first event and was busy typing away on her computer. Peter had determined he still fit into an old suit. Emily wanted him to look the part of the emcee. After spending the last week promoting the beach bonfire, Anna Mae was coming by the pub later that day to help locate karaoke versions of popular songs so they could have a wide selection.

Her eyes fluttered shut as she remembered the way Anna Mae had held her hand while they told her family their plans. Anna Mae had probably meant it as a friendly gesture, but Emily hoped it was something more. Her initial attraction had grown with every moment they spent together.

What's the point of a summer romance? Cassie's words echoed in her head. As much as she hated to admit it, her sister's question was valid. If Emily allowed herself to fall head over heels for Anna Mae, it would make going back to her real life in Southern Maryland that much more difficult.

The door to the pub opened, and Emily's cheeks warmed as Anna Mae walked in. Her feelings weren't the most important thing at that moment, and she needed to keep things professional between them. The priority was saving her father's legacy. She couldn't lose sight of that goal.

"Good morning," she said as she helped Anna Mae with the bag she was carrying and followed her to their usual booth.

"Hello yourself," Anna Mae said. After she set her things down on the bench seat, she threw her arms around Emily, almost knocking her over. Emily tentatively returned the embrace, her heart thudding against the walls of her chest.

So much for keeping this professional.

"Things are going really well," Anna Mae said as she released Emily and sank into her seat. "I loved how your family jumped right in."

Emily nodded as she slid into the opposite seat, trying to calm the tumultuous emotions running through her. "My sister is researching local trivia, but she's already put together a decent amount of questions for our first event."

"That's great." Anna Mae beamed, causing Emily's heart to skip a beat. "Now it's time to pick which nights each week would work for the different events and then get the word out."

"Well, in the past, we've done trivia on Wednesday nights and karaoke on Saturdays."

Anna Mae's smile somehow brightened. "Sounds good. We can try that for the first week and see how it goes." After pulling out her laptop, she set it on the table and began rapidly typing. "I can set up several events for different nights on social media that people can RSVP to, which will help give us an idea of how much interest there is. Unfortunately, there's no way to get an exact count because people often indicate interest without actually attending, but it will give us a ballpark and tell us whether the campaign is doing its job."

"Have you spoken to your dad recently?"

"No," Anna Mae said in a clipped tone. "But he'll arrive soon. I'm hoping by then to have some good news to share, even if it's simply that the social media buzz looks promising."

She was silent for a few minutes as she continued typing. Taking advantage of her distraction, Emily studied her. Anna Mae had left her hair down, and it hung in dark sheets around her face. She had a strong chin and a prominent nose, but her angular features were softened when she smiled. As she pulled her full bottom lip between her teeth, Emily's breath caught in her throat, and she wondered what it would be like to kiss that lip.

She blinked and shook her head, trying to control her thoughts. *This won't do at all.* Getting distracted by romance wouldn't help her reach her goal, and the last thing she needed was to start the new school year nursing a wounded heart. Besides, as she'd told Jen before she left, there was nothing wrong with her life or her routine.

Sure, it gets lonely sometimes, but it's safe. Predictable and secure. She didn't want to complicate anything, and starting something with Anna Mae was likely to be very complicated. After all, long-distance relationships rarely worked out.

"All right, the events are live on social media," Anna Mae said as she closed her laptop with a satisfied click. "It's not much, but it's a start."

Emily forced herself to smile.

But Anna Mae saw right through her as she frowned and grasped Emily's hand. "Something wrong?"

"N-No." Part of her wanted to pull away, but she relished the feel of Anna Mae's soft skin against her own. "I want this to go well for both of us."

"Well, we won't know if we're successful for a bit, so we might as well relax until the first event." She studied Emily's face. "Are you going to the beach bonfire tonight?"

"After all the work you've put into promoting it, how could I not? Besides, it's tradition. My family goes every year."

"Wanna be my date?"

With a pounding heart, Emily swallowed the hope that grew in her chest. Did Anna Mae have any idea how much a simple four-letter word meant to her? Part of Emily wasn't sure it mattered.

"Y-Yes," she squeaked. *Oh for goodness' sake.* She cleared her throat. "Uh, I mean, yes, I'd love to go with you."

"Good, that's settled then." Anna Mae's smile lit up the whole room. "Now, let's find some karaoke songs."

While Emily tried to focus, her insides were reeling. Was she really going on a date with Anna Mae? *Oh Lord, what on earth am I going to wear?*

～

At first, Cassie had started feeling much better about keeping the secret of her not-a-shark encounter, and she suspected that had a lot to do with Derrick asking her to go with him to the bonfire. She hadn't stopped smiling since.

That had all changed when news of Derrick's so-called "heroic" rescue spread like wildfire through the tiny town. Both the local newspaper and radio station had requested interviews. She and Derrick were meeting a reporter for lunch so he could get a photo of them together, and they were scheduled to join the morning show the next day.

She'd never been interviewed before, and the idea made her queasy. When Derrick asked her to keep the secret, she'd thought they just wouldn't correct the story, instead allowing people to believe what they wanted. But now, it wasn't so simple. They were broadcasting a lie. What would happen if they got caught?

Derrick had convinced her to go along with it by focusing on how much it would help him, and she had to admit that the opportunity to spend more time with her old crush won out over her better judgment. Still, her stomach churned the morning of the first interview, and she worried she wouldn't be able to go through with it.

At noon, she headed to Cafe de la Mer to meet the reporter and Derrick. The French bistro was an elegant spot for an interview, which only made her feel more like a fraud. Derrick was already inside, talking to a tall man with dark hair and striking blue eyes.

"Cassie," Derrick said as he approached her, taking her hand and lifting it to his lips. Her heart fluttered. A moment later, she was blinded by a bright flash. She blinked as tiny dots swam in front of her eyes.

"Apologies, Miss Gallagher," the dark-haired man said. "It was too perfect a moment not to take a picture." He held out his hand, and she shook it. "I'm Roger Simmons. I'm so pleased you could join me for lunch today. The whole town is talking about your harrowing ordeal, and my editor wants to feature your story on the front page of tomorrow's paper."

The queasiness increased, and Cassie struggled to regain her composure. "It's a pleasure to meet you as well, Roger."

The hostess signaled their table was ready, and Derrick offered Cassie his arm. Her face lit up as she took it, and they strolled into the restaurant together. Every eye in the place turned to look at them, and Cassie ate up the attention. *Maybe this interview won't be so bad after all.*

Once they placed their orders, Roger pulled out a notepad. "So, tell me, Cassie, what made you decide to be shark bait the other day?"

Cassie bristled at the phrasing of the question. "It wasn't by choice, I assure you." Her mouth felt dry, and she licked her lips. *You can do this. Just keep it simple, and don't go into too much detail. One lie wouldn't hurt anyone, right?* "I wanted to go for a quick swim before my shift at the pub, and I got a little more than I bargained for."

"I've been telling the city council for years that we need a better warning system for when dangerous predators are spotted in the water," Derrick said with a grave expression. "You may recall, Roger, I ran for mayor against Ryan, and it's unfortunate he won, as he has done so little for the town in the last few years."

Cassie blinked. Derrick had run for *mayor*? He didn't strike her as the political type.

Roger raised an eyebrow before glancing back down at his notes. "Er, yes, I do recall that. Um, anyway, Cassie, what was your first thought when you realized you were surrounded by sharks?"

Derrick tensed beside her, and Cassie laid a reassuring hand on his arm. Why the reporter had glossed over Derrick's comments was beyond her, but she understood his annoyance. It was his moment, and he deserved the spotlight.

"I was terrified," Cassie said with a moan, putting a clammy hand on her chest. *Ugh, everything about this interview feels wrong. Am I laying it on too thick?* She'd never told such a big lie before. But the reporter leaned in, his pen poised over his notepad, so she forced herself to continue. "I had drifted so far from shore, and I didn't have time to think." She turned adoring eyes to Derrick. At least that was easy. "I'm so lucky Derrick was on duty. He didn't hesitate to come to my aid." She purposefully avoided calling it a "rescue," but neither the reporter nor Derrick seemed to notice.

"And what were you thinking, Derrick, when you saw Cassie in danger?"

"That I needed to get to her as fast as I could," Derrick said without missing a beat. "I didn't know if she was hurt or bleeding, which could have attracted more sharks."

"Your quick thinking likely saved her life," Roger said, furiously jotting down notes. "Have you had training, or did you act on impulse?"

"It was a little of both," Derrick said. "I've worked as a lifeguard for several summers, but we've never had a shark come in so close before."

Cassie shifted in her seat, uncomfortable with how easily Derrick could spin the tale. *Perhaps he's had a lot of practice?* She pushed the thought away.

"Tell me more about after you pulled her from the water. What was going through your head?"

"She seemed to be going into shock, so I knew I needed to get her warm, which is why I took her back to my place." Derrick glanced over at Cassie with a heart-stopping smile. "In the ocean, I was so focused on getting her out of the water, I didn't have time to get a good look at her." He slid an arm around her, pulling her close to him. "But on the walk back to my place, I could see just how beautiful she is."

Cassie's cheeks warmed, and her smile stretched from ear to ear. "I'm so glad it was you." She grasped his hands as she gazed into his eyes, and suddenly, she realized she wasn't lying anymore. At least, not about this. "My hero." Another flash, but as she wasn't facing the camera, this one didn't bother her as much.

"And how do you feel about each other, now the danger is passed?" Roger asked, interrupting their moment. "Is this where the story ends?"

"I hope not," Derrick said, his eyes never leaving Cassie's.

"Me, either," Cassie breathed. Her heart pounded in her chest.

Derrick turned back to Roger. "Technically, this wasn't the beginning of our story." Cassie's heart swelled at the words "our story." "We went to high school together, but we didn't run in the same crowds."

"So this is your second chance at love?"

"Definitely." Cassie gave an emphatic nod.

"Would you say this is a dream come true, then, Cassie?" Roger nodded at Derrick. "Did you have feelings for him in high school?"

Her smile faltered. "I had a crush on him, yes." She cleared her throat. "But I always hoped to have a love like my parents did. They were high school sweethearts."

"Well, we may not have dated in high school, but fate has given us another chance, and I, for one, don't plan to waste it," Derrick said, squeezing her hand. "We're going to the bonfire together this evening. And tomorrow we'll be on the morning show with Deidre Lewis."

Their food arrived then, and they talked of other things while they ate. Now that the interview was over, her guilt subsided. It seemed to have gone well, and she hadn't technically lied about the sharks.

"Thank you for agreeing to meet me," Roger said as they left the restaurant. "My editor is going to love this article." He shook each of their hands. "Would you be open to a follow-up? I imagine readers are going to be interested to see where your romance goes."

Cassie shook her head, but Derrick beat her to it. "We'd love to!"

"Fantastic," Roger said. "I'll be in touch."

Derrick turned to her then, his blue eyes shining with enthusiasm. Cassie forced a smile as her stomach churned. How much longer could she keep this up? Continuing to perpetuate the lie wasn't what she'd signed up for when Derrick had asked her to keep the secret. But then, he pulled her into his arms, and she savored the warmth of his embrace, pushing away her concerns.

"Did you want to come back to the house with me?" Cassie asked, her voice hopeful. She wasn't ready to leave him yet.

"I wish I could, but I've got some things to attend to." While she tried to hide her disappointment, she must have been unsuccessful because he hurried on. "But I'm looking forward to our date tonight."

Cassie's heart soared. Their first official date. She'd fantasized about this for years, and now it was finally happening! Derrick lifted her hand to his lips before he left her. She wasn't sure if her feet ever touched the ground as she floated all the way back to the car.

After spending the rest of the afternoon alternating between trivia questions and daydreaming about Derrick, Cassie was surprised how quickly the time flew. She needed to get ready for the bonfire. Her face broke into a giddy grin as she picked out a cute outfit: a black blouse with a sweetheart neckline, a jean skirt, and strappy sandals. She pulled her auburn hair back into a messy bun. As she applied her makeup, she wondered if she'd been wrong about summer flings. Finding Derrick again made her realize how much she wanted this to work out. She'd dreamed for so long of the day he'd finally notice her, and she didn't want to let it go at the end of the summer. Maybe Emily was right, and she should consider moving back home.

On the other hand, Derrick would love the city. There was so much more to do there, and she imagined them together at all the hottest clubs. He'd miss the ocean, of course, but they could always come back to visit.

When she headed downstairs a little while later, Emily and Peter sat waiting in the living room while their mother adjusted a few picture frames along the wall. The doorbell rang, and Cassie's heart jumped in her throat. Derrick had said he would meet her there, but maybe he'd decided to surprise her instead. Her hope was short-lived as Emily opened the door, revealing a very stylish Anna Mae. When they walked back into the room, Cassie's eyes fell on their clasped hands. She raised an eyebrow, and Emily blushed.

"Are we ready to go?" her mother asked.

"Sounds good to me," Cassie said with enthusiasm. The sooner they got to the bonfire, the sooner she could see Derrick.

A few minutes later, they headed over to the beach. The air was cooler than she'd expected. Should she have chosen leggings instead of the skirt? But her outfit was too perfect.

Besides, Derrick can always warm me up. A mischievous smile played on her lips.

The closer they got to the beach, the more the air filled with the familiar scent of burning wood. Aside from the bonfire, the town always held a small festival on a street nearby, though it consisted of little more than a grouping of food trucks, a few games, and craft vendors. Cassie breathed in deeply as the tangy smell of barbeque meshed with the briny scent of the sea.

A crowd had already gathered around the gigantic bonfire, and several people were roasting smores. Cassie discreetly scanned the crowd for Derrick, not wanting to seem too eager. She glanced behind her to see if they had passed him and bumped into someone.

"Oh, sorry." She turned and met Ryan's gaze.

"No worries," he said with a grin. "I'm glad I ran into you... literally." His brows furrowed as he looked her over. "How are you feeling?"

"I'm fine," she said, waving a dismissive hand, though a stab of guilt hit her stomach. Somehow lying to a reporter was easier than lying to Ryan.

"I'm so glad to hear that," he said, turning to walk with her. "I wanted you to know I've approached the city council about better detection of potential threats. Not just sharks, but riptides as well. Your harrowing ordeal was the push they needed."

"I'm glad my near-death experience gave renewed energy to the cogs of government," she said, though a wave of nausea threatened to overtake her as she made the quip. She hoped the interest in her encounter would die down soon so she could stop lying about it.

Ryan chuckled. "That it did."

They stopped in front of the fire with her family. Cassie stifled a sigh. Standing with Ryan hampered her efforts to find Derrick, but she didn't want to be rude.

Someone tapped her on the shoulder, and she whipped around. Derrick gave her a lopsided grin, which released a kaleidoscope of butterflies in her belly.

"I'm glad I found you," Derrick said. "This place is a zoo." He handed her a red Solo cup, which, from the smell, she assumed was filled with cheap beer.

"Thank you." She gave him her best thousand-watt smile.

"You're welcome." Derrick turned. "Mr. Mayor."

"Mr. Barnes," Ryan said, and Cassie frowned at his clipped tone. It wasn't like Ryan to be so cold. "I didn't think you bothered much with town events."

"About as much as you care for its safety," Derrick retorted.

What was *with* them? Derrick had mentioned running for mayor during their interview, but that was years ago, wasn't it? They couldn't still be bitter about that, right?

Before she could press the issue, a sizzle of flame shot into the air, causing everyone to turn toward the fire.

"I'll see you later, Cassie," Ryan said. He glared at Derrick before spinning on his heel and stalking away.

"What was that about?" Cassie whispered to Derrick.

"Who cares," Derrick said with a shrug. His expression brightened as he gave her an appreciative once-over. "You look great."

"It's amazing what a shower will do for a girl."

Derrick grinned and threw his arm around her, pulling her against him. "I can't say I minded the half-drowned damsel look."

Cassie giggled, relishing the feel of his hard chest against her back. Was the night warming up or was it just his presence?

As the sun set on the horizon, a band began to play. Cassie and Derrick walked closer to the water, dipping their toes in the surf. The breeze coming off the ocean was cool, and she shivered. Derrick wrapped his arms around her. She sighed contentedly. If this was the start of a summer romance, she would take it.

Chapter Ten

PETER FOLLOWED HIS FAMILY AS THEY LEFT THE BONFIRE and headed toward the small fair set up off the beach. He glanced around, wondering if he would catch sight of Ricardo and hating himself for it. Ricardo was a distraction he didn't need, but he hadn't been able to stop thinking about him. His ability to compartmentalize was the only reason he wasn't further behind on his edits.

When his mother stopped at a quilting booth, he took the opportunity to survey the crowd. There was quite a nice turnout tonight, which boded well for Anna Mae and Emily's plans for the pub. Maybe that was all the town needed: a reason for people to visit.

As he turned back to his mother, he glimpsed a familiar face. He swallowed thickly as Ricardo moved through the crowd, an older woman tagging along behind him. When his eyes met Peter's, his face lit up, and he strode over to him.

"Peter, I was hoping to find you."

"Here I am," Peter said, internally cringing. *Real smooth.*

Ricardo gestured to the woman next to him. "This is my mother, Anita. Mom, this is Peter."

"Oh, I recognize you," Anita said, placing a hand on Peter's arm.

"You gave such a wonderful and funny speech at your graduation. I'll never forget it."

Mom appeared beside Peter before he could answer. "Wasn't it just the best?" She stuck out her hand. "I'm Julie Gallagher, Peter's mom."

"It's so nice to meet you." Anita clasped his mother's hand in both of hers. "I heard about the loss of your husband. I've wanted to stop by the pub, but I didn't want to overstep. How are you holding up?"

"As well as can be expected. Thank you for asking." Though Mom gave a bright smile, Peter recognized the pain behind it. She gestured to Ricardo. "Is this your son?"

"My pride and joy." Anita released her hand and slid her arm through the crook in Ricardo's elbow.

"I'm Ricardo. Nice to meet you." He took Peter's mom's hand, lifted it to his lips, and planted a brief kiss.

"My, my, aren't you a charmer," she said with a laugh.

"I try." Ricardo's gaze strayed behind her. "Where is the rest of your family? I was hoping to see all the Gallaghers tonight."

"Emily is off with her new friend somewhere, and Cassie was here a minute ago."

"Well, hopefully we'll run into them later," Ricardo said. "My mom and I were heading to get some boardwalk fries. Would you like to join us?"

"Why don't you two go on ahead and get something for all of us?" Mom said. "Anita and I will stay here and check out these quilts."

Ricardo shrugged and patted Peter's back. "Shall we?"

Peter nodded and led the way. It didn't help that a flash of heat had shot down his spine at Ricardo's touch. While the last thing he needed was to get distracted, he had to admit there was something about the way Ricardo was with his mother that made Peter see him in a new light. The jock bravado he recalled from high school seemed to disappear. Even now, as they walked away, Ricardo glanced back, presumably to check on Anita. It touched Peter's heart more than it should.

When they reached the food trucks, Peter noticed Ricardo appeared to find any excuse to touch him. Whether it was to move Peter out of the way of someone trying to get by or tapping him to get his attention, barely a minute went by where they didn't make physical contact. As they waited in line, Peter couldn't help wondering if he had somehow transitioned from a family outing to a date. And he wasn't at all sure how to feel about that.

"I'm glad I ran into you," Ricardo said, pulling Peter from his thoughts. "Though at some point, I would love to have a plan to see you instead of randomly bumping into you."

Peter blinked. He couldn't mean... Could he? His pulse picked up speed, but he wasn't sure what to say.

Ricardo turned to look at him and burst out laughing. "You should see your face."

Heat rushed to Peter's cheeks. He shifted away, as much from embarrassment as wounded pride. He hated being laughed at. It triggered painful memories.

"I'm sorry." Ricardo's smile faded. "I didn't mean to offend you. I just meant I'd like to take you out sometime."

"Why?" Peter asked without thinking.

Ricardo cocked his head. "Why not? I enjoy spending time with you."

Trying to sort through his thoughts, Peter ran his hand through his hair. "I guess I just don't understand the sudden interest. We went to high school together for four years, and when your jock buddies weren't giving me a hard time, you barely noticed me."

"Things change," Ricardo said as they reached the counter. He ordered two buckets of fries and sodas. When he turned back to Peter, there was a hint of sadness in his dark eyes. "Back then, I didn't have time for dating. Between school, lacrosse, and the odd jobs I worked to help my mom, I barely had time for myself, let alone a relationship." His eyebrows furrowed. "Wait, my friends were mean to you?"

Dropping his gaze, Peter squirmed. *So much for leaving the past in the past.* "Ah, I mean, it was no big deal." He forced a laugh. "You know how kids are."

Ricardo placed a hand under Peter's chin and lifted it, leaving Peter no choice but to look into his eyes. "I'm sorry. I didn't know."

A lump formed in Peter's throat. He'd never expected to hear someone from back then actually apologize. Wasn't that something that only happened in movies? But here was the person Peter thought of as an old rival apologizing on behalf of others. Someone who also had struggles no one knew about.

"You didn't do anything." Peter put his hand on Ricardo's arm. "But thank you. I'm sorry things were so hard for you and your mom."

Ricardo shrugged. "It's one reason I pitched building a resort here to my boss. My mom still struggles to find work. I send her money, but she resents that she needs it. A huge resort would be a boon for the town's economy and would provide people like my mom stable employment."

"That makes sense."

"So," Ricardo said, taking the food and drinks from the vendor. He turned to Peter with a wry smile. "Dinner?"

Peter laughed. "It's tempting."

"But you're worried about finishing your dissertation."

"I do have a lot on my plate. It's not that I don't want to. I'm simply not sure how I can swing it with everything else going on."

"Is there anything I can do to help?" Ricardo asked.

"Unless you want to help me emcee at the crazy events my sisters have concocted for the pub, I don't see how you could."

"That sounds like fun, actually. What sort of events?"

After Peter explained the plans, Ricardo expressed interest in pitching in. Peter tried to ignore the thrill surging through him.

"It's settled, then. I'll help with the events in exchange for one dinner."

As they headed back to their mothers, someone tapped Peter on the shoulder. He turned to find Anna Mae and Emily standing behind him.

"Oh, hey, sis. I'm glad I ran into you. There's someone I want you to meet." He started to introduce Ricardo but found the man was staring at Anna Mae with a peculiar expression on his face.

"Anna Mae," Ricardo said, his voice unnervingly cold. "I'd heard you were in town."

"Ricardo." Anna Mae matched his tone. "Come to take over another town with one of your outlandish resorts?"

"You wound me." He placed a hand over his heart. "You know, Sunrise Oasis brings an enormous boost in tourism to whatever lucky town we open in."

Anna Mae scoffed. "At what cost? The livelihood of the owners of the small businesses you run into the ground?"

Peter and Emily had stepped away from the sparring duo and exchanged an uneasy glance. Ricardo had insinuated he knew Anna Mae, but Peter hadn't expected their rivalry.

"This is the man I warned you about." Anna Mae turned to Emily, who looked as lost in translation as Peter was. "If he opens one of his ridiculous resorts in Blue Heron Bay, you can kiss your family's lovely pub goodbye."

Peter rocked back on his heels. Was that true? Would Ricardo's resort run his family out of business? He would have expected to feel devastated by this news, but if he was being honest with himself, all he felt was relief.

"That's not true," Ricardo said, sparing a quick glance at Peter. "We plan to offer all small businesses a chance to sell to us before we open."

"So your own Irish chain restaurant can move into their building? I can only imagine how much money you'll save using their décor and themes." Anna Mae shook her head. "Typical. And if they don't sell to you, you'll drive them out of business without a second thought." She waved a hand toward Peter. "You might have him fooled with your charming personality, but I've known you a long time, Ricardo."

"As if you're some saint." Ricardo glared at her and then pointed at Emily. "If her family's precious pub was on the lot where your father wanted to build, you'd do everything in your power to get it closed down so you could bulldoze it to the ground."

Anna Mae's eyes flashed fire. "That may have been true at one time, but unlike *your* organization, mine is capable of change and growth." With one last withering glare, she grabbed Emily's hand. "Come on. You shouldn't have to listen to this."

Emily glanced back at Peter. "Are you coming?"

With his ears ringing, Peter stood frozen. His gaze wavered between Ricardo and Emily. Finally, he shook his head. Emily's upper lip curled in disgust as she spun on her heel and stomped away.

"I'm sorry you had to see that," Ricardo said once they were alone again. "But I would have completely understood if you decided you wanted nothing more to do with me."

They walked over to a bench on the edge of the fair and sat down. Peter was silent as he tried to process what he'd just learned. Why wasn't he furious? After all, Ricardo hadn't been completely honest with him. And yet... he couldn't help feeling that selling the pub sounded like a great idea.

His chest tightened as he stared at the ground. *What is wrong with you?* The pub was his father's legacy. He shouldn't be so flippant about it. But it was clear his mother was struggling to run it on her own. And it wasn't like he and his sisters could drop everything and move home. They had built their own lives far from their tiny hometown. Besides, wasn't the mayor hoping to increase tourism? Wasn't that why he had pitched Anna Mae's hotel group? A resort would more than accomplish that.

"Honestly, you'd be doing me a favor," Peter finally said.

Ricardo frowned. "What do you mean?"

Peter sighed as he slumped down on the bench and looked at the sky. "I mean, selling the pub may not be such a bad thing."

Ricardo shifted beside him, and Peter sensed his discomfort. "I'll admit, I have monitored the business, and from what I've seen, things don't look good."

"My father was the heart and soul of that place," Peter said. "Without him, I don't know that we can keep it going. My mom tries, but she never loved it like he did." He rolled his head to the side so he could look at Ricardo directly. "Would you be interested in buying it?"

"We would give your family a good deal." Ricardo nodded. "Especially because Anna Mae was right about one thing. We'd save a lot of money if we could make use of what's already there. It wouldn't take much to update the décor to match our brand, and it's well located for where we're looking at putting the resort."

Rolling his head back to stare at the stars, Peter debated his next words. "Well, keep me posted on your plans, and leave my family and the pub to me. It'll take some effort, but in the end, they'll see reason."

～

Emily followed Anna Mae clear across the festival, stumbling often as she struggled to keep up. She'd never seen her friend so upset before, but anger turned Anna Mae into a speed walker. Her steps were determined and focused, whereas Emily was still reeling from the argument she'd witnessed only moments ago.

Her blood boiled at the memory of Peter's nonchalance over Ricardo's revelations. *Does my brother have a loyal bone in his body? How could he stay with that man after everything he said?* Emily shook her head, trying to fight back the tears pricking behind her eyelids. She wasn't like Anna Mae; her anger usually presented itself through a breakdown, not renewed determination.

When Anna Mae finally stopped marching across the festival like a general heading into battle, she spun around and embraced Emily. Since the tears were already threatening to break free, Emily stiffened at the contact.

"I'm sorry," Anna Mae said, pulling away like she'd touched a hot pan. "I thought you might welcome a hug after that awful conversation."

Emily took a deep breath in through her nose and released it through her mouth before she responded. "It's not that. It's not... you." She was trying to rein in her emotions. "I'm just so confused... and hurt."

"As you should be." Anna Mae grasped her hand gently, as if she was afraid Emily might explode or disintegrate. "The nerve of that guy. And to befriend your brother while he has these nefarious plans afoot."

"That's what I'm angry about!" Emily cried out. "Not that he involved Peter but that Peter doesn't seem to care. L-Like the idea of losing our father's legacy doesn't gut him like it does the rest of us. In some moments he almost looked... *relieved.*" Tears leaked down her cheeks, and she dashed them away. "I don't understand him. It's like I don't know him anymore."

"Oh, Emily." Anna Mae pulled Emily into her arms. "Don't cry. I promise I will do everything in my power to save Fiddler's Green."

Emily rested her head on Anna Mae's shoulder as she tried to stop the tears from flowing. She breathed in the sweet floral scent of Anna Mae's perfume. By the time she realized what a mistake that was, it was too late. Her mind was swimming with images of holding Anna Mae, running her fingers through her hair, kissing her...

She pulled away, but the magnetism was still there as her eyes fell to Anna Mae's lips, soft, and plump, and kissable. To her surprise, Anna Mae's brown eyes dilated as she gazed back. Without speaking, Anna Mae leaned forward, raising her eyes briefly to meet Emily's, as if in question, before moving to close the distance.

"Emily, there you are." Her mother's voice caused them to jump apart, and Emily took a ragged breath. "Have you seen Cassie?"

She shook her head as she cleared her throat. "Nope, can't say I have." She struggled to keep her gaze off Anna Mae. "Last I saw, she was with Derrick."

"Will you help me find her? Oh, and Peter. I'd like to get a photo of the four of us in front of the bonfire." Her mother's eyes grew misty. "For old times' sake."

Emily swallowed and blinked to fight back the tears pricking her eyes. It was a Gallagher family tradition to stand in front of the bonfire and take a photo, but it wouldn't be the same without their father.

"Of course," Emily choked out.

"I'll, uh, catch up with you later," Anna Mae said before walking away. Emily stared after her, the desire to follow and the need for space warring inside of her. What had just happened between them? Was Anna Mae caught up in the moment, or had she wanted to kiss Emily as much as Emily wanted to kiss her?

"Are you coming?" her mother asked, her tone sharper than usual, signaling her annoyance. With a sigh, Emily hurried along, keeping an eye out for her flighty sister and traitorous brother.

Part of her wondered if she should tell Mom what she'd learned about Ricardo's plans, but her mother had already been through so much lately, and Emily didn't want to add to her plate. First, she would find her errant siblings and give her mother a happy memory, and then she'd wring her brother's neck.

"There's Cassie," her mom called out, pointing toward a bench where Cassie and Derrick were taking photos with a group of college students.

"Hey, guys, look at this." Cassie held out the Polaroid. "Aren't we adorable?" She grinned as she turned to look at Derrick. To his credit, his smile was as big as hers.

Maybe at least one of my siblings has sense. Emily never imagined she'd find a day when she considered Cassie the reasonable sibling. But her sister's happiness brought her joy, even as her gaze strayed to a very unhappy face when she scanned the crowd for Peter.

Ryan was sitting at a picnic table, watching the interaction with a scowl. Emily's heart went out to him. He'd been so kind and attentive to Cassie since she'd arrived, but she supposed the heart wanted what it wanted.

"Are we gathering for the family photo?"

Emily jumped at the sound of her brother's voice and spun around to glare at him. "We were looking for you. Where were you?"

Peter jerked his thumb over his shoulder. "Over there."

"Everyone's here! Now we can get our photo." Their mom looked around before handing her phone to Derrick. "Would you mind taking it?"

Derrick nodded, and what was left of the Gallagher clan gathered in front of the roaring fire. Emily and Cassie posed on either side of Mom, with Peter in the back, since he was the tallest. It was almost like they had formed a protective barrier around Mom, lending her the strength and fortification she had lost since Dad died.

After snapping a few photos, Derrick handed the phone back and then leaned over and whispered in Cassie's ear. She giggled and said a quick goodbye before departing, hand in hand with him. When Emily looked back over at the table where Ryan had been, it was empty.

Chapter Eleven

CASSIE CHASED AFTER DERRICK AS HE RAN THROUGH THE festival. He'd told her he had a surprise for her, and she couldn't wait to see what it was. When they reached a dark corner with no one nearby, he spun around and grabbed her by the waist, pulling her against him. Her breath caught in her throat, and she looked up into those deep-blue eyes, wishing she could get lost in them.

"Where's my surprise?" Cassie asked breathlessly.

"Right here," Derrick whispered as he leaned toward her.

He's going to kiss me. Cassie's heart pounded in her ears. Her eyes fluttered shut, and she held her breath, believing in another moment she would know if this thing growing between her and Derrick was real.

Snap. Cassie's eyes flew open. *What was that?* Derrick frowned at something behind her. When she glanced over her shoulder, Ryan was leaning against a tree with his arms crossed.

"Ignore him," she murmured, lifting her hand to cup Derrick's cheek.

Ryan cleared his throat. "Cassie, may I speak to you a moment?"

"I'm a little busy." She rolled her eyes at Derrick, who grinned.

"It won't take long," Ryan said.

With a resigned sigh, she let go of Derrick and faced Ryan. "What is it?"

"Could you excuse us?" Ryan directed this to Derrick.

Derrick tensed behind her. She placed a comforting hand on his chest and tried not to get distracted by his muscles rippling beneath her fingers. His eyes met hers, and he gave a brief nod before heading back toward the fair.

"Well?" Cassie asked, letting her frustration color her tone.

"Look, I know this is none of my business, but I felt like I should warn you," Ryan said.

"Warn me?"

"About Derrick. He's not a good guy."

"Do you even know him?" Cassie put her hands on her hips.

"Unfortunately, yes." Ryan's green eyes filled with concern. "I want you to be careful. I'm afraid he's only interested in you for his fifteen minutes of fame."

"What?" Cassie gawked at him, her mouth falling open.

"His heroic rescue is all over the news, not only here, but statewide. And the local paper is loving the attention. Now that you two are out in public together, it's only going to get more sensational. And that's what Derrick is after: headlines and fame, in whatever way he can get them."

Cassie shook her head, not believing a word he was saying. When Derrick had asked her about doing more interviews, she'd refused. The guilt about lying was eating away at her. He was unhappy but hadn't pushed her to change her mind. And with as fast as the news cycled, they'd be forgotten in a few days.

"Do you understand what I'm saying, Cassie?" Ryan asked as he moved closer to her, searching her face. His hand found hers in the dark, and he gave it a squeeze, sending a tingle up her arm. "Derrick isn't interested in you beyond the story."

She snatched her hand back and stepped away from him, fury igniting inside her. *The nerve!* "Who do you think you are, Ryan? Coming here, pulling me aside, and telling me something you *think* about someone you barely know."

His eyes flashed, and his mouth set in a grim line. "I know more about Derrick Barnes than I care to."

The air between them crackled. She moved forward until she was pressed up against him, glaring into his face. Her heart pounded in her chest, whether from anger, fear, or something else, she couldn't tell, and in that moment, she didn't care.

"I highly doubt that." Cassie lifted her chin, giving him the haughtiest look she could muster. "You're just jealous." It was the only thing that made any sense. She'd turned Ryan down, and now he was bitter she had found someone else.

Ryan's expression darkened, and his eyes narrowed into slits. The force of his anger startled her, and she stumbled back a step.

With a frustrated sigh, Ryan ran a hand through his hair. "I thought you should know who Derrick truly is, but it appears you've already made up your mind about him... and me." Without waiting for a response, he turned and stormed away.

Cassie took a moment to calm her pounding heart. Perhaps she shouldn't have baited Ryan with that line about being jealous, but who did he think he was, meddling in her new relationship?

He may know Derrick, but he doesn't know me at all. I've always got my eye on the next best thing. New job. New hobby. New guy. My time with Derrick is no different.

She shook her head as she walked back to the festival to find Derrick, vowing to dismiss Ryan's so-called warning from her mind. But when she saw Derrick standing amidst a group of young coeds, her resolve faltered.

You're being ridiculous, she told herself. *Even if Derrick is only in this for fame, who cares?* She wasn't exactly searching for a happy-ever-after fairy tale herself. Okay, so maybe she did want to see if their relationship might lead somewhere. And sure, it was her chance to have what her parents had had, even if she and Derrick weren't high school sweethearts. But she wasn't stupid. They were both young and having fun. Besides, she would head back to the city at the end of the season. There wasn't much point in getting tangled up in strings neither of them needed.

Squaring her shoulders, she marched over to rejoin Derrick. When she tapped him on the shoulder, his dazzling smile sent her heart fluttering like a hummingbird's wings.

"Everything okay?" Derrick asked as he slid his arm around her waist and pulled her to his side.

"It is now," she purred, resting her head on his chest.

"Ladies, I'd like you to meet the woman of the hour. This is Cassie Gallagher, the cutest damsel in distress I ever did see."

The women cooed as they asked him question after question about his daring rescue. Cassie kept a radiant smile on her face, but after about ten minutes of listening to the coeds' nonstop praise of Derrick, she grew bored and more than a little irritated. She gently extracted herself from his arms.

"I'm going to get something to drink. You want anything, babe?"

"Sure, I could use a soda, thanks." He bent to kiss her cheek, which set off a warmth in her stomach.

Ryan doesn't know what he's talking about. But when she glanced back at Derrick, hoping he was watching her, he instead had his arms around two of the women while the third was snapping their picture. Her chest tightened. *Right?*

Days after Peter apparently failed to have the correct reaction to Ricardo's revelations, Emily continued to give him the cold shoulder, which bothered him more than he wanted to admit. At least Cassie seemed oblivious, caught up in her own little summer fling, and Mom was so happy to have her children home, she didn't notice the tension.

He made his way to Grounded for coffee and some peace. When he entered the shop, he checked for both a quiet, empty table and Ricardo.

As much as he didn't need the distraction, he wanted to see the handsome man again. They'd shared some moments Peter wouldn't soon forget, and he couldn't deny the attraction anymore. The other night had confirmed it was mutual. They were going to go on an actual, planned date at some point, but in the meantime, he wouldn't mind spending a few minutes here or there with Ricardo. Call it motivation to get his dissertation finished faster.

His usual table was open, but no Ricardo was in sight. Swallowing his disappointment, Peter sat down and opened his laptop. It was better

Ricardo wasn't here, as he needed to focus if he wanted to meet his deadline. Or, at least, that was what he told himself.

He began working through his next section of edits, and soon he became lost in the world of affordable housing. The hours breezed by as he worked, draining two or three cups of coffee in the process. He'd lost count. As he was finishing the last of the section, the chair on the opposite side of his table scraped against the floor. He jumped and gazed into a familiar pair of dark-brown eyes.

"You were off in your own little world," Ricardo said as he sank into the chair. "I called your name about four times, and you didn't even blink."

"Sorry," Peter said. "I guess I was in the zone."

"Edits are going well, then?"

Peter nodded as he finished the last of his umpteenth cup of coffee, grimacing when the cold liquid met his tongue. How long had he been sitting here?

"I don't think I've ever seen someone make that face at Grounded's coffee." Ricardo choked back a laugh. "And I should know, since I used to work here."

"It's not their fault I let it sit for so long," Peter mumbled, setting the cup aside and closing his laptop. "I didn't know you worked here during high school."

"It was one of my many part-time jobs." Ricardo shifted in his seat. "Has your family said anything more about our conversation last night?"

"No, though Emily's not exactly speaking to me right now." With a sigh, Peter leaned back in his chair. "But as far as I can tell, she hasn't broached the subject with my mother. They're baking for the strawberry festival tomorrow."

"I never understood the appeal of that event."

Peter laughed. "It's more of a fundraiser for the local farmers."

"Still doesn't make much sense to me." Ricardo gave Peter a quick once-over. "And you don't take part in the baking?"

Peter rolled his eyes. "I usually only bake at Christmas."

"Oh, you do?" Ricardo leaned forward, his brown eyes dancing with amusement. "And what do you bake?"

Peter's cheeks warmed, and he lowered his gaze to the table. "I've been sort of, uh, appointed as the family baker. But I mostly make cookies, pies, and other desserts for our family's Christmas dinner."

"Hmm, I'm not sure I'll be around for the holidays this year, but if I am, is there any chance you could save me a morsel or two?"

"I'm sure that could be arranged," Peter said as he lifted his gaze to meet Ricardo's. Christmas was six months away. Did this mean Ricardo had high hopes for their date? Warmth spread through his chest when Ricardo reached across the table to hold his hand.

"When do you think you'll be free for dinner?" The intensity in Ricardo's eyes almost made Peter forget to breathe.

"My schedule should free up after the Fourth of July."

"I'm going to hold you to that," Ricardo said as he squeezed Peter's hand. "But for now, I'll let you get back to your work." He gave Peter one last charming smile before heading to the door.

Peter's stomach clenched, but Ricardo was right. They could enjoy their time together that much more if he wasn't distracted by his deadline.

But when he opened his computer, he blinked when he saw it had shut down. He'd forgotten to plug it in. After digging out the power cord, he plugged the computer in to reboot. He opened his document, but he didn't see his latest edits. As he frantically searched to see if he had saved the document to a different folder, a knot formed in his stomach. Had he forgotten to save his work? The coffee shop's Wi-Fi was spotty, so he hadn't bothered to save to the cloud. Truthfully, he didn't trust it anyway, not with something as important as his dissertation. He wracked his brain. Had he opened the file from his hard drive or had he opened the cloud version on accident as a temporary file? He checked his downloads, but it wasn't there either. Maybe his computer had glitched? It wouldn't be the first time. Which was why saving often was something he'd drilled into his head for months to avoid just this situation. But because he was so distracted by Ricardo, he'd lost hours of work. He pressed his fists against his eyes.

He shoved back from the table and took his empty coffee cup to the trash. As he stood in line, he thought back over his work session, trying to recall everything he'd changed. He mentally kicked himself. How had he forgotten to save? The memory of Ricardo startling him came to mind as he grabbed without thinking the cup the barista had set down. He dropped it a second later as the heat from the steaming liquid burned through the thin material, and he quickly slid a cardboard protector on the cup with a frustrated huff.

Fresh coffee in hand and his mouth set in a grim line, he started working on the edits again with renewed determination. Maybe Emily was right about Ricardo being wrong for him, not because of Sunrise Oasis Resorts, but because his constant intrusion into Peter's routine was causing him to lose sight of his goal: finishing his Ph.D. The time had come to reevaluate his priorities because nothing was more important to him than finishing his degree.

Chapter Twelve

The Gallagher women were taking turns in the kitchen. While Emily and Mom handled lunchtime at the pub, Cassie was busy baking her famous strawberry shortcake cupcakes for the strawberry festival. This afternoon, they would switch, and she'd go to the bar while Emily and Mom baked strawberry cheesecake and strawberry blondies.

Cassie had always loved the town's annual events. They transported her back to her childhood, which was a time she missed more every day. She'd been in such a hurry to grow up, but now she wished she had that time back. Things were certainly simpler back then. Her father was still alive, the pub was thriving, and her siblings only squabbled over sharing toys or who got to enjoy batter off the beaters.

While she didn't know exactly what had happened between Peter and Emily, something was up. When she'd entered the kitchen that morning, she'd found them on opposite sides of the room with the tension as thick as cheesecake batter. She stifled a sigh as she poured her cereal. Their fights were rare, but long and drawn-out. It would be several days before everything was peaceful again in the Gallagher house.

Cassie put on some lighthearted music for background noise as she made dozens and dozens of cupcakes. It'd been a while since she last baked, and she wondered why she had put it off for so long. The tiny kitchen in her apartment wasn't quite up for a marathon baking session like this, but it would work for baking a batch or two of chocolate chip cookies.

Her phone went off as she took out what felt like the fiftieth batch of cupcakes. She grinned as she bent down to press the answer button with her nose; her hands were filled with baking trays. After tapping the speakerphone with her nose as well, she stepped over to put the trays in the oven.

"Hey, Derrick. What's up?" she called, closing the oven door.

"I wanted to see if you were up for grabbing a quick bite to eat."

"Mm, I wish," Cassie said. "I'm drowning in cupcake batter right now."

There was a moment of silence, and Cassie sensed his disappointment pouring through the connection.

"Ah, right, the strawberry festival. I forgot." His sigh tugged at Cassie's heartstrings. He must miss her.

"I'm free tomorrow, though," Cassie said, hoping to lift his spirits.

"Eh, tomorrow won't work. The reporter wanted to talk to us today. She has a deadline of this afternoon."

Cassie paused in her task of moving the finished cupcakes onto the cooling rack as she glanced over at her phone. *Wait... Another reporter? Hadn't they agreed not to do any more interviews? The lie had gotten out of hand.*

"Hey, do you think we could come by your house?" Derrick asked. "Maybe she could include some promotional information about the strawberry festival."

"Derrick..." Her teeth worried her bottom lip. "I thought we agreed to stop doing interviews."

"Who is it hurting?" Derrick asked. "Besides, I told you that this might help me get a promotion. Don't you want that for me?"

"Of course I want you to get promoted," she said irritably. His insistence that interviews were the way to do that was getting a little tired. *If his boss is going to promote him, wouldn't he do it because of merit and not because of publicity?* "But I told you, I'm not comfortable perpetuating a lie."

"But people are coming in from all over, hoping to catch sight of the sharks. My buddy's T-shirt shop is swamped with customers wanting special-edition shirts printed." When she didn't respond, he pressed on. "Isn't that why you're here? To promote the town and your family's pub?"

As much as she hated to admit it, he had a point. But she wasn't sure the correct way to do that was through false pretenses. After all, what would happen if the tourists found out it was all a lie? Wouldn't that hurt the town more than help it?

She focused on filling the baking pan with batter as she debated how to respond. As much as she hated to let him down, she just couldn't bring herself to continue perpetuating the farce.

"I'm sorry, Derrick, but I can't be a part of this anymore. If you want to continue to give interviews, that's your choice, but I'm done."

For a moment, she regretted her decision. *What if Ryan is right? What if Derrick was only interested in me because of this stupid shark story?* She held her breath as she waited for him to respond. Well, if that was the case, it would be better if she found out now.

He sighed. "Okay, I understand."

The disappointment in his voice was palpable. She braced herself, expecting him to tell her he didn't want to see her again. Or maybe he would just hang up and that would be that.

"Do you want to grab dinner tomorrow?" he asked.

She blinked, and her heart soared. "I'd love to."

"Great! I'll pick you up at six."

After disconnecting the call, she hummed happily as she removed another batch of cupcakes from the oven. She should trust her instincts more often. Ryan was wrong, and her date tomorrow with Derrick would prove that.

Emily was pleased the lunch shift was busier than usual. The town's strawberry festival was typically a big hit, bringing in people from all over the state. They would often stay overnight, which meant Fiddler's Green might see a crowd for dinner too.

She was also happy to be away from the house. Things with Peter were still tense. She was baffled by her brother's refusal to see Ricardo for what he was. But she tried to push it out of her mind. More important things were going on than some big resort executive blinding her brother to what was at stake. Wednesday was their first event at the pub, and everything needed to go well. It would crush her mother if they lost their father's legacy so soon after losing their father.

Anna Mae had promised to stop by the house later, and Emily's mind kept replaying their almost kiss. She still couldn't believe it. Had Anna Mae gotten caught up in the moment? Or was she looking for a summer fling? Though that wasn't Emily's style, she couldn't help wondering what it would be like.

It was unlikely they'd have a moment to themselves any time soon. When Cassie came to relieve her, Emily and Mom would spend the rest of the day in the kitchen. Anna Mae had offered to help, provided Emily was available to put the finishing touches on their plans for trivia night. Cassie had already loaded the questions and answers into their computer system. Everything was coming together perfectly.

As the crowds wound down, Emily walked into the back office, where Mom was working on payroll. Mom looked up as Emily knocked softly at the door.

"Is it time already?" Mom asked, shaking her head. "I seem to lose track of the hours."

"Not quite," Emily said. "Cassie isn't here yet, but she should be soon. Is there anything you need me to do before we go?"

"I don't think so, but check with Tony."

Emily nodded and headed to the kitchen. Tony was cleaning up after lunch and starting dinner prep. He greeted her with a smile.

"Mom and I are going to be heading out once Cassie gets here. Anything you need me to do?"

"Nothing comes to mind," Tony said as he ran a hand through his salt-and-pepper hair. He started filling the sink to wash the last of the lunch dishes. "It's a real good thing you and your friend are doing, trying to save the pub."

"I'd hate to lose this place." Emily sighed and leaned against the counter.

"Me too." After washing a pot and setting it on the drying rack, he glanced at Emily. "It's been hard on your mom, keeping it open, but it's a labor of love. She misses your dad."

"We all do, but I get it's worse for her."

"It's too bad all you kids moved away," Tony said. "If even one of y'all had stayed, Julie wouldn't be struggling so much."

"I wish I had gotten a teaching position nearby," Emily said. "I've suggested Cassie come home, since she's not thrilled with her latest job, but I'm not holding my breath."

"Do whatever you can to convince her." Tony faced her. "It'll be good for her and Julie."

Emily nodded and headed out of the kitchen. Convincing Cassie to do anything she didn't want to do was a next-to-impossible task, but perhaps her sister's growing interest in Derrick would help. She was so lost in thought she almost ran straight into Cassie on her way to the dining area.

"You okay, sis?" Cassie asked.

Emily took a deep breath. "I have a lot on my mind. You know, with the trivia night and what not."

"Understood." Cassie stepped back. "I baked over one hundred cupcakes today."

"You've been busy." Emily smiled. "Well, Mom and I better be off. Text us if you need anything."

On the walk back to the house, Emily tried to determine the best way to broach the subject with Cassie again. She wanted it to seem like moving home was her sister's idea, as Cassie was notorious for doing the exact opposite of what people wanted her to do. While they'd all inherited their father's stubborn streak, Cassie seemed to revel in it.

"Penny for your thoughts?" her mother asked as they reached the house. "You were awfully quiet on our way here."

Emily forced a smile. "Just running through the plans for the first event, that's all."

"Your father would have been so proud of the way you're working to save his dream." She unlocked the door and led the way to the kitchen. The room was clean except for several ingredients that had been left on the counter, including eggs, butter, and milk. "Looks like Cassie left our wet ingredients out for us."

"She's always been a by-the-book baker, despite how often she acts outside of the box."

Mom laughed. "Your sister follows her own path." Her blue eyes softened. "It's not always such a bad thing to blaze your own trail, you know." She went over to measure out the flour. "I know you and Peter look at Cassie's life and think she's unfocused and reckless. I can't say I don't worry about her myself, but I admire her for her resilience and her resourcefulness."

"She's like a cat who always lands on her feet," Emily said, rolling her eyes. Though she had to admit her mother had a point. Cassie, for all her fanciful ideas, seemed to have a knack for having everything work out in the end.

"An apt description, but one we could learn from. How does she do it? Where does she find the energy to run after life with wide-open arms, ready to embrace whatever comes next?" Her mother shrugged. "She reminds me of myself at her age. Full of romantic ideas." Her smile faded. "But my romance days are over. I'll have to live vicariously through my children."

Emily bit her lip. Was her mother about to launch into yet another lecture about the importance of settling down and how much she wanted grandchildren?

"Speaking of... That Anna Mae is a nice girl."

"She is." Emily ducked her head and stared at the cookbook. "I appreciate her help with the pub."

"Is that all you appreciate?"

"I barely know her," Emily said, evading the question. Mom made a disapproving noise in the back of her throat, but the tightness in Emily's chest relaxed when her mother didn't press her further.

As she cracked the eggs and discarded the shells, she thought about what her mother had said. "If you could be more like Cassie, what aspects of life would you run toward with open arms?"

Her mother blinked, but then her face grew pensive as her eyebrows pulled together. "Well, I've always wanted to travel. Your father was a homebody and never wanted to go anywhere for vacation if it required a plane, but I've always wanted to see Europe, Hawaii, various Caribbean isles."

"So why don't you?"

"For one thing, it's been less than a year since he passed, and I'm still trying to get my bearings. And for another…" Mom sighed. "What would I do with the pub?"

"You could close in the off-season."

"I've considered it, but then what would my staff do? This is their livelihood."

"I'm sure they could find something in the off-season, or live off their savings until you reopen," Emily said. "Or perhaps you could close for periods of time, like a month, to give everyone a break and to allow you to travel. I know of several restaurants in Ocean City that close for short periods in the off-season because it's more expensive to stay open when there aren't any customers."

"Maybe." Her mom didn't sound convinced. "Anyway, it's not something for you to worry about. I'm sure I'll get to traveling when I retire."

They mixed the batter and began filling the mini cheesecake tins. Emily kept sneaking glances at her mother out of the corner of her eye. Would she be able to travel more if Cassie was there helping her with the business? Did Emily trust her sister enough to handle things while her mother was gone?

As each batch finished baking, they set the trays on racks to cool. Once they completed the cheesecakes, they moved on to the blondies. Just as they were putting the first batch in to bake, the doorbell rang.

Emily wiped her hands on her apron, both to remove flour and because they were suddenly quite clammy. She opened the door and was greeted by Anna Mae's warm smile.

Anna Mae stepped into the house, taking a deep breath and closing her eyes. "It smells heavenly in here."

"We're on our last item for the festival," Emily said.

"Then I'm just in time." Anna Mae embraced her briefly, causing Emily's stomach to flip-flop. Warmth spread up her neck and over her cheeks, and she ducked her head as she led the way into the kitchen.

"Are you here to help us?" Mom asked as they entered the room.

"Sure," Anna Mae said, stepping over to the sink to wash her hands. Emily handed her an apron, careful not to touch her again. The kitchen was already warm enough without her cheeks turning red every other minute.

The blondies went much faster with three pairs of hands, and soon the women were sitting in the living room, relaxing after a long day. Anna Mae pulled out her tablet and showed Emily and Mom how the social media campaign was going.

"I think we're going to have a good turnout," she said, her voice filled with pride. "And if we make the night a success, hopefully these attendees will bring their friends to the next one."

"Fingers crossed," Emily said.

Emily and Anna Mae spent the next few hours going over the finer details of the trivia night, and by the time they were finished, their confidence was soaring. Emily hoped their work would pay off and the town of Blue Heron Bay would return to its high-tourism heyday. Maybe then the town council would reject any offer Sunrise Oasis Resorts put in, thus paving the way for Wakefield Hotel Group.

Chapter Thirteen

Cassie, Emily, and their mom arrived at the strawberry festival early. The convention center was already filled with other strawberry enthusiasts who were also setting up their areas and chatting with their neighbors.

Ryan stopped by their booth. He greeted the three Gallagher women warmly, but his eyes lingered on Cassie. Emily hid a smile. That man had it *bad*, though she couldn't understand why. As far as she could tell, her sister hadn't given him any encouragement, and physical attraction only went so far.

"How are things going with the trivia night?" he asked, turning his attention to her.

"Really well," Emily said enthusiastically. "Anna Mae's publicity has garnered a lot of interest on social media, and we're hoping for a good turnout."

"That's great news." Ryan smiled. "I plan to join in myself." He glanced at Cassie out of the corner of his eye. "I'm quite the trivia buff, but I'm not sure how I'll fare with the subjects."

"Might want to watch a few episodes of *Jeopardy*," Cassie said, and her teasing surprised Emily. "Wouldn't want to be eliminated in the first round."

Ryan gave a hearty laugh. "I'll try to find the time between now and then to do some research." He glanced at his watch. "Anyway, I need to head to the podium so we can get started with the festival. Thank you for your contribution, and I look forward to proving my skills next time I see you."

Emily forced a smile, but she side-eyed her sister. It almost sounded like Cassie was flirting with him, though maybe she was imagining things. When he was out of earshot, she leaned over and whispered, "What is up with you two?"

Cassie stared at her with wide eyes. "Nothing, why?"

"I don't know. I thought you were keeping your distance since you were spending so much time with Derrick. And I figured he'd take the hint. But just now, it seemed as if you were encouraging him."

Her sister snorted. "Ryan? Please. If I encouraged anything, it was just a little healthy competition." She shook her head. "Don't read into it."

Ryan's voice came over the loudspeaker at that moment to start the festivities, and Emily decided to drop it. Cassie was an adult, and Emily should trust she knew what she was doing. Still, Emily couldn't help feeling like there might be a spark between her sister and the mayor, no matter how much Cassie denied it.

Her phone vibrated in her pocket. It was a text from Anna Mae, and Emily's heart leapt into her throat.

My father's in town. Planning to show him all that Blue Heron Bay has to offer. See you at the festival in a few hours.

Emily practically bounced out of her skin. It was going to be a long morning, but as the crowds began to gather in the convention center, she hoped the hours would pass quickly.

When they finally arrived, Anna Mae made a beeline for their booth. Mr. Wakefield shared many features with his daughter. He had the same prominent nose, dark eyes, and black hair, although his was thinning and peppered with gray. His demeanor struck her as authoritative but not domineering as he smiled at the assembled crowd on his way to their location.

"Father, these are the Gallaghers, who I've told you so much about, minus one," Anna Mae said, and Emily raised an eyebrow at how formally Anna Mae addressed him. "Julie, Emily, and Cassie, this is my father, Harris Wakefield."

"A pleasure to meet you all," Harris said. His gaze fell on Emily, and she shifted her weight from foot to foot. "Miss Emily, I understand you have been instrumental in assisting my daughter with her publicity scheme."

Emily nodded. "We've been helping each other."

"I appreciate your enthusiasm to save your town and your family's pub, though I do fear it may be misguided."

Anna Mae visibly bristled at her father's words, but the pasted-on smile never left her face. "Father, you underestimate how successful we'll be."

"Oh, I don't doubt you'll be successful." Harris waved a hand. "I simply think your triumphs will do more to help Sunrise Oasis Resorts than they will our hotels."

"But if you listen to my proposal, we might be able to beat Ricardo at his own game," Anna Mae protested.

Harris's eyes rolled toward the ceiling, and Emily got the sense this was an ongoing argument between them. She snuck a glance at Anna Mae, who shrugged helplessly. Harris's reaction was not a good sign.

A lovely young woman with auburn hair and clear blue eyes stepped up behind Harris. Emily assumed she was there for a cupcake, but the haughty once-over Emily received when she went to hand her one stopped her in her tracks.

Anna Mae's eyes widened. "Leslie, what are you doing here?"

"Ah, good, you've arrived," Harris said, turning to Leslie. "Leslie's family is interested in partnering with us on the Blue Heron Bay project." He gave Anna Mae a stern look. "I know you believe in the power of marketing, but I believe in partnerships. A deal with Steele Hotels would go a long way to convincing me of the benefit of the Blue Heron project."

"It's good to see you, Anna Mae," Leslie said. Her voice was deep and husky, and the way she gazed at Anna Mae gave Emily a sinking feeling in the pit of her stomach.

"Uh, good to see you too," Anna Mae said. Leslie moved toward her with outstretched arms, but Anna Mae took a wide step back and held out her hand. Leslie accepted it with a frown.

What's their story?

Moving closer to Emily, Anna Mae put a hand on her back. Emily's skin warmed from her touch.

"Leslie Steele, this is the Gallagher family. They own Fiddler's Green. This is Julie and Cassie, and this"—she pushed Emily forward—"is Emily. We've been working together since I arrived in town."

Leslie narrowed her eyes at the ease with which Anna Mae touched Emily before she appeared to recollect herself. After giving a curt nod, she pressed her lips into a line that might have been her attempt at a smile.

"Your efforts are duly noted, and of course, bringing tourism to the town is important," Leslie said. "But unfortunately, I'm afraid it's not enough, at least, not to offset the risk to our respective companies." She held out a hand to Anna Mae. "But we shouldn't bore them with shop talk, right, darling?"

Darling? Emily blinked rapidly.

"I promised Emily I would go over last-minute details for our first pub event, which is later this week," Anna Mae said, her voice as firm as her hold on Emily's hand.

Leslie raised a thin eyebrow. "There will be plenty of time for that little gathering later." Her voice dripped with condescension, and Emily fought the urge to glare at her. "We have bigger fish to fry at present."

Anna Mae opened her mouth to protest, but her father stepped forward. "My apologies, ladies, but I'm afraid it is imperative I steal my daughter away." He took a cupcake. "My compliments to the bakers." With a warm smile, he walked away. Anna gave Emily's hand a reluctant squeeze before she released it and marched after her father.

"I wouldn't get too attached," Leslie murmured to Emily once Anna Mae was out of earshot. She smirked and sauntered out of the convention center.

"What was that about?" Cassie asked when they were alone again.

Emily shrugged, not trusting herself to speak. She was saved when a fresh group of customers came up to them at that moment. But inside, her emotions were at war. She wasn't sure what to think. *What history does Anna Mae have with that woman?* Her heart sank as another thought occurred to her. *Or is it* history *at all?* It wasn't like Emily and Anna Mae had had the exes discussion. For all Emily knew, Anna Mae was already spoken for.

Emily closed her eyes briefly and took a deep, calming breath. She'd avoided relationships for so long. Of course the moment she found someone she was interested in, everything became complicated.

The rest of the day went by in a blur, and Emily wasn't sure if she was happy or disappointed when her family started packing up their booth. They'd run out of baked goods and were more than a little tired. As they headed out of the center to her mother's car, Emily couldn't help checking if Anna Mae had returned, but there was no sign of her. Her ribs constricted and she struggled to breathe. She worked to keep her face neutral lest her family start asking questions.

If only she and Peter were on better terms. He was the person she most wanted to confide in, but he'd holed himself up with his dissertation since their argument. Besides, she was still aggravated with his flippant attitude toward the pub. She could only hope Anna Mae would stop by later that evening, even if only to finalize the plans for trivia night.

Peter had emphatically declared his intent to skip the strawberry festival, and when his family left, he'd set up his workspace to work on his dissertation. On the plus side, the silent house was aiding his efforts to catch up on the edits he'd lost.

Ricardo had texted him a few times since the previous day, but Peter was resolute in his decision not to allow any distractions to keep him from his goal, no matter how handsome they were. He suspected Ricardo would attend the strawberry festival, if for nothing else than to evaluate the success of Anna Mae's marketing efforts.

Emily still wasn't speaking to Peter, but he had bigger things to worry about. Tonight, he planned to address the proposed sale of the pub with his mother when he could find a moment alone with her.

At that moment, he wasn't focused on any of those things. As he plugged away at his edits, a sense of accomplishment filled him, and he diligently pressed on. He spent the entire day at his computer, only taking brief breaks. By the time the front door opened, signaling his family's return, his eyes were getting that gluey-glazed feeling, and his muscles were tense from sitting in the same position for so long.

After obsessively clicking save for the millionth time, he closed his computer with a satisfied snap. If he could find a few more hours in the next couple of days, he would more than beat his deadline. He opened his door and wandered downstairs.

Cassie was standing in the kitchen, washing out some containers they had used to transport their baked goods, but Mom and Emily were nowhere to be seen. Maybe they had gone to the pub to prepare for the dinner rush, if it could be called that.

"The prodigal son emerges from his hole," Cassie said when she turned. "How goes the dissertation?"

"Very well, thank you." Peter searched the kitchen for leftover goodies.

"Here." Cassie lifted a tin out of the cabinet and handed it to him. "We didn't take these with us."

Peter nodded and opened it, finding a few cupcakes within. After grabbing a couple, he closed the lid and returned the tin to its place. "How was the festival?"

"Busy." Cassie grabbed a towel from under the sink and dried the container. "We were completely wiped out by midafternoon."

"Was Ricardo there?" Peter asked without thinking.

Cassie raised an eyebrow. "Not that I saw." She put the container away before glancing back at him with a smirk. "He didn't visit you here?"

"Why would he?" Peter retorted, though his stomach flipped. He stepped into the living room. "Where are Mom and Emily?"

"The pub," Cassie said as she followed him. "They gave me the night off since Sundays are usually slow at the bar. Things are coming together for trivia, though I think Emily has some competition."

Peter whirled around in surprise. "Competition? For what? With whom?"

"Um, Anna Mae," Cassie said, her tone suggesting this was obvious.

Wait. Emily was interested in Anna Mae? They'd spent a lot of time together on the pub events, but he hadn't considered they were a thing. Come to think of it, he was shocked Emily hadn't mentioned it. They typically talked about everything. Even more confounding was the fact that Cassie, of all people, knew before he did. Had Emily said something, or had he simply not been paying attention? He stared at his younger sister. She wasn't usually the most observant person, or at least, she'd never seemed to be.

"Oh, right," Peter said quickly, hoping to cover his faux pas. "Who's the competition?"

"Some Paris Hilton wannabe," Cassie scoffed. "She's the daughter of the CEO of a hotel chain Anna Mae's dad wants to merge with, and she wants to do some merging of her own." Cassie side-eyed him. "If you know what I mean."

Peter laughed. "I take it you don't like her?"

Cassie shrugged one shoulder. "I don't know her. That's just the impression I got. Anna Mae didn't seem thrilled to see her though, but I guess Mr. Wakefield thought he needed some reinforcements if he has any hope of setting up a hotel here with Ricardo also sniffing around."

Peter bristled at her characterization but let it go. "Surely Anna Mae's schemes to increase tourism and the attraction of an upscale resort would bring in enough business for both ventures in Blue Heron Bay."

"Maybe, but I'd much rather have the new hotel. The carbon footprint alone from the type of resorts Ricardo's company builds would change the entire culture of the town. Not to mention that a place like that could put us out of business in a heartbeat since they're sure to have tons of different dining options built into their model." She shook her head. "Blue Heron Bay will be just another Ocean City in no time."

"And what, you don't think Wakefield will do the same?"

"Not from what I've seen. They work with the towns where they build to fit their hotels into the existing infrastructure. And they have brand loyalty, so they'll still bring in the tourists without destroying the quaint, small-town feel for the year-long residents."

Peter stared at her, speechless. His sister had been paying closer attention than he'd initially thought. Though he was surprised she was interested at all. In his experience, Cassie didn't bother with things that didn't directly involve her, and since she would go back to her real life in the city soon, he wasn't sure why she cared if the pub went out of business.

"I'm shocked you're still hanging around with Ricardo," Cassie said, giving him another side glance. "I'd have thought you'd steer clear of someone who might kill Dad's dream."

Peter shifted uncomfortably. *Great.* Now both of his sisters were questioning his judgment. It would be more difficult to convince his mother of the value of selling the pub if the family was divided. He'd not considered getting Cassie on his side because he expected her to be indifferent. Clearly, the sentimental value of the pub ran deep. He could only hope Mom would see reason.

"There's nothing wrong with keeping our options open," Peter muttered. Cassie looked up at him sharply, but he turned away. With a newfound determination, he decided it was high time he spent some one-on-one time with his mother. "I'm going to the pub. I'll see you later."

He slammed the door behind him before Cassie could respond and stomped down the driveway. But her words echoed in his head. Was he being a terrible son to consider the benefits of selling the restaurant? Of course he understood his family's reasons for keeping it. His father had loved that pub and poured his heart and soul into it. But Peter wasn't a sentimental person. If considering the practicality of the situation made him heartless, then so be it.

"Peter," a deep voice called from behind him. He spun around, and his heart flew to his throat while his stomach dropped. So much for avoiding distractions.

"Hello, Ricardo."

"I haven't heard from you. Have you gotten my texts?" Ricardo asked as he fell into step beside him.

"I've, uh, been busy with my dissertation," Peter said as he picked up his pace. Ricardo was enemy number one as far as Emily and Anna Mae were concerned, so it was unlikely he would follow Peter into the pub. More reason to get there as quickly as possible.

"I was hoping to make plans for our dinner. But I feel like you're avoiding me." His tone was so morose and confused it brought Peter up short. "Did I do something wrong?"

Peter sighed and rubbed the back of his head. "No, well, not directly."

Ricardo frowned and shook his head. "I don't understand."

As a businessman, Ricardo might understand prioritizing. Peter figured it couldn't hurt. "You remember how you found me working the other day at the coffee shop?" At Ricardo's nod, Peter continued. "I forgot to save my work and lost my edits, which constituted multiple hours of work. I was trying to avoid further... distractions."

To Peter's surprise and relief, Ricardo's frown cleared, and he smiled. "Oof. I've been there. That really sucks about your edits, but I completely understand the need to focus." He stepped back. "Let me know when you're ready to be distracted again." With a wink that sent Peter's heart racing, Ricardo walked in the opposite direction, leaving Peter alone on the sidewalk.

At least someone understands. And what a reward a date with Ricardo would be once he was no longer facing a tough deadline.

Fiddler's Green was unsurprisingly empty when he entered. The part-time bartender was leaning against the counter, watching a football game on the television. Emily was out in the house, cleaning up tables and setting out silverware in the futile hope of customers. Well, it might not be completely futile. Some patrons of the festival might come out of their sugar-induced comas to partake in slightly healthier sustenance.

Peter slipped quietly to the back office, where he was sure to find his mother alone. Now seemed as good a time as any to have a pragmatic discussion. Without the influence of his more sentimental siblings, he hoped he could appeal to Mom's rational side.

He knocked softly at the door and then opened it, finding her sitting at her computer, going through the payroll. Shutting the door behind him, he stepped forward and rested a hand on her shoulder.

She placed her hand over his and gave it a gentle squeeze. "You missed quite the crowd today."

"So Cassie told me." Peter bent to kiss her hair. "Need help?"

She shook her head. "Adding up employee hours is the easy part; it's trying to find the funds to pay them that becomes more difficult." With a sigh, she rubbed her temples. "I never realized how hard this would be without your father."

"Dad wouldn't have wanted you to stress like this," Peter said soothingly. He crouched down beside her. The office was cramped and cluttered, leaving little space to move around. "Have you considered your options?"

She turned her head, her blue eyes wary. "What options?"

"What I mean is, have you considered selling?"

She sighed. "Of course I have. But I can't do that."

"Says who? Emily? Cassie?"

"No, no, I'm sure if I decided I needed to sell, they would understand."

Peter pressed his lips together, deciding that disparaging his sisters would not win him any points right now. "Then who?"

"I made a promise."

"Dad would understand." Peter placed a hand on her arm. "He would have wanted you to be happy."

She closed her eyes, and a tear slid down her cheek. "I know, but other than you kids, this place is all I have left of your father. And with you all gone, I can't bear to lose the pub too."

Talk about a gut punch. How could he argue with that? He and his siblings had lost their father, but Mom had lost her soul mate. The grief etched across her face was proof enough of that.

"I don't hold out much hope Emily's schemes will be successful, at least not long-term," she said as she turned back to the computer screen. "But I don't have the heart to tell her that."

"She may be on to something," Peter said, though he couldn't keep the doubt out of his voice.

"Blue Heron Bay hasn't kept up with the modern world. It was meant as a place for families to get away from it all, have some peace, and truly relax." She twisted her wedding ring around her finger. "But everyone prefers the hubbub of Ocean City. They have the boardwalk, amusement parks, and every spot of land from the ocean to the bay is claimed by some sort of distraction."

Ricardo's plans would change all that for their town. From what Cassie had said and what Peter had discovered through his own research,

Sunrise Oasis Resorts boasted a plethora of options to keep every customer entertained, from the tiniest tot to the oldest retiree. They offered various choices to encourage guests to spend their time, and money, onsite.

Sadly, the simpler family vacations he recalled as a child were becoming a relic of the past. Kids didn't want to sit around and play board games with their parents. They were on the internet and social media, playing games on their phones or binge-watching shows on the various streaming services. The neighboring town of Ocean City had kept up with this change in interest, upgrading their arcades, creating more extreme rides, and phasing out older attractions.

His mother was right. Emily and Anna Mae's plans to draw tourism were only going to work in the short term. Wakefield Hotels ranged from boutique to family to luxurious, and Peter expected whatever they planned to build here would be some sort of hybrid. But it wouldn't be enough, and he suspected Anna Mae's father already knew that.

"Hey, Mom, can you come—oh, Peter, I didn't know you were here." Emily's tone cooled significantly after she noticed him.

"I made some real progress on my edits, so I thought I'd stop by and see how things were going," Peter said, keeping his voice even.

"What did you need?" Mom asked, seemingly oblivious to the tension between her children.

"Your help," Emily said. "We've had quite the influx of customers in the last hour, and I could use some extra hands up front." She shot a triumphant look at Peter, clearly encouraged that her work with Anna Mae was paying off.

"I'll come too," Peter said, ignoring the way Emily's mouth dropped open. "Maybe we should text Cassie."

"Oh, leave her be. She's got a date tonight," his mother said, waving a hand. "We can handle it with the three of us."

When they entered the front of the pub, Peter blinked at the crowd, and he caught Emily's smug expression out of the corner of his eye. They each walked to a section and began taking orders. Peter put on his best smile and greeted his first table. The place was full for a change, and he would make the most of it. But he had a sinking feeling in his gut that it wouldn't last.

Chapter Fourteen

Cassie stood by the window, waiting for Derrick. He'd promised to come by around six, and as soon as Peter had left, she'd rushed to get ready. Her excitement grew as the clock ticked closer to the hour, and when an engine revved outside, she raced to the front door and threw it open.

He honked from the driveway and waved. After closing the door behind her, she hurried to greet him, ignoring the pang of disappointment that he hadn't come to the house and knocked like a proper gentleman. She climbed into the car and leaned over to give him a peck on the cheek.

His eyes traveled over her, and when he met her gaze, he gave her a sexy grin. "You look amazing."

"Thanks," she breathed. "So do you." It wasn't a lie, not really. He always looked good, but she couldn't help feeling overdressed as she compared her black dress with a sweetheart neckline and spaghetti straps to his bright-orange Bermuda shorts and flowered Hawaiian shirt.

She cleared her throat and forced a smile. "Where are we going?"

"There's this great little dive across the town line," he said, backing down the driveway. "You're gonna love it."

As they crossed into Ocean City and headed for the boardwalk,

Cassie's heart sank. She'd hoped for a nice quiet evening together where they could really get to know each other, but the crowds alone would make that next to impossible. There wasn't a restaurant in the area that wouldn't be packed with people. Part of her would have been thrilled even to go to her family's pub if it meant she could have a moment alone with him.

When he pulled into the parking lot of Secrets, she choked back a laugh. This *is his "little dive"? Is there a soul alive on the Eastern Shore who doesn't know about this place?* Stifling a sigh, she followed him into the restaurant and hoped he would opt for a booth or table. She was *not* dressed to climb into an inner tube that evening.

"We'd like a booth in the back if you have one," he said, and Cassie's shoulders relaxed. But it was short-lived because the booth was right next to the kitchen. They'd be interrupted all evening by staff. With an internal groan, she slid onto one bench and blinked when Derrick slid in beside her.

"This is cozy, isn't it?" he asked, taking her hand and giving it a squeeze.

Well, that was one word for it, but she refused to allow herself to focus on the negative. A night out with Derrick Barnes was something her high school self could only have dreamed about. She wouldn't allow herself to be disappointed now.

Once they'd ordered drinks and dinner, Derrick slid his arm around her shoulders. "So, tell me about yourself, Cassie Gallagher. What have you been up to since high school?"

"Oh, you know, college, career—that sort of thing."

"Career, huh? What do you do?"

She grimaced. *Ugh, really?* She'd hoped for a more stimulating conversation. If she'd wanted to talk about her career, she would have gone out with Ryan. For a moment, she wondered what Ryan was like on a date. He probably would have taken her to a nice waterfront restaurant in town, dressed in a polo shirt and khakis. Maybe they'd take a stroll on the beach after.

What is wrong with you? There she was, out on the town with the man of her dreams, and instead of living in the moment, she was daydreaming about being with someone she wasn't even interested in.

She forced herself to focus on the conversation. Perhaps once they got through the boring parts, they could go deeper. There were many things she'd love to learn about Derrick, like why he'd never left town.

Finally, she said, "I'm a paralegal. I've been working at various large firms in D.C. as a temp."

"That's cool. You planning to go to law school?"

"No," she said, her tone curter than she'd intended. She cleared her throat and tried again. "I barely made it through my bachelor's, so yeah, law school isn't in the cards."

He chuckled and squeezed her shoulder. "I hear that. My dad really wanted me to go into government, but it didn't exactly work out."

"Is that why you ran for mayor?"

His face darkened. "Oh, that. No, I actually thought I'd enjoy politics. I mean, I know it's government, too, but since it's more of a leadership role, I felt it was better suited for me than the position my dad found me." Their drinks arrived, and he took a long sip before continuing. "I worked for Ryan for a time."

That caught her attention. "You did?"

"Not long, thank goodness. I guess I'm just not meant to be an underling. I tried to change the way he ran the office, but he didn't like it. And then he took it as a personal affront when I ran for mayor."

She still couldn't wrap her head around Derrick being the mayor of anything. He seemed too much of a free spirit to want to work in such a boring job. But maybe he had more in common with Ryan than she thought.

"Anyway, after that didn't work out, I contacted my old boss about being a lifeguard again. You know I used to do that over the summers in high school."

"That, I remember." Back then, she'd enjoyed checking him out on more than one occasion and always found a way to sit in his section at the beach.

Their food arrived, and she wracked her brain for a new topic of conversation. While she was curious about his job, particularly in the off-season, it wasn't exactly the kind of date talk she'd had in mind.

"Have you ever thought about moving away from here?" she asked as she dipped one of her fries in ketchup.

His eyes widened, and he cocked his head. "Why would I do that? Everything I know and love is here. There's the ocean and great surfing, not to mention my friends and family."

Disappointment dropped into her stomach like an anvil as the reality of how finite their relationship would be sank in. If she hoped to have any sort of future with him, she would have to move back home.

"You could always come back to visit," she said, though even she could hear how half-hearted she sounded.

He frowned as he took a bite of his burger. "I guess, but I think I would miss the waves too much." His brow cleared as he seemed to catch on to her meaning. "But you could always move back. I mean, there are tons of law firms in the area. I'm sure you could find a job somewhere."

That wouldn't pay anywhere near what I make in the city or even just outside it. But she forced a smile. "Maybe that could work."

The conversation fizzled after that, and Cassie stifled a sigh of relief when the bill came. But as she stood to leave, Derrick grabbed her hand.

"There's supposed to be a really great band later," he said with his sexiest grin. "Mind if we stick around?"

Torn, she bit her lip. On the one hand, she had dreamed of a night like this throughout her entire high school career, and that lovesick schoolgirl within begged her to stay. But on the other hand, she had begun to wonder what the point of it all was. He lived here, she lived in D.C., and long-distance relationships rarely ever worked. Besides, from what she'd learned since they'd started hanging out, they had almost nothing in common.

In the end, she agreed to stay. It'd been a while since she'd gone out on the town like this, and she didn't know the next time Emily would give her the night off from the pub. Besides, she reasoned she shouldn't be so hard on Derrick. Maybe she'd built him up so much in her head that she'd set her expectations too high. That wasn't Derrick's fault, and she shouldn't hold it against him. Something about him had held her interest in high school, and she owed it to her former self to discover what that was.

～

A few days later, Cassie arrived at the pub in the early afternoon to set up for trivia. They had closed between lunch and dinner, and she relished the quiet. Between her shifts at the pub and hanging out with Derrick, she hadn't had a moment to herself.

The door to the pub opened, and the bells she'd hung there rang out. "We're closed," she called without glancing up.

"I thought you could use an extra pair of hands," a deep, familiar voice said. Startled, she spun around, and Ryan stood before her.

"Oh hey," she said, and her face broke into a wide grin. They hadn't seen each other lately except for the brief moment at the strawberry festival, and she was surprised to find she'd missed his company.

He blinked and then gave her a hesitant smile in return. "I didn't think you'd be happy to see me."

She frowned. "Why do you say that?"

"We haven't really talked much since the bonfire." He ran a hand through his hair. "And I think I owe you an apology."

"Oh," she said, grimacing. *Right, I'm supposed to be mad at him.* "That."

"Yeah, that." He raised his hands as if to surrender. "I just thought I was looking out for you, but I realize now you don't need some old dude keeping an eye on you."

Cassie laughed. "You're not that old."

"Love the qualification there." Ryan grinned before his face turned solemn. "But seriously, you can take care of yourself, and it's not my business."

"It's fine, Ryan, really. I'm sorry I got so angry with you." She gave him a grim smile. "I can be a bit hotheaded when people tell me what to do, and I normally do the exact opposite... sometimes out of spite."

His answering laugh warmed her insides. "Truce?"

She stuck out her hand. "Truce."

Ryan took it in his and gave her a gentle squeeze. His touch sent tingles up her arm. As she gazed at him, his green eyes warmed to a fierce fire, and she quickly withdrew her hand.

He cleared his throat. "Anyway, I'm here to help. Put me to work."

"Um, s-sure," Cassie stammered as she tried to compose herself. *What was* that? She wasn't attracted to *Ryan*, was she? Nope, not possible. Sure, she'd missed spending time with him, but that was just as a *friend*, right? After all, he was totally not her type. And he was way older than her. Okay, well, maybe not *that* much older, but still. They were so different they might as well have been from opposing planets.

"Maybe I can help with that," Ryan said, pointing at the computer where Cassie was working.

"Hmm, this is kind of a one-person job," Cassie said. "But I could use some help decorating. I want to give this place a festive feel, you know? Especially since we're so close to the Fourth of July." She glanced around at the sparse decorations Emily had hung. "But I'm not sure we have anything else."

"I've got some stuff at my house. You're welcome to it."

"Really?" Cassie asked, clasping her hands over her chest and beaming at him.

"Sure. Anything for you," Ryan said, and the conviction in his tone made her traitorous heart skip a beat. What was *wrong* with her?

"Oh, anything, huh?" Cassie said, trying to lighten the mood. "That sounds dangerous." His mouth fell open, and she flashed him a flirtatious smile.

Stop it! This is not *happening.* Even if there was an attraction there, which there most certainly was not, it wasn't something she wanted to pursue. She'd literally just had her first official date with Derrick. Sure, it hadn't exactly gone the way she'd hoped, but she wanted to give them a real chance, even if it only lasted for the summer. Somehow she didn't think Ryan would be open to a summer fling.

"Um, I'll go get the stuff then and bring it back here," Ryan said, the flush on his cheeks deepening.

"That would be great, thanks." Cassie's cheeks were burning as well.

Ryan nodded quickly and fled.

Cassie distracted herself by double-checking the trivia questions and answers for grammatical correctness. She hoped someone else would arrive while he was gone. The thought of being alone with him again both worried and excited her, and she wasn't ready to deal with those conflicting feelings.

About a half hour later, the bells rang out again, and Cassie's voice caught in her throat when she glanced over. Ryan carried what looked to be a heavy box. She left the computer and rushed over to help him.

"Are there any decorations left at your house?" Cassie asked as she grabbed one side of the box and they slowly lowered it to the floor.

"A few." Ryan arched his back. He'd rolled up the sleeves of his white button-down shirt, putting his surprisingly well-defined forearms on full display. She averted her gaze.

"Well, thanks for, uh, donating these to the cause," she said. "I'm sure you're busy with mayor stuff. I won't keep you."

"Actually, I'm all yours." Ryan cringed, as if he couldn't believe what he'd said. "Er, I mean, I'm available to, uh, help, you know, decorate."

"Oh, you don't have to." Cassie thought fast. There was no way she was going to spend the next who-knew-how-long alone in the restaurant with Ryan and his distracting forearms.

"I insist." To her horror—and joy—he removed the button-down, revealing a tight undershirt as well as his impressive biceps. While he wasn't as fit as Derrick, he clearly took care of himself.

"Um, okay, well, uh, why don't you show me what you brought." Cassie stared pointedly at the box, but she could still see him in her peripheral vision.

Ryan crouched down and pulled the flaps open, revealing several types of decor. There were flags and streamers in an assortment of colors, several pom-poms, and balloons in red, white, and blue. This would make the pub pop.

"Wow, where did you find all of this?"

"My parents moved to Florida several years ago," Ryan said as he lifted various items out of the box and set them on the table. "They didn't want to haul all of this down the East Coast, so they gave it to me. But my place is small, and I'm not really into decorating for every season."

"Do you see them often?" Cassie asked.

He shook his head. "They come up now and then, usually to visit my sister." He gave her a sad smile. "She made them grandparents, after all."

Cassie wasn't sure what to say. She couldn't imagine what she would do if her mother moved across the country. It was hard enough without her father.

"Anyway, how do you want to decorate?" Ryan asked, effectively changing the subject.

"Well, there's a lot of red, white, and blue in here," Cassie said, gesturing to the box. "Which would work well with what we already have." She pointed at the rafters. "We can hang the flags there. Then maybe the streamers and balloons could be used on the booths?"

"Sounds good to me," Ryan said, watching her. She crossed her arms over her chest. Something about him made her feel ill at ease and excited all at the same time. Was it that he challenged her? Or that he was older and, somehow, she felt she needed to prove herself to him?

She picked up the streamers and began wrapping them around one of the support poles. Ryan followed suit and wrapped a different pole. He glanced up at the rafters again.

"Do you have a ladder?"

"In the back," she said. "I'll go get it."

"No need." Ryan headed for the storage area.

Cassie took advantage of his absence to reassess her feelings. *What is going on with you?* Ryan had always struck her as conventionally attractive, but his boring job and equally boring personality had been huge turnoffs for her. *Maybe it's just that I haven't gotten a good look at his arms before.* Shaking her head, she laughed at herself. Somehow a pair of muscular forearms didn't seem enough to make her suddenly do a one-eighty on her feelings.

It could also have something to do with her less than exciting date with Derrick. Though she'd tried to enjoy their time with no expectations, as the night wore on, she found herself increasingly disillusioned. But she had chalked it up to just being a bad night, and when Derrick had asked her about a second date, she'd readily agreed.

Besides, it wasn't her first experience juggling an attraction to more than one man. And it likely didn't matter as she was unlikely to end up with either of them. At the end of the summer, she would return to the city, Ryan would continue to be the mayor of Blue Heron Bay, and Derrick would do... whatever it was Derrick did in the off-season.

"Found it!" Ryan called as he came back into the room. He set up the ladder under the rafters and climbed up with a bunch of flags. As he stapled them to the beams, Cassie couldn't help admiring him from below. With his legs on separate steps of the ladder, she had a decent view of his firm thighs. He definitely didn't skip leg day.

She felt like she was seeing him for the first time. When he'd come into the bar the night she'd arrived, she'd pegged him as a stuffed shirt based on his questions about her career. But as she'd gotten to know him, she'd seen a different side to him. Like at the strawberry festival, when she'd teased him about studying *Jeopardy*, he'd been more fun, playful even.

He caught her staring and smiled. "What?"

Cassie ducked her head to hide her flaming cheeks. "N-Nothing. I just wanted to make sure you were doing it right."

Ryan laughed. "Is there a wrong way to hang flags from the ceiling?"

"I suppose not. But it's important everything looks perfect for tonight."

As he climbed back down the ladder, Ryan scrutinized her face. "I'm surprised you care."

"Because I'm flighty and self-centered?" Cassie asked, unable to suppress the edge in her voice.

"Is that how you think I see you?" Ryan frowned, and Cassie wished she'd kept her mouth shut.

"Of course not," she said hastily. "Forget I said anything." She moved to start inflating the balloons, but he caught her arm. He opened his mouth to say something, but the tingles from his touch spread up her shoulder and made her shiver, which Ryan misinterpreted as discomfort. His face fell as he released her.

"Sorry." He turned to move the ladder.

"Wait," Cassie said, catching herself and Ryan off guard when she grabbed his hand. "Why are you surprised?"

He looked down at their hands as he spoke. "I thought you went to the city to escape small-town life. If the pub goes out of business, your mom could move, and you wouldn't have to come back here anymore."

"I didn't hate small-town life," Cassie murmured as she let go of his hand and returned to the decorations. "I wanted to try something different."

"And? Do you like the city?"

"Most days I do. There's something to be said for being just another face in the crowd after living in the shadow of my perfect brother. I love the anonymity." She sighed. "But it gets lonely."

"Don't you have friends?"

"A few, but I wouldn't consider myself close with any of them." She taped one end of the streamer to the back of one booth. "I thought the city was big enough for me to find a place for myself, stake my own claim in the world, if you will. But I keep bouncing from job to job, looking for something fulfilling when the most fulfilled I've felt has been working behind the bar these last few weeks."

"So why don't you move back?" Ryan asked. Was she imagining it, or did he sound… hopeful?

"I'm not ready to admit defeat yet," she said.

He cocked his head as he considered this. "Would you be doing that, though? I mean, maybe it's not a battle worth fighting."

"Why do you say that?"

"Well, you went there for a change, right? But the change isn't what you expected. I don't think it's failing or 'admitting defeat'"—he held his fingers up in air quotes—"as you say, to try something new and realize it's not for you."

"I'm not sure I've given it a real chance."

Ryan leaned against one of the poles they'd already decorated and crossed his arms. "Okay, how long?"

"How long… what?" Cassie furrowed her brows.

"How long do you think you need to give it for it to count as a so-called 'real chance'?"

"I don't know."

"If you stay in the city for—what?" Ryan raised one hand. "Five years? Ten years? Is that a real chance?"

"Why are you trying to quantify it with a timeframe?" Cassie grabbed another streamer and stepped to the next booth.

"Because I want you to consider how much of your life you're willing to spend in a place you don't like before you decide you've given it long enough, before you try something that might actually make you happy." As he stepped toward her, he raised his arm as if to touch her before he let it fall to his side. "Take it from an old man. Life is short, and while you can't be happy every minute, you shouldn't waste it staying somewhere you've already realized isn't for you."

"But all my stuff is there," Cassie protested, though she could hear how stupid and half-hearted that excuse sounded.

"There are these newfangled things called moving trucks," Ryan said, his tone teasing. "They hold your stuff and help you transport it to anywhere you want to go."

"Oh, yeah?" Cassie retorted. "What if I wanted to go to Europe?"

He laughed. "It's just a more expensive form of shipping."

"That's true." They continued to hang the decorations as Cassie mulled over his words. Emily had suggested the same thing, though nowhere near as eloquently as Ryan had. What would it mean for her to move home?

"I can practically hear the gears turning in your head," Ryan joked. Cassie couldn't hide her smile, which he seemed to take as encouragement. "It's not something you have to decide today, tomorrow, or this month, but think about it. Especially if you're that unhappy in your current situation."

"I'll take it under advisement," Cassie said with a grin. And she meant it. Whether he had intended to or not, he'd given her a lot to think about. Her life in the city wasn't at all what she expected, and she had to admit coming home was sounding more and more intriguing. But was she ready to throw in the towel?

On the other hand, if she kept chasing the next best thing, she'd eventually burn herself out, both professionally and personally. And by that point, what happened in her future might no longer be her choice.

Chapter Fifteen

Emily flitted from table to table, arranging and rearranging the setup for trivia night. She couldn't sit still as anxious energy raged through her. A lot was riding on the success of that evening, not only for the pub but for the town as well, and she hoped their efforts wouldn't be in vain.

"For heaven's sake, Emily!" her mother cried out. "You're going to wear a hole in the carpet."

Emily glanced over her shoulder. Mom stood near the bar, glaring at Emily with her hands on her hips. But she couldn't obey her mother's orders, no matter how hard she tried. She briefly sat in a booth, surveying the way they'd laid out the pub for the night, but moments later, she was back up again, checking on the sound system and the screens.

"You need to calm down," Anna Mae murmured as she stepped up beside her and placed a reassuring hand on her shoulder. Emily looked into her deep-brown eyes, but instead of feeling a sense of peace, her anxiety only seemed to increase.

They hadn't seen each other since the strawberry festival. Anna Mae had texted she was unable to stop by due to business with her father and Leslie Steele. Emily tried and failed to quell the jealousy surging through her veins. As she glanced behind Anna Mae, she took small comfort in finding her alone.

"I'm trying," Emily finally said, clasping and unclasping her hands in front of her. Having some part of her body continuously in motion helped, but only a little.

"Look, we've done all we can to prepare. Now we need to make sure we deliver."

Anna Mae gestured to Peter, who was prepping to be the emcee of the event. Cassie was behind the bar and had concocted a special menu of festive drinks for the occasion. She and Ryan had worked all afternoon decorating the pub. Emily tried to find comfort in the fact her family had pitched in, but she couldn't help worrying everything was about to crash and burn in front of her eyes.

The event was due to start at six, and although it was only five, Emily's eyes kept straying to the door, wondering when the first customers would arrive. She stepped over to the bar, hoping Cassie could distract her.

"You look like you need one of these," her sister said, sliding a strawberry margarita in front of her. Emily narrowed her eyes. Cassie tended to be heavy-handed with her ratio of spirits to mixer. After a hesitant sip, she was surprised, not only that she couldn't taste the tequila but also at how delicious it was. Cassie had outdone herself.

"Wow, that's fantastic," Emily said.

"Jeez, try not to sound shocked," Cassie muttered.

Emily bit her lip. She needed to stop underestimating her sister. But before she could apologize, the bells on the front door jingled and Derrick walked into the pub.

He whistled. "It looks amazing in here." His gaze swept over the assembled Gallaghers and Anna Mae before they rested on Cassie. "But it all pales in comparison to you." He walked over and gave her a small peck on the cheek. Cassie flushed, and Emily found herself grateful Ryan had left earlier, though he promised to come back for the event itself. Part of her hoped Derrick would leave before then. The last thing their event needed was drama from her sister's apparent love triangle.

Anna Mae stepped closer to her, clasping her hand and entwining their fingers. With a deep breath, Emily worked to center herself. She had enough to worry about tonight without overanalyzing Cassie's love life.

People began arriving then, and Emily, Mom, and Anna Mae helped them find their seats. Cassie pushed Derrick out from behind the bar so she could concentrate on getting drink orders. That was where they hoped to make most of their money that evening.

When they were ready to start, Peter stepped up to the podium, where he would read out questions. Everyone had a small tablet on which to submit their answers. It saved time and alleviated the risk of people arguing over who had called out an answer first. The computer would note who entered the correct answer and when. Some tables had decided to play as teams, while others were playing individually. The prizes were mostly gift certificates to various restaurants or shops in town, though there was a hundred-dollar grand prize. But the goal was for people to relax, have fun, and, of course, tell their friends.

"Welcome, everyone, to trivia night at Fiddler's Green! I'm Peter Gallagher, and I'll be your host this evening. If everyone wouldn't mind doing a test run to make sure your tablet is working, we would appreciate it. Our test question is 'What date is always Independence Day?' Please choose a response from the four options, and once we've confirmed everything is in order, we'll begin!"

Emily walked through the pub, ready to assist anyone who was experiencing technical difficulties. The tightness in her chest eased as she noted the pub was full. Anna Mae's social media campaign had done its part. Now it was up to them to live up to expectations. As she was nearing the front of the pub, the bells on the door jingled, and her heart sank as Mr. Wakefield and Leslie Steele walked in.

"Father, Leslie, what are you doing here?" Anna Mae asked as she stepped toward them.

"We wanted to see what all the fuss was about," Leslie said, pulling Anna Mae in for a hug. Emily enjoyed some satisfaction when Anna Mae's spine went rigid from the contact.

Mr. Wakefield looked around the room. "This is a good turnout."

"For a restaurant of this size," Leslie said, with a haughty tone. Her eyes fell on Emily, and she gave her a sneer that, to an untrained eye, might have passed for a smile. "It's so... quaint."

Emily bristled at the description but maintained her composure. Regardless of their unspoken rivalry for Anna Mae's affections, it was quite a low blow to criticize the Gallaghers' pub just to get back at Emily.

"I hope you weren't planning to stay for the event," Emily said sweetly. "As you can see, we're at capacity."

"Not to worry, we only wanted to pop in for a minute to check it out," Mr. Wakefield said. "We should be going."

"Oh, but wouldn't it be fun to see how well Anna Mae's hard work pays off?" Leslie protested. "We should stay and support her efforts."

"Unfortunately, we can't—"

Anna Mae cut in, saying, "I'm sure we can find a table somewhere." When Emily turned to stare at her, Anna Mae raised her shoulders in an apologetic shrug.

After a brief conversation with Mom, Anna Mae put together a card table near the door and set up two chairs. As she was leaving the table, Leslie grabbed her hand and pulled her back. Anna Mae appeared to argue with Leslie but eventually relented and borrowed a chair from a nearby table to join them.

Emily couldn't believe what she was seeing. A moment later, Leslie turned to look at her and gave a triumphant smirk. It was all Emily could do to keep her expression neutral as she spun on her heel and fled to the office.

Peter was feeling pretty good. Everything was going smoothly as he called out questions and watched the screen to see who responded first. They were giving away prizes throughout the night for certain questions and at the end of each round. But he didn't miss when Ricardo slipped into the pub and over to the bar. Peter was concerned Cassie would throw Ricardo out or refuse to serve him, but she was kind and cordial, handing him an Old Bay Crush. He took comfort in the fact Emily had disappeared earlier, as he could only imagine how she would have reacted at seeing Ricardo in the place he was trying to drive out of business.

When they reached the end of the first round, he announced they would take a fifteen-minute break before starting the next one. Ricardo sauntered over to him with a smile that made Peter's toes curl.

"Hello there," Ricardo said. "How's the dissertation going?"

"Great," Peter said. "I'm ahead of schedule, and if this keeps up, I might send it back early."

Ricardo's dark eyes brightened. "Does that mean you'll be able to have some fun, then?"

"I think so."

"Good." Ricardo raised his drink toward Peter. "You owe me a date."

"I'm well aware," Peter said, laughing. "I'll let you know when I've submitted it."

"Sounds good." Ricardo gestured to the pub. "Nice turnout. Your sister must be pleased."

"You know, I haven't seen her in a while," Peter said with a frown. "I saw Anna Mae sit down with an older man and a young woman, but I'm not sure who they are. Her family, maybe?"

Ricardo searched the room, and then he shook his head. "Well, that is her father, but the young woman is her ex, Leslie Steele." He glanced back at Peter. "Though from what I understand, Leslie is hoping to reconcile. She's the heiress of Steele Hotels, and Wakefield has been trying to broker a partnership with them for years." He took a sip of his drink.

"How would a partnership impact your resorts?"

"It's hard to say," Ricardo said with a shrug. "It wouldn't be the best news, but then again, it may not matter. Unlike Wakefield, we have the capital for this venture, and we can move forward with it even if they build a hotel as well."

"Does your boss know that you have a personal interest in building here?"

"Not exactly," Ricardo said. "But I doubt he'd mind. This town is prime real estate for one of our ventures. My boss likes to be a big fish in a little pond, and I'm sure we'd bring in the tourism in no time."

"Then it sounds like you're a shoo-in for the development contract. What's stopping you from moving forward?"

Ricardo rolled his eyes. "Well, I haven't officially met him, but my understanding is the mayor specifically pitched Wakefield to the town because they don't have as large of a footprint as we do. While building here is good for my company and for my family, convincing the mayor and town council that we're good for the town is a different matter entirely."

Peter glanced over at Anna Mae, who looked miserable sitting next to her ex. Her eyes kept roving the room as if she were searching for Emily. Come to think of it, where was Emily? This was her event. It wasn't like her not to participate. Cassie was at the bar, tending to customers and shamelessly flirting with Derrick—much to the apparent and growing agitation of Ryan, who had recently arrived. When Derrick grabbed Cassie's hand at one point and twirled her around, Ryan jumped off his stool and stomped to the back of the pub. Was that where Emily had gone? Peter wished he had a moment to go check on her, but it was time to start the next round of trivia.

A knock on the office door startled Emily out of her pity party. She briefly considered turning off the lights and hiding in hopes whomever it was would go away. As if they'd read her mind, the knock came again, more insistent. With a resigned sigh, she pushed herself out of the chair and opened the door.

"Ryan! What are you doing here?"

"I noticed you weren't out in the pub, and I thought I'd check and see if you were okay." He stepped into the office and shut the door behind him.

"I'm fine," Emily lied. "You should go back out and enjoy the event."

He took one look at her face and shook his head. "First, I can tell you aren't fine." After searching the room for a seat, he pulled out an empty bucket and flipped it over before perching on it. "And second, I can't stand to watch another minute of your sister canoodling with that attention-seeking jerk."

"You mean Derrick?"

Ryan gave a curt nod. "Yes, him."

"What do you mean, 'attention-seeking jerk'?"

"Just what I said," Ryan said with a shrug. "Derrick craves the attention he's received since saving her life. She's confided in me that she's grown weary of the interviews, but he keeps trying to find ways to keep the story alive. And it's because that's all he wants: his fifteen minutes of fame. Once the camera lights turn to something else, he will too."

"What makes you say that?"

"Because he's done it before." The bitterness in Ryan's voice was unmistakable. "He doesn't care about anyone except himself."

"You sound as if you have a personal vendetta against him."

Ryan turned away. "It's a long story, but trust me when I say Derrick will move on to the next best thing once Cassie is of no further use to him."

Emily's heart sank. Her poor sister! Despite Cassie's questionable choices, Emily would hate for her to get her heart broken. She wasn't sure how serious Cassie was about Derrick, but she tended to follow her heart more than her head. Ugh, what a mess this summer was turning out to be.

"Enough about your sister. Why are you hiding out here?" Ryan asked. "Isn't this your event?"

"It's stupid," Emily said, dropping her gaze to her hands.

"Is it about Anna Mae?"

Emily nodded. While she knew she shouldn't get this worked up over a woman she'd known for less than a month, she'd never fallen so hard for someone in such a short period of time before.

"I figured," Ryan said with a sigh. "I saw the woman—Leslie, is it? I think she's a lot more interested in Anna Mae than Anna Mae is in her." He gave a humorless laugh. "It's easy to recognize unrequited feelings when you've experienced it firsthand."

"You should give Cassie some time," Emily said, lifting her head to look at him. "She's young—and naïve. If Derrick is who you say he is, then he'll eventually show his true colors."

"Yeah, but by then it'll be too late." Ryan's eyes were sad.

"Why do you say that?" Emily asked.

"I expect once it's all said and done, she'll hightail it back to the city, and who knows how long it'll be before she sets foot in Blue Heron Bay again." He leaned back against the wall and gazed at the ceiling. "Earlier today, she sounded like she was looking for something more from life, and I thought she might consider moving home. But if he breaks her heart, I know she'd rather be miserable in the city than risk seeing him happy here."

"She's miserable in the city?" Emily stared at him. While Cassie made it no secret that she didn't like her job, her sister being miserable in the city was news to Emily.

"Her ideas of what it would be like haven't panned out," Ryan said. "And that's why she jumps from job to job. She's trying to find happiness externally, and it's not working."

Emily considered this. It would explain a lot. Truthfully, the happiest Emily had seen Cassie lately was when she was bartending. She'd already broached the subject of Cassie moving home, but she could try again. Mom would appreciate the help with the pub, and Cassie's paralegal background might come in handy for some of the contracts and paperwork required to run things. Of course, that was assuming their efforts paid off and the pub remained open. If they failed, well, there wasn't going to be anything left there for any of them.

"But *you* shouldn't give up," Ryan said when Emily didn't respond. "I've seen the way Anna Mae looks at you."

"I don't know what the point would be," Emily said. Cassie's words echoed in her head. *What's the point of a summer romance?* "After the season ends, we both go back to our real lives, and then what?"

"That'd be up to you two to figure out. But enjoying someone's company, even if for a brief time, is never pointless."

Peter's voice wafted from the front of the pub. Ryan held out his hand.

"Come on. You can't hide here all night. After all, you worked hard to bring this event to fruition. Don't you want to see how it goes?"

Emily accepted his hand and allowed him to pull her to her feet. She had to admit he had a point. She had put a lot of work into the event, and she shouldn't let anyone ruin it for her.

Chapter Sixteen

Peter was wrapping up a successful trivia night, if he did say so himself. They were in the final round, and two teams were neck and neck for the grand prize. It amazed him how much random knowledge the participants possessed. If he hadn't had the cards in front of him, he would have been stumped on most of these. It was humbling, in a way. While he doubted he would ever need this information, he struggled sometimes to remember his expertise was in a particular field and there was a world of knowledge out there he hadn't studied.

Ricardo stayed with him, running to the bar to grab him drinks and helping him when the systems almost failed. As much as Peter appreciated his help, he kept a wary eye out for Emily. Anna Mae had glared daggers at Ricardo all night but made no move to approach him. In fact, Peter suspected she purposefully tried to keep Ricardo's presence at the event a secret from her father.

Peter called out the last question, and the team at table five, who had nicknamed themselves "Nessie's Guides," quickly clicked their answer. The computer system binged, confirming the response was correct.

"Congratulations, table five! You have won Fiddler's Green's first trivia night of the summer!"

The pub exploded in cheers and boos, any negative comments

coming from table five's rivals at table seven. It was all in good-natured fun, and soon the two tables were shaking hands. The winners came up to claim the grand prize, and Peter congratulated them. As entertaining as it had been, he was glad the night was over. Now, if he could only get Ricardo out of there before Mr. Wakefield or the other Gallaghers saw him.

A deep voice boomed, "Ricardo." When Peter and Ricardo turned, Mr. Wakefield stood behind them with his arms crossed.

"Mr. Wakefield," Ricardo said, his tone icy. Peter swallowed as his gaze flitted back and forth between the two men. He tried to take a deep breath, but the air was thick with tension as they stared each other down.

Finally, Mr. Wakefield said, "Ironic that you should come here. Seeing as this event was meant to save a pub your resort would shut down."

"On the contrary, sir, our resort would bring much-needed customers to small businesses such as this one."

Mr. Wakefield snorted. "Only after you've bought it for less than it's worth and turned it into some seedy tourist attraction."

Anna Mae had approached at this point and grabbed her father's arm. "Let's go. This is not the time or place."

"Perhaps not," Mr. Wakefield said without moving. "But he shouldn't be here. These people need to know what he's planning for this town."

"Since when are you the expert on my company's plans?" Ricardo retorted.

"I've seen it before. Your company is acquiring property up and down the East Coast in small towns like this one, building mammoth resorts, and shutting down small businesses along the way." Mr. Wakefield glanced at Peter. "Were you aware of his dealings?"

Peter nodded, surprised to be drawn into the conversation.

"But perhaps not the extent of them," Mr. Wakefield said. "It's shameful what he'll do to your family's business. You shouldn't allow him to stay any longer." He shot a baleful glare at Ricardo. "He's here for reconnaissance, and now he knows how you intend to save your pub."

"What's this about?" Mom asked as she stepped over to them. The conversation was becoming heated, and people turned to stare.

"It's nothing, Mom," Peter said quickly as he put his arm around her and began steering her away.

"Are you the owner?" Mr. Wakefield called.

Mom turned. "I am. What's going on?"

"You should know that this man"—Mr. Wakefield pointed a finger at Ricardo—"is trying to put you out of business."

"What?" Her eyes widened, and she looked from Peter to Ricardo. "Why? H-How? Peter? I thought he was your friend."

"He is," Peter hurried on. "It's all a misunderstanding."

Emily's voice rang out over the noise of the pub. "But it's not, Peter."

"What on earth is going on?" Cassie asked as she stepped from behind the bar.

"Tell them, Peter," Emily said, her tone demanding. "Tell them about Ricardo's plans." When he hesitated, she got right in his face. "If you don't, I will."

Peter looked around helplessly. Everything was being blown out of proportion, but he didn't know where to begin.

"Let me," Ricardo whispered to him, placing a hand on his shoulder and giving him a meaningful look. When Peter nodded, Ricardo turned to address his family.

"If I may," he said. "My company is checking out Blue Heron Bay as a potential resort location. I grew up here and was aware the town had fallen on hard times, so I pitched it to my boss as the perfect location for our next resort. As I was already coming home for a few weeks to visit my mother, it made sense for me to assess the area and report back. Sunrise Oasis Resorts is a well-known brand and would bring some much-needed tourism to this town." He took a deep breath, and after a quick glance at Peter, he continued. "But it is true we have an Irish pub under contract, and were we to build here, I would be interested in buying Fiddler's Green."

Mom gasped in surprise then turned accusing eyes toward Peter. "Is this why you asked me about selling?"

"It was simply a suggestion, Mom," Peter said, raising his hands in front of him as a shield, or in surrender. He wasn't sure which. "I know things haven't been going well since Dad—"

"At any rate," Ricardo said, "if the Gallaghers do not wish to sell, we will not force them to do so."

"Yet you'll still bankrupt them with your own pub!" Mr. Wakefield exclaimed.

"It's a risk," Ricardo replied with a grave nod. "But it's nothing personal, just business."

The patrons of the pub had mostly filed out, which meant a reduction in curious stares. But the tension was still suffocating, and Peter wished they could table this discussion until everyone had had a chance to calm down.

"Well, I hope this little event my daughter and yours have put together helps, but I doubt it will," Mr. Wakefield said to Peter's mom. "I just thought you should know you have corporate spies in your midst."

Ricardo rolled his eyes. "You're being overdramatic."

Mr. Wakefield glared back at him. "This pub is this woman's livelihood, so no, I don't think it's overdramatic to warn her of your plans. But we should go. I've seen enough."

He stormed off, with Leslie on his heels. Anna Mae paused for a moment, her gaze lingering on Emily. With a sigh, she shook her head and made to follow her father, but Emily caught her arm.

"Does this mean your father won't build here?"

Anna Mae shrugged. "At this point, I'm not sure of anything. I'll call you later." With one last withering look at Ricardo, she left.

Ricardo seemed to sense the growing hostility toward him. After giving Peter a reassuring smile, he took his leave. Soon, only the Gallaghers remained.

"So, how long have you been planning this?" Mom said, her blue eyes flashing as she stared at Peter. "Since before you came home?"

"Of course not," Peter said. "I only came home because Emily made me." The fire in Mom's eyes grew, and he quickly backpedaled. "I mean, of course I wanted to see what could be done to save Dad's legacy." Trying to maintain his composure, he took a deep breath. No sense in all of them getting emotional. "But when I saw the state of things and how stressed you seemed, it sounded like a viable option. When Ricardo showed an interest in the property, I was curious to see his plans." He held up his hands again as his sisters turned on him. "After Mom told me she didn't want to sell, I respected her decision and dropped it."

Well, that wasn't entirely true. But as he hadn't had a chance to discuss any deals with Ricardo in depth, it seemed logical to err on the side of caution. He was already in enough hot water with his family. Besides, there wasn't any harm in waiting to see how Emily and Anna Mae's plans panned out before broaching the subject again.

Emily scoffed. "I don't trust that guy as far as I could throw him."

"Then trust me." Peter crossed his arms over his chest and returned her glare, though his insides whirled. "I didn't realize how important this place was to Mom until I talked to her."

That part was true. The look on his mother's face when she told him the pub was all she had left of his father had gutted him. But it didn't change the reality of the situation. The pub was in trouble, and he doubted they would be able to save it. Still, that was a conversation they could have later, when their efforts to bolster business inevitably failed.

Emily's expression was doubtful, but she nodded. Mom appeared more hurt than angry by that point, and guilt stabbed at Peter's gut. He shouldn't have asked her about selling until he had a better plan. If he had waited, he wouldn't be in this mess in the first place. Cassie was the only one who accepted his words at face value.

One thing nagged at the back of Peter's mind. If, against all odds, their efforts succeeded in saving the pub, would Ricardo withdraw his pitch to build a resort in Blue Heron Bay? He'd made it clear he wanted to boost the economy of the small town, hoping to provide people like his mother with stable employment. Would he be so willing to abandon his plans, considering the impact on his mother?

Cassie woke up the next day tired, but content. Aside from the showdown at the end of the night, the trivia event had gone well, and she'd earned a lot of tips. The one sore spot was that Ryan had disappeared halfway through.

Her feelings were all mixed up. Derrick had hung out near the bar all night, and though they'd shared some laughs, she could admit to herself that their relationship didn't go any deeper than that. The guy she had built up in her head in high school had little in common with the man she was getting to know.

And then there was Ryan. After spending most of the afternoon with him setting up the pub, she'd started to see him in a different light. But many of the same issues she had with Derrick applied to Ryan too. Derrick had no interest in moving to the city, and Ryan was the mayor of the town. She could have no future with either of them once summer ended.

Needing to clear her head, she got out of bed and dressed for a run. It always helped her to sort through things when she was all muddled up inside. As she left the house and started at a quick walking pace to warm up, she debated heading to the beach but decided against it. Derrick was likely working today, and she needed some space. Instead, she stuck to the sidewalks around her mother's neighborhood and got a few laps in. When she arrived back at the house, out of breath but exhilarated, she checked her phone and saw a text from Derrick asking her to call him. Not ready to deal with him yet, she left it unanswered.

After a quick shower, she went into the kitchen to get something to eat before she headed to the pub. She'd offered to pull a double shift today to give Peter a chance to work on his dissertation and Emily some time to talk with Anna Mae about their next event. Cassie was excited about karaoke night. It'd been a while since she'd been to one, and she was itching to belt out some of her favorite songs.

When she walked in, Emily was sitting at the table with a bowl of cereal. Peter was nowhere to be found, though Cassie assumed he was hiding. Cassie still couldn't believe he'd wanted to sell the pub. Without even talking to Emily or Mom about it, Cassie knew selling was the last thing either of them wanted to do.

"It was nice of Ryan to help you set up yesterday," Emily said before spooning a bite of cereal into her mouth.

"Yeah, it's always faster with an extra pair of hands," Cassie said, pouring herself a bowl.

"He's been exceptionally helpful lately." Emily's gaze searched Cassie's face as she sat down at the table.

"He has," Cassie said cautiously. Where was her sister going with this?

Emily took a deep breath before she squared her shoulders and stared intently at Cassie. "He tells me you're unhappy in the city."

Cassie silently cursed Ryan for betraying her confidence. "I wouldn't say I'm unhappy, per se..."

"Then what would you call it?"

"It's not what I was expecting. I thought I would find the fast-paced environment exciting and that working in an office would be a positive change from waitressing." She frowned. "But the truth is, I hate it. I miss writing."

"Do you want to move home?" Emily asked, and Cassie was taken aback by her bluntness.

She gave a one-shoulder shrug. "I don't know."

They sat munching on their cereal as the words hung in the air between them. Was this going to further solidify her siblings' view of her as "flighty"? Poor little Cassandra couldn't hack it in the real world and came scurrying back to her hometown with her tail between her legs.

"It would be a good thing," Emily finally said.

Cassie almost choked on her cereal.

"You clearly love tending bar and meeting new people. Plus, Mom could use the help." Emily set her spoon down and pushed the bowl to the side, leaning her elbows on the table as she gazed at Cassie. "And with the hours you keep at the pub, you could pursue your writing here. Mom might promote you to manager at some point, which would mean you could find your own place."

Cassie mulled this over. Emily had a point. She could stay with their mother, helping not only with the pub but also with the house. Then later, when she was ready, she could strike out on her own again, but closer to home this time.

"But wouldn't that be a waste of my degree?" Cassie asked. She'd spent six long, exhausting years working toward her bachelor's in legal studies.

"You could always try a small law firm here, if you wanted," Emily said. "The degree is good as something for you to fall back on if you want to pursue similar work in the future. Besides, you could use some of your paralegal knowledge to help the pub. I'm sure Mom's vendor contracts will need updating over the years, and you can at least take a first look to see if there are any red flags."

"That's true." Cassie nodded. The idea was growing on her, especially due to the possibilities it gave her romantically.

"About your friend," Emily said, as if reading her mind. "He seems to love the spotlight."

"He does, but I think it's dimming."

"That's a relief." Emily put her bowl in the sink. "While I'm sure some of your celebrity status helped with our event last night, it would be nice if things got back to normal."

"Agreed."

Emily pursed her lips. "You know, Ryan really likes you."

Shooting her sister a glare, Cassie shoved another spoonful of cereal in her mouth. She was *not* having this conversation.

"He's not a bad-looking guy, though I'm hardly one to judge," Emily said with a laugh. "But he might be good for you."

Translation: he'd be a good influence on you. Cassie focused on her breakfast, refusing to meet her sister's gaze. Her conflicting feelings about Ryan weren't something she was ready to address with her sister now... or ever, especially since she couldn't quite articulate to herself how she felt. And she *definitely* wasn't going to date the man just to please her family.

"You could do worse, you know."

"And I could do a lot better," she shot back, pushing her chair back and stomping to the sink, no longer hungry. What she'd said wasn't fair, and she knew it, but her sister's words cut her deep. The fact that her family preferred Ryan over Derrick was no surprise. He was kind, sensible, and dependable. They would never associate those descriptions with her.

"I don't understand what you have against him." Emily came over to the counter and placed a hand on her back.

Cassie shrugged it off. "He's not the problem. What he represents to you is!"

Emily stared at her like she had two heads. "What is that supposed to mean?"

"It means I know why you're trying to push Ryan onto me. He's stable and mature, exactly what your flighty sister needs, right?" Cassie rolled her eyes and flipped her hair over her shoulder before launching into an imitation of Emily. "Maybe if Cassie finds the right match, he can tame her."

"That's not what I meant at all," Emily retorted. "You're not a wild pony on Assateague Island, but would it kill you to date someone who has their life together for a change?"

"That's a low blow, and you know it. Besides, how can you say that? You don't even know Derrick."

"I know enough. Ryan told me he's done something like this before with his fifteen minutes of fame."

Ugh, why can't Ryan just keep his opinions to himself? "Is this about the warning he gave me? He's just jealous, Emily. He asked me out and I turned him down, so now he's spreading false rumors about Derrick." Cassie shook her head. "Besides, Derrick agreed with me the other day that the shark story has gone far enough."

Emily raised an eyebrow. "What do you mean?"

Oh, no. "Just the interviews and media attention were too much," Cassie said, hoping to cover her gaffe.

"You called it a 'story.' Are you saying it's not true?"

Cassie shifted from foot to foot, wishing the floor would open up and swallow her whole. "It's mostly true."

"But not completely?" Emily rubbed her forehead. "You'd better sit down and tell me the whole story."

With a reluctant sigh, Cassie obeyed. She told Emily about being out in the open water and the crowd that had gathered on the beach. Then she explained how she immediately knew they were dolphins but Derrick had asked her not to say anything to help him get a promotion. Finally, she admitted that she'd told Derrick she was sick of the lie and refused to do any more interviews. Emily stayed quiet during her tale, but her brown eyes grew wider the longer Cassie spoke. When she finished, they sat in silence for a moment. While Cassie feared her sister's reprimand, a large part of her was relieved to finally tell the truth.

Finally, Emily said, "I'm afraid you're going to have to give one more interview. It's time to set the record straight."

"But then everyone will know Derrick and I lied!"

"Ryan is working on a petition for the city council to spend money researching warning systems to help protect beachgoers because of this story." Emily's lips set in a grim line. "Money the city doesn't have to spare. You must tell the truth before he presents it." She shook her head. "Derrick shouldn't have asked you to lie for him in the first place."

"It just got out of hand." Cassie hung her head in shame. Her sister was right, though she hated to admit it. Derrick was going to be furious with her, and she couldn't even imagine Ryan's reaction, but the lie had grown so much bigger than she'd ever expected it would.

When she didn't respond, Emily crossed her arms and glared. "Either you tell the media, or I will."

Cassie gave a defeated nod. It would be much worse if someone else broke the news. "I'll contact the reporters and let them know they need to retract the story."

"You might want to rethink your relationship with Derrick while you're at it." Emily stood and walked away, leaving Cassie wondering how long it was going to take her to dig herself out of the hole she'd dug.

Chapter Seventeen

D ESPITE HOW ANGRY SHE WAS WITH C ASSIE, E MILY WASN'T
sure if she should be giving her sister relationship advice. She'd tried and
failed to forget the way Leslie had hung all over Anna Mae at trivia
night. There was no real reason to be jealous. She and Anna Mae had
spent a lot of time together, and she'd thought something was brewing
between them after the bonfire, but since Anna Mae's father had arrived
in town, her focus had shifted. Still, Emily couldn't help the painful
twist in her gut whenever she recalled the image of Leslie's arm around
Anna Mae.

They were supposed to meet at Grounded that morning to go over
the final details for karaoke. They'd put together quite the list of songs
for the event, and their social media campaign was doing well. As much
as Emily looked forward to seeing Anna Mae and finalizing their plans, a
part of her was dreading the meeting.

Emily still dressed with care, choosing a warm yellow sundress that
gave her brown eyes a honeyed look. She pulled her hair back into a
braid and applied a small amount of lip gloss. Makeup had never been
her thing, but she'd experimented with small amounts since meeting
Anna Mae.

As she grabbed her purse, she saw Cassie had already left. The sound of clacking keys echoed from Peter's room, and Emily hoped he would be done with his dissertation soon. She was still angry, but she didn't want to spend the whole summer fighting with him.

The streets were bustling with people when Emily stepped out the front door. It warmed her heart. Whether they were tourists who had extended their stays or locals who were out for a stroll, it reminded her of how much she missed the way Blue Heron Bay used to be. If only she and Anna Mae could bring it back to its heyday.

Her brisk walk to Grounded helped to ease some of the lingering pain and jealousy from the night before. Anna Mae sat in a booth by the back window of the restaurant with two cups on the table in front of her. Emily slid into the seat across from her and lifted the cup tentatively toward her face. The velvety scent of hot cocoa flooded her nose, and she took a deep sip, relishing the warm chocolate flavor.

"I figured I'd order for you so we could get down to business." Anna Mae gazed at Emily over her laptop.

"Thanks." Emily set the cup on the table and wrapped both hands around it. "What's left to do for karaoke?"

"Not much." Anna Mae turned her laptop toward Emily. "Cassie concocted new ideas for drinks to serve, which is great. Each night should have a 'signature' cocktail to make things more festive." She pointed at a spreadsheet on the screen. "Last night's numbers were great, but I'd love to make them better. I'm launching this new ad today." She clicked a different tab on her browser and showed Emily the Facebook ad she'd created.

"That looks awesome."

"Glad you like it." She pulled the computer back around to face her as she typed. "I've got a similar one going up on a few other sites, and Cassie promised to make a video to appeal to the younger generation."

Emily was feeling obsolete. "Um, what do you need from me?"

"Do you think you could talk to Tony about incorporating some more festive food options?" Anna Mae asked, her dark-brown eyes meeting Emily's. "As much as I want to promote tourism for the town, I'd also like to garner some business for your mom. I noticed at trivia that few people ordered food. Maybe adding a few fun new appetizers or desserts would help with that."

"I'll talk to him," Emily said with a nod. She shifted in her seat. Was that it? Should she leave now?

"Great," Anna Mae said, her face breaking into a breathtaking grin. She shut her computer and shoved it aside, reaching her hands across the table. Emily cautiously took them in her own. "Now that the business talk is over, we can relax and spend some time together."

Wait, is this a date? She certainly wasn't expecting it to be anything more than a business meeting, but the look in Anna Mae's eyes told quite a different story.

"Aside from the pub, are you enjoying being home?" Anna Mae said when Emily didn't respond.

Emily nodded. "I love summer in Blue Heron Bay, and I'm looking forward to spending more quality time with my family." She gave Anna Mae's hands a gentle squeeze. "What about you? Will your father stick around for the Fourth of July?"

Anna Mae shook her head, a wistful look in her eyes. "No, he'll head back to Texas to spend it with my mother and siblings."

"Oh." Emily tried to hide her disappointment. "When do you leave?"

"No, you misunderstand," Anna Mae said with a laugh. "*I'm* not going home."

Emily frowned and leaned back. "You're not?"

"I don't leave until the deal is done," Anna Mae declared, but she didn't seem the least bit bothered by it. "My family is used to it. Since we're all grown and spread out over the country, we rarely get together except for weddings and funerals."

"Don't you get lonely?" Emily bit her lip. She hadn't meant to blurt that out. It wasn't any of her business.

Anna Mae shrugged. "Sometimes." She looked up at Emily from under her lashes, causing Emily's heart to flutter. "But right now, I feel less alone."

Emily swallowed thickly. If she'd harbored any further doubts about whether this was a date, they faded the longer she gazed into Anna Mae's eyes. Yet, she still couldn't shake the worry over Leslie's unwelcome appearance.

"Will, uh, Leslie be leaving with your father?" Emily asked, cringing internally at how obvious she sounded.

"If I had anything to do with it, she wouldn't be here in the first place." Anna Mae's brown eyes flashed.

"I take it the breakup wasn't amicable?"

Anna Mae released Emily's hands and sighed. "It's complicated. I was caught up in the newness of it all. Leslie was the first woman I was ever serious about. We were practically engaged. But she was much more focused on how our romantic union could boost our business prospects. She was always 'on.'"

"On?" Emily tilted her head.

Anna Mae drummed her fingers on the table as she seemed to search for the right words. "Like that guy your sister is dating, Derrick? He scheduled all those interviews, and even I could tell Cassie was getting sick of it. Leslie was like that. She always wanted our relationship to be part of the spotlight. I wouldn't call myself a private person, but some things should be sacred, you know?"

Emily nodded. That she understood. Though, if Cassie had been honest from the beginning, she could have avoided the whole situation. She forced the thought from her mind.

"I put my foot down about six months ago, and we had a huge fight. We took some time apart, and I realized the relationship wasn't what I wanted anymore." She gave a hollow laugh. "I don't even consider us friends. Everything is business with her. Her ambition never sleeps."

"She seems to still have feelings for you."

"Well, if she does, I can assure you it's one-sided." Anna Mae leaned forward. "I thought it was obvious that I'm interested in someone else."

Warmth crept into Emily's cheeks as she averted her gaze. She snuck a glance at Anna Mae and was rewarded with a bright smile that made her nervous but beautifully warm. Unsure what else to do, she cleared her throat.

"I'm glad you'll be here for the Fourth," Emily said. "You're welcome to join us. The fireworks are always a real treat."

"I'd like that," Anna Mae said, her tone sincere. Emily couldn't help the grin that took over her face, stretching from ear to ear. Maybe her soul mate hadn't been hit by a truck after all.

~

"So, Cassie, you requested this interview. Why don't you tell me what's on your mind?" Roger said, his voice kind.

She'd decided to go back to the original reporter who broke the story. Though he'd offered to meet her at a restaurant, she'd asked to come to his office. The fewer people who overheard their conversation, the better. While the truth was going to come out soon, she hoped meeting with the reporter privately would minimize the gossip before the article released.

Her hands fidgeted with the hem of her blue skirt as she nodded. "Thank you for meeting with me. I wanted to set the record straight." But with her heart jackhammering in her chest, the conversation was not going to be easy. To buy time, she allowed her gaze to travel around his office. Papers were scattered all over his desk, and clippings were pinned to the corkboard behind him. Somehow the clutter felt like a metaphor for the chaotic thoughts flying through her head.

Roger waved his hand. "Please, continue."

"The story Derrick and I told you wasn't the whole truth." With a sigh, she launched into what had actually happened. How she'd been swimming when people on the beach saw fins and thought the worst and how Derrick had come out to "rescue" her. "But then I called out to him to let him know they were dolphins, not sharks, and I was fine."

"Dolphins? Well, that's quite a twist, but I can understand why everyone assumed the worst. A dark-gray fin, from the shore, could easily be mistaken for a shark."

Some of the tension in her shoulders relaxed as she nodded. "Yes, they look very similar from such a distance, and the waves were rather intense that day."

"But if you realized it wasn't sharks while in the water, why didn't you tell everyone the truth?"

She bit her lip. *Here comes the hard part.* "Well, I had planned to. But when Derrick took me back to his house, he asked me if I would keep the dolphins a secret." She lowered her head. "At the time, I thought that just meant we wouldn't correct the story and would let people believe what they wanted. Then he started booking interviews, and I realized he meant to outright lie."

"And yet, you still went along with it."

"Yes." Her stomach twisted, and she squeezed her eyes shut as if she could block out the shame. Taking a deep breath, she continued. "It was wrong, I know. I'm truly sorry for my actions. There's no excuse for what I did."

Roger typed something on his laptop before he turned back to her. "What was your motivation, though? I don't understand why you continued to perpetuate the lie."

Her cheeks burned as she stared at her hands. "This is going to sound silly, but..." She shook her head. "You know how Derrick told you we knew each other in high school but didn't hang out in the same circles? Well, the truth is, I had a huge crush on him back then." As she said the words out loud, she sank lower in her seat, feeling more and more ridiculous. "A part of me was thrilled he'd finally noticed me, and I didn't consider the consequences of my actions."

"Unrequited love will make us do strange things." Roger chuckled, and she shot him a grateful smile. "What made you finally decide to come clean?"

"My sister, Emily." What Cassie didn't share was Emily's ultimatum. She was hoping for sympathy, and admitting that she only acted under threat of exposure wouldn't sound very sympathetic.

When the interview was over, she felt like a huge weight had been lifted from her shoulders. While it wasn't the hardest thing she'd ever had to do, telling the truth about the not-a-shark encounter definitely ranked in the top five. Though she suspected the fallout would be harsh and that the town might not be as forgiving as the reporter had been, she left the building with a lighter step knowing she'd finally done the right thing.

The article came out a few days later, and Derrick immediately started blowing up her phone. She kept her responses to a minimum. Part of her wondered if she should have warned him beforehand, but she was hurt and humiliated by the whole thing. If he truly cared about her, he wouldn't have asked her to lie in the first place. Maybe he didn't realize the repercussions of their actions either, but they both knew it was wrong. While she'd have to face him eventually, she was happy to put that off for as long as possible.

What she hadn't counted on was Ryan's reaction. He'd barely spoken to her. Although he came by the pub regularly, he spent most of his time with Mom. The few times they'd passed each other in the dining area, he'd given her a curt nod but otherwise hadn't acknowledged her presence. That cut her deeper than she'd anticipated, but she pushed those feelings aside because she didn't want to examine them too closely.

That night was karaoke, and Derrick had texted he would be there. She was nervous and on edge, but she knew she'd feel better after they talked. Derrick wasn't a bad guy. Misguided perhaps, but his latest text messages had been more apologetic. She hoped once they cleared the air, things would change between them, though she hadn't decided exactly what she hoped that change would be.

Fiddler's Green was filled with excitement as Cassie and her siblings set up for the evening. They had put together a robust list of songs, from old favorites to more recent releases. Cassie created a few specialty drinks, using the names of the songs. Her favorite concoction was Summer Lovin', which was a twist on a tequila sunrise. She expected it would be a big hit with the karaoke crowd, as it would give them all the liquid courage they needed in one glass.

The karaoke patrons began filtering in, and Cassie was set upon by those seeking her type of fortifier to enable them to sing their hearts out. She mixed, stirred, and shook her way through various cocktails, both themed and not, for the first hour. A few brave souls stepped up to the mic early on, but mostly, people seemed to be waiting for the alcohol to kick in. As the clock neared ten, more people signed up to sing, and Cassie hummed along to the familiar tunes, grateful for the distraction from her growing anxiety. Derrick had yet to arrive.

Finally, just after ten, he came in. Cassie signaled to Emily that she was going to take a break. When she walked over to him, he turned and opened the pub door, gesturing for her to go outside.

Once they were alone, she leaned against the brick wall of the building, bracing herself. But when Derrick stood beside her, she was taken aback by the remorse in his deep-blue eyes.

"Look, Cass, I'm sorry." He ran a hand through his blond hair. "Things got out of hand, and I lost sight of what mattered." When she didn't respond, he dropped his gaze to his feet. "I'm sorry you had to tell everyone the truth on your own, but I swear I would have been there if you'd let me know."

"I didn't know how you would feel about it all," Cassie said, her eyes narrowing. "Some of your text messages after the story broke suggested it wouldn't have gone over well if you'd had prior warning."

"I know." He rubbed his hand over his face. "I was just shocked and hurt. But I think you did the right thing."

"I *know* I did the right thing," Cassie said.

Derrick ducked his head and nodded.

"You never should have asked me to lie for you." She waited a moment to see if he would say anything else. When he didn't, she continued. "Is that the only reason you've hung out with me? Because I was helping you get your fifteen minutes of undeserved fame?"

His head shot up. "No! Of course not." He lifted his hand to cup her cheek. "I really like you, Cassie. And I was hoping to take you out again. I had a lot of fun on our date the other night."

Part of her still didn't trust him, but old feelings die hard. There was something about him she just couldn't seem to resist.

"I like you too," she murmured with a sigh. "Just promise me that the whole ordeal is over." She raised an eyebrow. "No more lies."

He lifted his free hand and held up three fingers. "Scout's honor."

While she was pretty sure he'd never been a Boy Scout, she decided it was good enough, at least for now. He'd have to earn her trust.

"So, I have an idea I'd like to run by you," he said. "You remember my old buddy Darryl, from lacrosse?" At her nod, he continued. "He's created this show in Annapolis where they do a lot of different stunts, mostly in the water with Jet Skis and boats and stuff, but they also do some stunts on land. Anyway, they're bringing their show to Ocean City next week, and I talked him into doing one here in Blue Heron. I know your family is trying to bring more tourism to the town, and I was thinking some of the proceeds could go to that effort, either to the pub or to the city's tourism budget." He smiled at her. "He invited me to perform as well, and I wondered if you might join me."

Despite her misgivings, her heart melted. *Wow, he wants to help save the pub? He must really care, not just about me, but about the town as well.* But she didn't know the first thing about stunt shows. "Uh, what exactly would that entail?"

"Well, for starters, if you could ask your sister's friend for help with PR, I would greatly appreciate it." He shuffled his feet. "And as for the show itself, I plan on doing some surfing stunts, which is easy enough, but I've been practicing on my dad's Jet Ski and thought I would do a few tricks with that as well. Would you be willing to ride with me?"

She'd never been on a Jet Ski before, but it sounded exciting. Sort of like a water motorcycle. She gave him her thousand-watt smile with an enthusiastic nod.

"Awesome! We can meet for lunch later this week and discuss all the details. For now, I'd love to hear you sing."

That was all the encouragement she needed. She spun around and pulled him back into the pub. Emily was going to be so happy to hear about the stunt show, and Anna Mae would jump at any chance to help spread the word about a town event. It was the sign she needed that everything would be okay.

Chapter Eighteen

PETER WAS PLEASED WITH THE TURNOUT. KARAOKE NIGHT was proving to be more successful than trivia. The patrons loved the song options, putting their own spin on them. While Cassie was gone, Ricardo had pitched in as bartender. Though Emily and Anna Mae had looked unhappy, they'd left him alone, much to Peter's relief. Even Leslie Steele had kept her distance when she'd arrived without Mr. Wakefield, but Peter assumed her interests lay more with Anna Mae than anything else.

During a lull in activity, Peter stepped over to the bar as Ricardo finished making a series of shots on a surfboard that Cassie had named the Big Kahuna. Her twists on popular drinks were a hit among the college crowd.

"What can I get you?" Ricardo asked as he typed into the computer.

Are you on the menu? Peter cringed, grateful he hadn't said that aloud. "Just wanted to check on you."

Ricardo gave him a charming smile, which set Peter's heart racing. "I'm doing okay, but Cassie is sorely missed. She's much more entertaining than me."

"I find that hard to believe," Peter said, giving Ricardo a quick once-over. His usual slicked-back hair fell in his dark eyes, which gave him an almost dangerous vibe. Peter wasn't the only one to notice. More than a few interested glances were coming Ricardo's way from all genders.

"I aim to please," Ricardo said with another wicked grin. His gaze swept over the room. "I have to say, Emily and Anna Mae have outdone themselves. This event is amazing."

"I'm surprised to hear you compliment Anna Mae," Peter said, incredulous.

Ricardo shrugged as he pulled out a cloth from under the bar and wiped down the counter. "I give credit where credit is due." He leaned forward. "Besides, they haven't run me out yet."

"We're too desperate when Cassie's on break," Peter joked. "But in all seriousness, we should talk about your resort plans. My family is still against selling, but I think they can be persuaded."

Ricardo leaned forward. "I'm listening."

"Would your boss be interested in keeping the spirit of Fiddler's Green alive?" Peter asked, trying to keep his voice low despite the volume in the pub. "I know the resort contracts with an Irish pub under its overall umbrella, but if we could meld my father's original vision with your version, maybe it would be more palatable to my family."

"I can't make any promises," Ricardo said. "But I can certainly talk to my boss about it and see if he's willing to work with us."

The door opened, and Cassie strolled in with Derrick in tow. Peter turned back to Ricardo. "We'll talk more later."

Ricardo nodded. "I'm going to hold you to that." The look he gave Peter filled him with warm anticipation. The sooner he finished his dissertation, the better.

"I take it you and Cassie still haven't talked," Emily said as she stepped up beside Ryan at the bar. The pub had closed a few minutes ago after another successful event.

He shook his head. "I'm not even sure what to say to her. I'm embarrassed for buying into her story, and I can't believe she went along with a lie like that." His gaze lowered to his half-finished beer. "She's not who I thought she was."

"I'm sorry." Emily put a hand on his arm. "While it's no excuse for her actions, I'm not sure she really considered the consequences."

"Clearly," he said bitterly before gulping down his beer. He glanced behind him. "Where is she, anyway?"

"She left with Derrick a few minutes ago," Emily said. "It seems they've patched things up." She rolled her eyes. "He wants me and Anna Mae to help with publicity for some stunt show he's putting on. Cassie didn't give me many details, but she did say he plans to donate half of the proceeds to helping promote tourism in the town."

If Ryan was surprised by this revelation, he didn't show it. "I hope that is a promise he intends to keep." He met her gaze. "But I'm concerned she's going to get caught up in his quest for fame again."

"I tried to warn her about Derrick after you told me your concerns. But I think it got lost in the revelation that she'd lied about the shark incident."

Ryan nodded, his green eyes grave. "I'd hoped she'd listen to someone closer to her."

Emily gave a hollow laugh. "I wouldn't exactly call us close." She moved to wipe down the last table and set the chairs on top. "Peter and I were like two peas in a pod growing up, even though he and Cassie are closer in age. I'd always wanted a brother, but Cassie was a surprise, to all of us." She smiled ruefully. "She came into this world like a hurricane, and I don't think her storm-force winds will ever calm."

"But you worry about her." Ryan stood and grabbed a broom and began sweeping underneath the tables.

"Of course I worry about her. She's my little sister, but that doesn't mean I *understand* her, and that's something she needs. Someone who gets her."

Ryan stopped sweeping and rested his chin on the hand holding the broom handle. "I'd hoped to get the chance to understand her, but after the lie she told, I'm not sure if I'll get it, or if I even want it anymore." He resumed sweeping. "I thought she was opening up to me, but apparently not."

"I know." Emily dropped her gaze. "I tried talking to her about you, but she wasn't very receptive."

With a frustrated sigh, he walked away to sweep behind the bar. Her heart went out to him. While he clearly cared a great deal about her sister, her concern for him went deeper than that. He'd been so kind to her family. Mom had told her that Ryan made a habit of stopping by most nights to check on her, and Emily assumed he was paying tribute to her father.

Emily went to do a last walk-through of the kitchen. Though she was worried about Cassie, she had other things on her mind. Her date with Anna Mae had gone better than expected, and she was looking forward to seeing her again.

However, she couldn't shake the feeling something was still brewing between Anna Mae and Leslie. Despite Anna Mae's dismissal of Leslie as an ex, when Leslie had arrived at karaoke night, notable sparks had been flying between them. It would make sense for the two women to rekindle their attachment, considering how often their professional relationship would bring them together. But Anna Mae had emphatically assured Emily she retained no residual feelings for Leslie, and she insisted their relationship was strictly business.

Regardless of how Anna Mae felt, Leslie clearly still held a torch for her, if her animosity toward Emily was any indication. While Emily tried her best to ignore them, she couldn't help mentally comparing herself to Leslie, and in her estimation, she always came up short. After all, she didn't have a multimillion-dollar hotel chain to her name, just a struggling family pub that might not last the summer.

Once she'd determined everything was ready for the next day, she returned to Ryan. As she approached, he looked up and smiled, but it didn't quite meet his eyes.

"Thanks for all your help tonight," Emily said.

"Anytime," Ryan said as he put the broom away.

They walked outside together, where the heat of the day was still hanging on.

"I can't believe June is almost over," Emily said, looking up at the star-studded sky. "Oh look, a shooting star!" They both followed its trajectory until it disappeared from view.

"Did you wish for anything?" Ryan asked.

"Probably the same thing you did." Emily grinned. Ryan dropped his gaze with a frown, and Emily wondered if she'd gone too far. "I'm sorry, I didn't mean—"

Ryan interrupted her. "It's okay." He ran a hand through his blond hair. "You're more likely to get your wish than I am. But it's no matter. I only hope, in time, Derrick will come to deserve her."

"What do you mean?"

Ryan sighed. "You might wonder how I know so much about Derrick. The truth is, I've known him for years, much to my regret. His father is a successful real estate agent in Ocean City, but since his family lives here, he was one of the former mayor's biggest campaign donors." He leaned against the building. "When Derrick got out of college, his father wanted him to make something of himself, so the mayor offered him a job with the town government." He glanced at Emily. "I was his supervisor."

"Wow. I had no idea."

"It's not something I like to talk about," Ryan said. "Anyway, Derrick was a terrible employee. He showed up late, if he came to work at all, and he did some nefarious things I'd rather not get into. Eventually, I had to fire him." He stared up at the sky. "As you can imagine, that didn't go over well. Derrick was furious. The former mayor had decided to run for county executive at that point, and initially, I was the town's favorite to be his replacement. Derrick ran against me, and, well, despite my credentials, running against a local is never easy as an outsider."

Emily made a derisive noise in her throat. *The idea of Derrick being the mayor of anything is ludicrous.*

"I'm sure you know, having grown up here yourself, how this town thrives on 'good ol' boy' politics. It was an uphill battle, but with your father's support, I won." Ryan's smile faded. "Unfortunately, the former mayor's daughter, a dear friend of mine, got caught up in the crossfire. He used her, much like he used your sister, to gain influence and fame. He pretended to care about her and made a huge show of their relationship, at least when there were cameras around."

"I don't think I've ever met her," Emily said, cocking her head as she tried to remember.

"She's a couple of years younger than Cassie. After growing up in the spotlight of this small town, her endorsement carried a lot of weight.

She was a sweet girl, drawn in by Derrick's charm, but once the election results were in and Derrick realized he'd lost, he dropped her and moved on to the next best thing."

"That's awful," Emily murmured. Her heart went out to the unnamed girl, but it brought fresh worry for her own sister. She wanted to believe Derrick was capable of change, but from what she'd seen thus far, she doubted it.

"I wish I had told Cassie everything the night of the bonfire, but my pride got the best of me when she called me jealous, and I didn't handle that conversation well at all." His chuckle was bitter and humorless. "In the end, I guess she was right, but I swear, my sole motivation was to protect her."

"She might still come around, you know," Emily said.

The look on his face told her he didn't believe that any more than she did.

"I won't hold my breath." Ryan bowed his head. "I'm sorry. I shouldn't have burdened you with this, but I thought you should know. Have a good night, Emily." He walked down the street, his usual brisk step heavy.

Emily headed back to the house, her mind filled with what Ryan had shared. Like his friend, Cassie had been completely taken in by Derrick's charms. He'd seemed genuine about his desire to help the pub and the town, but after the lies he'd told, Emily just couldn't bring herself to trust him.

Chapter Nineteen

Cassie bounced out of bed the next morning ready to start working with Derrick on the stunt show. Last night, he'd told her Darryl had scheduled a few interviews to garner publicity. A lot of thrill seekers who had heard about the shark story had come to town, and even though the fact that it had been a hoax was now well publicized, they'd hung around hoping to see a shark anyway. Who knew that a fake shark sighting would garner so much interest in her little town.

But her heart sank a little at the idea of more interviews. After the humiliating experience of coming clean, it was quite literally the last thing she wanted to do. She reminded herself of the benefit to the pub and forced herself to ignore the churning in her stomach. At least they weren't lying anymore.

After the interview, he would take her to the marina to start practicing his stunts on the Jet Ski. She was most looking forward to that. Several years ago, she'd dated a guy with a motorcycle, and the only thing she missed about him was that feeling of exhilaration with the wind in her hair. She imagined being on a Jet Ski would feel similar, though with the added fun of being on the water.

She dressed with care and did her makeup perfectly. Her roots were starting to show, and she'd need to dye her hair again soon. But otherwise, she was pleased with her reflection. Her auburn hair framed her face with beachy waves, and her hazel eyes were greener than brown today.

Derrick was picking her up and taking her to a local news station for the interview. Several people from the stunt show would be attending, so she hoped her part would be minimal.

When the doorbell rang, she bounded down the stairs and flung the door open. He stood there looking as handsome as ever with his blond hair slicked back and his deep-blue eyes giving her a quick once-over. He whistled, and his full lips lifted.

"You look amazing," he said, holding out his hand.

She slipped hers into it, and he gave her a squeeze before leading her to his car.

The drive to the studio was over quickly, and Cassie worked to keep the butterflies in her stomach under control. Flashbacks to the interviews she'd given recently were causing her anxiety, particularly the one where she set the record straight. Telling everyone she'd lied was one of the most humiliating experiences of her life. Would they bring it up today?

Several people from the stunt show were already inside when they were ushered to the greenroom. Derrick greeted them with high fives and fist bumps while Cassie loitered near the entrance. Shyness was out of character for her, but she couldn't seem to shake the growing discomfort.

"I'd like you all to meet my girlfriend, Cassie," Derrick said, gesturing for her to join him. With a deep breath, she stepped over to him, and he slid a reassuring arm around her waist. It took a moment for her brain to process the fact that he'd referred to her as his girlfriend. They'd never discussed labels, and she wasn't sure how she felt about it. While she'd agreed to give him another chance after their talk the night before, she'd assumed that meant they'd just continue casually dating. *"Girlfriend" has a whole connotation to it that I'm not sure I'm ready for.*

"Nice job, man," a man with short brown hair said as his eyes traveled over her. "I'd pull this one out of the ocean, too, sharks or no."

Blood rushed to her cheeks, and she stared at the floor. That was not at all what she needed right before they went on television.

"Hey, cool it, Darryl," Derrick barked, his arm tensing around her. "That's done and over with."

The guy held up his hands. "I was just messin' with ya, man. Lighten up."

To Cassie's relief, the producer came over at that moment to greet them and to inform them they had five minutes before they would be on air. Cassie stepped over to the mirror and made sure she was camera-ready.

As they were led out to take their seats, Cassie was pleased she and Derrick were placed on the far edge, away from the interviewer. The chairs were set up in a semicircle in front of a large window looking out over the ocean. She hoped that meant they wouldn't be the center of attention. But it seemed she was alone in that desire because Derrick scowled when he sat. Clearly, he was still hoping to be in the spotlight. Ryan's warning about Derrick's desire for fifteen minutes of fame echoed through her mind. She pushed the thought away.

"Good morning and welcome to *At Dawn's Break*. I'm your host, Dawn Harris, and today I have with me a local group who will be performing a thrilling stunt show right here in our town. From my right, we have Darryl Bannigan, Chris Pans, Michael Rex, Brittany Collier, Alice Cairns, Derrick Barnes, and Cassie Gallagher. Welcome, all." Dawn turned to Darryl. "It's my understanding you are the mastermind behind this show. Can you tell me more about it?"

Cassie breathed easier as the interview continued without requiring any input from her. Most of the stunts would include water sports, like water skiing, Jet Skiing, surfing, and speedboat races. She hoped it would be exactly what the town needed to garner more tourism.

Derrick suddenly nudged her, and she refocused to find Dawn and all of the other interviewees staring at her. She cleared her throat.

"I'm sorry, I didn't quite catch that."

"I asked if you were excited about performing stunts with Derrick."

"Oh, yes! Very excited. I've never been on a Jet Ski before, so I'll have to learn quickly. But I expect it'll be a lot of fun, and Derrick will keep me safe."

"Especially if there are dolphins around," Dawn said.

Cassie's heart sank, but she worked to keep her expression neutral.

"Now, Derrick, there have been some accusations coming from the city council about you cutting corners around safety. In fact, the mayor himself, Ryan Caulfield, has threatened to deny certain permits until the safety concerns are resolved. How do you respond to that?"

Derrick leaned forward. "Thank you for the opportunity to address this, Dawn." He faced the camera. "We are giving the city our full cooperation. I can assure you that no corners are being cut, and safety is our top priority."

"You and the mayor have butted heads before, haven't you?" Dawn asked. "Particularly during your campaign a few years back."

"Yes, but I think this time it's a bit more personal."

"How do you mean?" Dawn cocked her head.

Derrick grasped Cassie's hand, entwining their fingers. "Let's just say, I got the girl."

Heat rushed to Cassie's cheeks, and she yanked her hand away. *Did he seriously just drag me into their rivalry?* First, he'd called her his girlfriend, then he'd not only announced it to the world—er, well, their town—but he'd turned it into some sort of twisted love triangle. Her heart beat erratically in her chest. Dawn closed out the interview, but Cassie couldn't hear a word she said over the pounding in her ears. As soon as they were released from the stage, she cornered Derrick.

"What was that about?"

He shrugged, nonchalantly, like he hadn't just embarrassed her, again, on television. "I don't see what the problem is. We're together, aren't we? And why should we hide it?"

She pinched the bridge of her nose between her thumb and forefinger, something she had seen Peter do on more than one occasion when she had made some crazy statement. Suddenly, she completely understood how he'd felt.

"I never said we should hide it," she said, slowly, like she was talking to a five-year-old. "But there's a vast spectrum between 'hiding it' and announcing it on TV."

"It's not like this is a national channel." When she didn't respond, he cupped her chin in his hand and forced her to look at him. "But even if it was, I want the world to know how I feel about you."

Cassie took several deep breaths. There had been a time when hearing him say those words would have made her swoon. However, after the fiasco with the shark lie and the following humiliation, she'd quickly learned the value of keeping some things private.

He tugged her hand. "Come on, Cass. Don't be mad at me. I didn't mean anything by it."

Sucking in a calming breath, she nodded. She believed, deep down, that he meant well. His impulsiveness was simply a part of who he was. But something still needled her. If he truly only wanted to share their happiness, why had he mentioned it only after the news anchor had asked about Ryan's concerns?

Emily was pleased with the way karaoke night had turned out. While the pub didn't have any events planned for the evening, Anna Mae had told her to pay attention to the patrons on normal nights to see if there was a marked increase in customers. Correlation didn't mean causation, but Anna Mae had argued that more customers in the pub was a good sign overall for tourism in the town. Emily crossed her fingers for a lot of fresh faces that evening.

The one face she longed for most, however, was Anna Mae's. But she'd already texted Emily to say she wouldn't be by that day because she was meeting with her father. He wanted to review the numbers for the last two events they'd held, and then they had a meeting with Ryan to discuss the town's annual tourism. Emily tried not to dwell on the fact that this meant Anna Mae would spend the day with Leslie.

Peter came into the kitchen as Emily finished putting her breakfast dishes into the dishwasher. His brown eyes met hers, and he smiled wryly as he prepared a cup of coffee. Emily blew out a heavy breath. They couldn't keep walking on eggshells around each other forever.

"How's your dissertation going?" she asked.

"Almost done. I'm hoping to finish my edits by tomorrow."

"That's wonderful. I'm so glad you've made such progress." Emily leaned against the counter. "Look, I'm sorry I've been so harsh about Ricardo."

Peter shrugged. "It's okay. He wasn't exactly my favorite person, either, in high school, but I didn't realize he was Anna Mae's enemy number one when I ran into him at the airport." He cocked an eyebrow, and Emily laughed.

"He's not our enemy," she said. "But his interest in the pub caught me off guard." She stared down at the floor. "I'm not ready to give up on Dad's dream yet."

"I understand." Peter stepped closer to her. "It's not like I don't get how hard it would be. I'm simply trying to be pragmatic. Mom can't handle this on her own. And if things don't improve, I'd rather have a frank conversation now, while we're all here, than get a frantic phone call when I'm all the way on the other side of the country."

Protestations welled up inside her, but she tried to quell them. Peter wasn't wrong. And yet, they'd come so far. The two events they'd held were hits. If they could keep the momentum going, their mom could afford to hire more staff in addition to keeping the restaurant open.

"She might not be alone for long," Emily said. "I'm trying to convince Cassie to move home."

"Like that'll ever happen."

"You'd be surprised." Emily raised an eyebrow. "She's not as happy in the city as we all assumed."

Peter scoffed. "Forgive me if I have a tough time buying that."

Emily told him what Ryan had shared with her and what Cassie had confirmed herself. His disbelief was replaced by a frown of concern. By the time Emily finished her tale, he was pacing the length of the kitchen.

"Cassie moving home would be a wonderful thing on multiple levels," Peter said as he completed a lap. "Her legal background would aid Mom in researching any changes to the law regarding things like licensing requirements and zoning changes. Plus, the contracts, as you pointed out." He stopped and drummed his fingers on the counter. "But are you sure she's interested? This is Cassie we're talking about, and she's never been the most decisive person. Her whims are like Maryland weather. If you don't like them, wait five minutes."

"You have a point. Especially since I believe some of her sudden drive to return home is coming from her interest in Derrick."

Peter rolled his eyes. "Of course it is." They went over to the table and sat across from each other. "How do you feel about this stunt show?"

"That guy is as shifty as sand, and I don't trust him at all," Emily said, practically spitting the words. Rubbing her temples, she sighed. "But I can't deny that any event that brings in crowds is good for the town and the pub. But Ryan told me some... things that are concerning."

"What kind of things?"

As she relayed the story Ryan had told her about the mayor's daughter, Peter's eyebrows drew closer and closer together. He was clearly just as perturbed by Ryan's tale as she was.

"I can't say I'm surprised. I never believed Cassie would lie so much without encouragement. Don't get me wrong, I know she tells white lies when it suits her, but this was extreme."

"Exactly," Emily said. "And I'm concerned that because he's presented this stunt show as a way to help the pub, she's going to let her guard down with him again. I don't think he gives two figs about the pub or the town. He's only in it because it benefits him."

Peter scrubbed a hand over his face. "Though, I guess we should be a little wary about the story. We've only heard Ryan's side, and, well, he seems to like her. But his intentions may not be entirely honorable either. Have you told Cassie all of this?"

She sighed. "No. I have no idea how to, and she already bit my head off once for daring to interfere in her love life. But Ryan doesn't strike me as someone who would try to sabotage a relationship out of jealousy." Emily turned a sharp eye on her brother. "But while we're on the subject of love lives, what exactly is going on with you and Ricardo?"

"Nothing," Peter said, a little too quickly, in Emily's opinion. "Well, I mean, nothing... yet. We're supposed to go out after I finish the current version of my dissertation."

"Well, if you can convince him not to put us out of business, then I'll approve."

"And what about you and Anna Mae?"

"We're working together," Emily said, her tone insistent.

"Uh-huh. Is that all it is?" He leaned forward, resting his chin on his hand. "Even Cassie has noticed the amount of time you two spend together, and Cassie is probably the least observant person I know."

Emily's cheeks warmed under his scrutiny. "Fine. We had a date the other day. But there's a complication."

"Would that be Leslie Steele?"

Emily nodded. "They only broke up six months ago, and while Anna Mae has insisted it's over, I don't think Leslie agrees."

"I wouldn't worry too much," Peter said. "I know we haven't spent much time together since I've been home, but from what I've seen, Anna Mae is smitten with you."

"It's mutual." Emily ducked her head, hoping to hide her burning cheeks. She cleared her throat. "Anyway, I better get ready for my shift at the pub." She walked to the kitchen doorway and turned back. "Do you think Ricardo would be willing to help at the bar again tonight?"

Peter tilted his head to the side. "Cassie isn't working?"

"She asked for the night off so she could practice with Derrick."

"Figures. I'll ask him."

Emily climbed the stairs, relieved to have cleared the air with Peter. It never felt right when they fought. She pulled out the clothes for her shift, smiling to herself. Despite her dislike of Ricardo's business ventures, she was happy her brother had found someone. It looked like all the Gallagher children would have summer romances.

Chapter Twenty

AFTER SPENDING A FEW HOURS ON HIS DISSERTATION, PETER blinked when he reached the end of the document. Had he completed his edits already? He scrolled through, but there was nothing left from his advisor. He felt giddy as he backed up and saved his work. *This is a welcome surprise.* The first person he texted was Ricardo, but he kept his text simple and only asked if Ricardo could cover the bar tonight. Peter wanted to share his good news in person so he could see Ricardo's face.

He left his room and stepped over to Cassie's door. She hadn't made so much as a peep since she'd come back from her interview that morning. He knocked, and a mumbled reply came from within.

"How are you doing?" he asked as he entered the room. He found her sitting on the chair by her window, staring off into the distance.

Cassie gave him a small smile. "I'm okay. How's the dissertation going?"

"It's done!" Peter exclaimed. "Er, well, at least I'm done with the latest round of edits."

"That's wonderful news." To his surprise, Cassie stood and embraced him. "Now you can enjoy the rest of the summer."

He blinked, a warmth spreading through his chest at her obvious pride. Since they'd never been close, he'd always assumed she didn't care about his Ph.D. progress. But her reaction made him see her in a different light.

"I hear you aren't working tonight."

She shook her head. "I'm supposed to meet Derrick at the marina after he finishes his shift."

"How did the interview go?"

Her hazel eyes darkened. "Fine."

"Well, that sounded convincing," Peter said, trying to keep his voice light.

"They brought up the shark thing, of course, which I know I deserve," she said with a sniffle. "But then..."

He waited a moment, but when she didn't continue, he laid a hand on her shoulder. "Tell me."

With a sigh, Cassie told him how the line of questions had changed, focusing on Derrick's rivalry with Ryan. She shared how she felt when Derrick made it seem like she was some prize to be won.

"It just rubbed me the wrong way. He introduced me as his girl-friend and then announced it to the world." She leaned back in her chair. "I feel like I should be over the moon. I've only had a crush on him for, like, forever. But it bothered me, and I'm not sure I know why."

"He did ask you to keep a secret for him and then turned it into a much bigger lie."

"True, but I went along with it, even when I knew it wasn't right." She squeezed her eyes shut as if she could erase the memory of her actions.

Peter frowned. "Do you want to be in a relationship with him? He doesn't sound like a good guy."

She stood and paced the room. "Yes and no. If you had asked me before the whole shark debacle, I would have been more enthusiastic. But now, I'm not sure." Her lips curved in a bitter smile. "I should have stuck with my initial belief: what's the point of a summer romance?"

"Have to disagree with you there, sis." Peter crossed his arms. "I'm quite enjoying mine."

Cassie's eyes lit up. "I knew it!" She rushed over to him, her earlier aggravation forgotten. "The first time I saw him, I knew there was something between you. Tell me everything!"

Peter laughed. "There's not much to tell. But now that I don't have my dissertation hanging over my head, I'm hoping to spend more time with him."

"I'm so happy for you, Pete. You deserve some fun after all your hard work." She tapped her finger to her chin. "There are a couple of events happening in town this weekend that might be a fun first date."

"Oh? Like what?"

"There's Screen on the Sand," Cassie said. "And I believe they will have food trucks set up there. Willowwood is hosting Sundaes in the Park. Then there's the production of *The Wizard of Oz* the children's theatre is putting on."

"Those sound like good options," Peter said. "But I'll have to talk to Ricardo. He might have a favorite town event from his youth, or he might want to forgo them altogether." He glanced at his watch. "Well, I better get over to the pub. We'll miss you tonight."

She laughed and waved a dismissive hand. "It's one night, Pete. I'll be back to work tomorrow."

As he left her room, Peter checked his phone. Ricardo had texted back, confirming he'd come to the pub that night. Peter couldn't wait to share his good news. After devoting so much of his summer to his dissertation, he was looking forward to having a break and enjoying some time alone with the man who'd filled his thoughts since they reconnected on the plane.

When he arrived at the pub a little while later, he found it packed. He'd expected the dinner rush in a few hours, but it appeared to have started early. Emily ran past him to the kitchen, and he followed close behind.

"Where'd all these people come from?" he asked as he caught up to her.

She shrugged and typed an order into the computer.

"I wish I knew, but I'm glad you're here. We could use an extra set of hands."

"Where do you want me?"

Emily nodded to the front of the house. "Take section C. Chris is due for a break."

"What about you? Do you need a break?"

"I'll take one later," Emily said with a shake of her head. She glanced at him. "Please tell me you got in touch with Ricardo about tending bar."

"I did, and he's coming, though he won't be here until after five."

"We'll make do until then." Emily sighed.

The next few hours flew by in a sea of customers. By the time he found a moment to catch his breath, Ricardo was already behind the bar. His dark hair was slicked back, and he was wearing a deep-green button-down shirt. They hadn't had time to find him a uniform with the pub's logo.

"When did you get here?" Peter asked him as he slid onto a stool.

"About an hour ago. You looked pretty slammed."

"It's been like that for hours."

"How's the dissertation?" Ricardo wiped down the bar, and Peter was grateful for the lull in customers. But he didn't expect it to last long.

"It's done," Peter said with a triumphant smile.

Ricardo looked up, his dark eyes wide. "Done? Already?"

Peter nodded. "I finished the last of my edits this afternoon. I'll take one last look at it before I send it back to my professor, but otherwise, this round is over."

"So, does that mean I can finally take you out?" Ricardo leaned back and raised an eyebrow.

"If you still want to," Peter said.

"I definitely still want to." Ricardo slid his hand across the bar, and Peter was eager to place his own in it. "Would Sunday be too soon?"

"Sunday would be perfect."

"Good. And I hope to have more news about how we can incorporate the current setup of the pub. I sent my plans to my boss earlier today." Ricardo gave his hand a squeeze before turning to help a customer.

Peter waited while Ricardo finished up before speaking again. "Is he coming here?"

Ricardo shook his head. "No, but if we move forward with the deal here, he'll come up later this summer. Though, he might change his mind when he learns both Steele Hotels *and* Wakefield are sniffing around."

"He doesn't like competition?" Peter asked.

"Mm, I wouldn't say that." Ricardo set his elbow on the counter and rested his chin on his hand as he stared off into the distance. "This isn't the first time we've butted heads with the Wakefields, but it is the first we've heard about a partnership with the Steeles. It's a riskier venture to go up against both of them."

"Assuming they actually form a partnership." Peter leaned back and crossed his arms. "Which Anna Mae doesn't seem keen on."

Ricardo shrugged. "Anna Mae doesn't run the company. At least, not yet." He cleared his throat. "Anyway, enough shop talk. About our date…"

Chapter Twenty-One

EMILY COULDN'T WAIT TO TELL ANNA MAE ABOUT THE turnout last night. All their hard work was paying off. She only hoped the pub's success was translating to the rest of Blue Heron Bay. She had no doubt in her mind that once Mr. Wakefield heard the good news, he'd move forward with building a hotel.

As she entered the coffee shop, her eyes scanned the lobby for a familiar head of black hair. When her gaze alighted on Anna Mae, she rushed over to the table, grinning from ear to ear. But at the expression on Anna Mae's face, Emily's joy depleted, and she slid onto the chair across from her with growing dread.

"What's wrong?" Emily asked, not even bothering with pleasantries.

Anna Mae blinked, and her eyes focused on Emily for the first time. Her lips curved into a sad smile, and Emily slid her hand across the table. Anna Mae grasped it and gave it a grateful squeeze.

"I'm not even sure where to begin." Anna Mae dropped her gaze to the table.

"Your father's not moving forward with the hotel, is he?" All of Emily's excitement deflated. After everything they'd done, Blue Heron Bay still wasn't a good enough investment for Wakefield Hotel Group.

"Oh, he still wants to move forward," Anna Mae said, her brown eyes flashing.

Emily cocked her head. "Then I don't understand. Isn't that good news?"

Anna Mae pulled her hand away and folded her arms on the table, resting her forehead on top of them. Her silence did nothing to alleviate Emily's growing anxiety.

When Anna Mae finally raised her head, the fire had gone out of her eyes. "He'll only move forward if we merge with Steele Hotels." She heaved a sigh. "But every time I try to talk to Leslie about the partnership, she starts reminiscing about our relationship and we make no headway."

"Have you told your dad?"

Anna Mae pressed her hand to her forehead. "No. I need this deal to prove to my father that I'm ready to take over the company. If I tell him that I can't work with my ex, he'll see me as unprofessional." Rubbing her temples, she groaned. "To him, business comes before feelings."

"Is there any other hotel group you could partner with that would still achieve your goals without involving your ex?"

"No one my father trusts," Anna Mae said. "Part of me wonders if I shouldn't just entertain her and walk down memory lane for a while. Whatever it takes to close this deal."

Emily's heart sank. "But you wouldn't—I mean, you don't want to rekindle what you had, right?"

"Of course not! I told you already, I don't see her that way anymore."

Well, that was something, but was it enough? Emily's stomach churned as she tried to process this information. Would Leslie really delay, or worse, back out of a business deal because of unrequited love? It sounded ridiculous to Emily. After all, this was the twenty-first century, not a Jane Austen novel.

"But if she's using this deal as a way to reconnect with you, I think your father should know about that. It's highly unprofessional and borderline unethical."

"I know, and I'm sure he'd put an end to the deal if he knew, but then he'd also pull out of building in Blue Heron Bay, and I don't want that either. Not after we've come so far and done so much to help your family's pub." Anna Mae took a deep breath and forced a smile. "Speaking of, how did last night go?"

Emily wasn't sure what to say. Though things were looking up for the pub, the fact was, without something to continuously draw tourists in, they might have just been delaying the inevitable.

"It was a complete success," she finally said. "We had a great turnout."

"That's good news!"

"I thought so…" Waves of nausea threatened to overtake Emily, and she breathed deeply.

"Look, don't worry about the hotel." Anna Mae waved her hand. "I've still got some ideas up my sleeve to convince my father to move forward without the Steeles. And as you pointed out, they aren't the only hotel group out there. Why don't you grab yourself a hot chocolate, and then we can discuss where we stand with the fireworks tonight and Derrick's stunt show."

Emily went to the counter, not sure if she'd be able to stomach anything. Her thoughts spun as she placed her order and glanced back at Anna Mae. Was she about to lose her family's pub and the first real chance she'd had at love all at once?

It was the Fourth of July, and Peter was thrilled to have finished his dissertation edits just in time to enjoy it. His family had a booth at the fireworks where they'd sell beer and pub fare to the masses. For the first time, he was looking forward to a town event, and not only because Ricardo would be there. After spending most of June cooped up in his room, it would be nice to get outside and enjoy the warmth of summer for a change.

A knock sounded at the door, then Cassie flung it open, her hazel eyes bright. She'd been out with Derrick for days now, riding around on his Jet Ski, and it seemed to have lifted her spirits, the whole nonsense with the shark lies and Derrick's proclamation on the morning show apparently forgotten.

"Tonight is going to be so much fun!" she said as she came into his room.

"Sounds like you're in a good mood."

"I am." Lifting her arms above her head, she twirled around his room on her tiptoes. "I spent all afternoon practicing with Derrick, and I think our stunts are going to knock your socks off!"

"I can't wait to see it," Peter said, and he was surprised at his own sincerity. While it wasn't really his thing, Ricardo had vouched for the company sponsoring it. Apparently, he'd worked with them as one of his many jobs throughout high school.

Cassie stopped twirling and eyed his outfit, which included a polo shirt and khakis. "Aren't you a little dressed up for working the booth?"

"I'm not working tonight. Emily and Mom gave me the night off."

"Ooo, are you seeing Ricardo, then?"

Peter gave a nonchalant shrug. "Probably."

"Well, I still think you're overdoing it a bit. We're having crabs tonight, after all. You're gonna get covered in Old Bay."

He had to suppress a groan. As much as he enjoyed the Maryland staple, he didn't love the idea of working so hard for his food. That was one of the only things he and his father had agreed on, as Sean had preferred crabcakes to picking crabs.

"I'll see you downstairs." Cassie danced out the door.

With a wry smile, Peter shook his head at her antics.

A little while later, he joined his family in the living room. Emily and Mom had already loaded up the car with the last of the things they needed for their booth. Tony was meeting them there with some premade hors d'oeuvres, and he'd be working the grill for the night.

As they climbed into the car, Peter was filled with anticipation. Ricardo had texted earlier to say he had some news from his boss about the plans to buy Fiddler's Green. Peter hoped they'd get a moment alone away from his family to discuss it. Somehow it seemed too important to wait for their date.

When they arrived, he helped his family carry the keg and other alcohol to the booth. Cassie had planned another signature drink, this one called The Firecracker. It was a mix of a piña colada, a strawberry daiquiri, and a frozen Blue Hawaii, layered to form a red, white, and blue concoction. He expected it would sell well, given the patriotic holiday.

After everything was unloaded, he wandered around the setup, checking out other booths and keeping a watchful eye out for Ricardo. Just as he was about to head back to his family, someone tapped him on the shoulder.

Peter turned to see Ricardo. "I was looking for you."

"Well, here I am." Ricardo gestured to a picnic table. "Why don't we grab a snack and sit there."

They stopped at a booth selling fried cheese then brought their food back to the table. Peter snuck nervous glances around, hoping they were far enough away from his family that no one would overhear their conversation.

"So, I spoke to my boss, and he's open to the idea of incorporating some of Fiddler's Green's style into the new pub, but he needs to see it to get a feel for how to go about doing it. Is there any way you can get me some pictures without raising suspicion?"

To buy himself some time, Peter dipped a mozzarella stick into the marinara sauce and bit into it. The grease from the cheese flooded over his tongue. Then he said, "I'm sure I can make it work."

"Good." Ricardo reached into his pocket and pulled out a piece of paper. "Here's what we're prepared to offer your family."

The fried cheese seemed to lodge in his throat as he looked at how many zeros followed the first number. The offer was more than generous and would set his mother up nicely in her new life. Perhaps it was even enough to placate his sisters.

Ricardo chuckled. "I take it from your facial expression you're pleased."

"That's an understatement," Peter said once he'd recovered. "I don't see how my family could say no." Well, that wasn't completely true. Sentimentality held a lot of sway over the Gallaghers.

"Well, once you get the pictures, I can send them to my boss, and then we can start negotiations for how and when the sale will take place." Ricardo raised an eyebrow. "When do you think you'll share this with your family?"

"Share what with his family?" Cassie asked, making them both jump.

Peter grabbed the paper and slid it into his breast pocket. "N-Nothing. Why aren't you at the booth?"

"Mom sent me over here to ask you to come help out. We're swamped." Her eyes strayed to his pocket. "But what are you hiding?"

"It's none of your business," Peter snapped.

"Oh really? We'll see about that." She spun away from the table and raced back to their booth.

Oh no. Even though he was a full-grown adult, the very idea that his sister was about to tell on him still managed to strike fear in his heart. Peter jumped up and chased after her, ignoring Ricardo's protests.

"Mom!" Cassie shouted as she reached the booth.

Mom looked up, worry filling her blue eyes. "Cassie? What's wrong?"

"Nothing's wrong," Peter said quickly as he caught up to her.

"Peter is having clandestine meetings with Ricardo." Cassie's chin rose. "I think he's still planning on selling the pub."

"What?" Emily rushed over from the back of the booth. "Is that true?"

"N-No." Peter's heart pounded in his chest. "Cassie just misheard something Ricardo said and ran with it." Sweat built on his brow, and he tried to discreetly wipe it away. "You know how her imagination gets away from her sometimes."

That was the wrong thing to say. Cassie's eyes darkened. With one swift movement, she reached into his breast pocket and yanked out the paper. She scanned the numbers, and her mouth dropped open.

"Is that so? Then explain this!" With a triumphant look, she handed the paper to their mother.

Peter's heart sank. There was no way he could deny it now. And if the look on Mom's face was any indication, he was in deep trouble.

"Seriously, Peter? After everything Mr. Wakefield told us, you're still working with Ricardo? I can't believe you!" Emily shook her head and stomped away. Cassie bounced on her toes, as if she was debating between following Emily and watching Mom chew him out.

But Mom didn't look angry, just disappointed. "Why?" That one word from her was enough to cut him down to size.

"I just wanted to consider all of our options," he mumbled, staring at the ground.

Cassie clicked her tongue in disapproval then followed Emily, clearly deciding that comforting their sister was more important than enjoying his shame. When had she become the good sibling?

"I'm sorry, Mom. But let's be honest, the odds are stacked against us."

"Of course they are! You think I don't know that?" She crumpled up the paper and tossed it at him. "I just never thought you'd bet against your own family."

With that, she went back to work in the booth, leaving Peter standing on his own. He bowed his head, the guilt rushing over him. Clearly, he had underestimated just how much the pub meant to his family.

Chapter Twenty-Two

As things died down at their booth, Cassie left to find Derrick and a prime spot for the fireworks. She found him on the edge of the beach, having a heated discussion with someone she couldn't make out in the darkness. With bated breath, she inched closer, and the other person shifted into a stream of light coming off the road. It was Ryan.

"I have half a mind to revoke your permits," Ryan said, his voice rising.

"Oh, I'm sure the council would *love* that," Derrick said, leaning forward. "The town is barely making budget, and you want to kill a great source of revenue?"

"If they knew how many corners you cut, they wouldn't hesitate." Though it was hard to tell in the shadows, Ryan's face appeared to be tomato red. She'd never seen him so angry.

"It's not a big deal," Derrick said, waving a dismissive hand.

"You're putting lives at stake! Literally!"

"Chill out, dude. It's not that big of a deal."

"Not a big deal? It's against the law to jump another vessel's wake within one hundred feet."

Cassie's mouth dropped open. The jumps they'd been practicing for days were *illegal*?

"And who's going to measure it? You?" Derrick scoffed.

Ryan glowered at him. "I highly doubt that's necessary considering how close you're jumping. And none of you are even wearing PFDs!"

"Everyone on the team is a strong swimmer." Derrick put a hand on Ryan's shoulder. "Relax, man. It's all going to be fine."

Ryan shoved him. "Don't touch me."

"What's your problem?"

"You, you're my problem." Ryan got right in Derrick's face.

Having seen enough, Cassie rushed forward. "Hey, what's going on here?"

Both men took a step back, but they continued to glare at each other. With an exasperated sigh, Cassie moved between them.

"Derrick, why don't you go find us a seat for the fireworks? I need to talk to Ryan."

At first, she thought he wasn't going to listen to her as he refused to break eye contact with Ryan, but then he nodded and walked away. One problem down, Cassie spun to face Ryan.

"What was that all about?"

"I was expressing my concerns about the stunt show." Ryan crossed his arms and stared at the ground.

"And your concerns led you to almost knock Derrick out?"

His lips twitched. "I appreciate the vote of confidence, but that wasn't my intention."

"Then what was your intention?"

Rubbing a hand over his face, Ryan sighed. "I just want him to take more precautions. I thought I could appeal to his logical side, but frankly, I'm not sure he has one."

"Well, I do," Cassie said, gesturing to the sand. "So why don't we sit here, and you can tell me your concerns, and I can finally apologize for the shark story."

After a moment's hesitation, he nodded and sat down on the beach. "Do you want to go first or should I?"

"I will," she said then took a deep breath. "I'm sorry, Ryan. I should have said that a while ago, but honestly, I just couldn't face you. When

Emily told me you were planning on petitioning the city council for a warning system, I felt awful. I never expected the lie to turn into the mess it did, and I'm so sorry for dragging you, the town... everyone into it."

He gave her a small smile. "Thank you. I appreciate your apology." His face fell. "But I have to tell you that I was sorely disappointed. I expected that kind of thing from Derrick, but not from you. I thought you were better than that."

She swallowed and lowered her gaze. "I know. I have no excuse for my behavior. I never should have agreed to keep the truth a secret in the first place, let alone perpetuate the lie so openly."

Ryan was silent, which just added to the weight of her guilt.

"I understand if you can't forgive me."

"I wish you had come to me sooner. We could have avoided a lot of unnecessary drama if you had even just told me the truth privately." He placed a tentative hand on her arm. "But I was really proud of you for coming forward and owning your mistake. That took guts."

"I'd love to take credit for it," she said with a bitter laugh. "But Emily threatened to expose me if I didn't admit to the lie, so I wasn't as brave as you may think."

"Still, you accepted responsibility and did what you could to make it right. I can respect that."

She cleared her throat, hoping to shift the conversation. "So, tell me about the safety concerns."

"Jumping Jet Skis is dangerous under normal circumstances, especially with as close as you all have been practicing, but there's a hurricane coming up the coastline. It's not predicted to make landfall, but it might make the surf rough for several days." He blew out his breath. "I get that that may up the ante of the stunts and make them more impressive, but I wish Derrick would take more precautions to keep everyone safe."

She sat there a moment, absorbing everything he'd said. "And what was that about PFD?"

"Personal flotation devices. My understanding is that some of you are foregoing them to increase the thrill."

Her teeth worried her lower lip. What he said was true. Darryl had watched one too many *Jackass* movies and seemed to think personal safety equipment was an affront to his brand.

"I'm actually one of the ones who isn't wearing one."

Ryan's eyes widened in horror. "Cassie. No, that's too dangerous."

"But as he said, I can swim."

"Not in that surf! Even the strongest swimmers would struggle with the undertow. God knows if there will be riptides too. Please promise me you'll wear a life jacket." He grabbed her hand in both of his and squeezed tight. Her mouth fell open in surprise. He'd never touched her like that before, with so much feeling. The warmth of his hand spread up her arm, filling her chest.

"I promise." And she meant it. In that moment, she would do anything he asked of her, which surprised her.

As if he realized how intensely he was holding her, he let go and dropped his gaze. "Thank you. Please... try to talk some sense into him."

"I will," she said. He raised his eyes to meet hers again, and the intensity there took her breath away. Part of her knew she needed to leave, to go find Derrick, but the other part didn't want to, and she wasn't sure how to feel about that.

"I should go," he said, rising to his feet. He held out a hand to help her up. "I've got some mayoral duties to attend to."

With a quick nod, Cassie jumped up and hurried away. But she didn't immediately return to Derrick. She needed a moment to process whatever had just happened with Ryan.

She walked down to the shoreline and stepped into the tide, enjoying the water's cool caress. Maybe the calming influence of the ocean would help alleviate the storm of emotions swirling within her.

When she and Ryan had decorated the pub together, something had stirred inside her, but she'd refused to acknowledge it. He wasn't her type. And yet... It had bothered her more than she wanted to admit how much she had missed him after the truth about the shark story had come to light. She was glad they'd at least cleared the air; she just wished it hadn't come with complicated feelings. His pride at her coming clean, even if she couldn't quite call it bravery, had touched her heart. Then there was the way he'd looked at her tonight. Derrick had never once looked at her that way. Not even when he called her his girlfriend.

So, okay, obviously her feelings for Ryan went deeper than she'd wanted to acknowledge. But that didn't mean she had to act on them. At the same time, she found herself more disillusioned with Derrick than ever. While once upon a time, he might have been her dream guy, if she was honest with herself, he wasn't quite as dreamy as she remembered. Ryan's warning spun around in her head. Derrick had said the stunt show would help with tourism, but the risks he was taking seemed to be less about the town and more about Derrick's ego.

Well, she'd promised Ryan she would talk to Derrick. Maybe he would listen to her. They were together, after all. At least, for the time being.

Peter stood in front of the full-length mirror in his childhood bedroom, buttoning up a dark-blue shirt. His black hair was still damp from a shower, which surprised him considering how long it had taken to choose an outfit. He grimaced at his reflection. It was just a date. Nothing to get worked up over. Though it had been a while since he'd been on a date. There was also the fact that this felt like so much more than a first date, but even still, he shouldn't be so nervous.

Peter grabbed his wallet and shoved it into the back pocket of his khakis. He left his room and glanced over at Cassie's door. His family had barely spoken to him since they'd found out about Ricardo's offer, and he couldn't blame them. Although he'd apologized profusely, actions spoke louder than words, and the only way to lay their animosity to rest would be to call off the deal with Ricardo. That was something he planned to discuss with him over dinner.

The doorbell rang, and Peter's heart fluttered in his chest. Ricardo stood on the porch in a black leather jacket with his dark hair slicked back and a playful grin on his handsome face.

"You look good," Ricardo said as the front door shut behind them.

Peter met Ricardo's eye as he tried to ignore the warmth flooding his cheeks. "So do you."

"Shall we?" Ricardo gestured to his rental car.

They walked over and climbed in.

"So, where are we going?" Peter asked.

Ricardo gave an enigmatic grin. "You'll see." He backed out of the driveway and drove down Main Street. As they passed the pub, Peter felt a pang of guilt in his stomach. The parking lot was full. Despite his doubts, his sister's plans with Anna Mae truly seemed to be paying off.

When they continued over the two-lane bridge, Peter glanced at Ricardo. There wasn't much on this side of the bay, as far as he was aware. Then again, he'd only been back for brief visits over the last few years while completing his education. Things might have built up in his absence.

Ricardo pulled onto a side street, and Peter peered out the window, trying to decipher where they were. He'd never been to this part of town before. Bright lights shone through the encroaching trees, and a moment later, a well-lit building came into view. A multicolored sign blazed with the words "Cantina de Vida."

"I thought I'd introduce you to a bit of my culture." Ricardo parked the car. "I hope you like Mexican."

Peter swallowed. Did Ricardo mean the food or...? He nodded, afraid of what might come out of his mouth if he dared open it.

They entered the restaurant, and Peter took in the elaborate color scheme—blinding shades of blue, loud reds, neon greens, and brilliant yellows. A mural of mermaids with sugar skulls for faces covered one wall and extended to the ceiling. Peter had never seen anything quite like it.

"Beautiful, isn't it?" Ricardo asked.

"Very. How did you find this place?"

Ricardo shrugged. "I do my research. It's been on my list to visit, and this seemed the perfect opportunity."

He took Peter's hand and led him to the host stand, where a young man who couldn't have been more than sixteen was staring at his phone. He looked up as they approached.

"Seating for two, please," Ricardo said.

Peter continued to allow his gaze to wander over the decor. Who knew such a place existed so close to sleepy little Blue Heron Bay?

"If I'd known I was going to have competition for your attention, I would have chosen a less artistic location," Ricardo said, interrupting his thoughts.

"Sorry." Peter laughed. "It's just like one of those pictures that the more you stare at it, the more you notice."

"I'll take your word for it," Ricardo said, never taking his eyes from Peter's.

The intensity in Ricardo's gaze did nothing to calm Peter's erratic heartbeat. He cleared his throat. "Have you updated your boss on what's happening with the Steele/Wakefield partnership?"

"Not yet." Ricardo leaned back with a frown. "We're supposed to talk again on Monday." He shook his head. "But let's set aside the business talk for a moment. Tell me more about yourself."

"What do you want to know?"

"Why did you decide to go so far away for school?"

"Well, I got my bachelor's and master's in South Carolina via full scholarships to both. When it was time for my doctorate, the University of California offered me the most money."

"You must be pretty smart, then, to have gone so far in school without taking on significant debt."

Peter shrugged. "I was always a good student."

"You're being modest." Ricardo leaned forward. "You didn't get to be valedictorian of our class by simply being a *good* student. Some subjects may have come easily for you, but it probably took a lot of hard work and studying. And as I recall, you were also in a ton of clubs and ran track as well." He shook his head. "I'm not sure how you managed it all."

"It was a long time ago." Peter shifted in his seat. "Besides, you were a lacrosse star. Didn't that earn you a few scholarships?"

"Sure, but not a full ride. I'll be paying my student loans well into my twilight years." Ricardo flashed a grin. "Do you think you'll move back here when you graduate?"

"I haven't decided yet. It'll depend on where I get a job." He folded his hands on the table. "But I doubt it. I like it out there." He gestured to Ricardo. "What about you? Would you move back here?"

"It'd be nice to be close to my mom, but I travel so much, it likely wouldn't matter." Ricardo leaned forward. "But if I found the right place... maybe someone worth settling down with, I could be persuaded to find somewhere to call home."

Peter was saved from replying by the appearance of the server, but his insides were all a-flutter. They placed their orders, and Peter worked to get control of himself.

"Do you think you'll find a job in the government?" Ricardo asked when they were alone again.

"I'm more interested in a nonprofit. The government, even local, is so limited in what it can do. There's so much red tape. Nonprofits struggle with funding, which can limit their ability to make a difference, but that's where I'd do the most good."

"Any particular place in mind?"

Peter shook his head. "I have a few places I think would be a good fit. My plan is to start applying in the new year and have something lined up by the time I graduate."

"And then you'll change the world?" Ricardo said, his tone teasing.

"I wouldn't go that far," Peter said with a chuckle. "But I do hope to help as many people as I can. Housing is a tremendous problem, but there's such a stigma assigned to the homeless."

"I admire you for your optimism and desire to help." Ricardo rested his elbows on the table. "I've been pitching more locations lately to my boss that would boost the small-town economy, but sometimes I wish we did more for the communities we build in."

"You mean, other than shutter small businesses?"

"That's not the goal," Ricardo said. He sighed. "But it happens."

"Might I suggest altering your business model?" Peter leaned back in his chair.

"How do you mean?"

"Don't seek out small, struggling towns. Or, if you do, try to partner with the businesses instead of replacing them."

"It's not like we set out to put places out of business," Ricardo said in protest. "It's just a natural consequence. Our resorts provide everything a person needs." He tapped his fingers as he listed them off. "Dining, shopping, entertainment. So our clientele tends to remain on-site, which means the town sees more tourism, but other businesses don't benefit from it."

"Right, but maybe if you contracted with the small businesses to bring them under your umbrella? Then it's still a part of your resort. You're still offering customers what they want, but in a way that protects the autonomy of the business."

Ricardo shook his head. "My boss prefers to work with known entities. If a business is already struggling, is it because of a lack of tourism or because it's poorly run? Besides, there is a risk of lost revenue because we wouldn't own all the restaurants and stores outright."

"True. But if you create an affiliate program instead of bulldozing any business that tries to compete, it might also make your proposal more palatable to local governments that are averse to development."

The scent and sound of Peter's sizzling fajitas warned him of their food's arrival before it reached the table. The smell of sauteed onions, peppers, and well-seasoned grilled chicken hit his nose and caused his mouth to water. Ricardo had ordered the carne asada platter. Together, their food took up every bit of space on the table.

"So, how would that look for Fiddler's Green if we still opened a hotel here?" Ricardo asked as he dug into his steak.

Peter filled a tortilla with meat, veggies, and toppings before he responded. "We'd have to agree upon the terms, but I assume we'd model it after other similar affiliation programs. There would be some sort of incentive, both for our respective companies and the customers, for participating in the affiliate program." He took a bite of his fajita and savored the way the spices warmed his mouth. "And that might help offset some of the concern over lost revenue because you'd still be getting some sort of financial incentive or commission from the referral."

Ricardo's lips pulled up in a sexy grin. "I love the way you preface all of this with 'we.'"

Heat crept up Peter's neck, and he struggled with how to respond to that. "I, uh, well, I mean—"

Ricardo chuckled. "It's just a nice thought." He cleared his throat. "I see your point, but it'd be a hard sell for my boss. While the goal has never been to put places out of business, he hasn't minded that inevitable consequence when we've opened in small towns before. He prefers full control of everything offered at the resort."

"Think of all the money it would save your company if you didn't have to do it all yourselves. You could still offer a lot of the resort activities and options but at a reduced upfront cost, especially with an affiliate program."

"How do you mean?"

"Well, you'd build a smaller hotel, for starters." Peter took a sip of his margarita. "And you wouldn't have to build up the restaurants, stores, or activity offerings right away. For instance, in addition to partnering with restaurants through an affiliate program, you could partner with spas, hair salons, movie theaters, and other such businesses to give the customers a variety of choices with less front-loading for you in the beginning. Then, if the affiliates aren't performing as you'd like, you can choose to build your own amenities later."

They ate in silence for a while as Ricardo appeared to mull over Peter's idea. It didn't seem like that outlandish of a concept, as there were several rewards programs that included affiliates. But Peter understood the advantage of owning everything offered at a resort. For one, it was easier to maintain a certain standard.

Taking a deep breath, Peter went in for the real reason for his alternative suggestion. "Is there any chance you'd consider not building a resort in Blue Heron Bay?"

Ricardo rubbed a hand over his face. "I pitched this idea to my boss as a way to help my mom and give back to my hometown. I would hate to walk away when I'm so close to building something that I believe will do a lot of good. Besides, it wouldn't be good for my career to pull out now." His eyebrows drew together. "Why do you ask?"

"As I'm sure you gathered, after Cassie overheard us on the Fourth of July, my family has been pretty angry with me. There's no way they'll sell now." Peter sighed. "While I still think selling should be an option, it's not the right time."

Ricardo nodded. "I get it, and I don't want to run your family out of business, either." He drummed his fingers on the table. "Look, I'll tell you what, if Wakefield decides to move forward, I'll withdraw my pitch and propose another option instead."

"Thank you!" Peter exclaimed. "If I can help in any way, please let me know."

"Aside from finding a job," Ricardo said, clearly hoping to change the subject, "what do you plan to do with all your free time after you graduate?"

Get to know you better. Thankfully Peter managed to engage the filter between his brain and his mouth, and he took another sip of his margarita before responding.

"I have a few ideas."

"I hope I'm in some of them." Ricardo winked, sending Peter's heart into overdrive.

After they finished their meal, Ricardo took Peter's hand as they left the restaurant. When Peter started heading back to the rental car, Ricardo pulled him back.

"We're just getting started," Ricardo said, pulling Peter into his arms.

"Oh? What did you have in mind?"

"How do you feel about... dancing?"

"Dancing?" Peter tilted his head. "What kind of dancing?"

"The best dancing there is. Salsa!" Ricardo led him to the building next door. Beside the restaurant was a nightclub, Rueda de Fuego. Peter's mouth went dry, and his hands grew clammy. He'd never been salsa dancing before, and the last thing he wanted to do was look like an idiot in front of Ricardo.

"What's wrong?" Ricardo turned to look at him, but Peter avoided his eyes.

"Nothing, it's just, um, getting late, don't you think?"

Ricardo's face fell. "Oh, I didn't think it was that late. Did you want to go home?"

Peter sighed and dragged a hand through his thick hair. "It's not that. I—salsa dancing. I've, uh, never been."

"I see." Ricardo's eyes danced with amusement. "Well, if you're open to learning something new, I'd love to teach you."

"I'm afraid I have two left feet."

"I don't mind if you step on a few toes. It's why I have ten of them."

The idea of spending the rest of the evening in Ricardo's arms was tempting. Peter's only experience with dancing was from prom, and it wasn't something he liked to dwell on. But he could tell this was something Ricardo enjoyed.

"Okay. I'll give it a shot."

"Fantastic!" Ricardo grabbed his hand and pulled him toward the door. "You won't regret it."

They entered the club, and Peter's senses were immediately overwhelmed. Latin music pounded through the speakers, and an elaborate light show illuminated the dance floor. The air was warm and tinged with the scent of sweat. Quite a few other couples were already dancing. Peter swallowed thickly. Why had he agreed to this? Ricardo was going to be so embarrassed when he saw how much rhythm Peter lacked.

"You'll be fine," Ricardo shouted over the music, a gleam in his eye. He pulled Peter onto the dance floor and spun him around. Peter stood there facing him, unsure what to do and trying to tamp down the growing panic churning in his stomach. Those fajitas weren't such a good idea. If he'd known they were going to be physically active afterward, he might have chosen a lighter meal.

Ricardo put his arm around Peter's waist and grasped his left hand. He instructed Peter to step back on his left foot as Ricardo stepped forward on his right. The feel of Ricardo's hand on him and their close proximity messed with Peter's head. He struggled to concentrate on Ricardo's instructions, mumbling apologies every time he misstepped. But Ricardo's patience never faltered, and eventually, Peter had grasped enough of the steps to follow Ricardo's lead. He also had a new appreciation for female dancers as he wasn't used to doing everything backward, but at least he didn't have to do the steps in heels.

As the second song ended, Ricardo stepped away from him. "Need a break?"

Peter nodded, and Ricardo led the way to the bar. He ordered two margaritas and two waters. They settled onto bar stools and watched the other couples dance while they waited for their drinks.

"So, how bad was I?" Peter asked.

"You're a fast learner," Ricardo said with a smile. "Before you know it, I'll be spinning you all over the dance floor like that lady."

Peter followed his gaze to a blond woman in a red dress and stilettos who was, indeed, being spun around on the dance floor by her partner, a dark-haired man dressed in all black. He couldn't imagine he'd ever accomplish those moves, but he appreciated Ricardo's confidence in him.

Their drinks arrived, and Peter downed the water first. Even from the basic moves Ricardo had taught him, he was out of breath. He wasn't sure how much of that had to do with the dancing versus being in Ricardo's arms.

Ricardo finished his margarita and set the glass back on the bar. "Ready for round two?"

"Let's go!" Peter said with feigned enthusiasm, grabbing Ricardo's hand and pulling him to the dance floor.

Chapter Twenty-Three

C ASSIE WALKED INTO THE KITCHEN TO FIND HER BROTHER brewing coffee. They hadn't spoken since she'd discovered he was still plotting with Ricardo to take over the pub. Part of her wanted to go back upstairs and hide until he was gone, but she decided against it. After all, *she* hadn't done anything wrong.

"How was your date?" She tried to keep the venom out of her voice as she leaned against the counter.

Peter glanced up warily. "It went well." After pouring a cup of coffee, he reached into the cabinet and got her a mug too. "I told him I didn't want to move forward on selling the pub."

That wasn't what she'd expected to hear, but she kept her expression neutral. "Oh? How'd he take that?"

"He understood, though he isn't sure his boss will be willing to scrap the proposal." Peter carried his mug to the table and sat down. "But he promised he'd talk to his boss tomorrow. He'll stop by trivia afterward to give me an update."

"I suppose that's something," Cassie said, though she wasn't convinced.

"Look, I know I upset you all, but I promise, I'm on board with saving it. And now that my dissertation is done, I'll have more time to devote to the effort."

She lifted her coffee and took a sip, letting the warmth and caffeine flow through her. It was exactly the wake-up she needed.

"Thanks for the coffee," she said, sitting down opposite him. "I'm glad you've seen the light."

Peter chuckled. "I guess that's one way of putting it."

While she was still concerned that Peter and Ricardo were in cahoots, curiosity got the best of her. "Your date must have been pretty boring if all you did was discuss the resort's potential deal."

"That's not all we did," Peter said, ducking his head.

"What else did you do?"

At first, he stared at the table, and she wondered if he would respond. They'd never been very close, so she wouldn't blame him if he wanted to save the juicy details for Emily. But then a warm smile broke over his face.

"He took me salsa dancing."

Her eyebrows shot up. "Wow! Wait, is there salsa dancing nearby?"

"Surprisingly, yes. There's a place right across the bridge."

"Who knew?" She shook her head. "Did you step on his feet?"

Peter's eyes darkened. "No, though..." His ears turned pink. "There were a few close calls."

She laughed. "I've been a couple of times in the city. It's a lot of fun once you get the hang of it."

They continued to chat about his experience. For what felt like the first time ever, their conversation was pleasant without a hint of an argument. Cassie wasn't sure what to think. Most of her life, she'd been on the outside looking in on her siblings' close relationship. She'd resented it at first and then accepted it as just the way of things. To be forming her own bonds with her siblings now was both strange and welcome. She only wished it hadn't taken her father's death and a threat to his legacy to bring the changes about.

~

Can't make trivia. Explain later.

Emily swallowed her disappointment as she put her phone into her back pocket. She hadn't seen Anna Mae since their last meeting at Grounded. Despite her assurances that she wasn't giving up on Wakefield Hotel Group building in Blue Heron Bay, Emily couldn't help her pessimistic attitude. The town was a huge risk, and she understood why Mr. Wakefield wanted to go into it with a partner.

"You look like your dog just died." Cassie came out from behind the bar with a hand on her hip. "Which is weird since, as far as I know, you don't have a dog. What's up?"

Emily licked her lips, trying to moisten them, but her mouth was dry. "Nothing. I'm fine." She turned back to the table she was setting to avoid Cassie's scrutiny.

Her sister didn't take the hint. "Not buying it. I'm a better people reader than you and Peter give me credit for." She pulled Emily around to face her. "What's wrong?"

Emily sighed. "It's Anna Mae. She's just been busy with the hotel."

"I was surprised not to see her here tonight," Cassie said with a nod. "But that's a good sign, right? Her father hasn't pulled up anchor and moved on to a different city."

Cassie's face was so full of optimism Emily couldn't bear to burst her bubble. She forced a smile. "Yeah, it's good news."

"And I'm sure once they've hashed out all the details, she'll come rushing back here so you can moon over each other."

Heat rose in Emily's cheeks as she dropped her gaze. "We don't 'moon' over each other."

"Oh please," Cassie scoffed. "Between you and Anna Mae and Peter and Ricardo, I'm surrounded by lovebirds."

"Speaking of, where's Derrick this evening?"

Cassie lowered her head. "He's busy with the stunt show."

"How's that going?"

"Fine, I guess." While Cassie gave her signature one-shoulder shrug, something seemed off.

"Do you want to talk about it?"

"Not really."

"Is everything ready for trivia?" Emily asked, changing the subject.

"Think so," Cassie said. "I've got the questions and answers loaded into the system, and Peter's checking the sound." She gestured to the bar. "I spent the afternoon experimenting on a new signature drink. I think you're going to love it."

"What's it called?"

"Black-Eyed Raven!"

Emily raised an eyebrow. "Dare I ask what's in it?"

"It's actually the perfect beach summer combo," Cassie said. "It's got pineapple juice, blue curaçao, vodka, simple syrup, and rum." She grinned. "A tropical, beachy vibe that's such a dark purple, it looks almost black."

"I'll take your word for it." Emily shook her head. She wasn't sure where Cassie came up with these ideas, but they'd been a hit so far with their customers, so she couldn't complain.

"Trust me." Cassie walked back over to the bar, and Emily followed. "I was thinking we should add a wet T-shirt contest to our karaoke night."

"Yeah, I don't think that'll go over well with Mom."

"Well, it was worth a shot," Cassie said with a grin. "We need something to keep things fresh."

Emily gnawed on her bottom lip. Cassie had a point. They'd had quite the turnout for the first karaoke night. But if they didn't have any new song options, people might get bored and leave early, assuming they showed up at all.

"I'll talk to Anna Mae about it. See if she has any ideas."

Cassie nodded. Emily took a seat on a bar stool while her sister set up for the evening. The dining area was ready. Peter was messing around with the sound system on the other side of the room, lost in his own little world. He'd been in a good mood ever since his date.

"What do you think about Peter and Ricardo?" Emily asked, keeping her voice low. While she was happy for her brother, she still didn't trust Ricardo.

"Like I said, lovebirds." Cassie smirked. "Why do you ask?"

"I don't know," Emily murmured. "I know you told me that Peter is no longer trying to sell the pub to Ricardo behind our backs, but I'm still nervous about their relationship."

"You worry too much." Her sister rolled her eyes. "I've never understood why Ricardo's company wants to open a resort here, anyway. It's not the most exciting of locations."

"There's less competition here than trying to build one in Ocean City."

"I guess." Cassie didn't sound convinced. "But I wouldn't worry about it. Peter said he would convince Ricardo to reconsider building here, and I have no doubt he'll try."

"I suppose." Emily sighed. Cassie's dismissive attitude toward their tiny town brought up other concerns. If it wasn't a profitable venture for Ricardo's company, then what hope did Emily have that Anna Mae could convince her father of its potential?

"You're worrying about it, aren't you?" Cassie leaned across the counter and peered into Emily's face.

"Just a little," Emily said with a laugh. "Though it's more about the other thing you said."

Cassie frowned. "What thing did I say?"

"About it not being an exciting or profitable location. I'm afraid Anna Mae's father would agree with you."

"Tsk-tsk, such little faith. They're not really the same. For starters, a boutique hotel doesn't have the same profit margin to hit as a huge resort." Cassie pulled a wineglass down from above the bar and poured more than the standard five ounces of red wine into it. She pushed it toward Emily. "You need this."

"I've gotta serve tonight," Emily protested. "I can't drink this now."

"I disagree, but you don't have to chug it. Just take a few sips to settle your nerves."

Emily grimaced but did as Cassie suggested. Cassie's extended college program had kept her in the mindset of a young coed well beyond what was acceptable. *Chugging, indeed.* But Emily had to admit her sister was right. As she savored the subtle hints of blackberry and the full-bodied feel in her mouth, the tightness in her chest eased.

"Better?"

"Surprisingly, yes."

Cassie harrumphed. "Yes, because it's so shocking I could possibly be right about something."

Emily ignored the sarcastic tone as she took the glass of wine and went to do one last walk-through of the dining area. She was sure the night would be another success. The question was, would it be enough?

Satisfied there was nothing left for her to do at the front of the house, Emily went back to Mom's office. Her mother was staring at a spreadsheet and glanced up when she entered.

"These event nights have really made a difference," her mother said as she beckoned Emily into the room. "I don't know how I'll ever thank you kids for all you've done, or your friend Anna, for that matter."

Emily hid a smile. "We're happy to help."

Mom eyed the wineglass in her hand. "Starting a little early, aren't we?"

"Cassie." Emily said it like an expletive instead of a name.

"She's good at her job." Mom laughed. She met Emily's gaze with a speculative look in her eye. "Speaking of, has Ryan stopped by to see her?"

"I'm not sure, but I don't know if he'll bother. It seems like a lost cause."

"Too bad." Mom shook her head and dropped her gaze. "He's such a nice young man."

Somehow *young* was not the word Emily expected Cassie would use to describe him, but she kept that to herself. "It's unfortunate but unsurprising. She says he's not her type."

"What about you? Is Anna your type?"

Emily shifted in her chair, not sure she wanted to have this conversation. "It's Anna *Mae*, Mom. And we're still figuring things out."

Her mother leaned back in her chair, and Emily tried not to squirm under her scrutiny. "You seem... lighter when she's around. Freer."

"I'm not sure what you mean." Emily blinked innocently at her mother, but inside, her stomach churned.

"Don't give me those doe eyes. I'm your mother, and I know you. She's good for you. Brings you out of your shell."

She'd always seen right through Emily, through all of them, really. Her mother used to claim she got a "mother's handbook" when Emily was born, and she said it had been updated to accommodate her children's needs and unique quirks over the years. Emily assumed it was more maternal intuition.

"All right," her mother said when Emily didn't respond. "I won't press. But I hope you'll keep your heart open. You know how much it would mean to me to see you settled."

"I'm well aware." Emily forced a smile. Her mother had been pestering her about settling down for about five years, since she'd turned twenty-five. She'd tried to explain things had changed and people were marrying later in life, but her mother wouldn't hear it. Emily suspected a desire for grandchildren was behind her mother's pushing. But her mother was more likely to get them from Cassie than Emily or Peter. As much as she loved teaching, Emily appreciated that, at the end of the day, the children didn't follow her home. And Peter, well, Emily wasn't sure what his stance was on children, but somehow, she didn't think they were in his plans either.

The bells over the pub door jingled, and Emily bent down to plant a swift kiss on her mother's cheek before she headed back to the dining room.

An enormous group of university students had arrived together, clearly excited for another night of fun trivia. Emily walked up to them with a warm smile.

"Are you playing individually or in teams?" she asked.

"Teams," a blond woman said. She stepped to the side, followed by a young man with glasses and a petite woman with auburn hair and a bright-green shirt. The others in her party split off into groups of three, and Emily led them to a set of tables near each other. She took their drink orders and approached Cassie.

"Looks like a great group already!" Cassie grinned. The entire table had ordered the Black-Eyed Raven. Clearly, they were familiar with Cassie's crazy concoctions.

"I guess you're famous," Emily teased.

Cassie's smile faded as she set several glasses on the counter. "At least this time it's not for being saved from not-sharks."

"Well, you were never quite cut out to play the role of a damsel in distress, so I'd say this is a step up for fame."

"That's true." Cassie poured various spirits into the shaker and mixed them together before straining the cocktail into a glass. "Though I'm not sure how much a 'step up' alcohol is."

"Don't sell yourself short." Emily gestured to the dining area, which was filling up with more customers. "I'm not sure if the trivia questions or the drinks are what's bringing people back." She put the drinks on her tray and carried them over to the tables. Then she moved on to seat the next set of customers.

Peter had stopped messing with the sound system and was helping to seat and serve as well. They passed each other in the dining room.

"Maybe your crazy plan will work after all," he called.

"Or maybe it wasn't so crazy to begin with!" she shot back.

He grinned and continued to the bar to put in his drink orders.

Whether this would save the pub, and by extension the town, Emily didn't know. But one thing she was sure of: her siblings were amazing. Although it had taken Peter time to come around to the idea of saving the pub, she was convinced he was fully on board now. Calling them both home had been the best decision she'd made.

Chapter Twenty-Four

CASSIE WAS SUPER PLEASED BY ALL THE DRINK ORDERS FOR not only that night's signature drink but for her creations from previous nights as well. Emily's comment about her fame brought a smile to her face as she filled order after order. She was having so much fun that she almost forgot about her mixed-up emotions.

Almost. She could compartmentalize enough to get through her shifts, but it was always there. Derrick hadn't been any more open to the suggestion of taking more precautions when she'd suggested it than when Ryan had. In fact, it had led to an argument, and they weren't speaking at the moment. It made practices awkward, and if the show weren't bringing in so many tourists, she would quit.

Then there was Ryan. He hadn't stopped by the bar recently. She thought after she'd apologized that things would go back to normal.

Emily appeared and picked up the tray. "It's a madhouse out there." She headed back into the fray.

"Wait," Cassie called. "Have you seen Ryan?"

"'Fraid not."

Her sister rushed off to serve the next round of drinks. Cassie's teeth worried her lower lip as she tried to ignore her roiling stomach.

Maybe he was busy, mayoral duties and all that. But she feared he was avoiding her. She'd blown him off so many times. Perhaps he'd decided to lie low until after the summer was over, when she would be back in the city. Her heart sank. He'd checked in on her mother regularly since her father died. She hated the notion that she might be the reason he'd changed his routine, especially since her mother looked forward to his visits.

A sudden shout interrupted her thoughts. Ricardo was standing with her brother by the MC podium they'd set up on one side of the bar, and neither of them looked happy. Peter's face was redder than Cassie had ever seen it, and whatever he'd said to Ricardo only set his mouth in a grim line.

Cassie left the bar and went over just as Emily walked up as well. The pub was still packed, but her concern for her brother overcame what little work ethic she possessed.

"What's going on?" Emily asked, swiveling her head back and forth between the two men.

"He," Peter said, jabbing a finger in Ricardo's direction, "is a liar."

"I didn't *lie*," Ricardo said. "I just didn't tell you the whole truth."

"Lying by omission is still lying!" Peter shot back.

"Wait," Cassie said. "Is this about the resort?" She glanced at Peter, whose fists were clenched at his sides.

He nodded.

"Call it what you want." Ricardo sneered. "I did speak to my boss about pursuing other opportunities, but I didn't dissuade him from Blue Heron Bay."

"So, you lied," Peter said through clenched teeth.

"I did *not* lie. I told you if Wakefield moved forward, I would withdraw my pitch. My understanding is Steele Hotels has shot down the partnership, so Wakefield is pulling out. Which means it's the perfect opportunity for my company." Ricardo ran a frustrated hand through his dark hair. "You don't understand the pressure I'm under. Beyond the opportunities this deal will offer my mother, this is my big chance to make something of myself. There's a management position opening at my company, and this is my shot to prove I can handle the promotion." He shook his head. "I'm not willing to jeopardize that, not even for you."

Emily sucked in a breath, and Cassie moved closer to her sister. The news was not at all what she'd been expecting, and from the way Peter was shaking, he clearly hadn't expected it either.

"I can't believe I ever trusted you." Peter's voice rose with his rage. "You haven't changed one bit since high school. Still only looking out for yourself."

"That's not fair!" Ricardo shouted.

"What about the pub? What's going to happen to it?" Emily asked, her voice barely above a whisper.

"I don't know," Ricardo said, and some of the fire left his eyes. He turned to Cassie and Emily. "Please believe my company doesn't intend to put your pub out of business, but unfortunately, I can't guarantee its survival once the resort is in place."

"What about the affiliate program?" Peter stepped forward. "Did you bring up that suggestion with your boss, or was your interest in that all an act as well?"

"Believe it or not, I did pitch my boss on that idea." Ricardo crossed his arms over his chest. "But he didn't think it would be good for our bottom line, especially as we already have a deal with an Irish pub chain. You know that if your mom sells the pub, your family could make a great deal of money. And the offer to incorporate aspects of Fiddler's Green still stands."

"It's not about the money." Emily glared at him. "This is our father's legacy. It's all we have left of him, and we will not give it up without a fight."

"I'd reconsider that, if I were you," Ricardo said. "Once the resort is operational, it's likely to further exacerbate your situation. And if we can't move our partner into this space, then I expect we'll either find another location or build one, and at that point, this pub will become obsolete." He looked at each of them. "At least if you accept my offer, your mother will have a nice nest egg for her retirement."

The volume in the pub increased as the customers grew restless for the next round of trivia, and probably another round of drinks as well. Cassie glanced at her siblings, unsure what their next course of action should be.

"I really am sorry," Ricardo said. "But I wanted to tell you now before we approach the town council with a deal."

"Whatever. Just get out." Peter pointed at the door.

Ricardo stared at Peter for a moment, as if he was hoping he'd say something more, but Peter refused to meet his gaze. With a frustrated sigh, he spun on his heel and stomped out of the pub.

Emily moaned. "What are we going to do?"

"We'll have to figure that out later." Peter nodded to the dining area. "For now, we need to move on with the event."

They went back to their respective positions, or maybe *battle stations* was a better description. Cassie had a whole slew of drink orders waiting for her, and she got right to work, hoping to distract herself from the kerfuffle they had found themselves in.

Every free moment she could find, Emily texted Anna Mae. As Peter read out the latest question, she took advantage of the lull in orders to check her phone. Still no response. She tried to swallow her frustration, but it got stuck in her throat. Anna Mae had never been this difficult to reach before, and Emily tried to quell her nerves as her insecurity reared its ugly head. *Is Anna Mae with Leslie? Is that why she isn't responding?*

Leslie had never hidden her interest, and while Anna Mae had sworn to Emily that things were over between them, they had to spend a lot of time together to negotiate the deal. Had Anna Mae changed her mind? Emily squeezed her eyes shut, willing herself to calm down. Even if that were the case, Anna Mae wasn't the sneaking-around type. If she'd decided to give Leslie a second chance, she would tell Emily.

Or at least, Emily assumed she would, but the truth was, they'd only known each other for a couple of months. For all she knew, Anna Mae had left a trail of broken hearts in her wake and Emily was simply the latest to get burned.

She shoved her phone back in her pocket and forced herself to focus. Right now, the most important thing was dealing with the latest threat to her family's pub, and that was Ricardo's resort. If Anna Mae had abandoned their efforts, then Emily and her siblings would have to soldier on without her, regardless of how much it hurt.

"According to legend, in Bob Dylan's song 'Country Roads,' what Maryland road is he referring to?" Peter asked the remaining two teams of trivia contestants.

A young woman at the table nearest Emily started humming the tune, careful not to say the words out loud lest the other team overhear. Her black brows pulled together in confusion, and she whispered to her teammates. Emily hid a smile. The question was tricky because the song was entirely about West Virginia, but the legend was that Dylan and his co-writers had actually written it about Clopper Road in Maryland.

It didn't stump the other table though. A moment later, they submitted their answer.

"And we have a winner! Congrats to the Cool Crustaceans, you are our winners for trivia night!" Peter called out.

The bar erupted into cheers, as well as a few good-natured boos from the losing team. Emily went to help Peter and Cassie hand out the prizes, pleased with the success of another event. If nothing else, Anna Mae had shown Emily the power of marketing, and she'd learned enough to run a campaign on her own.

After the customers had left, the Gallagher siblings set about cleaning up. Emily had cleared most of the plates before the final round of trivia, and Cassie had shut down the bar after last call. Peter moved through the dining area with determined purpose, clearly still processing his argument with Ricardo.

With everything going on, they hadn't had a moment to sit down and discuss things, but as the dining room came back together from the chaos of the event, it wouldn't be long. Sure enough, Peter finished sweeping and slammed the broom against the wall.

"We need to talk," he said.

"Should I get Mom?" Cassie asked, gesturing toward the back office.

Emily nodded. "She needs to hear this too."

She pulled out a chair at a table in the middle of the dining area and sat down. Peter sat beside her. A moment later, Mom and Cassie joined them.

"So, what exactly did Ricardo say?" Mom asked, worry lines creasing her forehead.

"He spoke to his boss about other opportunities they could pursue for their next resort. While his boss was open to the idea, the news that Wakefield was pulling out gave them the green light to move forward with building here." Peter continued to explain the argument from the point where Cassie and Emily had arrived. Their mother's face grew paler with each word he spoke.

She put her head in her hands. "There's no way we can compete if they open their own Irish pub."

"Sure there is," Emily said, insistent. "You've seen how well our events are doing. If we can keep the momentum going into the off-season, everything will be okay."

"And how do you expect to do that between your teaching, Cassie's job, and Peter on the other side of the country?" Mom asked, rubbing her temples.

Emily suppressed a sigh. Her mother was right. Emily, Peter, and Cassie had run these events. There was no way one person could do it alone. Sure, they could hire more people, but more staff equaled more people to pay. She and her siblings had volunteered their time.

"I could move home," Cassie said in a low voice.

"You have a life in the city." Mom shook her head. "You all have lives outside of Blue Heron Bay, and I'd never ask you to give them up."

"I can come home on the weekends," Emily said. "And over my school breaks."

"Most of the customers we've had are from the university." Mom huffed out a breath. "And on the slim chance they stick around here for break instead of heading off to Florida or Cancun, they're more likely to spend it in Ocean City than come to this sleepy little town." She shook her head. "We need to face facts. Blue Heron Bay isn't what it used to be, and as things stand, it's unlikely to prosper without outside influence. I think we should consider selling."

Peter's head shot up, and he met Emily's gaze with raised eyebrows. She spread her hands on the table and shrugged, though her insides were reeling. Losing the pub would feel as if Dad had died all over again. But at the end of the day, it was Mom's decision. Their father had left the pub to her.

"Are you sure that's what you want to do, Mom?" Peter asked, laying a hand on her arm.

"Of course not," she said, her voice weary. "But you said they planned to drive us out of business either way. I'm not sure what other choice we have."

"I can try to talk to Ricardo again," Peter said, though his tone implied he'd rather do anything else. "Try to make him see reason."

"And maybe we can still convince Wakefield," Emily said. "They haven't left yet."

"Don't the town council and the mayor have to approve any new development?" Cassie had been quiet during the exchange, but her voice had an edge to it.

"I think so." Mom gave her a curious look. "Why do you ask?"

"Well, I can't imagine Ryan and the town council would want that much development at once in our tiny town. And I'd imagine they'd only give the go-ahead to the one they thought was best for the future of Blue Heron Bay."

"Ryan's goal is to bring tourism to Blue Heron Bay," Mom said. "If Wakefield is pulling out, he might not have a choice but to move forward with Sunrise Oasis."

"It's too bad Anna Mae and Ricardo hate each other so much," Cassie grumbled. "Maybe if they joined forces, their combined carbon footprint would be smaller, and they could tell Leslie Steele what she can do with her partnership."

No way. Anna Mae had made it clear she considered Ricardo enemy number one. But Peter looked thoughtful.

"We still have the stunt show," Cassie said when no one responded.

"But that's a one-time thing," Peter reminded her. "It'll bring tourists for the event, but that's it."

"Well, it may also remind people Blue Heron Bay is still here, which might help boost tourism over time." Mom sighed. "But I'm not sure it'll be enough."

"I could still talk to Ryan," Cassie said.

"It won't do any good unless we know for certain Wakefield Hotels is still planning to build here," Emily said.

"We can't just give up." Cassie slammed her hands on the table, making everyone jump. "Not after everything we've done to save the pub."

The bells over the door jingled, and all the Gallaghers turned. Emily expected it to be Ryan, but her heart swelled when she saw Anna Mae.

"Good evening, Gallaghers," Anna Mae sang out. "Sorry I couldn't make it tonight, but I wanted to see how things went."

Emily rushed over and embraced Anna Mae, her relief at seeing her again warring with her insecurities. "Oh, I'm so glad to see you. Did you get my texts?" Other questions bubbled up inside her, but she shoved them back down, not wanting to make a scene in front of her family.

"The cryptic ones saying SOS and telling me to come to the pub ASAP?" Anna Mae asked with a half smile. "Why do you think I'm here?" She glanced around the room. "What's going on?"

Emily filled her in on the disastrous conversation with Ricardo, and Anna Mae shook her head through most of it, a fire building in her eyes. When Emily finished, Anna Mae sank down in a chair and rubbed her forehead.

"I knew he wasn't to be trusted," she said.

"Is your dad still planning on building a hotel?" Emily asked.

Anna Mae looked at her for a long moment before answering, and Emily wished she knew what was going through her head. "Yes, he is still considering it."

"Well, that's good news!" Cassie jumped up. "I can talk to Ryan and—"

"Wait." Anna Mae held up a hand. "It's not that simple. With Sunrise Oasis going full steam ahead, my father is going to need that partnership more than ever." She shot Emily a meaningful look.

Emily's heart sank. That meant Anna Mae would have to spend *more* time with Leslie. And somehow, Emily knew that Leslie would use that time to her advantage.

Mom moaned. "So we're back to square one."

Anna Mae stood. "Not necessarily."

"Where are you going?" Peter asked.

"There's something I need to take care of, but keep the momentum going. You've got another karaoke event next week." She glanced at them each in turn. "Use it well." She met Emily's gaze, and for a moment, her eyes were sorrowful. Then she waved goodbye and ran out into the night.

The urge to run after her and demand an explanation was strong, but Emily remained rooted to her seat. What was going on? Why was Anna Mae ghosting Emily and acting so secretive? Was it because of Leslie? Emily's stomach churned at the thought. Anna Mae's lack of communication and her cryptic response to the question about whether her father was still considering building in town were not at all like the woman Emily had come to know. Or at least, not like the Anna Mae she *thought* she knew.

The Gallaghers looked at each other in silence, not sure what their next move should be. Emily was fresh out of ideas, and by the expressions on the faces of her family, she wasn't alone.

"If Anna Mae's father backs out, is that it?" Emily asked.

"I'm not sure what else we can do," Mom said.

Cassie gave her one-shoulder shrug. "No matter what happens, we'll make this summer our best ever and go out with a bang!"

Chapter Twenty-Five

Please call me. We need to talk.

Peter glared at his phone. It wasn't the first text message. He'd also received several phone calls, all from Ricardo. Perhaps he should consider changing his number, since Ricardo hadn't seemed to get the hint.

He shook his head, wishing he could go back in time and heed the warnings from Anna Mae, Emily, and Mr. Wakefield. How could he have fallen for such a snake? He understood ambition, and he couldn't fault Ricardo for having it, but the lying was something else. If Ricardo had been honest with him about his promotional opportunity, things might've been different. Instead, Ricardo had led him on, acting under-handedly, and now Peter was left with a mess and a bruised heart.

And to think, I almost lost my dissertation because of some guy. Peter's instincts had been right all along. Focus on the degree, then on getting a job, and then, maybe, he could consider having a love life. It was time to get his priorities straight. *No more distractions.*

Only... he could use a distraction from the pain. He opened his laptop, but his professor had sent nothing other than an acknowledgement he'd received the latest edits. It was unlikely new comments would arrive before the start of the next semester. Peter faced a long stretch of nothing but working at the pub and spending time with his family. All good things, but not enough to keep his thoughts at bay.

A knock sounded at his door. "Come in."

Cassie peeked in, her unnaturally red hair pulled back in a ponytail. "How're you feeling today?"

"Not great. You?"

She walked in and sat on the edge of his bed. "Worried."

"About the pub?"

"Among other things," she said with a sigh. She drew her legs up onto the bed and hugged her knees. "This summer isn't turning out how I thought it would."

"No, it really isn't." Peter propped himself up on his elbow.

"At least you're done with your schoolwork." She grinned.

Peter bristled at the simplistic label of "schoolwork" but couldn't help smiling in return. His sister possessed a resilience he'd never appreciated before. She held onto optimism even when things seemed bleak. That must be how she bounced back so quickly after her multitude of setbacks. If nothing else, she'd certainly had a lot of practice.

"I'm trying to convince Emily to close up the pub early tonight so we can go to the fire house carnival," Cassie said.

"They're still doing that?" Peter shook his head. *This town will never change.* The thought brought him up short because Ricardo's resort would bring significant change, and not for the better.

"Of course! It's one of my favorite events of the season."

"I haven't been in years," Peter mused.

Cassie snorted. "What? They don't have carnivals where you live?"

"They probably do, but they're more geared toward children."

Her eyebrow rose. "Are you saying you don't enjoy fried food or rides that make you queasy?"

"I never got why people enjoy making themselves nauseated on purpose, no."

She swatted him playfully. "You're no fun."

Peter pushed himself off the bed. "Well, if you want Emily to consider letting us out early tonight, we should probably get over there now."

"I suppose you're right," Cassie said with little enthusiasm.

"What? Tired of bartending already? Ready to return to the world of legal memos and researching case law?"

"Hardly." Cassie frowned. "But I will admit, working at the pub isn't the same now I know it might not last much longer."

"Where'd your optimism go?" Peter asked. He needed her to hang onto it now more than ever.

"I'll always have hope," Cassie said. She raised her eyes to meet his. "But even I can see the writing on the wall here, Pete. As much as I want to believe we can pull through, I expect I'll be back in the city, pushing papers, at the end of the summer."

Peter swallowed around the lump in his throat. The thought of losing the pub hurt his soul, but he hated the idea of his sister being miserable in the city.

"You could still move home, even if things don't work out at the pub." Peter moved next to her and slid an arm around her shoulders. "I doubt Mom has any plans to leave, and there are other places you could work."

"I don't want to waste my degree," Cassie said.

"Maybe Ryan could help you get a job in government? They probably have a legal division."

Cassie gave a noncommittal shrug. "Assuming he ever speaks to me again."

Peter leaned back and studied his sister. Moments ago, she'd put a positive spin on the summer by pointing out he'd finished another round of edits on his dissertation. But her defeatist tone didn't sound like the Cassie he knew. "What makes you say that?"

"He hasn't been by the pub recently, and it's my fault. I know he's avoiding me, but I wish he'd still stop by, at least to see Mom." She turned to look at Peter, and her forehead creased with worry. "I appreciated that he checked in on her when we weren't here."

"I'm sure he'll be back. He has a lot going on."

Cassie didn't look convinced. "Anyway, as you said, we should get to the pub."

Peter nodded, and Cassie left him alone so he could get ready. He'd noticed Ryan's absence the last few nights but hadn't thought much of it until now. Was Ryan avoiding Cassie? Peter couldn't very well blame him. A guy could only take so much rejection. But maybe Ryan had given up too soon. Peter couldn't put his finger on why, but something in Cassie's eyes made him think there might be more to her feelings for Ryan than just appreciating his concern for Mom.

The pub had another successful evening, even without an event planned. But Cassie couldn't bring herself to enjoy it. Her gaze kept straying to the door each time she poured another beer from the tap. Another night with no sign of Ryan. To think, when she first got here, she'd taken his words about seeing her around as a threat. Now, she wished they'd been a promise.

The bells on the door jingled, and she shot a glance at the new arrival. She blinked. It was Stephanie, Derrick's neighbor, the one who'd helped her after her not-a-shark encounter. Cassie had seen her a few times when she was with Derrick, but as far as Cassie was aware, she'd never come to the pub.

"Cassie, how are you?" Stephanie slid onto a bar stool.

"I'm doing well. It's great to see you." Cassie leaned against the bar. "What can I get you?"

"Do you make your festive creations on non-event nights?"

"I'm not supposed to," Cassie said. "But I can bend the rules for a friend."

Stephanie's eyes brightened. "Then I'd love a Black-Eyed Raven, please."

As Cassie gathered the ingredients and began mixing the drink, Stephanie asked, "Where's Derrick tonight?"

"Um, I'm not sure, actually." Cassie shook the drink and then strained it into a glass. After adding a straw, she slid it over to Stephanie. "I think he's coming to the carnival later."

"You're good for him, you know."

Cassie raised her eyebrows. "Why do you say that?"

"I've known him a long time." Stephanie sipped her drink. "Mmm, this is so good! Anyway, let's just say he seems more stable since you've come to town. I mean, aside from that ridiculous lie about the sharks."

Cassie wasn't sure how to respond to that. While she'd continued working with him on their stunts, they'd barely hung out outside of practice. He was still sore over her sharing Ryan's concerns about the unnecessary risks they were taking. Things had been strained between them, but she'd given up trying to talk sense into him.

"Are you coming to the stunt show?" Cassie asked, hoping to change the subject.

"Oh, you're still doing that?" Stephanie gave her a wary look that caused a quivering in her stomach.

"Of course. Why wouldn't I?"

"Derrick just said you were having second thoughts. Something about being too far out in the water for your comfort."

Cassie rolled her eyes. *Is he making stuff up again or is he just that terrible a listener?* "I'm more afraid of the potential for rough surf due to bad weather, but I made a commitment, and the show will be good for the town."

After finishing her drink, Stephanie smiled, but it didn't quite meet her eyes. "Thanks for breaking the rules for me." She slid some money toward Cassie and turned to leave but glanced back. "Promise you'll be careful."

Cassie furrowed her brow. "I promise?" She hadn't intended it to come out as a question, but Stephanie nodded, as if she was satisfied with the response.

That was weird. First, Ryan had warned her about the rough surf, then Stephanie made her promise to be careful. She shook her head, needing to clear it. Her gaze swept the restaurant until she saw Emily. Lifting one hand, she signaled she was going to take a break, and Emily nodded.

Once outside, she leaned against the wall of the building and slid down to the curb, unsure what to think. But she couldn't help the sense of foreboding that was pooling in her belly. Her muscles tensed, and she shook her arms to loosen them.

Footsteps sounded a few feet away, and she raised her head. Her already tumultuous emotions took on an even more frenzied state when her eyes met Ryan's.

"Cassie? What are you doing out here?"

"Just getting some air." She took a deep breath in demonstration, which helped to calm her, if only a little.

He sat beside her. "Are you okay?"

"I think so?" The uncertainty in her tone was clear.

His forehead creased as he looked her over. "What happened?"

"I don't know really. Derrick's neighbor stopped by, and we had a weird conversation."

"About what?"

Not knowing what else to do, she told him. Maybe he could shed some light on the cryptic message it felt like Stephanie was trying to pass along.

"While I'm probably not the person who should be commenting on Derrick's stability, I do echo her caution to be careful." He pulled out his phone. "The National Hurricane Center has tracked the storm much closer to us than they originally expected, though it'll still stay out to sea. The rough surf though..." His jaw clenched. "I have half a mind to cancel the event entirely."

"Don't do that!" The last thing the pub, or the town for that matter, needed was to have such a huge event cancelled when they were struggling to bring in people. "Maybe we could move the whole thing to the bay instead, where the water will be a little calmer."

Ryan didn't respond. She wanted to ask him how he'd been, why he hadn't been by lately, what had brought him there tonight. Yet she couldn't bring herself to do it. Seeing him again after so many days of silence made her feel... things.

"I'm glad you stopped by tonight," she said, breaking the silence.

His eyebrows shot up. "You are?"

"Yeah, it's been weird not having you around."

Ryan leaned back and studied her, as if trying to decipher the meaning behind her words. While she didn't want to give him the wrong idea, she wasn't entirely sure what that was anymore. Her thoughts were still too muddled from Stephanie's visit.

"I appreciate that you check in on my mom," Cassie said.

Something flashed across his face. Disappointment? It disappeared before she could fully register it.

"I owe it to your father," Ryan said, his tone cooler. "I wouldn't be where I am today if it wasn't for him."

Cassie nodded. She knew that, but somehow tonight it hit differently than the first time Ryan had told her. It wasn't like she expected he was hanging around for her, but her chest constricted, and she hunched forward, wishing she could become as small as she felt.

"Are you going to the carnival tonight?" Ryan asked.

"If I can convince Emily." It took effort, but she forced herself to look at him. His gaze was traveling over her in her fetal position. "You?"

"Kind of have to." Ryan gave a half smile. "Being the mayor and all." He glanced at his watch. "In fact, I need to head over now." His forehead creased again. "Are you sure you're okay?"

"I will be." It was as much a promise to herself as it was to him.

Ryan nodded. He hesitated a moment as if he didn't want to leave her but then pushed himself off the ground. "I guess I'll see you there."

"Save me a turn on the Scrambler," Cassie called. Ryan glanced back at her, an unreadable expression on his face. Lifting her hand, she gave what she hoped was a lighthearted wave.

Save me a turn on the Scrambler? Who says that? No wonder Ryan was avoiding her. If she were a traffic light, she would have caused an accident with all her mixed signals. She needed to figure out how she felt about Ryan and either make a move or leave the poor man alone.

Chapter Twenty-Six

EMILY SCANNED THE CROWD, HOPING FOR SOME SIGN OF Anna Mae. They hadn't spoken since the night before. Anna Mae had said she had something to take care of, and Emily assumed she would reach out whenever she was ready, but the waiting was difficult.

The carnival was set up at the fire station. Parents helped their little ones into the kiddie rides, while thrill seekers stood in line for the Zipper and the Drop Tower. There were character photos, a Bingo hall, and tons of food trucks. All the proceeds went to help the local fire station buy equipment and provide training for the year.

Cassie grabbed Emily's arm and pointed to the bumper cars. "We should go on those!"

"Aren't you a little old for carnival rides?" Emily asked, teasing.

But Cassie shook her head, her hazel eyes sparkling.

"Well, you go on ahead. Maybe I'll join you later." Though she had no intention of doing so. She preferred quieter rides, like the Ferris wheel.

Emily found Mom trying her hand at a water gun game. It was one Dad had helped them with when they were younger, lining up the gun with the hole before the water started spraying. With his guidance, they usually won, and Emily's heart squeezed at the memory.

The bell rang, and the water started spraying, but Mom was nowhere near on-target. Emily laughed and put her hands on her mother's, guiding them until she hit the bullseye. Unfortunately, by the time she did, one of her competitors had managed to blow up their balloon. It burst, and the bell rang again, signaling them as the winner.

"Ah well, it was worth a shot," Mom said, a bittersweet smile on her face. "I half hoped your father's spirit would come help me."

Emily's throat tightened, and she put a hand on her mom's shoulder. "I'm so sorry, Mom. For Dad, for the pub." Her head fell forward, heavy with grief. "I really thought we could save it."

"Hey now, hope is not lost. We've still got a few weeks of summer left." Mom pulled Emily into her arms. "And if it doesn't work out, I know your father would be proud of everything you kids did."

A screech cut through the air, the sound of feedback from a microphone getting too close to a speaker. Emily and her mother walked into the large tent that held the main stage. Her heart leapt into her throat when she caught sight of Anna Mae standing next to Ryan. But her joy was soon squashed when she noticed Leslie Steele and Mr. Wakefield with her. Were they going to announce a partnership?

"Good evening, everyone, and thank you for joining us for our annual fire house carnival," Ryan said. "I don't mean to interrupt the festivities, but I wanted to share a bit of news with you while I have you here this evening." Ryan motioned for Anna Mae, Leslie, and Mr. Wakefield to step forward. "As most of you know, I've been working to increase tourism in our little town, and I think you'll all be happy to learn I'm making progress in that regard. To provide further details on where things stand, I'd like to present Mr. Harris Wakefield." He moved to the side as Mr. Wakefield took over the microphone.

"Good evening. I am the CEO of Wakefield Hotel Group, and my daughter, Anna Mae, has performed due diligence on the town to determine if it's a good fit for our hotel. We have also worked to secure financial capital to ensure we can offer the best of our brand to the residents of this great town. I'm pleased to share that Wakefield is partnering with Steele Hotels in the hopes of building an oceanfront boutique hotel right here in Blue Heron Bay."

The crowd clapped politely, though Emily wasn't sure if the weight of the announcement had sunk in. After so many years of attempts to bring tourism back to the town, she couldn't blame the townsfolk for their skepticism. After all, why would this news be any different from everything else they'd tried?

"We'll be working with the mayor and town council as we develop our proposal and assess an appropriate site to build. And we'll be holding several town hall meetings that we invite all of you to attend so that you can hear our plans and ask any questions you may have. To further seal our relationship with Steele Hotels, my daughter would like to say a few words." Harris gestured to Anna Mae.

She glared at the stage and shook her head, refusing to move from her spot. But then Leslie pushed past her and grabbed the microphone.

"On behalf of Steele Hotels, I want to thank Anna Mae for ensuring the success of our partnership," Leslie exclaimed, her dark eyes scanning the crowd until they met Emily's. A sly, triumphant smirk pulled on her lips before she composed herself and continued. "*Together*, we hope to bring a new and prosperous chapter to Blue Heron Bay's history!"

Emily swayed on the spot, her heart sinking into her stomach. The way Leslie said the word "together" told Emily everything she needed to know, and Anna Mae's bright-red cheeks only further confirmed it. Though Emily couldn't tell if the color was from rage or embarrassment. Grabbing Leslie's hand, Anna Mae pulled her away from the podium before she could say anything else.

Emily couldn't move, couldn't breathe. She stood rooted to the spot, part of her hoping this was all a bad dream and she would awaken any moment, ready to laugh at her silly subconscious. Another part prayed for Anna Mae to seek her out. She believed if Anna Mae would just look at her, she would know if her worst fears had just been realized.

Cassie glided up beside her and grabbed her arm. "Come on, Emily. Let's go."

Emily allowed herself to be dragged through the carnival, her head bowed.

Mom and Peter were already at the exit, waiting for them. Her brother's lips set in a grim line while Mom hugged Emily. But Emily found no warmth in the embrace. Nothing could break through the cold settling around her heart.

Burying her feelings deep within, she forced a smile. She didn't want to cause her family to worry about her. If Mr. Wakefield was moving forward with the hotel, that was good news for them. She clung to the positive side of his announcement while shying away from the heartbreaking portion. If it would preserve her father's legacy, it was worth the sacrifice. Or at least, that was what she told herself.

"I'm glad Wakefield Hotel Group is going to develop a hotel here," she said, struggling to keep her tone neutral. Three heads swiveled in her direction, and their expressions told her they didn't buy her performance. "If it means Ricardo will think twice about building a resort, then there might be hope yet for Fiddler's Green."

"I don't care whether this helps or hurts the pub," Cassie said. "Nothing would make what just happened okay." She shook her head, her face almost as red as her hair. "I can't believe the nerve. Making an announcement like that? And not even the decency to give you a heads-up?" She glared back into the carnival. "It's funny Anna Mae hates Ricardo so much. From where I'm standing, they're cut from the same cloth."

"Enough!" Emily cut in, her voice breaking. "As much as I appreciate you being angry on my behalf, I won't allow you to speak ill of her." Tears sprang to her eyes, but she blinked them back. Her family stared at her, and she couldn't stand their pity. "Let's go home."

She walked forward, holding her head high, and prayed her family would follow without further comment. Though Cassie's words echoed in her head, she refused to give them any credence. Anna Mae wasn't like that. Emily had long suspected that when it came to a choice between herself and Leslie, there was no competition. Beyond their romantic history, Leslie had much more to offer than Emily ever could: a beautiful jet-setter with business savvy who could help Wakefield Hotel Group grow beyond Mr. Wakefield's and Anna's wildest dreams.

Who was Emily to that? A small-town nobody with a struggling family pub. She stumbled on the sidewalk as the painful reality hit her again. With a steadying breath, she regained her footing and tried to ignore the growing ache in her chest. She needed to get home. Once she was safely ensconced in her room, she could fall apart.

Peter tested the sound system for the umpteenth time that afternoon. The karaoke event was still several hours away, but he wanted everything to be perfect. As Cassie had stated, if Fiddler's Green wasn't going to make it, then they might as well go out with a bang.

Despite the news that Steele Hotels had merged with Wakefield Hotel Group, there was no sign that Ricardo's company intended to give up their plans for a resort. With that reality facing them, Mom had talked more and more about selling the pub. Peter smiled sardonically. Not long ago, that news would have been welcome, but recently, he'd grown to appreciate what his father had built. It was fitting that he figured out how important the place was just in time to lose it.

But the show had to go on, and Peter was ready to make their last few events the best they'd had yet. Cassie had insisted on having a themed night and suggested the '80s. She'd made all the previous themed drinks available as specials tonight with one notable addition: a Love Shack cocktail, named after the popular song. The name, and the cocktail, suited the event perfectly.

"Can you step away from the sound system for a minute?" Mom asked as she came up to Peter. "I need to talk to all of you."

A quick burst of emotion threatened to choke him. He'd seen Ricardo skulking around earlier in the day, and he assumed his mother had come to a decision. Ricardo had kept his distance from Peter, which was a small comfort, but it did nothing to assuage Peter's anger, both at Ricardo's actions and at his own stupidity in trusting him.

Cassie, Emily, and Tony were all seated at a table in the middle of the restaurant when Peter joined them. His mother gestured for him to sit before she began her spiel.

"First, I want to say I appreciate how hard you all have worked over these last several weeks." She gazed around the restaurant, a sad smile playing on her lips. "It almost felt like old times, having all of you home and pitching in at whatever job needed doing. Your father would be so proud."

Cassie sniffled beside him, and Peter's own eyes began watering. It was a small comfort knowing that his father hadn't lived to see his beloved pub sold out from under them.

"I'm sure you saw that Ricardo stopped by." Mom shot a quick glance at him before continuing. "He's made me a substantial offer on the pub, and I'm inclined to accept, but before I do, I wanted us to discuss it." She took a deep breath. "As you know, if we don't sell, it's highly likely Sunrise Oasis Resorts will put us out of business. It may not be immediate." She forced a laugh. "Lord knows we have the loyalty of the town. But I'm afraid we won't have the loyalty of whatever tourists the resort brings in. Truthfully, I'm not sure what Blue Heron Bay will look like with this new development."

"Just another overpopulated beach town," Cassie said. "All shiny and built up with no soul."

"Now, now," Mom scolded. "We shouldn't talk that way." She shook her head. "But you're right. I expect the resort will offer several amenities Blue Heron Bay doesn't currently possess. Whether that will be good for the town is something we'll have to wait and see." She stared down at her hands. "Well, at least the town will see. If I sell the pub, I plan to sell the house, too, and move away."

All three Gallagher siblings gasped. Peter's mouth dropped open. He'd never expected Mom would leave town. Travel more, yes, but not move permanently. His chest tightened. *Is this our last summer in our childhood home?*

"But where will you go?" Emily asked.

"I'm not sure yet." She shrugged. "Honestly, I wouldn't mind living a more transient life." Turning to Cassie, she smiled. "I'd love to travel, see the world. But I know I wouldn't love not having a home base for long."

"You could come stay with me for a while," Cassie said. "I have a spare bedroom in my basement apartment."

"I'd like to visit all of you." Mom looked at each of her children. When her eyes fell on Tony, she gave him a wistful smile. "We're getting ahead of ourselves, though. Tony, you've been with us since the beginning. What are your thoughts about selling the pub?"

Tony had been quiet during the whole of the exchange. He shifted in his seat, and Peter gathered he wasn't entirely comfortable being the sudden center of attention.

"Well now," Tony said. "I can't pretend to be surprised, but I am disappointed." He met each of their gazes before he spoke again. "Y'all are like family to me, and it's hard to imagine Blue Heron Bay without the Gallaghers." He ran a hand over his gray hair. "However, it's the right choice. Better to get out now while the pub is still worth something than to go under and be stuck with the debt."

"What will you do for work?" Cassie asked, placing her hand on his.

Tony gave her a warm smile. "Aw, you know me, Cass. I'm like a cat, always land on my feet." He squeezed her hand. "That's why you and me get along so well."

Cassie laughed, though it sounded hollow to Peter's ears. Everyone was silent as the reality of their situation sank in. He couldn't believe, after all their efforts, it had all come to naught.

Well, that wasn't entirely true. As he looked around the room, he couldn't help noting how much they all had grown, both as a family and individually. He'd seen his youngest sister in a different light. Though he'd never agree with her life choices, she'd developed an unshakeable resilience he admired. Emily had come into her own as well, pushing herself out of her comfort zone and embracing her inner leader. She'd risked her heart, and while it hadn't ended the way she'd hoped, he was proud of her for doing it. His mother had kept the pub going for as long as she could, even with the odds stacked against her, and he knew it was a labor of love.

As for himself, he had finished his dissertation, which was his goal, but he would be taking so much more back with him to the West Coast: a newfound understanding of the importance of family and a better balance in his approach to life.

"So, is this it, then?" Emily asked, tears filling her brown eyes. "Are we selling?"

"Ricardo gave me until Labor Day to decide, and I'd like to see how the stunt show impacts tourism," Mom said. "But I don't know that we have another option."

Emily nodded and ducked her head. Tony reached over and grabbed her hand, rubbing his thumb over Emily's knuckles. Everyone else joined hands around the table. The battle may have been over, but the Gallaghers would not go quietly.

"Then we better make tonight the best party this town has ever seen!" Peter said, and Cassie met his eye with a determined nod.

A few hours later, the first people began streaming in for karaoke night. From the looks of the growing crowd, their final event was going to be a smashing success.

"You should be proud," Peter called out to Emily, who was passing with an empty tray.

Emily's smile was weak. "I just wish it had been enough."

"Dad would have wanted it this way."

"What do you mean?" Emily tilted her head.

Peter gestured to the dining area. "He loved seeing this place filled with happy people." He looked back at her. "And he would've wanted us all together to say goodbye."

Emily nodded, her eyes shining with unshed tears. She ducked her head and hurried back to the bar. As he was struggling to keep his own emotions in check, he understood how she felt. Tonight shouldn't be about what they were losing, but what they had accomplished. He forced himself to focus on that positive.

The first brave soul of the night approached. A young brunette with teased-up hair and a multicolored outfit moved toward him. She caught him gawking at her getup and struck a pose.

Peter laughed. "What would you like to sing tonight?"

She flipped through the songs and picked one of his least favorites. He suppressed a groan as he noted her name and the song title.

"Thanks," he said with a forced smile. "I'll call you up in a few minutes when we're ready to get started."

The woman flashed him a grin before dancing back to her seat. It hadn't occurred to him to dress to the theme, and his blue button-down dress shirt and black slacks stood out in the sea of bright Lycra.

"No worries, big brother," Cassie said as she sidled up beside him. In her hands was a denim jacket and aviator sunglasses. "I've got finger-less gloves, too, if you want them."

"Thanks... I think," Peter said, shaking his head.

Cassie laughed and held out her arms so he could see her outfit. A green miniskirt over bright-pink leggings paired with a colorful shirt and a jean jacket of her own. She'd also teased her hair.

"I... Wow," he finally choked out.

"I'm getting into the spirit of things!" She glanced at the front door. "We're about ready to get started."

Peter nodded. "Sounds good."

Cassie walked back over to the bar, and Peter turned on the sound system. "Good evening, everyone, and welcome to another karaoke night at Fiddler's Green!"

The crowd cheered, and Peter's chest ached at what he didn't say, what he *couldn't* say. Would it be one of the last karaoke nights ever at the pub?

"If you haven't signed up yet, what are you waiting for? We're going to start things off in just a minute, so come on up and pick your song!"

A line formed soon after Peter's announcement, and the clipboard quickly filled. He smiled as he prepared to cue up the first song. His heart was heavy but full. The night was going to be bittersweet, and he planned to savor every minute of it.

Chapter Twenty-Seven

CASSIE WOKE THE MORNING OF THE STUNT SHOW WITH mixed emotions. On the one hand, this was the last major event the town would put on before the end of the summer, and she wanted it to go well. But on the other hand, Ryan's and Stephanie's warnings had plagued her mind for days. The rough surf had already caused several riptides, and the lifeguards had issued red flags, warning swimmers it wasn't safe to go in the water. It wasn't quite bad enough to close the beaches entirely, but she was still nervous.

With a quivering stomach, she dressed and prepared to head down to the marina, where she'd meet with Derrick and the rest of the stunt show to go over the final plans for the day. She almost hoped they'd cancel the show, or at least postpone it until weather conditions improved.

When she arrived, Derrick rushed over to her and engulfed her in a hug. She forced a smile, hoping he wouldn't see the trepidation in her eyes. Aside from practice, they hadn't spent much time together. Between his lifeguard duties and her shifts at the pub, there just wasn't enough time in the day. Though, if she was being honest, she also couldn't bring herself to make the effort to see him. Her attraction to him had cooled significantly since she'd witnessed his argument with Ryan on the beach.

"You ready for this?" Derrick asked, his blue eyes gleaming with excitement. She tried to match his enthusiasm, but her stomach was in knots. Even there in the marina, the water of the Assateague Bay was choppy. The erratic movement of the dock and the boats tied to it made it difficult to maintain her balance. She could only imagine how much worse it would be when they got to the ocean.

"Are you sure this is a good idea?" she asked, her gaze straying back to the water. "Maybe Ryan's right. It doesn't look safe."

"Oh, please." Derrick scoffed. "Since when do you listen to that guy?" He swept his arm toward the sky. "It's a beautiful day. The sun is shining, and the breeze coming off the ocean is keeping the August humidity at bay. Besides, it's a *stunt* show. It's supposed to be a little dangerous."

"This is more than a 'little dangerous,'" she said, putting air quotes around the last two words. Her lips pressed together as she crossed her arms. "I think we should postpone."

"What's this I hear?" Darryl came up behind Derrick. "You wimpin' out on us, man?"

"No way!" Derrick shot her a glare. "She's just got cold feet, but we're fine."

"Hope so. Cause this show is costing me a pretty penny, and I need you to be one hundred percent on board." His brown eyes swept over Cassie. "Don't worry so much, doll."

She resisted the urge to roll her eyes. If there was one good thing about getting the show over with, it was that she wouldn't have to spend another moment with that guy. Ever since the interview, he'd made her skin crawl.

After he exchanged a few more words with Derrick, Darryl walked away. Alone again, Cassie took the opportunity to try to talk some sense into him.

"Derrick, if we're going to do this, I think we should take some extra precautions and maybe change out some of the routine."

"Why are you being like this?" He crossed his arms and narrowed his eyes.

She took a step back, shocked by his change in demeanor. "Being like what? Sane?"

"Wow, okay." His eyebrows drew into a scowl. "Are you trying to pick a fight right now?"

"I'm trying to appeal to your logical side, but now I'm starting to think you don't have one." Her hands clenched into fists. It was the only way to keep them from shaking.

"Jeez, Cass, I'm doing this for *you* and your family's pathetic little pub. But hey, if you want to back out, that's fine by me." He sneered. "You're easily replaced."

She staggered as if he'd hit her. He might as well have. *Pathetic little pub? Easily replaced?* Her stomach roiled as she stared at him, dumbfounded. *Everything Ryan said about him was true. He couldn't care less about me.*

But what could she do? The pub needed the publicity, and she feared if she backed out now, he'd renege on his promise to donate half the proceeds to the town's tourism budget. Assuming, of course, that he hadn't lied to her about that, too, like so many other things. Even if the pub went under, she wanted to do whatever she could to help her hometown. And if that meant doing this stupid show with this awful man, it seemed a small price to pay.

"So, what's it going to be?" His blue eyes, once so beautiful to her, were as cold and hard as sapphires. "Are you going to stick to your commitment?"

Straightening her shoulders, she nodded once. "I'll do the show, but after that, we're done."

It was his turn to stagger back. "What?"

"You heard me." Heat flooded her veins as her anger grew. "I don't deserve to be treated like this. I'm only doing the show because of my 'pathetic pub,' as you so rudely put it. After that, I'm out." Her lips quirked up in a half smile. "Besides, as you said, I'm replaceable, so really, it's no big loss, right?"

With that, she spun on her heel and marched away, needing some space. There wasn't much time before they had to ride out to start the show, but she couldn't stand to look at him for another minute. Not after the things he'd said.

Emily sat with her mother and brother on the beach, pleased with the turnout. People peppered the sand for miles with blankets and umbrellas, waiting for the show to start. Her eyes kept searching the crowds for some sign of Anna Mae. Despite everything, Emily still hoped for a chance to talk to her, if for nothing else than to thank her for all she'd done to try to save the pub.

"It looks rough out there," Peter said, holding a hand to his forehead to shield his face from the sun. "Is there any chance they'll cancel?"

"I doubt it," Emily grumbled. Somehow, she didn't think Derrick would let anything stand in the way of him achieving more notoriety.

She'd tried to like him, for Cassie's sake, but she couldn't quite bring herself to do so. While she appreciated his efforts to make things up to her sister, something about him just rubbed her the wrong way.

Music started playing, and she glanced behind her at the speakers that had been set up along the sand dunes. The first of the stunt acts roared out onto the open water. Six water skiers, three men and three women, were pulled along by two speedboats. They waved at the crowd as they went past, then the men did a quick flip, landing cleanly back on their skis. Applause sounded around her, and she joined in, half-heartedly. The rough water made it difficult to see what they were doing, as the skiers kept disappearing behind the waves.

After performing several different flips and tricks, the skiers slowly joined together behind one of the speedboats, with two of the women climbing on top of the men's shoulders. The last woman scrambled to the top of the human pyramid, and they waved to the crowd. As the boat turned to head back in, they hit a huge wave, and the skiers toppled, the woman on top screaming as she went down.

Emily's hand flew to her mouth as a collective gasp went through the onlookers. A moment later, the boat circled back to pick them up. Counting in her head, she breathed a sigh of relief once all six people had climbed out of the water.

"That was close," Mom murmured, her hand over her heart. "I hope Cassie has better luck during her stunts."

Unfortunately, the treacherous surf proved to be a hazard to all the acts. So far, no one had been seriously injured, but the closer they got to Cassie's performance, the more agitated Emily became.

She turned away during a break to see Ryan walking across the beach, a life jacket on his back and something orange in his hand. Lifting an arm, she waved to him, and he came over.

"Cassie is up next," he said as he sank into the sand beside her. His face was creased with concern. "I hope she was able to talk some sense into Derrick. It's dangerous out there." He gestured to his orange flotation device. "I've brought this in case things go wrong, and the Coast Guard is on standby."

Just then, six Jet Skis came roaring into view. Ryan crossed his arms over his chest as his eyes narrowed. Emily followed his gaze. It was hard to tell from a distance, but it didn't look like all the riders had on life vests.

Ryan swore. He stood and marched over to the shoreline, craning his neck to get a better look. Filled with dread, Emily followed him. The six Jet Skis split up, with three of them riding to the opposite side of the performance area. At an unseen signal, the groups of three raced toward each other. The ones on the right lifted to jump the wakes of the ones on the left. Two of them succeeded, but the one nearest to the shore was too close. It crashed into the other Jet Ski, and Emily's mouth fell open in horror as the vehicle tipped over, a familiar head of red hair falling into the ocean.

"Cassie!" she screamed. Her heart stopped as she waited for her sister to resurface.

The other five Jet Skis surrounded the one that had been knocked to its side. After some shouts and scrambling, one rider was pulled out of the ocean.

"Cassie?" she whispered. Ryan turned to look at her, his lips set in a grim line. He shook his head. She sank to the ground as her brother and mother came running up next to her, both screaming for her sister.

That was all it took for Ryan to rush toward the shoreline, where a dinghy was waiting. He threw the flotation device into the dinghy and dragged the boat into the water. There was no way he was going to get to her sister in time—he was too far away. Emily needed to stand, to get her family away from this awful scene, but she couldn't seem to find the strength.

Everything felt like it was moving in slow motion. Four of the Jet Skiers and a Coast Guard boat searched the area for any sign of Cassie while the other Jet Skier helped Derrick right his vehicle. Emily stared hard into the water, praying for a miracle.

For several minutes, all she heard was the blood rushing in her ears, louder than even the pounding of the surf. But then, there was a commotion beside her, and she turned. A man with binoculars was shouting something.

"What is it?" Peter said, running over to the man. "What do you see?"

"Take a look." The man handed him the binoculars.

Emily forced herself to her feet and took her mother's hand, pulling her over to where Peter stood.

A heartbeat, then another, before her brother finally said something. "I see Ryan. He's got her."

Their mother collapsed onto the sand, sobbing uncontrollably. Emily knelt beside her, but her heart was still in her throat. They were too far away to see if Cassie was still alive.

"They're pulling her onto a boat. We need to get to the marina, now!" Peter handed the man back his binoculars and thanked him before leaning down. "Mom, we've gotta go. Can you stand?"

After she gave him a weak nod, Peter helped their mother to her feet. He held out his hand to Emily, and she gratefully accepted it.

They ran as fast as they could over the hot, uneven sand. As they approached the stairs to go over the dunes, a familiar figure stood at the top of them.

"Ricardo," Peter growled. "Get out of the way."

"Look, I know I'm the last person you want to see right now," Ricardo said, holding up his hands as they reached the landing. "But my car is here, and I can get you to the marina much faster than you can walk."

Peter looked about ready to protest, but Emily was faster. "We would really appreciate that." When her brother shot her a death glare, she glared right back. "He's right. We walked here, and we'll never make it before the ambulance arrives."

With a groan, Peter nodded, and Ricardo led the way to the car. They all jumped in and took off at top speed.

Chapter Twenty-Eight

CASSIE WOKE TO A POUNDING HEAD, WHICH WASN'T HELPED
by the incessant beeping beside her. As she opened her eyes, she stared at
an unfamiliar tiled ceiling. With a frown, she rolled her head to the left,
wincing as the pain intensified. An IV tower next to her held various
bags filled with fluids. She followed the tubes to the blanket covering her
arm. She lifted her right arm, yelping as pain shot through it. After
flexing the fingers on her left hand, she tentatively moved it and pulled
back the covers, gasping at the sight.

A cast covered her right forearm, but bruises extended out to her
bicep. She lifted her left hand and gently prodded her head. Her eyes
squeezed shut, and she released a low moan as the pain reverberated
through her skull. The hair near her temple was shaved, and her fingers
traced the line of several stitches.

"Ugh," Cassie cried out. *What happened?*

"Cassie?" a familiar male voice said. A moment later, a pair of
concerned green eyes was staring down into hers. "You're awake." The
relief in Ryan's voice was palpable. "Oh, thank God." He reached over
and pressed a button above her head.

A woman wearing blue scrubs appeared in the doorway. Her dark hair was cut short and graying near her temples. "Ah, Ms. Gallagher. You gave us quite a scare." She stepped over to Cassie and examined her vitals on a screen, which Cassie understood was the source of the annoying beeping. "How are you feeling?"

"Awful," Cassie croaked. She tried to clear her throat, but it was dry and sore. "Where am I? What happened?"

"You're in the hospital," Ryan said. He blinked rapidly as if he were holding back tears. "You were knocked off the Jet Ski and hit your head pretty hard."

"Broke your arm too," the nurse said. She glanced at Ryan before turning back to Cassie. "This young man saved your life. Pulled you out of some pretty treacherous water." She gave Ryan a stern look. "I'm going to tell her family she's awake. We need to limit her visitors for a while, so you best take your leave."

Ryan nodded. After the nurse left, he squeezed Cassie's left hand. "I'm so glad you're okay."

He turned to go, but Cassie pulled him back. "Wait! Is what she says true? Did you really save me?"

"I pulled you out of the water, but it was a joint effort."

"Tell me more. Please."

His lips curved up. "I will, later. Right now, your family needs to see you, and you need rest." When she glared at him, he gave a short laugh. "I promise, Cassie, I will regale you with the whole tale when you're better."

She pouted but released his hand. The smile he gave before he left stirred warmth deep inside her chest.

One by one, her family came in. The first to enter was Mom, and Cassie's eyes filled with tears at the worry lines on her mother's face. She wrapped Cassie in a gentle hug, careful of her many bumps and bruises.

"My baby," she cooed, smoothing Cassie's hair. "We've been so worried."

"How long have I been here?" Cassie asked.

Her mother's hand stilled on Cassie's head as her blue eyes searched Cassie's face. "Ryan didn't tell you?"

"He told me I hit my head and broke my arm, but then he had to leave."

"You've been here for a couple of days."

Cassie's eyes widened. "Days?" She stared at her mother. "Did I miss Labor Day?"

Her mom laughed. "Not yet, though you're cutting it close."

"Oh good." Settling back on her pillow, Cassie rubbed her head. "Hopefully I'll be out soon."

"You shouldn't rush it," she said, her smile fading. "Your injuries are pretty extensive, and you've only just woken up."

"But I don't want to miss the family cookout!" Cassie pushed herself up in bed. Pain shot through her, and she sank back down with a groan.

"Shhh, my darling, it'll be okay. If needed, we can always postpone it."

Cassie scowled, which morphed into a grimace as it pulled at her stitches. "It's not the same."

Mom patted her head. "All that matters is we'll be together." She glanced over her shoulder and sighed. "Your siblings want to see you, so I better go, but I'll come back as soon as I can."

Emily was her next visitor. "Is this payback for making you tell the truth about the sharks?"

"Ha ha," Cassie said. "I suppose I've been a bit accident-prone lately."

"You're just lucky they always end with a handsome rescuer," Emily teased.

Cassie regarded her sister. "You have a point. I am lucky." She shook her head. "Sounds like I'm lucky to be alive."

Emily held up her hand, her forehead creasing. "Let's not think about that."

"Sorry," Cassie murmured. "Ryan really saved me, huh?" She smiled. "I guess I owe him."

"Does this mean you might give the poor man a chance?" Emily arched an eyebrow.

Cassie laughed and then winced. *Ugh, this broken body is for the birds.* Her sense of humor would not bode well for healing.

"I don't think he'd want to date me looking like this."

"You haven't seen him the last few days," Emily said gently. "He's been a wreck."

"Has he?" Cassie tried to hide the interest in her voice.

Emily nodded. "I'm sure if the nurse hadn't kicked him out so we could visit, he wouldn't have left your side."

Cassie bit her lip. She wasn't sure what to do with that information. The warmth in her chest returned.

"Well, anyway," Emily said, misinterpreting Cassie's silence for exhaustion. "I'll head out so Peter can come in, and then you should get some rest."

"Wait," Cassie said. "Can you ask Ryan to come back?"

Emily stared at her. "Are you sure? You shouldn't push yourself. You've been through a lot."

Cassie nodded. "I'm sure." When Emily still looked doubtful, Cassie gave her best puppy-dog eyes. "Please?"

"I'll see if I can find him," Emily said with a sigh.

Peter rushed in next. "How are you feeling, Cass?"

"I'm still kicking."

He grinned. "You must be okay if you're back to joking." He gently took her hand. "You gave us a terrible fright, you know that? Mom about had a heart attack watching it all unfold from the beach."

"Can you fill me in? My memory's a bit fuzzy, and Ryan didn't have a chance to share many details."

"One of the other Jet Skis tried to jump your wake too early and crashed into you. You hit your head as you fell into the water and were knocked unconscious. If it hadn't been for your life vest, you would have drowned. You've been in and out of consciousness the last few days."

Cassie worked to keep her face neutral, which, with as much pain as she was in, wasn't hard. The reality of just how dire her situation had been sank in.

"There's actually someone else who'd like to see you, if you don't mind," Peter said, dropping his gaze. His cheeks turned red, and he shuffled his feet. "When we were racing to the marina, we ran into Ricardo. He gave us all a ride to the hospital, and he asked me to let him know when you woke. He's waiting outside."

Cassie's eyebrows shot up before she could stop herself. *Ugh.* That hurt. Her throat worked as she tried to swallow, wishing she had some water. When was the last time she'd had something to drink?

"Does that mean you've forgiven him?"

"I wouldn't go that far," Peter said. "But I'm glad he was there. I'm not sure any of us were in a condition to drive."

"Well, I suppose I can see him." Cassie settled back on her pillows. "But just for a minute."

"Thanks, sis." He patted her good hand. "I'll come back later to check on you."

It was a few minutes before Ricardo came in, and Cassie started drifting off. But the sound of her door closing jolted her awake, and she followed his movements with her eyes, not bothering to turn her head.

"I'm glad you pulled through." Ricardo thrust his hands into his pockets.

"Thanks for helping my family." Cassie tried to keep the bitterness out of her tone, but it wasn't easy. Knowing that that man and his stupid company were taking away the only piece of her father she had left was too much to bear.

"Of course. I'm glad I was there to help."

At that moment, Ryan appeared in the doorway. He glanced at Ricardo before looking at Cassie. "Sorry, Emily said you wanted to see me, but I can come back."

"Actually, I'd like you to come in." Cassie beckoned him, an idea forming in her head. "Sit down, please, both of you."

Ryan took the chair by her bed while Ricardo moved to the one nearest the door. With a deep breath, she debated her next words. Her brain was fuzzy, with all the pain medications she suspected were being pumped through her IV. But she forced herself to focus, as she wanted to make sure she said this right.

"Ryan, I know you know that Wakefield Hotel Group is working with Steele Hotels to build a hotel in Blue Heron Bay, but I'm not sure how much you know about Ricardo and his company's interest in the town."

Ryan frowned as he looked at Ricardo. "I'm familiar with his plans, and I stand by what I told the council. That's a lot of development for our little town."

"It'll bring in much-needed tourism," Ricardo said, crossing his arms.

"He's right," Cassie said. "It will, but at a cost." She turned her head to look at Ryan, ignoring the throbbing ache. "Ricardo's company wants to buy Fiddler's Green and move their own Irish pub into it. Their resort stands to put a lot of places out of business, like Grounded."

"He'd have his work cut out for him between convincing the council and securing all the necessary building permits." Ryan's lips set in a grim line. "And I'm certainly not inclined to approve something like that." His eyes narrowed at Ricardo. "We support small businesses here."

"Ah, but once they hear how much revenue the resort will bring in, they'll feel differently," Cassie said. She sighed and closed her eyes. It was all coming back to her. Contracts and administrative law, where the two intersected. Maybe her paralegal degree was going to be worth something after all. "My mom is considering selling, but I'd hate to see my father's legacy end this way." She opened her eyes as the final pieces of her plan fell into place. *Why not try to mend my sister's broken heart as well?* "I believe we can all agree that this town needs something to increase tourism. It's also clear that Sunrise and Wakefield are interested in moving forward with building here, but I don't think Blue Heron Bay can support both a boutique hotel and a sprawling resort without significantly altering the quaint charm the town already offers."

Ryan pursed his lips as he stared at Ricardo. "I don't suppose there's any way you and Anna Mae would be willing to work together to this end?" Cassie hid a smile. He caught on quickly. Or he just knew her better than she'd realized. Her heart fluttered, but she couldn't get distracted by that now.

Ricardo shook his head. "My boss would never go for it. Our companies are longtime rivals. Besides, building a smaller resort would hurt our bottom line. Our customers expect a certain level of decadence when they book with us."

"Well, would you at least be willing to meet with Anna Mae and get her thoughts?" Ryan asked.

Ricardo looked back and forth between Ryan and Cassie before blowing out a breath. "I suppose it couldn't hurt." He stepped closer to Cassie's bed. "But I wouldn't get my hopes up. Sunrise Oasis Resorts has big plans for this town, and I believe with a little persuading the town council will come to see it's the best move. My company isn't likely to change its entire business plan for a small family pub."

"What about you?" Cassie asked, challenging him. "I know you like my brother. Would you consider pursuing a different plan for his sake?"

"I—" Ricardo gaped at her, open-mouthed. He collected himself and grinned. "You Gallaghers are something else." After a moment, he nodded. "As long as the impact is also beneficial to my mother, I would consider it. But I'm not the ultimate decision-maker here."

"I have faith in your powers of persuasion." Cassie yawned and immediately regretted it. Was there a facial expression she could make that wouldn't hurt?

Ryan stood. "We should let you rest."

"I know where Anna Mae is, if you have time to come with me." Ricardo gestured to the door.

"Ryan, wait."

He glanced at Cassie and then nodded to Ricardo. "Just give me a minute."

When they were alone, Ryan stepped back to Cassie's side. "What is it?"

"I just wanted to say thank you." She sniffled, biting back tears as her brother's words echoed in her head. "For saving my life."

"It was nothing," Ryan said, his ears turning pink. "I'm just glad I got to you in time."

"You're wrong," she whispered. "It was everything. Peter told me what the doctor said. If you hadn't asked me to wear the life vest, if you hadn't been there, if you hadn't—" She choked on a sob.

"Shhh." Ryan placed a gentle hand on her left arm. "The important thing is you're on the mend."

Her eyes widened. "Wait, what about Derrick?" She shook her head, surprised it had taken her this long to ask about him. "Is he okay?"

"He had a few bumps and bruises, but nothing compared to your injuries." Ryan moved his jaw, as if there was more he wanted to say.

"You should know that I broke up with him before the show started."

If he was surprised by this news, he didn't show it. She moved to cover his hand with her own, and pain shot up her right arm. Instead, she shifted, trying to hold his hand. Understanding dawned on his face, and he grasped her left hand. She gave him a meaningful squeeze as she gazed up at him. Something in her eyes must have told him everything she couldn't say. A sweet, shy smile played on his lips, and he bent closer to her. She closed her eyes, preparing herself as the beeping behind her grew in tempo, but to her utter disappointment, Ryan's lips pressed against her forehead. When he pulled away, she pouted, and he laughed.

"Get better first," he said, and the promise in his voice made her smile, which surprisingly didn't hurt.

"Come back soon?"

"I will, I promise."

He left her then, and Cassie stared up at the ceiling for a long time, reassessing everything she'd thought she'd known about herself. The old Cassie never would have given Ryan a second glance. But somewhere along the line, she had changed. Some of that had to do with the pub. She'd never fought so hard for something in her life. What started out as a way to get time off work had turned into a crusade that meant something to her. And now, she had to contend with the fact that she'd fallen for someone she never expected to.

Cassie couldn't help rolling her eyes at the audacity of the last part. Her mother would be thrilled, as would Emily and Peter. They'd pushed her toward Ryan since the moment she set foot in town, but she'd resisted because he didn't fit her usual MO. Even when she'd realized she was attracted to him, she fought her feelings because she didn't want to settle for anything less than a passionate and fairy-tale love, like what her parents had. When Derrick had showed up to save her from a pod of dolphins, she thought she'd found it. But Derrick had been all smoke and mirrors, building up his fame, first through his not-so-heroic rescue and then through the stunt show that had nearly cost her life.

She shifted in the hospital bed. *Of course it took me almost dying to*

admit how I feel about Ryan. Typical. I suppose I've always been one for dramatics. But now that she knew, she couldn't wait for him to return.

Emily sat in the waiting room with her mother. Peter, Ricardo, and Ryan had rushed out moments before, saying there was something they needed to do. She couldn't imagine what required all three of them, but she was too worried about Cassie to dwell on it for long. Besides, she couldn't say she was sorry to see Ricardo go. While she appreciated his willingness to drive her family to the hospital, she wasn't ready to forgive him. Even if he paid a handsome sum for the pub, it wouldn't be worth it, not to her.

The extra help Mom had hired to staff the events had allowed the family to spend a significant amount of time at the hospital. Peter and Emily had split the shifts between them to make sure at least one Gallagher was in the pub to oversee its operation, but Mom had refused to leave the hospital. Now that Cassie was awake, Emily hoped Mom would be more amenable to getting some rest in a real bed. As it was, her mom was nodding off in the chair beside her.

Emily tapped her on the shoulder, startling her awake. "You should go home. Cassie's going to sleep most of the day."

"I don't want to leave her alone," Mom said, shifting in her seat.

"I'll stay. But based on what the doctor said, the danger is over. Now, she needs to rest and heal."

"For me, the danger is never over with you kids." Mom glanced over at Emily with a half smile. "I'm your mother, after all. Why don't you go? I'll be fine here on my own."

"Are you sure?" Emily asked. She hated to leave her mother, but she could really use a shower and a nap. None of them had slept much the last few days.

"Go." Her mom waved her hand toward the door. "I'll call you if anything changes."

Emily gathered up her things. She glanced back at Mom, who had pulled out a book. Hopefully, the doctor could give a prognosis for Cassie's recovery soon. Better still, she hoped they would release Cassie before Labor Day. She'd overheard her sister lamenting the idea of being stuck in the hospital for the holiday.

She pulled out of the parking lot and headed down Main Street. Blue Heron Bay was busier than she'd seen it in a long time. Emily's lips turned up in a wistful smile at the success of Anna Mae's efforts.

The thought of Anna Mae made Emily's chest ache. With everything that had happened with Cassie, she'd been able to push the memory of seeing Anna Mae with Leslie from her mind. Emily bit her lip as she drove down the streets toward her childhood home. Perhaps Anna Mae hadn't told her that she'd had a change of heart to spare Emily's feelings. Or maybe she had only flirted with Emily to encourage her cooperation for the plans for the hotel.

Regardless of the reasoning, Emily was heartbroken and angry at herself for allowing it to happen in the first place. She'd come home to help her family's struggling business, not find love. Her initial impression of Anna Mae as worldly and sophisticated should have clued her in to the fact she could never measure up. Besides, wasn't she happy with her life the way it was in Hidden River? She had her students, her house, and most of her family within a few hours' drive. If she really wanted to find love, she shouldn't be looking for it in a town she no longer lived in, and especially not with someone whose job required such extensive travel year-round.

She pulled into the driveway and shut off the car, shaking her head. They were too different. She'd known that from the beginning, but she'd allowed herself to believe they could overcome it. Well, she wouldn't make that mistake again.

As she walked into the house, her phone buzzed. It was Peter.

"Where are you?" he asked as soon as she answered.

"At the house," Emily said, bewildered. "Why?"

"I need you to meet me at Grounded."

"Now?"

"Yes, now! It's important."

Emily shut her eyes, fantasizing about her inviting and comfortable bed upstairs. Would she ever see it again?

"What's so urgent?" she asked, trying to keep her frustration out of her tone.

"You'll see when you get here." The line went dead.

Seriously? Emily clenched her hands into fists. What could possibly require her to rush over to the local coffee shop now? Cassie was awake and on the mend. Mom had been fine when she'd left her. If it was pub-related, he would have asked her to meet him at Fiddler's Green. And why couldn't he just tell her on the phone? Hadn't her nerves suffered enough?

With a groan, she marched back to her car, her temper flaring. Her brother was testing her patience.

Chapter Twenty-Nine

PETER'S LEG BOUNCED IMPATIENTLY AS HE WAITED FOR HIS sister to arrive. Anna Mae and Ricardo had left to talk to their respective companies about their plans, and Ryan was heading back to the hospital to be near Cassie.

When the door opened and Emily appeared, Peter jumped up and waved enthusiastically. He blinked when Emily rolled her eyes at him and stomped over to his table. What was with her?

"I'll have you know I'd gone home to take a nap when you insisted I meet you here," Emily groused as she plopped down in her seat. "So please tell me what was so important that it required me to lose more precious sleep."

Peter stifled a laugh. His sister should really try a cup of coffee, or at least a five-hour energy drink. When he didn't immediately respond, she crossed her arms over her chest and glared at him.

"Sorry, I didn't know you were going home to nap, but I have some exciting news to share." He took a deep breath then paused for dramatic effect, which only increased his sister's annoyance. "I just left Ryan's office, where I met with him, Ricardo, and... Anna Mae."

Emily's mouth dropped open. "What? Why?"

"Cassie shared our concerns with Ryan about the resort in hopes he might be able to do something as mayor. He met with Anna Mae and Ricardo to discuss if they'd be willing to go into a joint venture that would preserve the soul of the town. Anna Mae was on board immediately, and even said that if her father refused, she'd be willing to move forward without him. But Ricardo…" Peter blew out his breath. He was still angry at Ricardo, but it wasn't important to the current story. "Anyway, he said he'd speak to his boss about it and agreed that if Anna Mae was willing to move forward without her father's backing, he would consider doing the same, without Sunrise Oasis."

Emily's eyes widened. "Wow, that's… Wow."

"Right?" Peter smiled. Finally, Emily was showing the right level of enthusiasm. "Anna Mae plans to give her father an ultimatum: either agree to build in Blue Heron Bay without Steele Hotels or she walks. She'll leave the company entirely."

"But how does Steele Hotels feel about that?" Emily asked.

"They didn't discuss that," Peter said. "But I'm not sure Anna Mae cares. Apparently, she wasn't thrilled with the stunt Leslie pulled at the carnival."

If his sister had a reaction to that revelation, she didn't show it. "Okay, but why did Cassie think Ryan should be the one to suggest this? Didn't he already know about the planned development of Blue Heron Bay?"

Peter explained how Ryan knew about the resort but was unaware of the specifics of Ricardo's plans and how he suspected a resort requiring so much change in the town wouldn't go over well with the council.

"This is a lot to take in." Emily put her head in her hands.

"I know, but I wanted to tell you as soon as possible. Regardless of whether Anna Mae and Ricardo strike a deal either on their own or with their respective companies, the town will not take any action that would jeopardize small businesses like Fiddler's Green. Ryan has a list of similar hotel chains like Wakefield, and he's prepared to pitch to others if this deal doesn't go through."

"So… the pub—we can keep it?"

"Well, so long as we can keep it profitable," Peter said, hedging. The resort was only one of their problems, but if the town could find a hotel chain willing to build here, they'd have a better chance of increasing tourism.

"Still, that's something." Emily's eyes brightened. "And to think, this all started because of a suggestion from Cassie, of all people."

"Maybe that knock to her head shook something loose," Peter joked. "Or perhaps she just had ample time to work it all out while she was unconscious."

"Whatever it was, I'm proud of her."

Peter was finishing his shift at the pub when the bells on the door jangled. He looked up with a frown. Who was coming to eat at three o'clock in the afternoon? His lips pressed together when his eyes met Ricardo's. Despite Ricardo's promise to speak with his boss, Peter wasn't sure if he could ever fully trust him. He'd already been burned once.

"How'd it go?" Peter asked, folding his arms across his chest.

"Surprisingly well," Ricardo said, pulling the baseball cap off his head and running a hand through his thick black hair. "I should have known it would be all about money for my boss, though."

"What do you mean?" Peter cocked his head. As far as he could tell, Ricardo's company stood to lose more money than they'd gain.

"Well, merging means less upfront investment on our part. Wakefield will carry some of that burden. But my boss also liked that it would diversify our portfolio of properties, which will help expand our brand."

Peter laughed. "I guess I hadn't thought of it that way." He searched Ricardo's face for any trace of deception.

Ricardo held up his hands. "I promise, there's no further threat from us to the pub. And the hotel is sure to bring in a lot more business, so it should only help the town." He lowered his hands and his head. "I'm sorry, Peter. I never meant to hurt you." His fingers fiddled with his hat. "As much as I wanted to help my mom with stable employment, truthfully, I was blinded by my own ambition."

"I appreciate your apology," Peter said. Part of him yearned to go to

Ricardo, pull him into his arms, and say everything was forgiven. But he wasn't ready.

"Do you..." Ricardo stopped and shifted his weight from foot to foot. He twisted his hat. "Could we maybe start over?"

Peter sighed. "I'm just not sure I can trust you."

Ricardo's face fell. "Then, perhaps, I'll see you sometime when I'm in California."

As he turned away, Peter's heart lurched in his chest. He couldn't let him leave, not like that.

"Wait," he called, crossing the room. He grabbed Ricardo's arm. "Come to our Labor Day cookout."

Ricardo blinked and staggered back. "What?"

"The cookout," Peter said. "We're having it at the house. I'd love to have you and your mom join us."

"W-We'd be honored."

"Great." Peter gave his arm a squeeze before releasing it. "I'll see you then."

Later that evening, Emily was clearing the last table of the night. She was more than ready to shut down the pub and go home. The bells on the door jingled, and she spun around, ready to give whoever had the audacity to come in that late a piece of her mind.

"We're clos—" The word died on her lips. Anna Mae stood before her.

"I'm not here to eat," Anna Mae said. She took a hesitant step forward then stopped. "I'm assuming you heard that the partnership with Steele Hotels is off?"

"I have." Emily lifted her chin, hoping to hide the emotions that were warring inside of her.

"You should know that Leslie and I... We aren't together," Anna Mae said.

"I'm sorry to hear that." Emily chose her words carefully. Her emotions were all over the place at seeing Anna Mae again.

Anna Mae stared at her. "Are you?" She bit her lip. "I had hoped... Well, I suppose it doesn't matter, but I wanted to explain myself to you."

"What's to explain?" Emily clasped her hands behind her back to hide their trembling. "You got back together with your ex. It's not a crime."

"That's just it," Anna Mae said, her voice animated. "We didn't get back together. What Leslie said at the carnival was a lie." She rushed over to Emily, taking her hand. "I know I've been spending a lot of time with her, but it was to make this deal go through, to save your family's pub. That's all." Her lips twisted. "Unfortunately, she read into that more than I expected, then she told my dad that we had some big announcement. I had no idea, but that's why she said what she did at the carnival. I confronted her about it and told her in no uncertain terms that we were never getting back together." She squared her shoulders. "When I talked to my dad, I explained what happened, and he promised me that he wouldn't try to merge with Steele Hotels again in the future."

Emily blinked, not quite believing her ears. While she wasn't surprised by Leslie's antics, it didn't explain why Anna Mae had kept her distance.

"Say something," Anna Mae pleaded, her dark eyes searching Emily's face.

Pulling her hand away, Emily took a step back. "Why are you only telling me this now? The carnival was over a week ago. Why didn't you come to me sooner?"

At that, Anna Mae stared at the floor. "I was afraid you wouldn't take my calls." She raised her eyes to meet Emily's. "And I was hurt too. I told you so many times that there was nothing between us. After Leslie implied we were back together, I didn't know what else I could say to convince you we weren't."

That hit Emily square in the chest. While Leslie's deception had certainly aided her doubts, her own insecurities had almost cost her a relationship with the most amazing woman she'd ever met.

"I'm sorry," she mumbled. "I just can't imagine why someone like you would want to be with someone like me."

Anna Mae rolled her eyes as she pulled Emily into her arms. "Then let me show you." Her hand caressed Emily's cheek, then she leaned forward and kissed her.

When Anna Mae pulled away a moment later, Emily's heart pounded in her chest. Anna Mae gave her a tentative smile, but then her chocolate eyes melted, and she pulled Emily back to her, sliding her hands into Emily's hair and kissing her passionately.

"Now do you believe me?" Anna Mae teased.

"Completely and totally," Emily whispered. She pulled Anna Mae tightly against her, relishing the warmth radiating between them.

"There's more," Anna Mae mumbled against Emily's shoulder.

"Oh?" Emily stepped back, not sure her heart could handle much more at this point.

"Now that we've executed all the paperwork, my dad wants me to start looking into our next venture."

Emily shifted her weight to her back foot. "Oh, I assumed you'd stay here and oversee the project."

"Aside from promoting our hotels, my job is more about seeking future locations for the company to consider."

"Where will you go next?" Emily asked, slumping into a chair. She should have known it couldn't last. Her heart ached, but she swallowed her pain and composed her expression. It wasn't Anna Mae's fault. It was just part of her job.

"Actually, my dad was interested in Southern Maryland." Anna Mae's dark eyes met Emily's briefly. "There's some place called Solomon's Island that sounds promising."

Emily blinked at her, not sure she'd heard her right. "Solomon's... That's right near me."

"Is it?" Anna Mae asked, a coy smile playing on her lips. "Interesting." She pulled out the chair next to Emily and sank into it. "Well, I'm not familiar with the area, and I could use a tour guide who could show me the best spots. Know anyone?"

"I might," Emily said, playing along. She placed her hand in Anna Mae's. "But it'll cost you."

"I hope I can afford it."

"You can, I'm sure." Emily gave her hand a brief squeeze. "Just a few thousand kisses."

"Well then." Anna Mae leaned forward. "Consider this a down payment." She pulled Emily in for another sweet kiss.

Chapter Thirty

CASSIE SMILED AS HER MOTHER PULLED INTO THE DRIVEWAY. She was thrilled to be out of the hospital and back home, especially as it was the start of Labor Day weekend. She'd worked hard to convince her doctors she was well enough to convalesce at home, and they had agreed, though they warned her to take it easy.

Emily and Peter were standing on the porch, awaiting their arrival. They both waved as Cassie climbed out of the car. Her legs were still wobbly from spending so long in bed, but her strength improved each day.

"Welcome home." Emily pulled her into a hug, a gentle one since Cassie was still badly bruised.

"I'm making all of your favorites." Peter opened the front door for her. "Cajun crab and shrimp mac and cheese, Caesar salad, garlic bread, and strawberry cheesecake for dessert."

"Sounds heavenly after hospital food," Cassie said. She walked into the house and collapsed into a recliner. The scent of melted cheese and roasting spices filled the air, and she sniffed appreciatively. "But that's quite a feast. Isn't it just us tonight?"

Peter shrugged. "Then we'll have leftovers for a while."

Cassie nodded, pleased that they'd agreed to her request for a quiet family dinner. Ryan, Anna Mae, Ricardo, and a few others would join them Sunday for the cookout.

Her mother went to help Peter in the kitchen while Emily sat across from Cassie on the couch. It felt good to be home. No more incessant beeping or being poked and prodded while she tried to sleep. The doctors were just doing their jobs, but Cassie's patience grew thinner and thinner the longer she stayed in that hospital room.

"So, tell me what happened with Anna Mae and Ricardo," Cassie said, startling her sister. "Ryan told me they'd convinced their companies to move forward with a partnership, but he didn't give me a lot of detail."

"They both threatened to quit and form their own company." Emily shook her head. "I had no idea. Peter told me about it after they'd decided to move forward together. But after hearing your idea that they join forces, Ryan, Peter, and Ricardo went to find Anna Mae and get her input. She didn't even hesitate to agree."

"Have you seen her since then?" Cassie hoped this meant their relationship was on the mend. Ryan told her Leslie Steele had left town, which she assumed meant that the partnership, and their relationship, was off.

"Briefly." Emily smiled. "She has had little time between working with the lawyers to dissolve the agreement with Steele Hotels and forming a new one with Sunrise Oasis Resorts." Leaning her head back against the couch, she stared at the ceiling. "But I hope to spend some time with her this weekend before I have to go back to Hidden River for school."

"I'm so glad everything is working out with you two," Cassie said. "What about Ricardo and Peter? Have they patched things up?"

"I'm not sure. Ricardo is still planning on assessing new towns on the West Coast for the development of their next resort. I imagine he'll see Peter while he's out there."

Peter entered the room and gave a silly bow. "Dinner is served."

Cassie giggled. "Well, thank you, kind sir." She held out her left arm. "Can you help me up?"

Her brother came to her side and wrapped her arm around her back to help her out of the chair. She walked into the kitchen to her usual seat, pleased he had served a meal that wouldn't require her to use a knife. Her right arm was stuck in this stupid cast for another few weeks.

"Before we eat," Mom said as she scooped a heaping portion of the mac and cheese onto Cassie's plate, "I just want to say how much I appreciate you all." Her blue eyes glistened with unshed tears as she looked around at the three of them. "Your father would have been so proud of you. How you pitched in and worked hard, trying to save his legacy. I wish he could have seen it."

The Gallaghers were quiet as they spared a thought for the loss of their beloved patriarch. Despite how happy they all were to be together, their joy was subdued.

After dinner, the family gathered outside at the firepit. Marshmallows, chocolate, and graham crackers were set up nearby, along with metal skewers. Peter lit the kindling and stoked the fire.

"I'm going to be sad when you all leave on Tuesday," Mom said as she settled into a chair.

"We'll be back before you know it," Peter said, picking up a skewer and stabbing a marshmallow.

"Actually," Cassie said, "I'm not going anywhere."

Her family stared at her, speechless. Emily was the first to find her voice. "What do you mean?"

"I mean, I'm moving home." She reached into her pocket and pulled out an apartment ad. "I've been thinking about it a lot, no thanks to you and Ryan's heavy hinting." She shot a look at her sister, who raised her eyebrows in feigned innocence. "And I've found a place I think would work. It's not far from the pub, and it's something I think I can afford with tip money until I figure out what I want to do with my life."

"That's wonderful!" her mother cried. She pushed out of her seat and rushed over to Cassie, throwing her arms around her.

"Oof." Cassie winced. "Careful, Mom. Broken, party of one, over here."

"When did you have time to find an apartment?" Peter asked.

She stared down at her hands. "Before the accident." Lifting her shoulder in a shrug, she smiled. "I thought it couldn't hurt to look. I had a nurse sneak my phone in so I could email the owner from the hospital. I'll still need to go back to the city to get my things, but if someone can give me a ride, I can sign the lease tomorrow."

Two days later, Peter and Ricardo set up tables in the back yard. They were expecting quite a crowd for the cookout, and they wanted everyone to sit together, family style. On the deck, Tony was working the grill, and the savory scent of burning charcoal and grilled meat drifted through the air. Ricardo's and Peter's moms were in the kitchen making strawberry shortcake.

"Thank you for inviting me." Ricardo brought two chairs over to the large table they'd created and pushed them in. "I'm really sorry for all the trouble I've caused."

Peter groaned. "Please stop apologizing. You saw the light in the end, and that's all that matters." Over the last several days, Peter had come to forgive Ricardo. When he'd seen how hard Ricardo was working to make sure the partnership between Sunrise Oasis and Wakefield Hotels would go through, it touched his heart. It was clear Ricardo was doing whatever he could to help his mother and save Peter's father's legacy. It was impossible to stay mad at him.

"True." Ricardo surveyed their progress. "And it was worth it. I can see now why your family loves the pub so much."

Peter moved next to him and slid his arm around Ricardo's shoulders. "The pub isn't the only thing I've learned to love this summer."

Ricardo stared at him and blinked rapidly. Peter's gaze swept the yard, pleased to see they were completely alone, for once. He lowered his head and pressed his lips lightly against Ricardo's. Well, he'd intended to make it a light kiss, but Ricardo had other ideas. Ricardo wrapped his arm around the back of Peter's neck, pulling him closer and deepening the kiss. When they stepped back from each other, Peter's heart was hammering in his chest.

"Peter, I—"

"Shhh." Peter held up his finger. "I'm sorry it took me so long to come to my senses. I hope you can forgive me."

"Forgive you?" Ricardo laughed. "You were looking out for your family. I'm sorry I broke your trust." He leaned forward, kissing Peter again. "I just have one favor to ask."

Peter raised an eyebrow. "And what's that?"

"Save me a dance when we're back on the West Coast."

Chapter Thirty-One

CASSIE GLARED OUT HER WINDOW. HER FAMILY HAD insisted she stay in bed while they set up everything outside. They claimed she was still too weak to help and it would be better for her to rest.

But she was tired of resting. She had been confined to a hospital bed for days, and now she was stuck in her room while everyone went off to have fun without her.

A familiar beat-up pickup truck pulled up in front of the house, and Cassie's sour mood was soon forgotten. Ryan climbed out and headed to her front door. Cassie squealed and hurried down the stairs as fast as her broken body would let her, wrenching the door open and wincing slightly at the pain that reverberated up her arm.

"Shouldn't you be resting?" Ryan asked as he came inside.

Cassie harrumphed. "I've rested enough." She wrapped her good arm around him. "Besides, aren't you happy to see me?"

"I'm always happy to see you, even when you're annoyed," Ryan teased. He helped her to the couch. "How are you feeling?"

"Better every day. Especially now that you're here."

A slow, shy smile overtook his face, and Cassie's breath caught in her throat. How she'd ever thought of him as boring escaped her. She had been so very wrong about a lot of things.

"Now that you're resting appropriately, I suppose I can give you this." He handed her a box wrapped in sparkly paper.

"A gift? What's the occasion?"

He raised his eyebrows. "Do I need an occasion?"

With childlike glee, Cassie tore open the present one-handedly. Inside of the large box were two smaller boxes. Cassie ripped open the first one. She frowned at first, but when she realized what it was, she glared at Ryan.

"Really?" She held up a pool float. It was a ridiculous inflatable pink unicorn.

Ryan widened his green eyes in faux innocence. "I thought you'd like it, given your penchant for swimming." His grin was lopsided.

"Not funny!" Cassie attempted to cross her arms over her chest, but it didn't quite work with the cast.

"It's a little funny," Ryan said. "But it's not your actual gift." He gestured to the other box. "Open that one."

She raised an eyebrow, but her curiosity got the better of her. Inside the second box was a small leather notebook. The cover was engraved "To Cassie, may you always follow your dreams. With love, Ryan."

"'With love...'" Cassie read aloud.

He met her gaze and then gave a solemn nod. "I do love you. I think I fell in love with you the first moment I saw you."

Impulsively, Cassie leaned forward and kissed him. She poured everything she wasn't sure how to say into her kiss, and he responded with a fiery passion she wouldn't have expected of him. With great care, he wrapped an arm around her and pulled her closer.

They broke apart to catch their breath. Cassie's insides melted, and her eyes shone with unshed tears. To think, she was once willing to throw all this away for some old high school crush.

"I have something for you too." Cassie stood, her knees still weak from that kiss, removed a key from her pocket, and held it out to him.

"Is this the key to your heart?" Ryan joked.

"Not exactly," Cassie said, rolling her eyes at his silliness. "It's a key to an apartment in town."

Ryan stared at her. "Then you've decided? You're moving back?"

Cassie nodded. "I think I decided a while ago, even if I wasn't ready to admit it. I'll email the temp agency my resignation, and I'll need to go back to the city to pack. But yes, I'm coming home."

It was Ryan's turn to be impulsive, and he grabbed her, careful of her broken arm, and pressed his lips against hers with such warmth and love, it took her breath away. Her heart was bursting with joy.

"I may be able to help you find a job in the city legal department," Ryan said as he released her. "I've heard our paralegal is retiring."

"That'd be good. But I also hope to continue working at the pub and helping my mom while also pursuing my writing."

"Whatever will make you happy." The look in his eyes told her he meant it.

Emily came to tell them the food was ready, and Ryan helped Cassie out to the back yard. Clouds had gathered, blotting out the sun. A cool breeze ruffled her hair, hinting that autumn was on the way.

As they walked outside, her eyes alighted on her family. Emily and Anna Mae were pouring drinks while Ricardo and Peter helped their mothers carry various dishes to the table. Tony brought over a platter of burgers and hot dogs, and everyone took their seats.

Cassie closed her eyes and smiled, happy to be alive and with her family. Her father would have loved to see them carrying on his end-of-summer tradition. When she opened her eyes again, everyone was talking and laughing as they passed food around the table.

She tapped her glass with her knife. All eyes turned to her.

"I'd like to make a toast."

Glasses were raised around the table, and Cassie grinned cheekily.

"To summer romances!"

Epilogue

PETER STOOD AMONGST HIS FELLOW GRADUATES AWAITING the distinguished hooding ceremony. The autumn, winter, and spring seasons had passed in the blink of an eye. He'd finally finished his doctorate, and his dissertation advisor was smiling at him from the stage. Somewhere out in the crowd, his sisters, mother, and Ricardo were watching, and he stood taller, if that was possible, as he filled with pride. After all the hard work and hours he'd poured into this degree, it felt like his life was truly ready to begin.

"Peter Sean Gallagher, PhD, Urban Planning and Development," the UCLA president said.

Peter walked onto the stage and turned to face the audience. Laughter rippled through the audience as Peter had to stoop so the professor could put the hood over his head. He shook his professor's hand and the hand of the university president. On the other side of the stage stood Ricardo. Peter frowned. *Why is he up here? He's supposed to be sitting with my family.*

Before Peter could say anything, Ricardo rushed forward and dropped to one knee. "Peter Gallagher," Ricardo said, his voice loud and clear. "The only thing that would make this day more perfect would be if you would agree to be my husband. Will you marry me?"

There were gasps in the audience as everyone waited for Peter's response.

First, he nodded, then when he finally found his voice, he choked out a "Yes, of course."

Ricardo stood and pulled him into a tight hug before he gave Peter a heart-stopping kiss. Instead of a ring, Ricardo had bought him an expensive watch, which he fastened onto Peter's wrist.

They couldn't spend much time together as there were still several people waiting to be hooded. The rest of the ceremony went by in a blur for Peter as he kept reliving the moment Ricardo had dropped in front of him on stage. After the last graduate had received their hood, the president made some closing remarks and ended the ceremony.

Peter rushed off to find Ricardo and his family. His mother caught his eye first and hugged him.

"Congratulations, Peter!" she cried out, engulfing him in a hug. "Such a joyful day!"

Emily and Cassie shared their congratulations as well, but Peter barely heard them as he turned to Ricardo. He didn't speak, just pulled him in for a passionate kiss.

When he pulled back, he rested his forehead against Ricardo's. "I can't believe you just did that."

Ricardo grinned. "Surprised?"

"That's one word for it."

"So, when's the wedding?" Cassie asked, patting Peter on the back.

"More importantly, *where* is the wedding?" Emily asked.

Peter and Ricardo looked at each other. "I suppose the most obvious place would be Blue Heron Bay," Peter said.

Ricardo smiled. "It is where we first met."

"Oh, and we could have the rehearsal dinner at the pub!" Mom exclaimed, clapping her hands together.

"How's that doing, by the way?" Peter asked as he shifted so he was beside Ricardo. "I meant to ask sooner, but things have been crazy with all the graduation preparation."

"We're still very much in the black." Mom put an arm around Cassie. "And Cassie has been helping me with contracting with local farmers, so we've altered the menu to a more farm-to-table feel."

Peter laughed. "How does Tony feel about that?"

"He hasn't said anything to suggest he's unhappy." Cassie shrugged. "But it's been really good for business."

"And the hotel?" Peter directed that question to Emily.

"It's coming along nicely, though Anna Mae has her hands full with the Solomon's Island project these days."

"Will you be coming home this summer to help out?" Mom asked, her gaze moving from Peter to Ricardo and back again.

"They have to," Cassie said. "They have a wedding to plan."

"Actually..." Peter cleared his throat. "I'm starting a new job."

"Way to bury the lede!" Emily playfully punched his arm. "Where?"

"Habitat for Humanity. I'll be working as the assistant director of housing."

A noise at the front of the auditorium caught their attention. The president of the university was tapping the microphone.

"Thank you all for coming. We invite you to a reception to honor our graduates in the main hall."

As Peter's family filed out with the rest of the crowd, he took a moment and turned back to look at the stage. While he still had the graduation ceremony itself to look forward to, he couldn't imagine anything would top his experience that day.

Engaged and hooded all in one evening. Who could ask for more?

"Are you coming?" Ricardo called from the back of the empty auditorium.

Peter nodded and walked down the aisle toward his future.

Also by Katie Eagan Schenck

When Cardinals Appear

When Swans Dance

When Doves Lament

A Home for Christmas

Acknowledgments

While this story was mostly inspired by Jane Austen's *Sense and Sensibility*, it came to me, almost fully formed, because of a tweet.

I had already planned on a modern twist on *Sense and Sensibility*, but the tweet was from the (at the time) executive director of Hallmark Publishing. She was looking for a book with *Love, Actually* vibes that took place at Christmas and followed three storylines that intermingled. Yes, *The Tides That Bind* started as a Christmas story.

Unfortunately, Hallmark Publishing is no more, but I will always be grateful to Bryn Donovan for her inspirational tweet. After following her suggestion to make it a summer story, she later served as one of many editors on this story.

Additional thanks go to my thesis advisor, Shelley Evans at Queens University of Charlotte, who served as the first editor of this book. And to the talented editors at Red Adept Editing who assisted with polishing prose and ironing out the last few kinks in the story.

As always, I want to thank my late mother. The promise I made to her led me to write my first book, and it is in memory of her faith in my abilities that I've continued to pursue this dream.

I want to thank my siblings and their partners, to whom this book is dedicated, for constantly demonstrating that love really is love. I hope I've made you proud with this latest novel.

A great debt of gratitude goes to my father and stepmother for their unwavering support. I'm not sure my father actually reads my books, but I appreciate that he faithfully delivers the signed copies to my stepmother every Christmas.

Many thanks to my cover designer, 100 Covers. Thank you for making this process as easy and painless as possible!

And last, but certainly not least, thanks to my husband and daughter. While my day job continues to wreak havoc on our lives, I appreciate the support from both of you that allows me to continue to pursue my passion. I love you.

About the Author

Katie Eagan Schenck writes sweet romance and women's fiction that warms the heart and gives all the feels. She has an MFA in creative writing from Queens University of Charlotte. When she's not writing she's either drafting regulations for the federal government, baking delicious treats, or binging Hallmark movies. She lives in Maryland with her husband, daughter, and their three cats.

facebook.com/keschenck

instagram.com/keschenckauthor